What would you do if . . .

The body artists could make you into anything you
  wanted?
The illness you bore could save the very lives that it
  destroyed?
The whole city knew who killed your daughter, but
  didn't care?

Have you ever wondered . . .

What they think about you on the other side of the
  mirror?
How it would feel if everyone could read your most
  intimate thoughts?
How many lifetimes you might have lived to get one
  life right?

Have you ever hoped to escape . . .

A city that knows your every thought?
A prison on one of Jupiter's moons?

**Creative and entertaining adventures that will
take you into new realms of imagination.**

What has been said about the
L. RON HUBBARD
PRESENTS
WRITERS OF THE FUTURE
ANTHOLOGIES

"This has become a major tributary to the new blood in fantastic fiction."

GREGORY BENFORD
AUTHOR

"From cutting-edge high-tech to evocative fantasy, this book's got it all—it's lots of fun and I love the chance to see what tomorrow's stars are doing today."

TIM POWERS

"I recommend the *Writers of the Future* Contest at every writers' workshop I participate in."

FREDERIK POHL

". . . an exceedingly solid collection, including SF, fantasy and horror . . ."

CHICAGO SUN TIMES

"A first-rate collection of stories and illustrations."

BOOKLIST

"It is rare to find this consistency of excellence in any series of science fiction and fantasy stories. The well-deserved reputation of L. Ron Hubbard's *Writers of the Future* has proven itself once again."

STEPHEN V. WHALEY
PROFESSOR ENGLISH & FOREIGN LANGUAGES
CAL STATE UNIVERSITY, POMONA

"The untapped talents of new writers continue to astonish me and every WOTF volume provides a well-spring of the greatest energy put forth by the ambitious writers of tomorrow."

KEVIN J. ANDERSON

"This contest has changed the face of Science Fiction."

DEAN WESLEY SMITH
EDITOR OF *STRANGE NEW WORLDS*

"Over the long haul the *L. Ron Hubbard Presents Writers of the Future* books have continued to support the creation of new science fiction writers and styles. Some of the best SF of the future comes from *Writers of the Future* and you can find it in this book."

DAVID HARTWELL

"Not only is the writing excellent . . . it is also extremely varied. There's a lot of hot new talent in it."

LOCUS MAGAZINE

"As always, this is the premier volume in the field to showcase new writers and artists. You can't go wrong here."

BARYON

"*Writers of the Future* is the leading SF pathway to success."

ALGIS BUDRYS

"This contest has found some of the best new writers of the last decade."

KRISTINE KATHRYN RUSCH
AUTHOR & EDITOR

SPECIAL OFFER FOR SCHOOLS AND
WRITING GROUPS

The seventeen prize-winning stories in this volume, all of them selected by a panel of top professionals in the field of speculative fiction, exemplify the standards which a new writer must meet if he expects to see his work published and achieve professional success.

These stories, augmented by "how to write" articles by some of the top writers of science fiction, fantasy and horror, make this anthology virtually a textbook for use in the classroom and an invaluable resource for students, teachers and workshop instructors in the field of writing.

The materials contained in this and previous volumes have been used with outstanding results in writing courses and workshops held on college and university campuses throughout the United States— from Harvard, Duke and Rutgers to George Washington, Brigham Young and Pepperdine.

To assist and encourage creative writing programs, the **L. Ron Hubbard Presents Writers of the Future** anthologies are available at special quantity discounts when purchased in bulk by schools, universities, workshops and other related groups.

For more information, write

Specialty Sales Department
Bridge Publications, Inc.
4751 Fountain Avenue
Los Angeles, CA 90029
or call toll-free (800) 722-1733
Internet address: http://www.bridgepub.com
E-mail address: info@bridgepub.com

L. RON HUBBARD

PRESENTS

WRITERS

OF THE

FUTURE

VOLUME XIV

L. RON HUBBARD

PRESENTS

WRITERS

OF THE

FUTURE

VOLUME XIV

The Year's 17 Best Tales from the
Writers of the Future®
**International Writing Program
Illustrated by the Winners in the**
Illustrators of the Future®
International Illustration Program

With Essays on Writing and Art by
L. Ron Hubbard • Anne McCaffrey
Eric Kotani • Vincent Di Fate •
Michael A. Stackpole

Edited by Dave Wolverton

Bridge Publications, Inc.

The Dhaka Flu: ©1998 Richard Flood
Nocturne's Bride: ©1998 Brian Wightman
Jenny with the Stars in Her Hair: ©1998 Amy Sterling Casil
Spray Paint Revolutions: ©1998 J. C. Schmidt
The Disappearance of Josie Andrew: ©1998 Ron Collins
Waiting for Hildy: ©1998 Chris Flamm
Valuable Advice: ©1998 Anne McCaffrey
Agony: ©1998 Ladonna King
Metabolism: ©1998 Scott Nicholson
Silent Justice: ©1998 Maureen Jensen
Our Mission to Dream: ©1998 Vincent Di Fate
Cyclops in B Minor: ©1998 Jayme Lynn Blaschke
Broken Mirror: ©1998 David Masters
Red Tide, White Tide: ©1998 T. M. Spell
On Writing Science Fiction: ©1998 Eric Kotani
Literacy: ©1998 Stefano Donati
The Dragon and the Lorelei: ©1998 Carla Montgomery
Red Moon: ©1998 Scott M. Azmus
The Third Agenda: ©1998 Michael A. Stackpole
Faller: ©1998 Tim Jansen
Conservator: ©1998 Steven Mohan, Jr.
Illustration on page: 31 István Kuklis ©1998
Illustration on page: 37 John Lock ©1998
Illustration on page: 65 Paul Marquis ©1998
Illustration on page: 95 Paul Marquis ©1998
Illustration on page: 110 Eric L. Winter ©1998
Illustration on page: 142 Eric L. Winter ©1998
Illustration on page: 176 Sherman McClain ©1998
Illustration on page: 181 Paul Marquis ©1998
Illustration on page: 194 John Lock ©1998
Illustration on page: 247 John Lock ©1998
Illustration on page: 286 John Philo ©1998
Illustration on page: 329 Eric L. Winter ©1998
Illustration on page: 347 Dionisios Fragias ©1998
Illustration on page: 393 Christopher Jouan ©1998
Illustration on page: 417 Rob Hassan ©1998
Illustration on page: 450 Rob Hassan ©1998
Illustration on page: 481 Christopher Jouan ©1998
Cover Artwork: "Island City in Blue" © 1998 Paul Lehr

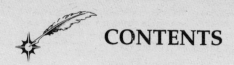

CONTENTS

ON TO THE FUTURE

Written by
Dave Wolverton

Fifteen years ago, L. Ron Hubbard initiated the *Writers of the Future* Contest in an effort to help discover aspiring authors of science fiction and fantasy. Since Hubbard passed away, Author Services, Inc., has handled the contest administration, while Bridge Publications, Inc., has continued to publish this annual collection of winning stories.

Five years following the start of the writing contest, Author Services, Inc., established a complementary contest for illustrators based on Hubbard's wishes.

In the ensuing years since its inception, we've published about 250 new authors and over 100 illustrators —many of whom have gone on to start their own successful careers. Algis Budrys, the Coordinating Judge of the contest at its start, continues to be a judge, as do some of the other original contest judges.

As of this year, we will be making some minor adjustments to the rules for the writing contest. (Please refer to my article at the back of this book if you are interested in submitting.) Also, I'm happy to announce that we are adding a new judge for the writing contest. Eric Kotani, a longtime friend of the contest who writes hard science fiction, will act as one of the professionals who reads our finalist stories and selects the prize winners.

At the same time that we have gained a new judge, it is with deep regret that I announce we've lost one also. Paul Lehr, a phenomenally talented illustrator, helped teach for many years the illustrators' workshops and was instrumental in the selection process for our winning illustrators. Paul passed away in late July, due to cancer. He was deeply loved and will be as deeply missed. I'd like to extend our heartfelt condolences and our thanks to his wife Paula, and to his family and friends.

• • •

Once again, we have a very talented collection of artists to introduce. The stories this year are often thought-provoking, but, first and foremost, entertaining and imaginative. Some of these authors are already selling to major markets and establishing themselves as professionals. For all these authors, we hope that this contest serves as one rung on their ladder to success. The illustrators also show a great deal of rising talent.

So, without further ado, on to the future. . . .

THE DHAKA FLU

Written by
Richard Flood

Illustrated by
István Kuklis

About the Author

Richard Flood grew up in Chicago and lived in San Francisco for a while before earning a degree in English at UC Berkeley. He now lives in Bucks County, PA, near Philadelphia.

Richard has been a science fiction fan all his life. While at Berkeley, he won a share of the prestigious Eisner prize for a selection of a novel in progress, and he won a Crothers Short Story Award. During that time, his fiction appeared in several literary magazines.

Since then, Richard has worked as a small-press editor, technical writer, and computer programmer.

Like a couple of other authors in this book, Richard has been a finalist in this contest before. His story "Eyes of Light" was published in 1996. Since we allow authors who have not published more than three stories and who have not placed in the contest to continue to enter, Richard sent us this fine tale and won first place for his quarter, qualifying him for the $4,000 grand prize.

About the Illustrator

István Kuklis was born in Hungary in 1958 and, like many artists, got detoured on the road to life before he came back to illustrations in 1989. He likes to show his work in competitions, and is especially interested in both fantasy and science fiction. He says that he likes to emphasize the importance of the first impression, but that a meticulous and elaborate illustration can give more than momentary pleasure.

From the somnolent quiet of the Bombay red-eye, Kalpana Shah lurched into sound, light, and gleaming corridors of the Dhaka International, this year's "world's busiest airport," all chrome and bright plastics.

She turned left and pushed into the flow of bodies, onto a slidewalk, angling into the fast lane. She was not on the contagion team, but for a *Stage 1* she still had to be on-site within ten hours. Thanks to Indian Airways, she was now cutting it close.

Halfway down the first conveyor, she stopped abruptly behind a large family and their collection of luggage. They ignored her "Excuse me's," proffered in four languages. Sighing, she put down her bag. Dots of color appeared in the air like transparent confetti. She slid into a holographic cloud.

Assullam walaikum. Assullam walaikum. Hello. Welcome to Bangladesh, home of the famous pink pearls; the world-renowned carpets; the saris of finest, number-one, world-class silk—only two thousand laka, first-class discount pricing.

Each projection had a louder, faster barker than the last—bazaar stalls in fast-forward. She frowned, and wondered what the nuns at her girlhood school would think of such cut-and-paste English.

As she cleared the strand of commercials, an elderly woman began coughing violently on the opposing walkway, leaning into her path.

Kalpana groaned. *A lovely bouquet of anthrax, memsahib. World-class, number-one.* She made a mental note to take some immunogen snake oil when she reached the hotel.

Near the exit, she wove through a chaos of people, into the hooting of bus and taxi horns, the suffocating humidity. Rain streamed down outside the overhang. A mob of drivers formed a flattened arc facing the new arrivals. None held up her name or even a garbled approximation.

Thunder crackled across the sky.

She checked her watch and cursed silently, moved onto the taxi stand. Scanning, she quick-stepped into a back seat festooned with advertisements and pictures of saints—turbaned, white-bearded Sikh patriarchs, one hand raised in blessing; blue-skinned flautists; and the ubiquitous Bangla Cola.

"*Assullam walaikum,*" said the driver, smiling behind an impressive black mustache.

"*Walaikum salaam.* But English, please. To Manikganj." She gave him the hotel address.

"You have come from Delhi?" asked Mr. Mustache, eyeing her in his rearview mirror. "You will be shopping while you are here? I can recommend many fine stores—fine silk, gold products, silver."

"No," she said curtly. "I am here on business."

The rear-seat display hissed to life amid cymbal-and-bass clamor. A stadium-sized sari shop, camera motoring up and down the towering aisles.

"Could you turn it down, please?" she shouted. "It's a long drive. I'd like to have a little sleep."

He looked puzzled.

"Sleep!" She pointed to her ears. He nodded, finally. The display went silent and dark.

"Ah yes," said the driver, clearly annoyed by this probable loss of commissions. "Very sorry. Later perhaps, yes?"

Kalpana shrugged. She took a one-hour dose of sopor, sublingual, and contacted the local node of her security service, setting her palmkit on *Monitor*. Mustache seemed benign enough, but one could never be too careful.

She lay back in the seat. Outside, the rain etched vertical lines in the air. She thought of her father, lover of rains and night, strange man, long gone.

"Beware those," he'd told her once, "who love the day too much, and who fear night." What was she then—six? seven? He was full of spooky admonitions.

She was so young when he left—*pater absconditum*—abandoning his family to relatives, not even waiting the traditional seven-times-seven years for renunciation. He was mostly a vague dream in her memory. The few sayings, the large eyes, the gentle gaze. These she remembered.

•••

J. Rao, the chief scientist of Rahman Research Center, stayed glued to his semitransparent screen when Kalpana appeared, finishing work on what seemed to be a spreadsheet of some kind.

After several minutes, he finally looked up, unsmiling. "It is not *my* opinion," he said, "that this—problem—requires neurological study. The contagion unit is already here. However, study is required."

Kalpana said, "Perhaps you can give me some idea of *why* I am, as you say, 'required.' I've been told very little."

J. Rao sat back, pursing his lips slightly. "We do work with infectious diseases here—mostly primate research, nothing exotic. In the past week, we have had two problems. First, a mutant strain of myxovirus. A virulent, odd strain. Second, one of our researchers allowed herself to be contaminated with this virus."

"What class of myxovirus?"

"Ortho, though it appears an anomalous mutation."

"Influenza, then," Kalpana raised an eyebrow. "Not often a neurological impact."

Rao began to speak, stopped himself, then continued. "Yes. The contagion unit found neural abnormalities in all six victims, perhaps a result of high fevers. Hence, a call to UN Medical; hence, you. Six infected, ten others under tight quarantine. This strain is highly contagious. However, we seem to be lucky—the infectees had minimal contact with others."

"How long is the infectious stage?"

"A day or two, we think. No more than three. By the beginning of the third day, victims are incapacitated. The six here have been comatose for three days."

At Rao's suggestion, they donned safe suits and visited the quarantine ward where five of the six infectees were kept.

They included three lab workers, a cleaning lady, and Ram Sen—a young boy who worked as a lab helper, errand boy, and general mascot of the facility. He was Rao's nephew. A sixth man, the boy's neighbor—apparently some sort of criminal—was kept under separate lockdown.

Rao followed Kalpana as she visited each bed. All five patients looked gravely ill, puffy-eyed, pallid, feverish. She attached sensors and used her palmkit to take neural readings of each one, ending with the boy Ram Sen.

As she finished her first circuit, the contagion crew entered in their powder-blue UN gear. Rao went quickly to the door, almost salaaming them in. He gave Kalpana a perfunctory introduction, then invited her to leave by suggesting that she continue her work later.

•••

In her hotel room, Kalpana awaited analysis of the first scans, sleepless. It was night, but she kept all of the lights up.

When she was able to sleep, it was this way, in brightness.

She smiled to herself. Night-troubled, rain-hating, rational—not her father's girl. Never to be.

The room screen glowed, oozing multiplexed news and commercials.

She sighed. Tonight felt like another sopor night.

A newscaster's talking head promised "Eight hundred dead in Mahabilipuram—next." But she was not falling for the hook "next," probably a damned *yuga*, and anyway, she was not interested in today's disaster. By voice, she faded most of the channels, brought her comm queue to the foreground.

Nothing much, though. Solicitations from several vendors of fine technology, an update on state employee benefits. A birthday luncheon. A note from Bobby Kuphal that wouldn't convert into text. She considered bouncing it, unread, but curiosity prevailed. She accepted the message and awaited the pineal connection.

Nothing happened; cheap hotel electronics striking again. She slid off the end of the bed and stood near the screen, cupping the cool, hand-sized dome atop it, submitting her handprint. By the time she settled back onto the bed, her pineal interface was kicking in, spraying cold light before her mind's eye.

Bobby's thin, dark features appeared. "Too much work, K," his disembodied face said, smiling puckishly. "Got to take time off. Here I am skiing the Himalayas and you are nowhere to be found. Speak to me."

A little clip of him disappearing down a slope, and *poof*, back to the overlit hotel room. She frowned. Text would've been sufficient, yes? But that was Bobby.

Vacation? Not now. Not anytime soon, most likely.

She asked for her earlier tomograms of the plague victims, studying brain cross sections on the screen, finding a few thermal irregularities, maybe even lesions in the reticular formation of the patients.

Something happening in the amygdala, too, posterior. What had she read on that recently? She could not recall.

She clipped a few zoomed views and dispatched them to another analysis server in Bangkok. Their oddball AIs always came up with a different perspective. Perhaps by morning she would receive something.

In any case, the damage was quite subtle. From a neurological view, at least, none of these people had suffered serious harm. Good news for them.

•••

The next day, Kalpana arrived at the Rahman Center early to take blood and cerebro-spinal fluid from the patients. While working beside Ram Sen, she felt a presence, as if someone had entered the room.

She turned and gave a start. Ram Sen's large, open eyes fixed on her in a gentle stare, warm and unblinking.

"Can you speak?" she asked in English, not sure if it was a language he understood.

"Yes." His eyes followed her as she moved closer, though his head and body remained still.

"Do you know where you are?"

"The moon?" he said. "You are a moon person?"

"It is a safe suit," said Kalpana. "You are ill."

"A joke," said Ram Sen. He flashed a toothy smile. He had a pleasant face, with the jut-mouthed features common in South India. "I work here, you know. How are the others?"

"We don't know yet. Everyone else is still—asleep."

Ram Sen gave a tiny nod. "Coma—I am not *that* young. I think I will be okay, but the others, a few are quite old. This is why I ask."

"Yes."

"What day it is?"

"Wednesday, twelfth of May."

"Four days, then," he said, looking concerned. "You must feed Hanuman."

"Hanuman?"

"My monkey," said Ram Sen. "I keep him in a cage during the day, or he gets into trouble. So he has not been fed."

"I will have someone take care of it."

"Good. Thank you."

For several minutes, neither of them spoke. Ram Sen studied her with a soft, steady gaze, smiling vaguely. The unease that usually accompanied such silence was strangely absent. Kalpana's breathing slowed, a warm comfort spreading through her body.

Long ago, she had felt this way. At times during her childhood. Alone in the small garden behind her home, or with her father, sitting in a warm breeze. Silent, thoughtless, happy. She had forgotten.

After a minute or two, Ram Sen blinked slowly. "I must now sleep."

"Wait."

"The fever—I am very tired." His eyes closed. Their short exchange had exhausted him. Quickly, she left the quarantine ward.

J. Rao sat at his desk, searching through data on his screen.

"Ram Sen has awakened. He spoke while I was in the ward," Kalpana said.

J. Rao turned slowly from his work, seeming mildly annoyed. "He is awake now?"

"No, not anymore. He spoke with me for a minute or two."

Rao brought up a video window. "This just happened?"

"Yes, just now."

He replayed the brief dialog with Sen a few times. "He seems weak, tired," he said finally. "To be expected, I guess. He is not himself. It is a good sign, though. This is excellent news."

"He seems," said Kalpana, "an impressive boy."

Rao's brow furrowed. "Sen?"

"Ram Sen. The sick boy." Kalpana stared, puzzled by his response.

"Sorry. Impressive? Sen is a good boy," said Rao, "but he has few ambitions, and his attention wanders. His life revolves around bad movies, girls, and his motor scooter. He is my brother's youngest son. I know him quite well."

•••

Later that day, Ram Sen was awake when she returned to the ward, propped up in his bed reading a book. Some color had returned to his face. The swelling around his eyes had decreased.

"So," he said, "have you visited Hanuman?"

"No, Sen, I have not had time yet."

"Please *do* this," he said. "And I must ask you another favor—please set him free. I will not be returning there."

"I am sure," said Kalpana, "you will be out of here in another week or so."

"No matter. I will be headed west."

"West? You should not travel. You are recuperating from a serious illness. Why would you do this?"

Ram Sen looked her over carefully. "I am not sure I will tell you. You are one of them, are you not?"

"I don't know," she said. "What 'them'?"

"This brotherhood of the cutting and shrinking, the bright lights. This is your religion."

Sen was starting to annoy her. What permitted him such generalizations and hasty judgments? "I have no religion."

"Everyone has religion."

Kalpana laughed nervously. "I do not think it is quite that easy. Or so bad."

He turned that quiet, serious gaze on her, not at all a silly adolescent. "It is worse than you think. But I will tell you anyway. Do you know Arunachala?"

"No. What is it?"

"A sacred hill in Tamiland, in South India, revered for thousands of years. It has several temples. It is my home, and I must return there."

·   "Your home is nearby, in Manikganj. Were you not born here?"

"There is more than one home," said Ram Sen. "Anyway, I must go to Tamiland."

Kalpana smiled. "Your uncle will not allow it. You are rather young to take such a trip alone."

"I was confused yesterday," said Sen, unsmiling. "Like many. Like *you*, I see. Now I am not."

He would live in a temple? She did not like this personality change at all. Was it of a neurological origin? She would have to study the scans again. He seemed very lucid, but not himself, not the boy Rao had described. She hoped it was temporary.

He gestured toward the other patients, rather pompously, she thought. "Now we choose again. I am not confused anymore. Everything is changed."

•••

The next morning, two more patients woke. The first, Dr. Pandya, a heavy, fiftyish researcher for the center, spent most of her first hour weeping uncontrollably. Dr. Pandya showed neural signatures like Sen's, but slower in their progression.

After the weeping subsided, Kalpana introduced herself and told Pandya as carefully as she could about the possible neural consequences of the illness. "If you are ready, I'd like to do a series of perception tests."

"I don't know," said Dr. Pandya, in an incongruous schoolgirl voice. "I do not think so."

Her regressive behavior was odd, but not altogether surprising, given what Kalpana had seen so far. She rescanned the woman as they spoke. "It is important that we understand the effects of the illness. We cannot treat it or prevent its spread if we do not understand its nature."

Dr. Pandya smiled, glassy-eyed, her voice growing more normal. "I have made a grievous error."

Pandya had had nothing to do with the virus's release, so her guilt had to be part of her emotional exaggeration. The microscreen on Kalpana's scanner showed the same heightened activity in the amygdala she had noticed the night before. "What error? This is not your fault."

Dr. Pandya began weeping again. Kalpana stroked her hair, though it was difficult to comfort someone while wearing a safe suit. "You are not responsible for this. What troubles you?"

"I have lived the wrong life."

Kalpana thought of Sen. *Everything is changed.* She prepared to hear how Pandya longed for a cave in the Himalayas, surviving on mountain water and *prana* alone. "I was to be a dancer, you know."

"A dancer?" said Kalpana flatly, unable to suppress a memory of DisFeed hippos dancing in tutus. Pandya's physique was not a dancer's.

"I know it seems absurd now. But as a young girl, I was quite good. And to dance, to study the traditions, this was my love."

"Your parents interfered?"

"No, they were not like that. It was my own decision, my own fears. I chose something safe, and which I was also good at."

Kalpana decided to defer the perceptual tests, happy with the additional scan for now. She excused herself, and picked up the receiver on a nearby phone.

The next patient she needed to see was a Mr. Prabhu, or Mr. Lockdown, as Kalpana was coming to think of him. But she'd need Rao to give her access to Prabhu.

Rao did not answer his extension, though the phone-indicator showed him at his desk. She beeped him and waited.

Dr. Pandya hummed a traditional melody, lost in her memories.

After a few minutes, it became obvious Rao was not going to return the call. Frustrated, Kalpana decontaminated and went to his office.

•••

Rao sat at his desk, as expected, across from Goodacre, the head of the contagion team, a blue-eyed, handsome Brit with a small gray mustache. Goodacre had led his crew into the quarantine room on that first day, when Rao had evicted her.

"Why did you not answer my page?" Kalpana asked.

"As you can see," said Rao, "I am meeting with Dr. Goodacre. There are important matters."

"I will see Prabhu now," she said. "I have examined the others."

Goodacre smiled wanly at her.

"Sit down, please," said Rao.

She sat.

"Dr. Goodacre feels that the outbreak is now contained."

"We are lucky," said Goodacre, "that the contagion is brief, perhaps not even forty-eight hours, and that all of the carriers traveled little. Had even one of them gone into Dhaka—" He shook his head.

The tenor of the conversation bothered her, this air of finality. She surreptitiously pressed the send button on her equipment. In keeping with procedure, the data storage was their property, and all it contained. But no matter what happened, she would retain *something* to analyze in her personal files. "How can you be sure?" she asked.

"We can't, of course," said Goodacre. "Not completely sure. In this work I find certainty to be a character flaw. We will continue to monitor the contact points of all the infectees. But we *are* certain that they have passed through the communicable stage."

"Yes. Well, my work is not finished. Something odd is going on with Pandya and Sen—personality change. I suspect there may be a neurological cause. I would like to examine Mr. Prabhu, and return tomorrow to finish with Pandya and Sen."

"Mr. Prabhu," said Rao, "is a street criminal. It does not make sense for you to visit him at this time."

"Surely someone can accompany me," said Kalpana. "Has he shown violent behavior?"

"There is certainly that potential, yes," said Rao. "In any case, such a visit is not necessary."

Goodacre nodded, smiling sympathetically.

"We don't know that," said Kalpana. "The neurological work has barely begun. I require more data."

They both looked at her silently, wooden-faced. Rao cleared his throat. "We appreciate all you have done, Ms. Shah."

How magnanimous, she thought. "Don't give me that! I insist on seeing Prabhu."

"Anger," said Rao, "is bad for the blood. Very bad, very heating. You must calm down. In our view the crisis is over. Further testing is a waste of government funds."

"I insist," said Kalpana. "You are bound by the rules of the Johannesburg Strictures."

Rao sighed. "You are an uncooperative woman."

What, she wondered, were they up to? Probably the usual—nothing more than the standard turf-politics. Rao had seen her as an annoyance all along, a non-doctor and non-Bangladeshi forced on him by bothersome protocol.

"Dr. Goodacre," said Rao, "has transmitted his signature to your organization. The *Stage 1* is officially ended. Further investigation is now at the discretion of this center. I must ask you for your data."

He held out his large, fleshy hand. Kalpana detached the data cartridge and flipped it on his desk.

• • •

She had the taxi drop her off a half-kilometer from the hotel, and went into an office building, down to a mallway that connected hotels with local businesses. She wanted to walk a little, away from people, away from the beggars and street hawkers.

Below, midafternoon, turbaned security guards outnumbered the shoppers. She thanked the nameless gods of shopping areas, and walked at a slow pace.

To her right, in the low-rent strip near the ceiling, an old LED ticker dispensed fragments of local and world news: movie stars, financial deals, portents of war or peace. Opposite, holographic projections of American cartoon characters careened through a narrow slice of space, chirping in Bengali.

Light shows sparkled in store windows, explosions of color and geometry. Perfumes oozed from the sari and pearl shops. *Pink pearls, the wondrous, of Bangladesh.*

She could not shake the strange discomfort that had been with her ever since she left Rao's lab. She felt at once anxious and exhausted, disjunct, as if her nervous system carried some unknown toxin.

She was not angry. She had been through enough similar nonsense to know that one's anger had to be brief and precise, if expressed at all. Those who did not learn this ended up unemployed, or cardio statistics.

The first few times she'd fallen victim to office politics, bad management, or leering incompetence, she'd been less circumspect, but that seemed like long ago. One could not survive in this work without patience and resiliency. This business with Rao was all too typical, and she should not let it trouble her.

Still.

She walked on, feeling short of breath. Did she have a physical problem? No, not likely. She got plenty of exercise and ate well. The insomnia was her only persistent problem.

A mild anxiety attack, then. For some reason, she was not handling the day's frustrations well.

She breathed slowly, deliberately, nearing the hotel entrance.

The last stores on both sides sold music and had the usual blaring displays. In one, a virtual Neelam—India's current box-office queen—wriggled in a tight sari, singing about lost love, backed by the smarmiest Indian orchestra Kalpana had heard in a while. On the other side, some Western head-banger band leapt around a morphing stage, seemingly into Kalpana's path, posing, spewing vocals that approached white noise.

She stopped for a moment to watch. The odd dual concert was funny, silly. But touching her face, she realized she was crying.

•••

Before bed, in her bright room, she composed a software search robot to find recent material on the amygdala, hoping to locate the reference she vaguely recalled. She released it onto the net and fell back on the bed, engaging an occasional ritual, thinking words into a buffer somewhere back home:

Father, leaver,
Do you still know me?
Do you still live,
bearded, emaciated, ashen?
The little girl
you once knew is gone.
She has done well
If not to your liking.
But her work helps others.
She is kind to them.
She gives to the poor
When she can,
Heals the many.
Still,
There is a sorrow deep inside her,
Even in greatest happiness.
She thinks it is yours, this wound,

Given long ago.
How does it heal?

K.

•••

At 1:00 A.M., she awoke suddenly from sopor-induced sleep, wide-eyed. She had been dreaming. Some mission with her family, deep in a vast mine in the south. There was a sense of great portent, but she could not recall why. Like so many of her dreams, it was all half-formed, half-remembered, inconclusive.

Then there was a trip through a dark graveyard, warm, windy. Slate gravestones worn smooth with age, small and oddly cylindrical. Her father was there, frail now, with a wispy beard. He smiled and reached to her—electric-shock touch, hot and sharp. She'd lost consciousness.

Now she sat in bed in her artificial day, sleep gone again as quickly as desert rain. And she had hours to kill. Her flight did not leave until the late afternoon.

She asked the TV to power up, checked messages. Meeting notes from the office, confirmation of a technology class. And another jot from Bobby K, this one wearing the God's-hand icon of an interactive clip. Date and time only fifteen minutes ago, world-time.

She invoked it: "Touch me."

The interface worked this time. There was a brief, chittering synchronization, radio neurons forming in the air. She ascended through a dome of white light.

She saw Bobby, or his recording, watched him from the air as he schussed down a difficult slope, visored and slim, royal blue against the white background. Then a voice-over—generic announcer voice:

"The slopes of Hardwar—finest in the Himalayas. From around the globe, skiers come to experience the legendary snowpack. Of Hardwar."

Now he was snowboarding, doing 180s in the air.

Enough filler, Kalpana thought. Where are you? These clips were designed to cover the time it took the other party to connect.

The snow fluoresced slightly, then she was beside him, holding his virtual hand as they descended a slope now covered with ribbons of color.

"2001," said Bobby, smiling at her, eyes still hidden behind his goggles. "The ski experience."

"You need a better writer," said Kalpana, though she felt happy to see him. Like many clips with expired copyrights, the material had been endlessly abused in commercials: SoyBoy, Delhi Deli. Still, in tastelessness, none equaled the notorious clip of Moses coming down from Sinai with a double six-pack of Bangla Cola.

"How about something more quiet," she said. "I need it."

They dissolved to a rain forest, near a narrow waterfall and lagoon. She lay on warm, soft moss. Animal noises were muted, and insects edited out.

She wore a red-and-gold sari, Bobby's preference, her hair down. Bobby sat beside her, cross-legged in a white lungi, showing off his slim, muscular torso.

"I wish you were real," he said. "But I can still give a ghost backrub. How is the trip? Job got you down?"

She considered how much to tell him. He had a sympathetic ear, but with a limited attention span. He understood her work only in the simplest sense.

"It's been a bad day," she said. "A local M.D. and a British one wouldn't let me finish my work."

He rubbed her feet. "Old-boy network?"

"I don't know," she said. "Not really. I don't even know why it's bothering me so. These things happen."

"You need some time off," said Bobby. "A little vacation. Let me conjure something."

"I don't—" she said, enjoying this realm of peace, but already the rain forest wing decayed into red-green-blue.

● ● ●

Newark, from the air, glittering towers of the rebuilt city looking across the Hudson to dead New York. Kalpana felt a warm summer breeze on her face. "So, where to, flyboy?"

"Millennium Ballroom, of course."

She could finally see his nice eyes now, dark and playful in the dim, sourceless light. The Millennium was an occasional hangout, five glassine floors of sound and light, bodies in motion. It was a place she often enjoyed, good for blowing off steam. Usually.

"No, Bobby," she said. "Not right now." Before the words were fully spoken, they segued again.

A white beach in the sun. Cancún perhaps, or Jamaica. They strolled hand in hand, barefoot, warm sand between their toes. She could smell the ocean, feel the breeze. There were people on the beach and in the water, swimming, power-skiing, paddling languidly in bright plastic contraptions. Snippets of music drifted on the breeze as they passed—Caribbean and western. The beach was not crowded, but it was still too much. She still felt a vague, visceral illness, like mild motion sickness. "This is a little better," she said, looking up at him. "But make them go away."

He stopped walking, gave a pained smile. "I can't. This one's not mine, and I don't have write-access."

The light and sound streamed in odd, swirling patterns, blurring. She could not focus, Bobby's face a blurred, low-res mask of concern. Something pressed on her chest, her throat, blocking her breathing. She coughed, choked, dropped to the ground. Her own voice seemed to call from somewhere far above: "Bobby!"

• • •

Eyes held closed, she lay on her bed in the hotel, a wetness across her chest and beside her. Nasty sour smell all around.

Lovely, she thought, sitting up carefully. Vomit disconnect—the best kind. On occasion, motion sickness intruded on flights in virtual space.

She rang the front desk to report the mess, peeled off her kaftan and got into the shower.

Later, as the maid changed her sheets, she sent a message to Bobby so he would not worry, then powered off the TV. When the maid left, she sat motionless on the edge of the bed, wondering about her return to Bombay. It seemed less and less appealing. If she left, she would be miserable for a month, unresolved. She had given in easily, too accommodating to these bureaucrats. She was learning bad habits.

She would contact Rao again, even call in some favors from the home office if necessary. She was not done just yet.

She laid back. She felt surprisingly, happily sleepy. Sleep-compatible, for once. She yawned. It was still very early in the morning. Rao could wait a few hours. She was not going to let this slumber opportunity get away.

• • •

Kalpana awoke thinking of Sen and the stupid monkey. She had promised she would check on the creature, but had not gotten around to it. She did not want to face Sen again having let it starve.

She dressed, checking her mail by voice. Last night's robot was a good one, apparently, its work filling her search queue. Atop the list of abstracts was the clip she had viewed a few months before. It was the work of some dead neurologist's avatar, entitled *Immortality and the Posterior Amygdala*.

The lofty title implied more than the study actually delivered. It focused on a group of pathologically morbid patients. Past research had suggested hyper-activity of the posterior amygdala in such cases. This study had used a drug engineered to normalize this pathology. It worked so well that two patients who received early, higher doses went from a phobic paralysis to exaggerated, even reckless, behavior.

Though the match was not exact, the study's tomograms resembled those she had seen in recent days.

She archived the material, then dug through her pocketbook and found the key Sen had given her, called a cab.

• • •

The home of Sen and the infamous Prabhu was ten minutes away, on the eastern side of Manikganj. It was a drab, concrete structure, prisonlike save for small Muslim verandas jutting from most of the rooms.

No caretaker could be found, so Kalpana climbed the stairs to the second floor and located Sen's room. Inside, the monkey's cage was opposite the door, near a window. Her heart sank as she spied it. The monkey lay on the bottom, a tawny mound of fur, unresponsive to the noise of her entry.

She started across the room to the cage, but stopped herself halfway. Hanuman's food dish was still half full. He had not starved. Kalpana felt in her bag for her biomask, ever careful, whispering, "Wouldn't want to catch what Sen had."

She stood, looked downward, laughed softly to herself. It sounded so strange, alien, like her mother or aunt speaking through her. She surveyed the neatly barren room. *Father, vanisher—do I stand in the graveyard?*

She took a slow breath and put the mask back in her bag. Even if the monkey was infected, who knew whether it would be contagious, anyway. Several days had likely passed since onset.

When she drew near, Hanuman opened watery eyes, alive after all. Sad little monkey-face, sniffling, suffering, but surviving, it seemed. He sneezed on her hands as she cleaned his cage, and she promptly washed them, some habits unbreakable. The creature had a bad wheeze, but there was really not much she could do beyond provide fresh food, water, and a few kind words. Somehow, she felt it would survive.

She disposed of her cleaning materials, sent herself a reminder to call the landlady in a couple of days to have her set the monkey free, and left.

•••

Back at Rao's lab, everything had turned cordial. Rao smiled and postured. She had sent a flurry of messages upstream, requesting intervention, and guessed his superiors had enumerated to him the various local powers of the Pan-Asian Medical Council.

"Of course, we never meant," said Rao, grinning like a fool, "to imply you cannot complete your work here. Only that we now assume official responsibility."

Whatever *that* meant. One had to be very careful with the vagaries of bureaucratese. *New—fact-free!* Such people must be made to capitulate, like stubborn children. "So, you will allow me to see all the patients?"

"Yes, of course."

"You will allow me to complete my work as I see fit?"

"Yes, certainly."

"You will allow me to see Prabhu?"

"Yes." His smile was growing tired.

"Good," said Kalpana. "The contagion—have there been any new cases?"

"No," said Rao, "I am happy to report there are none. The early quarantine was a success. We are fortunate."

She asked for her data cartridge. "I would like to see Sen first, then Prabhu and Pandya."

"You may not see Sen," said Rao. "You are unable to see Ram Sen."

"I thought," she said, her tone as grim as she could make it, "we had reached an understanding."

"I am very sorry."

"*Why* am I not allowed to see him?"

"It is an embarrassment, really. He is not here. He escaped yesterday during a linen-change. We have not been able to locate him since. Goodacre is not happy. Not at all."

Kalpana maintained her frown, fighting off an impulse to laugh. "When did this happen?"

"In the afternoon, not long after you left. In fact, if you have any notion of where we might search for him—"

She nodded, feigned a moment of recall. "He spoke of visiting an uncle in Khulna. Yes. I would look into that."

Then she excused herself, not wanting to laugh in Rao's face.

She visited the dreaded Mr. Prabhu, now deep in an expected reexamination of his lifestyle. Despite the ominous descriptions, he was a nervous, dark-skinned, tiny man whose crimes against mankind mostly involved pickpocketing and minor fraud. He had, however, spent much of his fifty-odd years in prisons.

"Everything is change, now," he told her in Bengali, echoing Sen.

"Han," she said. *Yes.* "How so?"

He did not know Hindi, Marathi, or more than a few words of English. He rambled briefly in one or two languages she could not even identify—Naga? Manipuri?—then dropped back into Bengali. "It is death sentence."

She asked him to clarify, and labored through his response, struggling with the odd hill-dialect Bengali he spoke. Standard Bengali would've been challenge enough.

He spoke of his days in prison, of the "dead" there. By this, she slowly realized, he meant those scheduled for hanging. He had seen men put to death, been with them in the months before they were hanged. He had seen a few scheduled to die and then pardoned.

They were all, he told her, the worst of men, even the reprieved. These men, if spared death, only returned to their criminal habits. Not one changed.

"But—" He held up a finger for emphasis, flashed a toothless smile, nodded. "But. While death. While—" He drew the shape of a noose in the air and touched his eyes, signaling sight. "While noose, then it is change. Then, men is change."

When she left, Kalpana planted a big kiss on Rao, leaving him in a state of moral shock. It was something he needed, in ways he had yet to understand.

•••

On the flight out, she pored over neurological references and her data, looking for closure. The observer kind, at least.

She pulled up background on brain structures, on the amygdala. Almond-shaped, hence its name, it nestled in the temporal lobe, and had long been associated with base emotions or fears.

She reviewed the paper her robot had tracked down, thought of Sen and Pandya. *Death-walis.* Death saints. Prabhu had used this term to describe his death-row friends. Saints for a time. Made reflective as long as the sword hung over them.

All of the patients had lesions in the portion of the amygdala now associated with the mortality sense. *Everything is changed.* Sen and Prabhu both sensed the nature of what the virus had wrought in them, confirmed by this scan data.

Unlike Prabhu's death-walis, though, this change was not born of external threat. This sentence was cellular, immutable. *Everything is change.* No return to old ways.

Kalpana looked out the window at the approaching green-and-tan haze of the Indian coastline. She felt a little warm. Her heart beat quickly, and her throat felt a little sore. She closed her eyes and took a long slow breath. No pardon.

• • •

Arunachala's main temple was a circus, a huge, smoky enclave with pyramidal gateways, each one layered with grotesque icons in the South Indian style. Gods on shelves, they always seemed to her, weird knickknacks.

Inside, in the dusk, the courtyard was full of people —families jabbering loudly in Tamil, children scurrying about, various animals. To her right, a Brahmin ran a pet-the-baby-elephant franchise for the children. Another, just behind them, seemed to be juggling.

She found a priest who spoke English, and described Ram Sen to him. He nodded and took her into a building where a young shaven-headed boy wanted ten rupees to anoint a Shiva statue on her behalf.

They went to another, larger stone structure, and waited for a large family to move from the entrance.

Illustrated by István Kuklis

They descended concrete steps, ducking a low stone ceiling. At the bottom, a small crypt-like room was lit by oil lamps.

Ram Sen sat there atop a concrete block, his dark eyes glinting in the low, flickering light. He jumped up and gave her an enthusiastic hug. "Doctor K, you have found me!"

He asked about the other patients. She told him they seemed to be recovering much like he had.

"And Hanuman—you kept your promise?"

"Yes," said Kalpana. "But he was sick. The flu, I think. I gave him fresh food and water."

"The flu," Sen echoed, slowly.

"This place," said Kalpana, gesturing upward. "This temple is total chaos."

"In its way, this is like anyplace else," he said. "But there is power here. I stay in the quiet rooms, where the current is strong."

Now he looked in her eyes, his brow slightly narrowed. That gentle, thoughtful gaze. "And you," he said. "How are you?"

Kalpana reached in her handbag for a tissue.

"You have the flu?" asked Sen.

"I think so. Hanuman, I suppose."

"You came here sick? You came through airports this way? Dhaka, Madras?"

"Yes, yes."

"Hm." He frowned, rubbed his chin thoughtfully. "And now?"

"I have some vacation time."

"But," said Sen, "you are not going home to rest."

"I think I would like to see the world. Athens, Moscow, Bangkok, JFK, Heathrow."

"You are sure of this? These are not good places to be sick."

"Yes," said Kalpana, "I have thought about it quite a bit." She lowered her eyes, thinking of her father again. Across the years, despite everything, there was still some thread. Something about all of this was his.

"One or two days, yes?"

"I figure about fifty hours before I am laid out," she said. "That should put me across the Atlantic safely, even with a few delays."

He nodded solemnly and smiled, not a boy's grin, but the qualified joy of one who saw the limits of things, the sorrow and ending in every bright, dancing surface.

For what seemed a long time, they sat in silence, in the dim stone enclosure of the room, gazing at each other, nothing more to be said. Finally, she took a deep breath.

"I must leave now," she said. "There's not much time left."

He leaned to her and gave her another hug, long and heartfelt.

Outside in the noisy courtyard, she sneezed as she pushed through a clot of people. For a moment, she felt guilty, but she recalled Sen's words. *Like anyplace else.* She passed the elephant and juggler again.

And as good a place to start, she thought, as any other.

NOCTURNE'S BRIDE

Written by
Brian Wightman

Illustrated by
John Lock

About the Author

In 1986, Brian Wightman says that he fell asleep on a zabuton in a rock garden in Kyoto. He awoke with a pen clutched in his hand, and knew then that he wanted to be a writer.

Since then, Brian has managed to feed himself by working as a bagel baker, chaplain, youth worker, organic cook, and window washer. He currently manages a support program for people recovering from mental illness. His work has previously appeared in Tales of the Unanticipated and Xizquil.

Brian is currently working on a science fiction novel set on a transformed future Earth.

The fine tale that follows won first place in its quarter, and bodes well for his career.

About the Illustrator

John Lock says that in his thirty years, he doesn't remember a time when he was not drawing—but does remember the first time he saw a Frank Frazetta cover. From that moment, he knew that the destiny of his artwork lay in the realm of imagination.

While in college, his professors told him that fantasy art was a waste of time, but to the chagrin of his teachers, the only fantasy piece he was allowed to create was praised as one of his best works.

During the past fifteen years, he has worked on perfecting his techniques with an airbrush as well as exploring other media and styles. He has done some limited work in the fantasy and science fiction fields, but it wasn't until he won this contest that the doors burst open and the hope of fulfilled dreams rushed in upon him anew.

He recognized her from the picture: a tall woman, young and uncertain. She sweated in a black, high-collared dress. Her hair was tied back in a foreign fashion; it had been passed through a long sleeve, or wrapped in a wide scarf perhaps. The last ends of it curled out of the scarf down near her waist. The scattering of short-haired native girls behind her were laughing and reuniting with kin, but she stood straight, her hands clasped together at her waist, her eyes scanning the road in the other direction. A large handbag sat on a trunk close beside her.

He started to walk up to her, then stopped two paces away, remembering that Old World people preferred to speak to others from a distance. "Chloe?"

She looked at him uncertainly. "Hames?"

Of course, she would have been expecting her fiancé to come in person.

"Ah, no. I'm his brother. Reed."

He held out his hand to her and she took it uncertainly. Around them the other passengers were already loading bags into trucks, or dragging them down to the docks to waiting boats.

"Where is Hames?" She spoke with a throaty accent, the way Old World girls in videos always talked.

"He couldn't come. He's busy with the harvesting, you know."

Illustrated by John Lock

She looked up at the reddish glow on the horizon that marked the sun, hidden behind the thin sheet of clouds. "What time is it?"

"It's just a little before noon."

"How long do we have before night?"

"Twenty or thirty days."

She looked back at him, her expression blank. "I meant today."

"Yes. Of course. Almost two hours."

"Thank you. Are you going to take me to Hames, now?"

"Yes. Of course. We'll be there by nightfall. Just across the straits, up the finger bay. I've got my boat here."

She picked up one end of her trunk as he reached for it.

"Here," he said, "I'll get that."

She stepped back, as if it were a concession to him, but she took the handbag off the trunk and held it against herself. Reed suddenly got the impression she had not been far from her luggage on her whole journey.

Her trunk took up most of his boat, making it unstable and low in the water. He stood on the gunwales to balance the boat with his weight, then offered to help her in, but she was already settling herself on the edge of the seat in the bow, her hands once again folded on her lap. He started the electric motor, and unfolded the arm so he could guide it from his standing position. The other boats were slipping quietly into the dimness to their private destinations. Reed pointed their boat across the strait and opened the throttle.

The flyer that had brought her lifted off with a rush of wind and noise. The sudden roar cut them off from each other, they could not speak and be heard. When it faded away they were alone on the water, no one else in sight.

Chloe opened a button at her throat.

"You say it's almost winter?" she said.

"Yes."

"It's hot." But still she sat with her legs together and her hands folded in her lap.

"It will cool off later. You won't want that dress again before deep winter."

"What is it you call winter here? You have your own name for it."

He hesitated. "Actually, we divide up the year into twelve seasons, not four. This is Sleep. You might want to cut your hair, too. It tends to rain a lot this half of the year. It's hard to keep things dry. There's a story of a foreign diplomat who wore his hair tied up in a knot on his head. After two months of never drying out , it started to mildew and he had to shave his head."

For the first time, her face cracked a thin smile. One hand came up and touched the braid at the back of her hair. "It's never been cut before," she said to herself. She looked out over the water again. She had to be uncomfortable, perched on the edge of the seat that also supported her trunk.

"Looks like it might rain again, soon," he said, looking at the sky. "I think we'll make it, though."

"Tell me again why Hames couldn't come," she said, twisting around on her seat.

Reed cleared his throat. "Well, it's the last harvest, you see. We only have so long to get the crops in, before . . . before winter."

"Famine," she said. "That's what you call winter, isn't it? No, don't shelter me. I live here, now. I want to know."

"It's not so bad as that. There's always fish. And we keep good grain stores."

"How long does Famine last?"

Reed hesitated.

"Tell me."

"Here, six hundred and forty-two days. From the last sunset to the first sunrise."

She looked into the bottom of the boat, considering this. "Almost two years," she said to herself.

"You must be very brave to come here," Reed said, trying to be positive and not knowing how. "If I got the chance, I'd leave. For the chance to have the sun rise every day. . . . Here when it finally does come up, we get so much of it . . ."

"And in between are the seasons you call Pestilence and Death; yes, I know. Am I so brave? We had four seasons of death in the Old World. Here there's only one."

She looked out over the water and Reed thought she didn't want to talk anymore.

Breakers swelled up as they emerged from the harbor onto the open straits. Reed balanced the top-heavy craft with his weight. He felt safer standing. He felt in control. The wind picked up. The rain was not far away.

"Is it true that mores in the New Worlds are more conservative than in the Old?" she asked suddenly, catching him by surprise.

"Ah. I don't know. What do you mean?"

"I've heard that on some worlds people do not bare their knees, for example."

Reed laughed. "In the other half of the year, you keep yourself covered. The sun is your enemy. Now, we have darkness for our modesty."

She pulled off her knee-high, animal-skin boots, then she arranged her skirt so it fell just above her knees. Her face was damp with sweat or spray. But then her hands folded in her lap again.

"How much farther is it?"

Reed pointed ahead to a narrow opening in the dark-green shoreline. "That's the finger bay. Hames lives about an hour up there. Later in the year you'll be right on the waterfront, but now we've got a short walk once we land."

"You don't live with Hames?"

Reed smirked. "Hames is a good enough farmer to make it on his own."

"So why did you come to get me?"

"I had the time."

"You're not a farmer?"

Reed cleared his throat. She had caught him in an uncomfortable lie. "Everyone's a farmer, this time of year."

She didn't confront him about the apparent contradiction, but he had to explain. It was odd, covering for his older brother this way.

"He's really a good farmer," he went on, talking because he had to say something. "Almost the perfect farmer."

"What is a perfect farmer like?" She still watched the coastline drift by them. "We don't have farmers in the Old World, anymore. The soil's poison, you know."

Reed cleared his throat again. He was digging himself in deeper. "The perfect farmer knows his land. He knows its chemistry, how it holds water, how it loses water, how it changes through the seasons. He knows his crops, what they will get from his land and what he will need to give them. He knows the rain and weather, and what he needs to do to deal with it."

"But what's he like as a person?"

Did she read his mind? Or was it just Hames? Hames had always loomed larger than life. Even when he was silent, he filled a room with his presence. Certainly, Reed's older brother, Chloe's fiancé, had filled the boat to overflowing.

Reed really owed his land to Hames, not their parents. The land of their parents had been difficult land. Part of it was steep and rocky, the other was drowned in the briny floods of Famine. Father and Mother planted bread and other salt-marsh plants during Pestilence, but bread wouldn't keep well through the oppressive heat of Drought, and it sold poorly in markets. Most people had more of the salt-marsh than they could stand. When the chance to grow returned in the season of Death, hayfair would endure the dry, salty land. It would keep through Famine, but it was tough and unpalatable, poor food for a poor family.

After his second year, Hames decided to improve the land. The valuable foods that could be grown on Nocturne needed flat fertile land out of reach of the salty waters. Through the whole of Famine, while Father and Mother fished the seas, Hames dug into the high hill-sides. He indentured himself to a neighbor, promising to labor in their fields come Pestilence, for help in the dark season. Reed was only a child then, only a little over a year old. He was sent to mind the traps in the shallows and dig for shellfish at low tide. But Reed got to watch as Hames, the tender young adolescent, terraced their slopes and transformed their salt-marsh into a prime farm. That year, Father and Mother raised apple root, red oats, and fey berries. They sold the delicacies and ate the grains through Drought. When Famine came once again, Hames had a new plan.

"This land is too small for three or four adults to work together. It's a waste of time. I'm going to work Regan's farm up the bay."

"Don't be ridiculous," Father said. "We don't have the money, even for that old piece of marshland."

"I've bought it on mortgage," Hames answered. "It can be terraced the same way as our land was."

"Regan's cousins won't mortgage that land to you," Father grumbled, thinking that would end the argument.

"They already did," Hames said and left the table.

Regan's cousins, not knowing what to do with the marshy land left in their care by Regan's death earlier in the year, had had difficulty finding a buyer. They had only received offers from poor farmers of unknown repute, or from wealthy men who had made a business of renting useless land to ignorant immigrants. Next to these, the young Hames was a proven farmer, a youth who would do whatever had to be done to make his payments.

Reed labored on, tending his parents' traps in the shallows and digging in the mud, while Hames expanded the family fortunes, built his own farm and his own house.

That year, at the very beginning of Drought, Father died, leaving Reed and his mother alone on the plot of land that was too small for three or four farmers. Reed found himself standing in the midnight sun beside Hames's grain shed. If he opened the gate, the grain would spill out on the ground. The top layer would dry out and crack in the hot Drought sun. Vermin, if they found the mound of unprotected grain, would burrow into it. Perhaps they would lay eggs that would destroy the entire store, all that had been grown for the long dry season ahead. Hames would never suspect that the villain had been his own brother.

Reed stood in the hot sun with his hand on the bolt. He dreamed of Hames's return home, his defeat in this venture of independence. With one jerk of the hand, Reed would bring back together the family that had been splintered.

He thought of that moment many times when he worked alone beside his mother that year. He would see himself going back, drawing the bolt, watching the golden red grains spill through the door into a growing cone on the dusty ground. He knew exactly how it would have looked.

Mother died next Pestilence. Hames offered to share a portion of the wealth he had accumulated alone on his new farm, but Reed declined. This was his penance for his fantasies: he ate none of the grain he had plotted to ruin. From that day on, he and Hames were equal. Reed worked alone the land that was too small for three or four.

•••

"You don't like him, do you?" Chloe twisted around to look at Reed.

He laughed uneasily. "You have no mercy."

"Am I acting like an Old World girl? Crass and direct?"

"No."

"Well, I won't change overnight."

"Nobody asked you to."

"Well, that's good. I changed worlds, but I didn't change myself."

"Right."

"So why don't you like him?"

Reed sighed. "Because I'm his younger brother. Because he is the perfect farmer, and I'm not."

"Is that why you came to get me? You're a sloppy farmer? You can take the better part of the day off even in the middle of the last harvest, even if it isn't your wife you're going to meet?"

Reed nodded. "Yes. That's right."

"Does this make you less of a man?"

"No."

"Just making sure I understand Nocturne's values."

She turned and looked out at the coastline, dark lines in the failing light. They were approaching the finger bay. The sky hung heavy with rain. The sun could not have dipped below the horizon already, but the thickening clouds had obscured all trace of its orb.

He offered her a piece of apple root. Her face cracked a smile again. She apologized, saying she hadn't eaten since, oh, since before she boarded the flyer, some six hours ago. She grimaced at the sweet and sour taste, but she ate all he gave her.

"The air smells funny here," she said.

"I've heard the air on the Old World smells like sewage."

"That's not true. Most of it, most of the really dangerous residue, you don't smell at all. But there isn't any life to it. It's like . . ." she looked back at him and her face fell. "You wouldn't have the least idea what I'm talking about. Any comparison I could think of . . . you have never heard of."

She turned away again, and trailed one hand overboard.

"Don't," Reed said softly. "You don't want to dangle your hand in the water. When the tide's coming in, there are darts in the shallows."

She snatched her hand back. "So what would Hames have done if you had been a more perfect farmer and not wanted to lose harvest time coming to get me? Let me wander aimlessly until I tried to swim for it and got my head bit off by a dart? Whatever that is."

"One of our version of fish. They're not that bad. They're no bigger than your little finger. But they hurt."

"Quit doing that."

"What?"

"Dodging my questions. Is that a Nocturne thing? I told you I'm a crass and direct Old World girl, I'm used to getting things laid out straight for me. I live here now, I need to know these things."

"Yes, of course. You're right. It's not a Nocturne thing. It's just me."

"Well, answer my question, then. What would he have done?"

"There's a ferry that runs up the bay in about two hours."

"But you volunteered to come get me instead, and he thought this was a good idea?"

"No. I . . ."

She struck her trunk with her fist. "Say it!"

Reed started. Her blank composure had only been a veil. She was tense to the point of snapping. "I told him he was a jerk, and he said that if I thought it was so important, I could go pick you up myself. So I did."

She rolled her eyes. "How old are you, Reed?"

"I turn four in Fisher—the start of Famine. Why?"

Her brows drew together, then she hung her head in her hands. "So that's, what, twenty-four of my years? Twenty-three? I don't know. It's too much to take, all at once."

"Do you like Hames?" Reed finally dared.

"What's to like? I don't see him anywhere."

"Well, I assume you sent messages."

"You believe in love, don't you, Reed?"

"You don't?"

"Love is a freedom. Maybe you can afford it, here on Nocturne. I had a choice. I could have fallen in love on the Old World, and died, or I could come here, and live. That was more than I wanted to pay for love."

Reed looked away from her eyes. She was what she called herself, an Old World girl, crass and direct.

"You may find you get along with Hames well," he said. "He doesn't believe in love either."

When he glanced back, her face had fallen again, and he thought, strangely, that he might have hurt her.

"But he is, really, a very kind man," Reed added. "And you must like him some. There must have been other options, after all. And some folks do just come. Mostly men, or families, but some women come and join squatters' collectives on the islands. You chose to be a picture bride. And you chose Hames. There must have . . ."

He faded out as he saw her glaring at him.

"Yes. Some folks do just come," she said. "What is it you call those people?"

"I've never said that," he said slowly.

"Maybe you haven't. But other folks say it. What is the name for people who come here with no money or kin?"

Reed shook his head.

"I'll help you. They're only good for one thing. Rather than send people, the Old World might as well send . . ."

"Fertilizer."

"Thank you. My brother fertilized Nocturne. He came here three years ago. My years. It was, I think, the second season of spring. What you call Pestilence. Gary was going to squat on an island, and then when he had got himself settled I was to come out and join him. But things didn't go quite right. The first island your development council sent him to was nothing more than rock and water. Nothing grew there. So he went back for another recommendation. He spent more of his money getting around to the other side of the pole.

"That island had good soil. It also had a dozen squatters on it already, who were feuding. One group shot at him, another took him in. But they just wanted to use him. Gary wrote back. He said one day he was hauling up traps in a little bay, and someone shot the man in the boat with him. The guys on the shore kept telling him they weren't going to hurt him, he should just come ashore and join their side of the feud. Gary sat there, covered with the blood and brains of the dead man, the boat bobbed and turned on the waves, and they shouted and laughed from the shore. Eventually the boat turned until the bow was pointing out to sea. So Gary just turned it on. They shot at him, but they missed.

"He drove that boat until the battery went dead. Then he put out the oars and rowed until he came back to the mainland. He did find a couple places that might have worked out, but they had collectives on them. You had to buy into them, and he was out of money. The last message I got from him said he'd found some scorched land on an island far from the pole. There was no one else on the island, but he'd rather that than go back to the place he had been. But by then it was—what is the third season of Pestilence?—First Harvest, and he was tired, poor and sick. According to the notice I got a year later, Gary only lived a few days after that last letter. It was a common fever. Something he could have easily avoided, if anyone had been there to tell him how to do it."

Chloe looked at Reed fiercely. "I intend to live."

"Hames will treat you well," Reed said softly. "Unless this whole region starves, you won't. This is a hard world, but you couldn't live with a better man to help you face it."

"You think less of me, don't you, for coming here to be his bride. You're offering me kindness, but it is the kindness of pity."

"No."

"Yes. I don't need pity. I'm not giving up anything. You think I'm giving up something very important, but you're wrong. It's not that important. I'll still have me. I can still be the person I want to be. And having Hames or you or anyone else around won't change that. I accept changes, I don't surrender to them. Don't laugh at me!"

Reed stopped smiling. "I wasn't laughing. I was just thinking. You remind me of Hames. You two will either fall in love, or you'll kill each other."

Chloe turned around and rode in silence for a while. The rain finally started, a light mist on a blustering wind, not enough to really wet their hair. Reed expected more, but instead of turning into driving rain it faded, leaving them damp and heavy in the growing gloom. Reed caught a glimpse of a large form perched in a tree by the shore.

"Look over there," he pointed. "An owl. First one I've seen this year."

She followed his finger.

"Real owls?" she asked.

It spread its wings and swept down, plunging into the water, then lifting off suddenly with a fish-shaped shadow dangling from its talons.

"No," she said. "That's a Nocturne owl."

"Yes," Reed said. "Nothing from the Old World would live here."

"Except us." Chloe sighed. "I'd better see what this world looks like while the light lasts. Do your trees lose their leaves in winter, like ours?"

"Yes. Almost the whole world goes dormant. Only the seas are still alive."

"Maybe we should follow their lead, and hibernate until spring."

"I hate spring. There's a reason why it's called Pestilence, after all. More people die in Pestilence than in any other season, unless there's some problem with the stores. Death is my favorite season. It's the only peaceful one we have. But Famine isn't bad. You'll learn to like the dark."

"I don't doubt I will. A part of me liked that this was the season you were going into right now. I could have waited a little longer, you know. I could have come closer to the end of Famine. But it seemed right to restart under cover of darkness, give myself some time before I was forced to see what I had done by the light of day."

"So you do have doubts."

"Who wouldn't? But when the sun rises in the spring, I will look around and find that I am still me." She picked up her braid and cradled it in her hands.

"And your children?"

Chloe dropped the braid. "Children?"

"It's possible. Hames will expect it. You could have two before sunrise. Hames will think it's a good idea, in fact, because it's possible you might lose one in Pestilence."

"Now you're being nasty," she said, with startling clarity. "You really do dislike your brother, don't you?"

Reed opened the throttle instead of answering. The wake built up a roar behind them, and the waves slapped harder against the bow. Chloe braced herself against the jarring bounce of the boat.

"What about you, Reed?" She raised her voice over the increased noise. "You're going to be my brother-in-law. Who the hell are you? Are you married?"

He shook his head.

"What is it that you do better than Hames?"

"Don't."

"No. I want to know. It's dark, you can't see my face. The world's shutting down; no one will know until the sun rises two years from now. Hames is the better farmer. Is he the better man?"

"No."

"Why not?"

"I'm kinder."

The rain started again, heavier, large drops that struck with a perceptible impact. It would wet them thoroughly in a moment. The waves lapped almost to the gunwales, and rocked the boat. Reed throttled down.

"I used to have to be better than him at everything," he said, as if to himself. "But not anymore, not really. We've picked our fields of expertise, as it were. He's the better farmer. I'm the better man."

"And I, between you, am disappearing into darkness." Chloe faced forward and folded her hands again on her lap.

They didn't speak for the last fifteen minutes of the trip. Reed ran the boat up on shore and tied off to a tree. Chloe let him carry the trunk. Hames's summerhouse was a small cottage on stilts, surrounded by a wide veranda. The front door stood wide in welcome, though Hames rode his harvester at the far end of the field. A single lantern hung from the porch rafters, bathing the entrance with a soft yellow glow. They mounted the stairs and sat in the split-cane chairs to the side of the door. Hames saw them. He stopped the harvester and came to meet them. They waited while he trudged through the muddy field, and the rain fell heavier and harder.

Hames stopped at the foot of the stairs and stroked his beard, looking at her. Chloe sat straight and rigid, as she had stood on the landing pad. She had buttoned the top button of her dress. Neither of them spoke. Hames grunted softly, then climbed the stairs. He came to her, stood too close to her, and touched the long braid that hung down until its end lay in her lap.

"How long does it take," he said, "to grow hair like that?"

"Nineteen—I mean, three years."

"It's pretty. Well, this is your home, now. No need to wait here like a guest. I've got to finish the harvesting. Too much more rain and the grain'll split its husks. Reed, you show her the house? Help her settle in?"

"Hames," Reed said. "If it hasn't split yet, it won't be split by tomorrow."

Hames snorted. "I didn't make this place by harvesting tomorrow."

"But . . ."

"But what?" Hames challenged him.

"But it's your business, not mine."

"Mm." He turned and walked back down the stairs.

Reed sighed. "Well, shall I show you inside?"

"No," she said. "I'd rather sit here awhile. Do you have a drink, here? We call it coffee, back on the Old World. Roasted beans steeped in hot water. Do you have something like that?"

"I don't know. There's cone. It's a tuber we roast and steep. Would you like some?"

"Yes. Yes, please. Just make it up the way you usually do, and bring it to me."

She sat in her chair, her hands primly folded, but her eyes pleaded. Reed could not resist desperation. "I'll be right back."

It only took him five minutes to boil the water and steep the ground root. When he brought out the tray with steaming cups and biscuits, she was not on the porch. Her trunk and handbag were also gone. A square track in the mud showed where she had dragged the trunk back down the path to the waterfront.

Reed put the tray down and trotted after her. He wanted to call out but didn't dare. He had an irrational fear she would try to drive away in his boat and over-turn it in the middle of the bay, but when he got there she was sitting on her trunk beside his boat. She had changed clothes. She wore a loose cotton shirt and a pair of shorts. She had hacked off her hair just above her shoulders. She looked at the braid in her hands, still wrapped in the scarf.

"Chloe?"

"Tell me something, Reed." She looked up at him. "This farm of yours, this less-than-perfect farm: could you use help on it?"

"What do you mean?"

"What I said. Another pair of hands, to help you bring in the harvest before the grain splits, seeing as how you're a day behind already, as it is."

Reed didn't say anything.

Chloe lifted the end of the severed braid and brushed it against her nose. "The way I figure it, Gary died because he didn't know what he was doing and didn't have time to learn. But if I worked with you for a year, I might know what I was doing. I could get that land he'd come here for. You believe in love, so you wouldn't have to marry me. So do you want a partner?"

"I couldn't do that to my brother."

"The hell you couldn't. Help me get my trunk in your boat, and let's get going. I'm hungry and tired, and I don't want to sit here until tomorrow."

Reed didn't move.

"What?" she asked.

"A year's a long time."

"Until spring then. Just through the night, then we'll look at things again when the light of day returns. Help me, Reed. I want to make one last choice while I still can."

"You're going to make a lot more than that, I think." He took hold of the handle at one side of her trunk.

JENNY, WITH THE STARS IN HER HAIR

Written by
Amy Sterling Casil

Illustrated by
Paul Marquis

About the Author

Amy Sterling Casil wrote her first novel—
"Freddy the Friendly Butterfly"—at the
age of five. Since then, she has moved up in the world. She has
been a finalist in this contest in 1995, 1996, 1997, and 1998.

I find that interesting. Though the stories we see are
always anonymous, her quality shows through. Amy's work
is always thoughtful and often poignant or gut-wrenching.

Her finalist story for this contest, "Johnny Punkinhead,"
was published in The Magazine of Fantasy and Science
Fiction, and a sequel to that story, "Chromosome Circus,"
will also soon appear in the same magazine. In the meantime
she has recently sold to Talebones Magazine, and she just
placed in this contest. Her prize-winning story, a powerful
tale called "My Son, My Self," will appear in next year's
Writers of the Future anthology.

Her stories have won her honorable mention in The
Year's Best Fantasy and Horror and in The Year's Best
Science Fiction anthologies.

Amy received her MFA in creative writing at Chapman University, and is a graduate of Clarion East. Since 1994 she has moderated the Science Fiction Writer's Workshop on America Online, and she currently teaches writing through AOL's Online Campus, UC Riverside Extension, and the Novel Advice online site for writers. She also writes for Speculations *magazine, and has published poetry and nonfiction in women's and literary magazines.*

About the Illustrator

Paul Marquis was born in 1973 and raised in the San Francisco Bay area. While at San Jose State University, he stumbled across several talented teachers who taught him that he could obtain anything he wanted. He took it upon himself to expand his "meager" skills by obtaining gallery spaces before having done any work, thus adopting the sink-or-swim outlook he needed to survive as an illustrator. He had three exhibitions before he ever took a single illustration class, and he had three more exhibitions before he graduated.

While he loves painting and drawing, he pursues writing and acting as he finds time. His long-term goal is to follow in the footsteps of James Cameron, Tim Burton, and Clive Barker—three artists who started small and eventually turned to the ultimate canvas.

Spitz was improving Jenny Julian's face when she brushed her fingers across his carmine velvet mask. For ten years he'd been her outlaw cosmetic surgeon, yet she'd never seen his face. The red velvet was a stage curtain between Spitz and the straight, unmodified world.

He smoothed the mask with a nervous hand. "I thought you weren't coming back," he said.

"The mole, just there, under my eye," she told him.

Spitz sighed, like a sleepy child. "This is the last time. I thought you'd made it out."

"No," Jenny said. She turned and he pulled her back with gentle pressure on her cheek.

"You said you'd fallen in love with a man."

She bit her lip. "So I did," she murmured. And so she had.

Spitz continued his work and Jenny was glad that he didn't press harder. "There's only so far you can go without people knowing," Spitz said. Jenny felt the warm drip from the pipette as he applied new tissue. "Even someone like me has limits."

She opened her mouth. "Could you lengthen my incisors?"

Spitz's eyes, like dark olives, blinked through the mask. "That's bizarre."

"Something dangerous." Jenny smiled.

"You're hunting again, aren't you?" Spitz looked past her shoulder, his gaze fixed somewhere on the blank gray wall of the treatment room.

"Hunting? I'm free. I thought I'd visit the Norton Simon. They've got a show on the Renaissance and the Reformation."

Spitz peeled his latex gloves with a snap. Again, the childish sigh. "You were beautiful when you came in," he said. "I don't say that to everyone. To anyone."

Jenny crossed her legs and rested her chin in the palm of her hand. "I was not," she said. "I had a hideous pug nose."

"If I told you it was you all along, would you believe me?" He stepped toward her, then hesitated. The crepe rubber soles of his shoes squeaked on the linoleum floor.

She put her arms behind her head and eased back in the soft beige leather chair. "Lengthen my incisors," she said.

His shoes squeaked again as he walked away. "Tomorrow," he said. "I've got a full schedule."

"You always had time for me before," she called and lazily began to climb from the chair.

Spitz turned. He inclined his head slightly, the mask harlequin-like, and she imagined that underneath his face was a skull, no flesh at all, just those shiny dark eyes set in dry bone.

"You're like my hairdresser, always wanting to dictate the cut," she said.

"You don't have a hairdresser," Spitz replied.

"I did have one."

"That was then, this is now."

"Wasn't that from a book?"

Spitz chuckled and his larynx bobbed up and down. "You read that, too? You're showing your age." Then, he paused. "Jenny, you did say it was the end—last time."

"You can't give it up, can you?"

He shook his head, and for a moment she thought he might peel off his mask.

"I'm worried about you," he said.

"My bills are always paid," she told him. She rose and strode by him, giving a brief squirt of pheromones from the implanted glands along her collarbone. She heard his small groan, which meant either frustration or enjoyment, and she smiled, though she knew that she should not have dosed him.

"Tomorrow at nine," he told her. "Don't be late."

"Ah, another time, Spitz. I'm off to the museum," she said. "Perhaps I'll climb the Burghers of Calais."

In a room down the hall, a woman cried, "No, no, no, no, no." Sometimes, the procedures done by Spitz and his colleagues were painful.

"Where taste and artifice meet in pain," Jenny said as she exited the treatment area. "Isn't that a good advertisement?" Each time she visited Spitz, she tried to offer a new slogan, preferably one with masochistic overtones. Usually, he would laugh, but he merely turned away, so Jenny laughed for him.

The two auburn-haired receptionists laughed with her, but in Jenny's heart, she felt only cold emptiness. Spitz hadn't wished her happy hunting. He hadn't wished her anything at all.

•••

"I can't let you in without a ticket," the young man at the door told Jenny. His chin was dark with stubble and his chest strained the seams of his navy jacket with the Norton Simon logo embroidered on the pocket: one of the hypermasculine boys, so pumped with hormones that Jenny feared she'd sprout hair on her upper lip if she touched him.

A slim man with a shock of curly gray hair spotted her, and his eyes narrowed. Jenny felt certain she'd never seen him before, but he ambled over as if he knew her.

"She's a guest," he told the guard. "I'm sure you've just forgotten your ticket."

"Of course," she said. She followed him inside. Once they were safely past the desk, she turned with a Jenny smile. "I've never seen you before in my life."

"You have," he said. "We were at U.C.L.A. together."

"Oh," she said, and considered saying he was mistaken, but then she remembered that he'd taken her to a basketball game, and he'd tried to kiss her in the Pauley Pavilion. "Avi," she said.

"In the flesh. You look fabulous."

His eyes glittered. What a little hawk nose he had. "Thanks," she told him. "Believe it or not, I came on business. Shall we catch up later?"

His smile faded. He turned away and his shoulders hunched in his worn tweed jacket. She nearly called him back, but instead pressed two fingers to her upper lip and scanned the gallery. Along the wall were Rembrandt van Rijn's paintings, most of the guests crowding before them. Two obviously modified women lurked near the bar, blue-black feathers crossed over their cup-like breasts. Birds were in this season, Jenny recalled. These two looked like a pair of predatory crows.

She approached the Rembrandts and for a moment hunting was forgotten, because here was the old man himself, hurt eyes glaring amid folds of flesh, all the pain and humiliation and dignity of age, painted in three-quarter view from the right, with the light of a Dutch oil lamp streaming down the canvas. She wanted to touch the thick, impasto brushstrokes which made the face seem real enough to kiss. What a thing, to kiss Rembrandt.

"Amazing, isn't it?" It was a deep voice, slow, slightly European.

After a moment, she said, "You've been watching." She allowed herself a sidelong glance. Dark skin, a hint of jowls, but just a hint, and the charming affectation of silver-framed glasses: an intellectual who wished to show it.

"I try to keep an eye on all the works of art here," he said.

Jenny bit her lip. Could he possibly realize she was modified? Another sidelong glance: no. It was as it seemed, a line. She released a bare whiff of pheromone from the tiny glands along her collarbone. "You're a guard?"

He laughed. His eyes, hazel, with green rimming the irises, narrowed just a bit with the pheromone. "Some people tell me that I run this place."

There were choices to be made, and she made one. She would be a gamine, with wide eyes. "Mr. Gustafson?" He was nearly half a head taller than she and oh, did she love big men, not like the puffed boy manning the door, but like this one. She'd flipped through the profiles of those she might find this evening, her adventure in the art world, and she'd liked his the best. He wasn't the wealthiest, by far, but he had power, and there were other enticements.

He looked past her shoulder, and for a moment she thought she'd lost him. His eyes came to rest near a clutch of Picasso sketches and he pointed at a woman with a dark pageboy, with the glossy face of someone who'd had her skin regrown, and very recently. "My wife. She wouldn't appreciate that I'm about to ask you to call me Mark."

"Oh," Jenny said, and looked at her Italian leather pumps, which had cost enough to feed a poor family for a year. "I see."

He smiled. "What brings you here?"

"Miracles," she told him, and the Rembrandt glowed as if lit from within the canvas. To have been so near the painting was as sweet as a spoon of fresh peach ice cream. Before the last time had ended (*he* had gone; *he* had left her) she'd begun to imagine, as a baby learns to walk, that there were more pleasures than the hunt. She glanced at the wife and nearly said, "It's been lovely, Mark, but I have to go."

"Have you been in the sculpture garden recently? We have a Henry Moore and—"

"I was thinking I'd like to climb the Burghers of Calais," she said, then she laughed. His face lit and he laughed with her as she linked her arm in his. "You don't believe me," she said. "Perhaps I'll climb your Henry Moore. Smooth, is it?"

She made herself seem small as they left the gallery. Birds were in that season, and Jenny needed no feathers. She decided that Mark would like it if she trembled, and she did tremble, when he kissed her. She climbed through the hole in the belly of the Henry Moore, which was a huge lumpen sculpture, smooth to the eye, but rough to the fingers, the product of a man who had seen women as vessels of clay, of earth, as things to bear water and babies.

"I don't even know your name," he said after the kiss.

She rested her cheek against the cool, carved granite.

"Jenny," she told him.

"The stars are shining in your hair," he said.

She knew that.

•••

The first night, she took him to a hotel only a block from the Norton Simon. Once, she had lunched there with a girlfriend, when she'd had only three modifications: her awful pug nose, her teeth, and the widening of her eyes. Nothing more than any woman would do, if she had the money. For years she had remembered the polished brass fittings in the lobby, set in veined green malachite. It was thus a sweet, delayed pleasure to take Mark on the white Queen Anne bedspread, though she only delicately used the pheromones, for he did not need them.

In the morning, his eyes were greener than they had been the night before, or perhaps it was only the memory of the green polished floor in the lobby.

"I never . . ." he said, hoarse. His face was rough with stubble and she loved it, but she only smiled a little.

"Neither have I," she said. She meant it, the same way she always meant it, because each one of the hunted was unlike the others; each one was like a mouthful of rich dessert, to be taken carefully, to be savored.

They were together, often, after that, and she allowed him to come to her apartment in the High Tower, that old beige stucco block concealed in the Hollywood Hills.

Illustrated by Paul Marquis

Still, he did not say the mantra, though the look on his face was unmistakable, the pure joy when he came through the door.

After three weeks, she allowed herself a little wine, real and bitter, though it never affected her as strongly after the modifications as it had done before. They made love and he kissed the mole on her left shoulder, the one Spitz had created just that morning, a tiny dark beige oval.

She almost felt, at that moment, as she'd felt with *him* before it had crashed, and she shut her eyes tight, feeling Mark inside of her, wishing that she could forget herself, but it was impossible. Every tissue in her body was working, more inside than out, for Spitz had made her the perfect lovemaking machine, and hadn't it been exactly what she wanted? She couldn't forget, as her body was caressing Mark, like a gently stroking hand.

And that morning, Mark said the mantra.

"I love you; my God, I've never been with anyone like you." He buried his head in her hair. "I want to marry you. I want you to have my children."

"Oh," she said, and he took that as a yes, and she stroked his head and his neck and his shoulders. "Oh."

She expected to feel the disappointment which always followed the completion of the hunt, that sinking dread which meant there was little left but to move him along, but she didn't know what she felt. Perhaps fear.

"Mark, you're already married," she whispered. "You have a little boy and girl." The pictures had been in his wallet. Sometimes he talked about the children, though never his wife.

"There has to be a way to work it out," he said. "I'm telling her tonight."

She didn't know, but could imagine, what he'd already said to his wife to excuse his long absences. "You're off to work," she said. He caressed her lips, just a light brush of his fingers, and started for the shower.

While the water ran, she heard him singing, and he had a very nice voice, a rich baritone.

"You should have gone into opera," she called. She opened her data terminal and logged on.

"I can't hear you," he said.

"A very nice voice," she murmured. From his wallet, she slipped his ID card and his bank card. She had so many prints of his retina that Spitz had told her there was a ridiculous overabundance in making the prosthesis. The prosthesis was cold, like an oversized fish scale, when she slipped it over her eye.

The bank-net admitted her quickly, but her heart froze when she heard a thumping from the shower. She relaxed when she heard a muffled laugh and "I dropped the soap."

She turned aside and let her terminal's little scanner examine the prosthesis, counting slowly to seven, and it bumped her into Mark's banking menu.

He had more than she'd thought in his main account: 2.1 million. She saw a second account, less than a hundred thousand, and this, she decided, must be for the children. Also, a checking account. She considered a moment, then transferred an even two million into the account of Edna Macomber, who was also Jenny Julian, when Jenny Julian traveled on the continent, as she did, twice a year, wearing St. John knits and a cap of dark, curly, implanted hair.

She was reclining on the bed when he came out, a pale blue angora blanket thrown across her legs.

"I don't know how I'll get through the day," he told her. His cheek felt smooth and buttery as he kissed her, and he smelled deliciously of cologne.

"You'll do beautifully," she told him.

Green eyes. She wondered how she would look with green eyes. Then, she thought of Spitz, and wondered if he had time today to lengthen her incisors.

"I'll call tonight," Mark told her.

"Oh yes," she said. "Please." She had tucked the prosthesis under her tongue and she pushed it out, slowly, as soon as he left, and held it high so that it glittered in the pale morning light.

•••

Spitz was abnormally silent as he worked on her mouth. "Maybe," he told her, as he rearranged the bite guard and set to work on the other incisor, "maybe you shouldn't come back."

Jenny squirmed and Spitz put his hand on her shoulder. He continued to work on the tooth as he talked.

"It's all getting a little weird for me," he said. "Negative energy." He slipped the bite guard from her mouth and handed her a cup of cinnamon-flavored water. She spat into the sink and watched the pink liquid swirl down the drain.

"You're serious," she said, staring into the smooth basin.

"Here's the mirror. Have a look." He yanked the overhead mirror down, turned the frame light to bright, which was of klieg-light intensity, and dialed the mirror to the highest magnification. Her mouth looked raw and vampirish, with bloody gums. She turned away.

He walked around the chair and tried to force her to look again in the mirror. "Spitz, why—"

"Look, it's exactly what you wanted, isn't it?"

"Yes," she said, hoping it would satisfy him. "It's exactly right."

"As always. At your service."

She tore off the blue gown he'd draped over her chest and threw it at him. "You're the one who educated me about the prostheses. You've been making them!"

He shrugged, and for a moment she thought he'd unmask himself, but he merely began to arrange his instruments in a neat line. "I just don't want you to come back, Jenny. Can you understand that?" She thought he might be crying. She leapt at him and tugged at the back of his mask, where dark curls escaped between the laces.

He grabbed her wrists and they struggled like that for a while, he grunting and she gasping for breath, until she finally released him and stepped back.

"I'm sorry," she said.

He wouldn't look at her.

"It was your idea, most of it," she said. Her body hurt more than when he'd changed her the last time, made her "perfect." That pain had been deep in her belly, but now, the pain was like a stabbing knife under her breastbone. She massaged her ribs and leaned against the padded chair.

Spitz gasped near the instrument tray, and he gave her a sidelong glance. "It's your black lump of a heart," he said, then he laughed. "Whatever's left of it."

The pain melted into a hot flash of anger. "Damn you," she told him. She was going to say more, but she realized that she didn't need Spitz: there were people in Europe, people who wouldn't question. If she didn't like the incisors, an old-fashioned dentist could handle it, though lab-grown tissue was tough and it would take longer than a normal tooth to cut down to size.

Jenny ran out, and she would not go home, because by this time there would certainly be a querulous message from Mark, wondering, because his bank would have given him notice that two million had been transferred to a Swiss account held in the name of Edna Macomber. Mark would go home that evening, not to tell his wife he was leaving her, no, but perhaps to make amends, and to lay plans to cover the loss of the better part of his money. And perhaps, since he was bright, he would have the consoling thought that it had not been real, that he'd only been taken by a mod, a criminal, someone who hunted. Jenny, who preyed.

It would be bad for Mark, but not as bad as it had been for Jenny when it had all gone wrong, when *he* had left her.

Jenny took a cab up to Sunset and got out at a corner where she remembered a small outdoor cafe. The cafe was dark, but she saw the glittering neon sign of a night-club halfway down the block.

Raw music and lights assaulted her as she entered. Girls who wore breathing tubes danced in jelly on the other side of the dance floor. They writhed like snakes. These were not merely mods, but hypermods, perhaps seventeen or eighteen, changed so greatly that they were only tenuously human.

She sat at the bar and ordered a drink and received a strange look from the bartender, who looked like a man but, Jenny decided quickly, was really a woman.

"Milk," the bartender told her.

"All right," Jenny said. She had a stim-pill in her pocket for all-night emergencies, but she merely fingered it and watched the jelly dancers gyrating. They were green and phosphorescent and as slender as twelve-year-old boys.

She sipped the milk and it burned her lips. It was not milk, but something else, something worse. She gagged.

"It's strong, if you're not used to it," someone said.

She turned to see a hypertrophied bundle of muscles with the head of something Hitler may have once dreamed. "You've had a bit of work," she told him.

"Uh-huh." He flexed his bare golden arm. "Care to dance?"

She went with him and as soon as they were on the tiny dance floor, the blond giant grabbed her waist and hoisted her over his head. He began to twirl, slowly. As Jenny spun, she saw the faces of the people of the club, some of them not faces at all, but pale masks the color of dough, with black holes for eyes. Around their necks were cravats colored citron and flame red and lemon yellow so brilliant it was like a slap in the face.

"Jesus God, put me down," she said. The giant continued to spin. There were things in the crowd, with faces like fleshy cabbages, gaping at her with jagged-toothed maws.

"Put . . . me . . . down!" She cuffed his ridiculously tiny ear and he stopped.

Slowly, the giant lowered her to the floor. "I'm sorry," he said. "Maybe you had too much juice."

She looked in his tiny blue eyes and decided they were as dumb as a gerbil's, though the wrong color. "I hardly tasted it."

"Well, let's just sit and talk."

She smoothed the shoulders of her jacket. "I think I need to go somewhere else."

The nightmare faces she'd seen from above looked more human now, but hardly normal. They were all modified, every one of them, and none of them subtly. She began to walk away when the giant called out, "I was kind of looking forward to talking with you. I've never talked to a classic mod like you."

She turned. "What?"

"You're pretty, for an older woman. I was going to ask who did your work."

The place stank like a brothel with all the pheromones the customers were exuding. "You don't even know what you're talking about. My God, the Butcher of Buchenwald must have done your face."

Lines creased the giant's forehead, and that, with the lowering of his golden brows, made Jenny step back. "I always heard you classics were snobs. Get out, bitch." He stepped toward her and the pounding music stopped. The jelly dancers quit undulating.

She drew her jacket close and told herself she was not like the freaks in this place, not at all.

The giant held up something slim and silver. "Now, I've got this." Her spare credit chip. He'd prized it from her pocket as he'd lifted her over his head for the sickening ride.

"You moron," she said, softly now, since the noise was gone. Her ears ached. "How long have you had it?"

"What? Since I took it. Bet there's a lot on it, too." What glittering, piggish eyes he had. The jelly dancers stared, faces blank like slack green dolls.

"This is the first time you've grabbed a platinum card, isn't it?" She estimated that he'd been fingering the card for at least twenty seconds. In less than ten seconds, the card would recognize that it was not her hand which held it.

Jenny counted under her breath.

"What the—" The giant screamed when the card sprayed fluorescent dye over his bare arm. The card began to glow. It burned away, then he dropped the smoking bits which remained. The crowd surged forward.

"I'll eat *oo*," she thought she heard one of the jelly dancers say.

Jenny ran. There were no cabs out. She ran down Sunset, past runaway, pimply kids who could barely afford tattoos, much less real modifications. They'd been on the Boulevard for years, the boys who looked for men, and the girls who'd do anything at all for a hot meal or a warm bed and more than anything for a taste of stim or wine or the ever-present cigarettes, which were the one constant, other than dirt and hunger, in their fearful lives. Her boots hurt, but she kept running. After a block, she sensed that the bar people had stopped their pursuit, but she didn't turn. She ran nearly a mile, to Franklin, heart pounding, lungs searing. Her left foot throbbed from blisters as if she'd dropped a brick on her toes.

She tried to flag a cab which waited at the light, but the blandly smiling driver looked past her and sped away. She was limping badly when she reached the High Tower and leaned against the cold stucco wall of the elevator vestibule.

Once inside, she slipped her left boot off and her toes were covered with blood. Spitz, she thought. Spitz would know what to do. She went to her terminal to call him, and saw that a message was flashing. Mark. It had been sent much earlier in the day.

Mark's face was white and strained. "Tell me it's not true," he said. "You can't have done this—" She cut him short and dialed Spitz's home line.

"Spitz, help me. I hurt myself. I need to—" She stopped. Spitz had a protection program running. It gave her menu options and she selected "message." Spitz's face appeared, and she sighed in relief, but quickly realized it was just a recorded drone.

"I know it's you," the recorded Spitz said. "I knew you'd call. You're a thief and you're lying to everyone, Jenny. I don't know you anymore."

"You bastard," she whispered in reflex. She felt a cold knot of fear in her stomach.

"You can get help," Spitz continued. "There are a lot of places. A lot of numbers. I'm sending them right now."

"I need help with my foot," she said.

"Just call one of the numbers. There's a 24-hour line, right in Hollywood."

"You prick." She keyed him to electronic oblivion. Then, she staggered to her bed and buried her head in the covers. Something was happening to her face: it felt horrible, tight around her eyes, and her mouth trembled. There was no one she could call, no one she could trust, if not Spitz, for *he* had left her, and Mark would never speak to her again, even if she gave all the money back. She sobbed a long while, and when she finally lifted her head and gazed across the basin, the sky was turning pink in the east and the lights were going off.

She went to her terminal and entered her banking program. Her hands looked so pale and frail: the skin was fragile, even wrinkled here and there. Her fingers trembled as she asked for a credit issue from the account of Edna Macomber. It would take a few minutes for it to imprint a new chip, like the one which had disintegrated in the giant's hand. Three million, she told the bank. Payable to Mark Gustafson.

She showered, soaping the blood from her foot, and afterward she bound the raw blisters with tape. She dressed and slipped the chip in her pocket. It was now fully light, and it took only a few minutes for her cab to arrive. She stared at the morning world from the cab, a world she had not seen for years, the early risers along the residential streets, joggers, women with dogs, small children leaving for school.

Mark's house was a substantial Spanish mansion in Brentwood. She knocked on the door and stared up at the security camera. No one answered. She knocked again, and heard padded feet approaching on the other side of the door.

The door opened a crack and a small voice said, "Who are you?" Jenny caught a glimpse of dark, shiny hair. This was Mark's boy.

"Is your father home?"

She heard the girl whispering behind him. "No, my mom's home."

Jenny took a deep breath. "Well, I have something to give her. I won't stay long."

"Are you a friend of Daddy's?" The girl, this time. The door opened halfway.

Jenny stepped inside. The boy wore gray, furry puppy slippers, and the girl, white slippers with kittens on the toes. Jenny knew nothing about children. These two, with their innocent eyes and smooth dark hair, made her want to bolt and run, hoping to catch the cab as it drove away.

Instead, she asked, "Where's your mother?"

"In the bedroom," the boy said. "She was crying." The girl nodded, solemn.

"Upstairs? You show me." Jenny bit her lip and followed the children up the winding stairway.

Mark's wife lay in bed with the covers pulled around her neck. She looked startled when the children came in, then put her hand to her mouth when she saw Jenny. Her eyes were red and swollen, cheeks drawn.

"You're the one," she said.

Jenny nodded. The children seemed frozen. "Don't be frightened," Jenny said. She took the credit chip from her pocket.

"I don't know why you're here," Mark's wife said.

Jenny approached the bed. The blood was rushing in her ears. Mark's wife wore a sleeveless white cotton gown. The bedspread was white cotton, Queen Anne, the bedroom done all in white. Orchids sat in a clear glass vase on a marble table. Jenny had dreamed once of such a bedroom, all done in white, with exquisite flowers.

At the door, the boy had his arm around the girl's waist. "Mom, are you okay?"

Jenny put the chip on the bedspread, near the edge of the bed. "This is a credit chip," she said. "It's worth three million, in Mark's name."

"The money doesn't matter," Mark's wife said. Her voice was slurred, the words indistinct. There was something strange and unfocused about her eyes.

Jenny leaned over the bed and saw an open pill bottle and a glass next to the vase of orchids. "Have you taken something?"

Mark's wife sighed, then her eyes fluttered shut. Jenny picked up the bottle: an antidepressant. "How many?"

She didn't answer: the wife's eyes opened briefly, then fell shut again. Ice went down Jenny's spine and she turned to the boy. She struggled a moment to find the right words. "I think your mother has taken some medicine. Too much medicine. Do you know how to call emergency?"

The boy nodded.

"Do it now," Jenny said.

The boy and girl hesitated, then Jenny heard their slippers padding away. Mark's wife moaned, and a bubble of saliva came from the corner of her mouth. Jenny's stomach roiled as she got Mark's wife over her knees, head hanging down. She opened her mouth and forced her fingers inside. You could just run away, she thought.

"Please be okay," she told Mark's wife. "Please."

By the time the paramedics arrived, she'd gotten Mark's wife to vomit nearly everything. There were bits of pills in the mess, so many.

"I'm so sorry," Jenny said as they put Mark's wife on a stretcher. No one seemed to know what she was talking about. One paramedic thought to tell her that Mark's wife would be okay.

She found the credit chip amid the confusion in the bedroom and pressed it in the boy's hand. "Give this to your father," she said. "Tell him it's from Jenny. Tell him I'm sorry."

"Are you a police officer?" the boy asked. Jenny shook her head.

When they started to ask her name, she ran.

•••

Jenny called Spitz every day for three weeks. He never accepted one of her calls. When at last he answered, for a moment she couldn't speak. Spitz had changed masks: now he wore forest green.

"I just want to talk to you," she said at last.

"About what?" His voice was neutral.

Jenny bit her lip to keep it from trembling. "I gave the money back," she said. "All of it, and an extra million. His wife tried to kill herself, but she's okay now." Jenny had called to check. The boy had answered, saying, "Mommy's okay."

"Christ," Spitz said. He paused and shuffled some papers. "Come by at four." He rang off before Jenny could reply.

Spitz made her wait, and wouldn't come near her as she reclined in the beige leather chair, her thighs tense, muscles corded like rope. He fiddled with his instruments until she finally spoke.

"Can you put me back the way I was?"

His shoulders tensed. He shook his head.

"Something, then, at least a little bit."

"Your face," he said, voice thick. "I could do your face. I can take the glands out, some of the other stuff."

Jenny stared at the ceiling. "I know what you said before. I'd never be normal inside again. No babies."

He nodded. "Jenny, I've been helping kids," he said. "For free. Serious cases." He swiveled the tray around and put his hand behind his neck. His fingers worked, and she watched him, her throat swelling, as he unlaced the mask.

"Spitz, you don't—"

The green velvet mask slipped away.

"You're like a boy," she whispered. He did not really look like a boy, but his black eyes were warm in his face, which was not a skull, but a perfect, longish oval. He had generous lips, almost feminine, and a bumped Roman nose. Not at all handsome. There was a small pimple next to his lip. She touched it gently, wonderingly. Nothing had been done to Spitz's face: ever.

He cupped her face in his warm, soft hands. He looked in her eyes for a long moment, and how different his eyes looked now without the mask, how very different.

"I can do your nose right now," he said.

"Back to ugly pug," she said, then laughed.

"It was never ugly," he told her. "I said that on the first day."

He worked a long while, and it was dark when he finished.

"There's a deli down the street," he said. "They have egg creams and seltzer."

"I would like that," Jenny said. "Do we sit at a counter?"

He nodded. "All the regulars sit at the counter." Jenny understood that the deli was where Spitz went without his mask.

In the days when Jenny had worn a white cotton nightgown, her aunt had taken her to a deli counter after school, and Jenny was allowed to order ice-cream sundaes, which came with a triangular cookie made of the same crackly beige stuff as an ice cream cone. She had always asked for peppermint ice cream, with the candies melting gooey red into the ice cream, cool and delicious.

"Do you think they'd have peppermint ice cream?" she asked and there was suddenly a tightening in her chest and an exploding sadness in her heart. "Spitz," she cried.

He bent over the beige chair and took her in his arms. "Yeah, they've got peppermint," he said, "and peppermint syrup too."

The peppermint ice cream was delicious, and the egg cream cold and smooth, the chocolate syrup mixed just so with the milk, and the seltzer squirted into the glass so that the foam exploded over the top. The straws were striped red-and-white paper and the seats hard red leather.

Later, Jenny and Spitz walked down Hollywood Boulevard toward Gower Street. "We're walking on the stars," she told him—beneath her feet, Mack Sennett's star. The bronze plaques stretched on, shining and smoothed over the years by countless passing pairs of feet, as far as Jenny could see.

HOW TO DRIVE A WRITER CRAZY

Written by
L. Ron Hubbard

About the Author

L. Ron Hubbard's remarkably productive writing career spanned more than half a century of literary achievement and enduring creative influence. Its scope and diversity eventually embraced more than 550 works—over 60 million words—of published fiction and nonfiction. And though he was always, quintessentially, a writer's writer, his zest for adventure, his inexhaustible curiosity, and his catalyzing personal belief that one should live life as a professional led him to impressive accomplishments in other fields—as an explorer and prospector, mariner and aviator, filmmaker and photographer, educator and artist, composer and musician.

Growing up in the then unsparingly rugged frontier country of Montana, he was riding horses by the time he was three, and had been initiated as a blood brother of the Blackfeet Indian tribe by the age of six. While still a teenager, before the advent of commercial air transportation as we know it, he journeyed more than a quarter of a million miles by sea and land into remote areas of the Far East largely untraveled by Westerners, intensively broadening his knowledge of other peoples and cultures.

In later years, as a master mariner and helmsman, he led three separate voyages of discovery and exploration under the flag of the prestigious Explorers Club.

Returning to the United States from the Far East in 1929, L. Ron Hubbard studied at George Washington University where he became president of both the Engineering Society and Flying Club, and wrote articles, stories and a prize-winning play for the school's newspaper and literary magazine.

A daredevil pilot, he barnstormed across the United States in gliders and early powered aircraft, became a correspondent and photographer for the Sportsman Pilot, *one of the most distinguished national aviation magazines of its day, subsequently worked as a successful screenwriter in Hollywood, and, when only twenty-five, was elected president of the New York chapter of the American Fiction Guild, whose membership at the time included Dashiell Hammett, Raymond Chandler and Edgar Rice Burroughs.*

All of this—and much more—over the breadth and range of his professional career found its way into his writing and gave his stories a memorable authenticity, and a fascinating sense of the way things credibly might be in some possible future or alternate reality, that continues to attract and engross readers everywhere.

Beginning with the publication in 1934 of his first adventure story, The Green God, *in one of the hugely popular all-fiction "pulp" magazines of the day, L. Ron Hubbard's outpouring of fiction was prodigious—often exceeding a million words a year. Ultimately, it encompassed more than 260 published novels, short stories and screenplays in virtually every major genre, from action and adventure, western and romance, to mystery and suspense, and, of course, science fiction and fantasy.*

Mr. Hubbard had, in fact, already achieved broad popularity and acclaim in other genres when he burst onto the landscape of speculative literature with his first published science fiction story, The Dangerous Dimension, *in 1938. But it was his trendsetting work in this field, particularly, that not only helped expand the imaginative boundaries of the genre, but established him as one of the founders and principal architects of what remains its most celebrated—and legendary—period of productivity and literary invention, the "Golden Age of Science Fiction" of the 1930s and 1940s.*

Such timeless L. Ron Hubbard classics of speculative fiction as Final Blackout, Fear, Ole Doc Methuselah *and* Typewriter in the Sky, *as well as later, precedent-setting novels—the ultimate alien invasion story,* Battlefield Earth *and the sweeping* MISSION EARTH® *ten-volume dekalogy— continue, meanwhile, to appear perennially on bestseller lists and garner critical accolades in countries around the world.*

L. Ron Hubbard's extraordinary fifty-six-year career as a professional writer was distinguished, equally, by his deeply felt and lifelong commitment to helping other writers, especially beginners, become better, more productive and more successful at their craft. This culminated in 1983 in his establishment of both the Writers of the Future Contest—*now the largest and most successful merit competition of its kind in the world—and the annual anthology of the winning best new, original stories of science fiction and fantasy.*

The companion contest for Illustrators of the Future, *for whose winners this anthology also provides a major international showcase, was inaugurated five years later.*

Mr. Hubbard's initial work with fledgling writers, however —undertaken even as he himself, still in his twenties, was swiftly rising to national prominence—found telling expression in lectures to student writers at Harvard and George Washington Universities and on other campuses on techniques for launching their careers.

He also began, as early as 1935, to publish sharply practical "how to" articles about writing as a craft and profession, which appeared in major writers' magazines for many years and continue to be used today in writing courses and seminars and as the basis for the Writers' Workshops held each year for the winners and published finalists of the **Writers of the Future** *Contest.*

In the pointedly tabular essay that follows, L. Ron Hubbard explores, with brevity and customary wit, a potentially inhospitable piece of literary terrain all too familiar to the new—and often to the seasoned—writer.

1. When he starts to outline a story, immediately give him several stories just like it to read and tell him three other plots. This makes his own story and his feeling for it vanish in a cloud of disrelated facts.

2. When he outlines a character, read excerpts from stories about such characters, saying that this will clarify the writer's ideas. As this causes him to lose touch with the identity he felt in his character by robbing him of individuality, he is certain to back away from ever touching such a character.

3. Whenever the writer proposes a story, always mention that his rate, being higher than other rates of writers in the book, puts up a bar to his stories.

4. When a rumor has stated that a writer is a fast producer, invariably confront him with the fact with great disapproval as it is, of course, unnatural for one human being to think faster than another.

5. Always correlate production and rate, saying that it is necessary for the writer to do better stories than the average for him to get any consideration whatever.

6.   It is a good thing to mention any error in a story bought, especially when that error is to be editorially corrected as this makes the writer feel that he is being criticized behind his back and he wonders just how many other things are wrong.

7.   Never fail to warn a writer not to be mechanical as this automatically suggests to him that his stories are mechanical and, as he considers this a crime, wonders how much of his technique shows through and instantly goes to much trouble to bury mechanics very deep— which will result in laying the mechanics bare to the eye.

8.   Never fail to mention and then discuss budget problems with a writer as he is very interested.

9.   By showing his vast knowledge of a field, an editor can almost always frighten a writer into mental paralysis, especially on subjects where nothing is known anyway.

10.   Always tell a writer plot tricks as they are not his business.

SPRAY PAINT REVOLUTIONS

Written by
J. C. Schmidt

Illustrated by
Paul Marquis

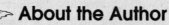

About the Author

J. C. Schmidt was born in Eugene, Oregon, in 1972 and currently lives in Seattle, Washington.

He would like to dedicate this story to John Damon, for getting him started. He'd also like to thank Rita Conley for her help and encouragement. And he'd like to send his love to his family: Kree, Emma, and Ondine.

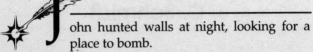

John hunted walls at night, looking for a place to bomb.

He was the guy everybody was looking for. The Chambers of Commerce in three neighborhoods had put a price on his head. Community organizations had condemned him. So he played it James Bond, hustling around in back alleys and sneaking up fire escapes; a hip-hop ninja with a license to deface.

Halfway through the night, as he leapt from roof to roof, he found what he was looking for: a plot of naked wall with "bomb me" written on it in letters only John could see. He stood back and looked at it to get a sense of scale, his blunt, powerful fingers rapping an anxious staccato beat on the leather of his shoulder bag. He turned around to look at the view. During the day this wall was a visual scream to the listening eyes of the walkers and the drivers on the streets below. Whatever was said by this wall would be said loudly. Currently the wall had nothing to say. By day its voice was a dull, noncommittal bluish gray. By night it was muffled by a freak shadow, a hanging flower arrangement that blocked the street lights just so and turned the wall's voice to a conspiratorial whisper. The wall was begging.

On the roof of the one-story building that stood adjacent to his target, John removed his shoulder bag and set out the tools he would need to inspire the wall: some rope, a grappling hook, a fall harness, a gas mask, and several new cans of spray paint.

•••

"What the hell does it say, anyway?" Sara asked, looking at the wall piece with a dubious expression.

John leaned forward and looked out the window of the coffee shop they were sitting in to get a better view of the large painting on the wall across the street.

"It says 'revolve,'" he replied in his low, almost inaudible voice. "S'matta? You can't read English?"

"That may be English, but that's not the Roman alphabet."

"Sure it is," John said, offhandedly. This was an old argument between them. "It's just done differently. 'Sides, the art should clear it up pretty good even for the truly lily white, such as yourself."

Sara looked again at the wall piece, which depicted a spinning globe surrounded by cartoon-like renditions of various historical figures, ranging from Joe Hill to Malcolm X, with the word *revolve* written in cryptic graffiti letters underneath. John's little tag/signature was worked inconspicuously into the lower left-hand corner: "Gypsy Poet."

She wasn't the only one looking. A group of college students stopped on a nearby corner, pointing and talking animatedly. She wondered if it was because of the quality of the art, the content, or the coup; John had done the whole piece in a single night, right on the Ave., which was the main drag of Seattle's University District. The Campus Police had to be furious.

"Damn, John," she said, returning her focus to him. "You kicked your own ass this time. I'll give it to you. That's the best one you've done yet."

John smiled, clearly pleased with the praise.

"So what's next, Canman?" she asked, sipping her Mexican hot chocolate.

"I dunno," he replied with a shrug. "Whatever. See if they go over this one. Take another crack at it if the light's still good for it later."

"No new pieces in mind?"

"Naw. This stuff is work. The nights wear me out. Messes me up at my day job."

Sara sighed and looked into her cup. John's job was low stress, low commitment, and low pay. He worked at a bakery, making bread, cookies, rolls, and other various and sundry. Sara's job at one of the area's leading software companies paid ten times what John's did, but sometimes she wondered if he wasn't getting the better deal. His job had withstood his being arrested twice for piecing. If something like that happened to her, it would be all over.

"Besides," John said, breaking into her train of thought, "the Forces of Evil are everywhere. I gotta be selective about my locations."

"They still don't climb walls?" Sara said.

"Nope. Just me and the Invisible Spiderman. Only wall climbers I know of so far."

"That still sucks," Sara said. "That you can't do the nice safe ground-floor walls."

John shrugged again.

The Forces of Evil were part of John's pet theory about people who ruined his pieces with cheesy tags and the like. It was John's belief that they were part of a unified front that had co-opted the graffiti movement in an effort to cancel its potential for social change. *Counterrevolutionaries* was his word for them. He said he thought maybe they were funded by the same people who had thought up *Hard Copy* and the *National Enquirer*—people who turned information into an input storm of meaningless garbage. People who took all the news out of the News, so you couldn't tell what was really going on anymore. Sara admired the theory, at least in the abstract.

"So when you gonna quit that lame-ass computer job and come piecing with me?" John asked.

"Soon as you stop wasting your time with that bakery job and submit some of your stuff to a gallery," Sara shot back.

"Shit, man," John said, wrinkling up his nose in distaste. "What would be the point? Stuff's in a gallery, nobody sees it but some rich kids. That," he said gesturing at the wall piece, "will at least be in the *U. W. Daily*. Might even make it into the *Stranger*. Citywide newspapers, baby. Not to mention all the people who'll see the original."

"Yeah, but it's the rich kids you want to reach. They're the ones with all the power to change things."

"I'm not after forced change through money and economics," John said for the millionth time. "I'm after spontaneous mass conversion through ideological superiority. Revolve, right? The earth doesn't spin because some white dude with a beard stands there spinning it. It spins because it's in the nature of the thing. All the parts of it spin on their own, and what you get is a mass revolution."

"John," said Sara wearily. "Do you honestly think anyone gets all that from that piece?"

"No," John said. "Not directly. But it puts the idea in their heads, so they can chew it over for a while. If they're into it, it'll come to them. Then they'll start to revolve on their own, falling into the mass revolution."

"Unless the Forces of Evil get to them first," Sara said with a wry grin. She was somewhat surprised to see a brief shadow of worry pass over her friend's face before it was replaced by a mirror of her own expression.

"To the fall of the Forces," John said, raising his mocha. Their mugs rang quietly off one another in the dim gray light from the window.

● ● ●

Full moon, the mother moon, she followed him across the rooftops, giving her blessing to his quest.

The Forces of Evil were abroad tonight. He could smell 'em; irritating little Bellevue wiggers with their weak-ass tags. John had plans in the works for them. But the time was not yet right. The message wasn't at its full strength yet. The word wasn't sufficiently out.

John picked a likely target and went immediately to work. The spot itself was not terribly auspicious, but the location was prime; the wall of a burned-out warehouse near the Alaskan Way viaduct. Commuter territory. Bored people, pinned in traffic, anxious for distraction—even something written on a wall. Word-out heaven.

John decided to be direct and topical. He threw up his grapnel and climbed about three-quarters of the way up the wall. From there he kicked off and began to describe slow pendular arcs back and forth across the worn brick. His top-of-the-line spray paint did its top-of-the-line best to cling to the wet and moldy masonry.

When he had completed as much of the picture as was within reach, he played out the rope and lowered himself down the wall, adding more paint to his work as more of it came into reach. The Gypsy Poet doing his best impression of a dot-matrix printer.

He had nearly reached the end of his piece when a spotlight pinned him to the wall. He looked over his shoulder at the viaduct behind him. A police car had stopped in the breakdown lane with its searchlight focused on him.

Shit, thought John. The city guard.

"Stop right there, kid," said the police officer over his loudspeaker.

"Or what?" John shouted through his gas mask as he began to swing back and forth again. "You'll shoot me?"

The police cruiser cut its light and sped off toward the nearest exit so it could double back around on the street grid and get to John. He figured he had about forty-five seconds to complete his quest for the night, then boogie.

He made two more swings, adding just enough detail to make the piece coherent. He would have liked to do a once-over and add some chrome, but there wasn't time. At the end of his second pass he dropped down to the adjoining rooftop and shook his grapnel loose with a single expert flip of his rope. He was coiling the slack when he heard the police car pull up on the street below.

John ran toward the fire escape on the side of the building opposite the police car. When he got there he saw two bicycle cops pounding up the stairs. Apparently the car had called ahead.

"Goddamnit," John said mildly as he ran for the median edge of the building and looked down to make sure the street was clear of police. It was.

"I sense the hand of the Forces of Evil in this," he muttered.

"Freeze!" shouted one of the bike cops as he topped the fire escape and shone his big six-cell Mag-Lite® at John.

John took half a second to judge distances and jumped off the fifth-floor roof. As he did so, he threw his grappling hook out in front of him with his left hand and clipped the rope into the carabiner on the front of his fall harness with his right.

When he had fallen about halfway, his grappling hook wrapped around a power line and his rope snapped taut. His trajectory began to curve. His life flashed before his eyes as the path of his fall took him toward the ground. He was trying to remember the formula for measuring the velocity of a pendulum when he skimmed past the concrete at what seemed like the speed of light. Just as he began a sigh of relief, he slammed broadside into a parked car.

The last things he heard before blacking out were the sound of breaking glass and the rending pop of his shoulder snapping out of its socket.

•••

The midnight phone call that woke Sara brought bad news, as midnight phone calls tend to do. John was in jail. No, the hospital. No. John was in a hospital under guard. Apparently he had fallen off a building while running from the police. The only number he would give for next of kin was Sara's. Which, she supposed, was close enough to the truth that the differences didn't matter. Before going to the hospital she called her parents' lawyer and arranged for him to take John's case in the morning.

Illustrated by Paul Marquis

John was being kept at Harborview, in the trauma ward. The police officer who met her in the waiting room told her that John had dislocated his shoulder, cracked two ribs, and possibly given himself a concussion.

"Which isn't nearly as bad as it could be after what he pulled," the officer concluded. His name tag informed Sara that she was talking to Officer Danvers. She took the name down in her mental notepad.

"Are you the arresting officer then?" she said, trying to get a handle on the situation.

"No. I was just on the scene. The arresting officers are Comstock and Bates."

"Bates?" Sara said before she could think better of it.

"Yeah," said Officer Danvers. "Poor woman. Everybody down at the station calls her Norman."

Sara laughed with Officer Danvers, and found she was beginning to like him in spite of herself. She shook it off. For the time being at least she would have to be careful with people in uniforms. They had John in custody.

"Can I see him?" she asked Officer Danvers.

"Sure," he said. "Right this way."

He led her down one of several corridors that fed into the lobby. Doctors and nurses walked past, doing their medical thing.

"What did you mean by what you said a minute ago? About 'what he pulled'? I thought he fell."

"Not hardly," Danvers replied. "Jumped. Off a five-story building. I just about shit my pants when I saw him do it, pardon my French. Threw a rope around a power line in midfall and tried to pull a Tarzan on us. Crazy thing is, if he'd been a better judge of how much play there was in that power line he might have actually made it."

"Jesus Christ," Sara muttered as they arrived at a door with a police officer standing next to it.

"Is all of this just for him?" Sara said, realizing she'd seen at least four officers since she'd entered the building.

"Oh, not at all," said Danvers. "Harborview is where we bring anybody who gets hurt in an arrest, or is already hurt when we get there. Cop central."

"Oh," said Sara, trying to digest the thought. Failing.

"Just go on in," Danvers said. "He's not restrained. Once he woke up he seemed pretty rational, so right now we're working on the assumption that he's just stupid, not crazy."

"Oh," said Sara again. Unable to formulate a reply, she pushed through the door. Danvers and the other officer waited outside.

Inside, the room actually looked fairly comfortable for a hospital. A guarded hospital. John sat in a bed located in the far corner of the room. His arm was in a sling and he wore a hospital gown. Four other beds in the room were currently empty. John watched television. Sara gathered from this that he was either extremely nervous or extremely bored. He was vehemently anti-television most of the time.

"So what was the piece?" she said by way of a conversation starter. He turned off the TV and looked at her, obviously glad to have something else to focus on.

"It was beautiful," he said, holding up his good hand and shaping the lines of the piece in the air before him. She walked across the room and sat down in a chair next to the bed. "Right there on the Alaskan Way viaduct. Quickie fast easy piece. Car drivin', with a big old cloud of smoke coming out of the exhaust pipe. Skull and crossbones in the smoke cloud. In the back seat of the car are some monkeys doing the 'see no evil, hear no evil, speak no evil' thing. In the front seat is a guy with one of those big yellow smiley faces. Political and topical right in their face."

"Yeah," said Sara. "But you're bashing carpoolers there. That's more environmentally sound than a single car driver you know."

"Pish," John said disgustedly. "Carpool, my big white ass. It's still cars. Those things are dangerous and bad for the air. Oughta be outlawed. If people'd bring their businesses into the city, folks wouldn't need to drive anyhow. And it would be better for the city's tax base, which would improve social services in the city. The willingness to drive all goddamn day so you can live in the suburbs and work in the city—or, these days, the other way around —is part of the whole mess. Forces of Evil type stuff."

"I drive to the suburbs to do my job," Sara pointed out.

"Yeah, I know. But I love you anyway."

"Thanks," she replied sarcastically. "So what's this I hear about you jumping off of buildings?"

"In a single bound," John said with a grin. "Dude hadn'a parked in a loading zone I'da been home free. Fucked his car up pretty good though, so I guess we're even."

"John, that was nuts. It's just a misdemeanor. You've already got two. Why'd you jump off a building to avoid a third?"

"Because I won't get probation on this one. I'm gonna have to do time in County for it. And I'm too close to do time. Besides, I'm worried about what might happen in jail. The Invisible Spiderman hasn't pieced in a couple of months. I'm wondering if the Forces of Evil haven't stepped up their attacks. In jail I'm vulnerable."

"Wait a second. Back up. Too close to what?"

"To getting the word out," John said.

"John, did you smack your head? You don't normally sound this crazy to me."

"No. I'm just telling it straighter than usual."

"Why?"

"Because I need to ask a favor of you, and you need to be up-to-date."

Sara sat back in her chair and regarded him suspiciously. She had known John a long time, and she'd always known that he had a sort of weird streak in him. John was fundamentally a believer in magic, in spite of his urban and decidedly post–Industrial Revolution personality. Most of the time he kept his more far-out views on reality to himself or turned them into a joke, for fear of sounding like a crackpot. In spite of his discretion she had long suspected that it was John's mystical beliefs that motivated many of his life choices and most of his day-to-day behavior. She had an uncomfortable feeling that he was about to admit as much to her. She wasn't sure how she felt about the prospect. It was, in large measure, John's willingness to feign normalcy that had allowed them to remain friends for so long.

"What kind of favor?" she said, her tone telling him clearer than words what was going on in her head.

"Don't freak out. I'm not going to ask you to do anything that goes against your grain. Just hear me out on something, and then do me this favor. After that it's up to you."

"Okay," she said. "Let's hear it."

"All right," John said. "I don't know how much time we have here, so I'm gonna give you the short version. Just listen, and remember it later on.

"You basically know where I'm at politically. I'm not going to go into too much detail about it. Just know that my motivations for that scene have always been spiritual. I guess they are for everybody, but they're especially so for me. Reason being that, for me, the whole spiritual thing has always been solid reality."

"John," Sara said, sounding tired.

"Just chill," John said, motioning her to be quiet with his good hand. "I'm just telling you this. You don't have to believe it right now. You don't have to believe it later either, but you might want to. All I'm saying is that there's more out in the world than what's dreamt of in your philosophy. Dig?"

"Okay," Sara said. "Given."

"All right," John said again. "Given that there's more to things than meets the eye, I'll tell you now that for me the Forces of Evil are a real thing. They're a paradigmatic force that I do battle with by launching my own counterpropaganda campaign against them. The Forces of Evil tell people it's okay to drive their cars. They tell people it's okay to eat beef. They tell people the status quo is in their best interests. They tell people a lot of bullshit. And to my eye that's all one unified force. The Forces of Evil. Usually they don't manifest in a local way. It's not all masterminded by an individual or a group of individuals that can be isolated and dealt with. But it's a coherent spiritual mass, nonetheless. It moves in a unified way that involves social and spiritual inertia. Just like my revolution, only different. The Forces of Evil are the white guy with the beard. They make shit spin the way they want it to, regardless of what's natural for it to do.

"My gig is that I counteract their inertia with complex runes of open-mindedness, scattered around the city. My pieces are inoculations against spiritual ebola and gangrene of the imagination. I'm striving for thoughts made real; material manifestations of hope. If that makes sense."

"Sure," Sara said. "It's crazy talk. But it makes sense."

"Cool," John said. "So here's the thing. I think my number's up. Sometimes you can just read this shit and you can tell that somebody's about to get whacked. There's nothing specific to indicate that's what's gonna happen. It's just like when you're reading a book and you can tell a certain character is going to get killed because that's the way these kinds of books work. Well, I think the Forces of Evil are going to come after me in County."

Sara looked at him sadly. He was really completely over the edge. Now that she was seeing him talk about it she realized that he had been for some time, and she simply hadn't noticed.

"Yeah, yeah," John said reading her expression. "I'm nuts. Whatever. All I'm asking for now that you've heard my little rap is just this one favor. I'm allowed to have crayons in County, but somebody's gotta buy 'em for me. I'm gonna be flat broke by the time I'm done paying the fines on this caper. So all I'm asking of you right now is that you buy me some crayons while I'm in the slam. If I make it out, I'll let you buy me therapy. If I don't, all I ask is that you follow your conscience."

Sara sat in morose silence and stared at her crazy friend.

"Sara," he said sharply. "Snap out of it. Will you do that for me? Buy me the crayons?"

"Sure," she said. "Buy you crayons. Got it."

"Okay," John said with a smile. "Then we're cool. I'll see you around. And listen. Don't tell anybody I'm crazy while I'm in, okay? If you have to think that, then let's talk about it when I'm out. Like I said, I'll even let you send me through therapy."

"Okay," Sara said, getting up to leave. She paused at the door and looked back to see John settle into his bed and fall quickly asleep.

• • •

When John disappeared from the King County Jail, Sara insisted on seeing his cell. John's lawyer had also been her parents' lawyer, so she was connected enough to the situation to have the legal leverage necessary to force her way in.

The cell was cordoned off from the rest of the cell block by lines of yellow tape. The Deputy Warden told her that they weren't putting any more prisoners in the cell until they could figure out how John had escaped.

"So it's exactly like it was when your guards noticed he was missing?" Sara said, stepping under the tape and looking into the small cell with its two bunks, a sink, and a toilet.

"Yeah," said the Deputy Warden. "Well, almost. We tumbled it pretty good after he escaped. Looking for tools or holes or loose bricks or something. We didn't find anything like that."

Something in his tone made her glance up at him. His expression told her he was leaving something out.

"What did you find?" she asked.

"Shank," said the Deputy Warden after a pause, "his cellmate, had a sharpened spoon in his bunk. We think that might be why your friend chose to escape. I mean really; there's not many other reasons to make yourself a fugitive over a six-month jail sentence."

Sara felt the color drain from her face, but she managed to keep her composure. She turned away from the Deputy Warden and walked into the cell.

For the most part it was like many of the jail cells she'd seen in movies and on television. The one notable exception was the full-sized drawing of a door on the wall opposite the bunks. It wasn't a normal door, such as one would find in a modern house. It was an old, handmade-looking thing, with large iron binders holding the planks together. A cast-iron ring served as the handle. Sara walked over to the drawing and examined it. The detail was remarkable. It almost looked real. She reached out to touch it. When her skin met the wall she was half surprised not to feel time-worn oak under her fingertips. Instead she encountered a smooth waxy texture.

"Thoughts made real," she whispered as she moved her hand over it, letting the texture sink into her mind.

"Crayon," said the Deputy Warden from the entrance to the cell. Sara jumped and glanced back at him apprehensively.

"It's really an amazingly good piece," the Deputy continued, banally oblivious to her reactions. "Sort of medieval-looking. Very realistic."

Sara just stared at him. She had an idea that she might start laughing, but somehow she restrained herself. Instead, after a final glance, she turned and walked quickly out of the cell, leaving John's door behind.

• • •

In the pale light of the waning moon, the Gypsy Poet Too stood back and looked at the finished piece. It was by far her best yet. The product of lots of practice, and no few daring escapes from the police graffiti squads. As she looked it over she reached up with a paint-stair ed hand and scratched her head. A small cascade of flour drifted onto the shoulder of her sweatshirt.

Her software job hadn't been able to withstand her late-night hours. Instead she was flipping pizzas at Zeke's for about an eighth of what she had been making in the office. Mostly the job was fine. The hours were flexible, the people friendly. But it seemed like no matter how much she brushed or showered, she could never get all the flour out of her hair.

The night was quiet around her. This piece was in a relatively isolated location, in marked contrast to her last several, one of which had been plastered onto a freeway sign on the Interstate 5 bridge that ran over the ship canal. That one had made the front page of the *Seattle Times'* local section.

She didn't expect any trouble with this piece though. It wasn't anything topical or political. It wasn't in an obvious place. It was just a carefully rendered drawing of a door, located in a back alley of the downtown area. She had all night to sit and stare at it if she wanted. Nobody would mess with her.

She settled in with her sleeping bag and a bottle of Coke, watching the door like a television. The weather was good. It was nearly summer solstice. Very nearly the earliest dawn of the year.

In the twilight of that dawn she heard the sound she'd been listening for: the slow grinding of rusty hinges. Sara smiled broadly under her black wool fisherman's cap and watched her friend come home.

THE DISAPPEARANCE OF JOSIE ANDREW

Written by
Ron Collins

Illustrated by
Eric L. Winter

About the Author

Ron Collins lives in Columbus, Indiana, with his wife, Lisa, their daughter, Brigid, and a terribly spoiled cat.

Ron says that he is the type of person who can gleefully spend a full week in the National Air and Space Museum, and who still gets a little emotional when thinking about the engineers and astronauts behind the US space program of the 1960s.

He has always enjoyed a good success story.

He graduated from the University of Louisville in 1984 with a degree in mechanical engineering, and immediately went to work developing electronics systems for navy aircraft.

Somewhere along the line, he drifted back to writing and delved into the basics with his usual fervor.

A few years later, he attended his first science fiction convention in Columbus, Ohio. One night he found himself sitting in an otherwise empty hotel lobby at one o'clock in the morning with Mike Resnick, Lois McMaster Bujold, and

Dennis McKiernan. They graciously included Ron and his wife in their conversation, and for the next two or three hours, they talked about everything from writing to selling, to marketing, to how the publishing industry works.

Ron went home more determined than ever to learn about this craft.

Ron has recently published stories in Marion Zimmer Bradley's Fantasy Magazine and in Dragon. In 1997, he was thrilled to sell Mike Resnick a story for his anthology Return of the Dinosaurs, and now he appears with this fine tale.

You'll definitely be seeing more of Ron's work in the future.

About the Illustrator

Eric Lama Winter was born in Washington, D.C., and currently lives in Germantown, Maryland. He is a self-taught artist who works in a variety of mediums. He has found inspiration from a number of artists and filmmakers, including Frank Frazetta, Frank Kelly-Freas, Roger Dean, Syd Mead, Ralph McQuarrie, and Michael Whelan.

Currently, he is trying to shift from being a part-time to a full-time illustrator.

A new child floats in my section today. He's number B86-97 and he feeds from tube twenty-eight, about halfway up, his shoulder pressed flat against the glass. I look at his chart. He's an early second tri who still weighs less than a pound. That tells me all I need to know.

His mother was cranked.

Tube twenty-eight. The number echoes in my thoughts like a distant police siren in the middle of the night. I came to the office this morning ready to sing, but suddenly I want to be doing almost anything else. It is not B86-97's fault though, and I try hard not to blame him for my suddenly foul mood.

The uterine chamber is over four meters in diameter and three meters high. It sits in the middle of the darkened office, its three-finger-thick Plexiglas sides held together by evenly spaced steel rods. Filtration hardware is crammed into its base, a half-meter-tall section of dusty black motors and tubes that smell faintly of warm machine oil. An aluminum hand-ladder mounted to the chamber's side leads to the insulated stainless cap, complete with a round hatch for fishing kids out at birthing time.

Inside the chamber, the children float in synthetic amniotic fluid that is corn-syrup golden. Vertical columns of soft lighting illuminate the chamber from within, allowing for proper monitoring, but not radically altering the children's growth process. Occasional bubbles rise through the fluid, weaving their way through masses of arms and legs and tiny heads with closed eyes and open mouths. I put my palm against the Plexiglas where B86-97 floats. The chamber is heated by elements that rise from the floor like brittle stalagmites, or perhaps like iron rods in a medieval torture chamber.

Warmth flows into my hand.

Ninety-six children float in my chamber today.

The steady throbs of heartbeats resonate through speakers embedded in the stainless caps: false sounds of a nonexistent mother. They echo in the morning silence.

The vibrations are supposed to make the children comfortable. I guess they work. But the heartbeats ring hollowly inside me today. A taste of desperation coats my mouth.

I smile despite the pain this child unwittingly brings me. "Good morning, Kyle," I say. That is the name I give to B86-97. Kyle Lincoln. I gaze into his tightly scrunched face and say his name three times inside my head to make sure I will remember it. I was never good with equations or history or economics—or anything else like that. But I can put a name to a face.

I pull my hand back, the heat of the chamber lingering like a stolen kiss.

Kyle Lincoln is curled around tube twenty-eight, absent-mindedly fingering its connection to his belly.

Josie Andrew was on that tube yesterday.

A sour ball forms in my stomach. Josie's DNA scan must have turned up something this time. He was only five months along, far too early for birthing. As usual, no paperwork is on file concerning Josie's whereabouts. Nothing to indicate he was ever here. Nothing tying

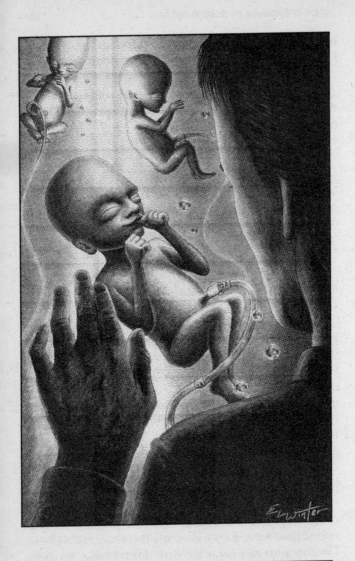

Illustrated by Eric L. Winter

him to feeding tube twenty-eight, or letting anyone know he needed extra vitamin K in his diet.

Nothing to say he used to smile when I sang to him.

Returning to my desk, I see a memo on my screen, the Calvin Birthing Center logo—the intertwined CBC done in royal blue and Hollywood gold—in the corner:

I'm certain everyone knows the Federal Child Care Commission will be here tomorrow to perform their annual licensing review. We know everyone is aware of how important this process is to our future. The auditing team will be looking for examples of our company's desire to care for the infants in our charge and our compassion for their rights as human beings.

Please take a few moments to review your records to help us put our best face forward. . . .

I click the memo away, thinking of Josie.

He was a big child for his age, nearing three pounds. He often sucked on his thumb, rubbing his lips around the knuckle and feeling the bone that had already formed underneath. Josie's smile, instinctive or not, made my heart soar. I'm certain it wasn't my imagination that the other children seem to gravitate toward him, too. Touching him idly, seeming to want to be close to him.

I began singing to him two months ago.

That evening had been rainy, I remember, and I hadn't wanted to leave. There wasn't anything at home for me anyway, and after thirteen years with the company, the chamber had begun to make me feel uncomfortable in a way that was somehow important. The day shift had already left, and the night crew was still gathered around the cafeteria, trading whatever stories they usually traded.

I stood in the empty lab that evening and stared at the children as they floated in golden fluid.

A memory flashed through my mind: Me as a kid, standing next to my father in the morning while he shaves, my eye-level coming to the edge of the sink. I tiptoe up to see shaving cream and black whiskers floating on the surface of the water.

I remember him singing to me. His voice deep and comforting, a warm, woolen blanket of sound that makes me feel safe to start my day.

•••

I couldn't tell you why, but standing alone in the chamber that night and gazing at the pool of lost children, I started to sing a song my father used to sing to me.

"You are my sunshine, my only sunshine . . ."

And Josie smiled, stopping when I stopped and smiling again when I started. His reaction stirred something inside me, something I had lost years ago. From that point on, I made it a habit to sing him a song every morning when I came in, and again every evening before I left.

Josie never failed to respond.

My own reaction surprised me.

Josie Andrew made me feel something I had never felt before. It was a feeling of connection, like having a length of fishing line tied between us that was so fine as to be invisible. But when he smiled at the sound of my voice, I felt the pinch of that line's pull, firm and strong. Undeniably there.

At first, I found myself hurrying the morning along so I could make it to work a little earlier every day. Then

I started getting up before the alarm clock rang, and even eating a full breakfast—something I stopped doing more years ago than I can remember. I even sang in the shower to warm up my voice.

I began to wonder about Josie's future. Perhaps he could be a scientist, like I would never be. Or a lawyer. Or maybe he would entertain—I could see him as a comic, standing amid howling laughter from a roomful of people. For the first time I found myself looking at the roster of prospective parents, wondering who might make my new friend a good home.

At one point, I even thought about . . .

But that is past me, I know. Fanciful thinking at best, anyway.

Kyle Lincoln feeds from tube twenty-eight now.

Josie Andrew will never be a scientist, or a lawyer, or a comic, or anything else. He is dead, rotting away where the company sends kids who fail DNA scans, kids who will not turn a profit because their genes are coded for Alzheimer's, or SIDS, or whatever.

The government took abortion away, saying we would not kill as a society. I am not a politician. I don't know if this is right or wrong.

I am a technician in a birthing center, a man who does his job without asking too many questions. All I know is that the government has given us a new procedure, prebirth delivery, so that a fetus that would have been aborted can live and grow in birthing chambers.

But this same government says we cannot "play God." We can understand, but cannot change. The law says we must test for genetic makeup to protect prospective parents and employers, but the same law says we cannot modify or alter the children's fate if the tests are positive.

For what must be the thousandth time I ask myself why I am doing this. My skin tingles and my head hurts. Then I think of the landlord shaking his fist under my chin, the refrigerator that sits empty in my kitchen. The money does not come in fast enough as it is, and a thirty-five-year-old man without a degree does not easily find a job in this day and age.

Still, the memo clings in my memory like the smell of landfill.

. . . *our compassion for their rights as human beings.* . . .

I cannot help but wonder what defect Josie inherited that signed his death warrant.

•••

I was twenty-two years old when I took this job. Sheila had just told me we were having a baby, and I was shaken to my roots. I needed a reasonable cash flow, and six semesters at Jefferson Community had pretty much let me know I wasn't going to get a degree in anything. Not knowing what else to do, I took the job at CBC.

At first, the kids just seemed to be shells waiting to be filled, dangling from their umbilical tubes like apples growing from the branches of a tree. My work was low level, taking fetal readings and making feeding adjustments based upon what the other techs told me. I was a floater, available for anything from janitorial cleanup to the midnight shift.

My first dumping occurred after two weeks.

I'll admit I was naive. I had no idea what my boss meant when he said it was time I had a chance to "go to Kelley's."

Kari Jones and I loaded plastic bags into the back of a pickup truck. I remember the smell of the diesel engine idling as we loaded black garbage bags into the back. The bags were heavy, and they made ugly slick sounds over the rumbling of the diesel as they hit the flatbed. Their bright yellow plastic ties looked like artificial butterflies against the black bags. I worked hard that night, grabbing two sacks at a time and hauling them aboard, trying to show off.

Yes, I was married, but I was young, and Kari was an attractive woman in her own way—slim and short, with brownish-red hair that curled past her shoulders and the heady air of worldly experience.

Kari told me to get in. The cab smelled of stale cigarette smoke and wintergreen air freshener. She threw a wrinkled blue bandanna onto my lap and laughed at my befuddled expression.

"Just wait, you'll be glad you have it," she said.

It was early spring. The night was overcast, the clouds reflecting a ghostly sheen of the city's light. The air was pre-rain heavy, and the windshield frosted on the inside so bad we had to wait for it to clear before we could leave.

Kelley's landfill was south of town. Kari stopped the truck and opened the padlocked entrance. I remember thinking it was odd she had the key. At that time, the idea of the company paying someone to look the other way had never even crossed my mind.

The truck's wheels crunched over metal and plastic. Headlights sliced erratically through the mist, exposing dead refrigerators and piles of refuse. There was no wind. I gagged against the stagnant odor. Kari tied her bandanna around her head and drew it over her nose. The voice of experience.

I quickly did likewise.

It took fifteen minutes of driving to reach the right place.

With the headlights off, the landfill was suffocatingly oppressive. We climbed into the back. For several minutes we flung sacks out into the inky void. One by one, they disappeared into the darkness, landing with wet impact amid the rest of the city's waste.

We made small talk on the way back, me fantasizing that Kari would stop the truck and suggest we do something I would regret later. It didn't happen, of course. I am embarrassed to admit I don't remember even being curious about what was in the bags that night.

The next day, however, I noticed we were missing two children from my chamber. When I asked my supervisor about them he grew quiet, then said simply, "They're gone. If you want to keep your job here, don't ask again."

My stomach burned like I had swallowed a handful of burrs. Something in his tone reminded me of the chill of nighttime air on my bare arms as I threw plastic bags into the landfill.

A month later, my wife Sheila miscarried.

She mourned for several weeks, but I'll admit I felt relieved. We had never talked about children before we married, and I never found the right time to tell her I am sterile. The child had been someone else's. I thought I loved Sheila enough to forgive a single mistake—or maybe I was just too embarrassed to own up to the truth at the time. Whichever, I figured she never had to know. But deep inside, the idea of raising another man's child had made me queasy, and the daily discussion of Sheila's pregnancy was a constant reminder of her betrayal.

Her miscarriage let me off the hook and meant I didn't have to face the question.

For days after that, I stood before the chamber and watched the children float. They grew larger day by day, month by month, becoming real people. I began to notice how each one was different. And I began to name them.

Megan Diane had a birthmark on her left hip and would hold her face up to listen to the artificial heartbeat. William Wallace was bold, struggling against the fluid, and even beginning to swim among the children in his last month. Seeing them in this new light made me feel tiny, small.

The chamber held from fifty to a hundred children at any one time. Professors. Bus drivers. Waitresses. Football players. Engineers. Every chamber was priceless, the future of the world.

That was when I began to realize I wanted to be a father.

When I suggested that maybe we could adopt, Sheila yelled and screamed at me, telling me I was stupid to think we could just "buy another dog to replace the one we lost." We drifted further apart over the next six months. When she turned up pregnant again, we both knew it wasn't my child.

She packed up and moved in with the guy the next day, and that's the last I ever saw of my wife. It's okay, though. An uneducated man like me is probably unfit to be a father anyway.

In the meantime, I had gone back to Kelley's three times.

• • •

It is, of course, illegal as hell to kill a fetus, regardless of its genetic makeup. The company does it to boost profit, though, knowing that a child with multiple sclerosis or AIDS or Huntington's disease is never going to earn out what it costs to raise them.

Everyone knows this except, apparently, the FCCC.

I sit at my desk and think of Josie Andrew. My heart sinks and I find it nearly impossible to breathe. The pressure is too much. I cannot stay here today. I stand up, my chair rolling across the floor as I walk breathlessly toward the door. The dark silhouette of my own shadow slips before me, outlined in the chamber's thin golden light. Josie's face sits inside the void, smiling at me, reacting to the tone of my voice.

The door is heavy, its knob cold against my hand.

I slip out to the hallway and press my back against the sterile white wall. My breath comes in thick lungfuls.

I am thirty-five.

I am unmarried.

And I will never be a real father.

I feel the presence of every child that has disappeared from my birthing chamber without record. Their tiny fingers gather around my throat. Josie's face lingers behind my closed eyes and I realize I cannot live with this any longer.

Josie Andrew is dead, robbed of his chance to make an impression on the world. Is there a worse fate?

I can think of only one.

I am thirty-five, I think again. No one knows I even exist. I am as good as dead, as dead as Josie Andrew.

I turn and race down the long white hallway. The air outside is December cold. I go to my car and start the engine.

There's something I have to do.

•••

Razor wire lines the top of the chain-link fence. It catches light from the full moon and gleams gun-barrel blue. The rotting stench is thick as gravy.

I stop my car in the shadows across the street and look at my watch. Ten minutes past one. The car door creaks as it opens. I shut it as quietly as I can. To the left is a run-down body shop, to the right is a barren field littered with dried husks where corn may grow next spring. The only sound is the wind whipping in from the northwest.

Despite three sweatshirts and a jacket, I shiver. Donning my work gloves, I stride to the fence. Tools jangle softly as I move. The flashlight beats against my thigh, and the wire cutters are cold on my hip. I reach for the surgical mask wrapped around my neck and pull it over my nose. It cuts the scent so it's almost bearable.

A thin layer of frost covers the galvanized iron of the fence.

The wire cutters are awkward.

I slice vertically through the fence, opening a slot nearly two meters tall. Using heavy pliers, I pull the fence backward at the bottom to leave a triangular opening.

I toss the cutters away and slip quietly into Kelley's landfill. The grass is dead, tall and coarse. My boots whip through it with harsh tearing sounds.

I crest a hill.

The landscape is postnuclear.

Broken shards of the world are scattered across the hillside, skeletons of human need: rusted metal that might once have been a washing machine, old lumber, shattered glass, plastic, bits of furniture.

Moonlight underlines everything in stark black shadows.

I continue.

I follow the same path I have driven so many times in the past. How many black bags have I thrown into this void? Pink and brown faces from the chamber stick in my mind, and for a moment my breathing fails me.

Still, I move forward.

Kelley's is a large landfill.

I'm certain it is my imagination, but the ground grows more slippery as I go, and soon I feel I am skating on a layer of grease and grime. Or maybe blood and gristle.

My stomach churns acidic. I am glad I have not eaten this evening.

In something under an hour I arrive at the place.

I would know it anywhere, surrounded by black mounds that seem to close over the area, protecting the world from the wickedness of the deeds I have committed. An ominous silence covers this artificial valley. The ground here is slick, wet with frost. For the first time, I reach for my flashlight and expose the area before me.

I have never really seen it before.

A bulldozer has pushed everything into large piles. Burial mounds, I think, remembering a slice of my American history from Jefferson Community. Still, they cannot hide what I have come to find. Black plastic bags are buried in the refuse, almost hidden from sight. A single yellow twist tie blazes vividly in the beam of my flashlight.

Suddenly I am colder than I can ever remember being.

Josie Andrew is in one of these bags. I can feel it in my bones. I set the flashlight at an angle to illuminate my work and walk to the mound of garbage. It is maybe four meters tall.

I put my gloved hand against the pile and climb to its top. A torn screen door is the first thing to go. I fling it away with both hands, and it flies into the darkness like a giant silver Frisbee. A soggy mattress is next. Then a rusted pan.

The work warms me.

Blood pulses through me, filling my body, my heart thumping proudly against my chest. I am here to find Josie, I tell myself. His lifeless body will speak to the FCCC auditors in ways more eloquent than I ever could. I am here so he can make his mark in this world.

And, maybe, I am here to begin making my own mark.

Perhaps again it is my imagination, but suddenly I hear another heartbeat, smaller, faster. More of a rasping *swish swish* than a solid *thump thump*. It is a sound I have heard a thousand times before. A fetal heartbeat. Josie Andrew.

Without realizing it, I find myself singing.

For my father

WAITING FOR HILDY

Written by
Chris Flamm

Illustrated by
Eric L. Winter

About the Author

Chris Flamm grew up in rural Pennsylvania and started her writing career at the age of five with an illustrated exposé about life in the coastal South called Glamour Girls of Miami Beach. This was soon followed by other masterpieces, such as Chiung and the Golden Butterfly, the tale of a Chinese girl who spends inordinate amounts of time chasing a butterfly.

At the age of nine, Chris discovered science fiction. She spent most of the rest of her childhood interviewing mad scientists and trying to contact aliens through telepathy.

After graduating from Indiana University, she moved to the Pacific Northwest, where she worked as a jewelry designer and silversmith. She lives in Portland, Oregon, with her husband, who is attending law school, and with her wonderful children.

So far, she says that the only alien she has been able to contact telepathically on a regular basis is her cat, Zandar.

I t was on one of the new grav trans that I met Hildy, though, of course, that wasn't her name then. I was on my way home from Dalhassy, in the middle of the continent, to where I lived in Renchester, on the coast—a good seven-hour ride on one of the old trans, but only about an hour on the Mountain-to-Coast grav trans.

In fact, I wished that the ride took a little longer because it was almost half an hour before I worked up the courage to speak to Hildy. I watched her get onto the trans at the Montgarten stop. She somehow looked familiar, though I don't know why. She was nicely built, with reddish hair and a light sprinkle of freckles—a look that I have always found attractive. But I don't think it was her physical appearance that I found familiar; it was something about her—her essence, or whatever it is that you want to call it—that seemed to draw me. It felt as if I knew her.

I never did actually work up the courage to sit by her. Instead, she came to me, smiled, and sat down. Do you know what the first words she said were? She said, "Do I know you from somewhere? You look familiar."

We talked for a few minutes and compared places we'd been. We'd grown up several thousand kilometers from each other. It was unlikely that we had met through our work; we were in completely different fields. She'd been off-planet, but I never had, so that was out. In fact, we quickly exhausted the possibilities. Yet the feeling persisted that we somehow knew each other.

My stop came and I had to get off—regretfully—to gather my things, and take the tube home to where my wife had dinner waiting.

We smiled at each other and Hildy waved as I went through the exit. I hadn't asked where she lived. I didn't know where she worked. I knew her name, RoseEllyn Dumont, and that's all I knew. On a planet of three trillion people, that's not enough.

That was the first time.

•••

The second time, I was a river guide on a remote stretch of the Fanfassing where it crosses the Upper Yinnish Peninsula on Berthehaven. Hildy had just come on-planet and she wanted to go to Frethewater, in the east, in search of certain metal ores that could only be found in that region of our world.

She told me that her name was Anna Held, and she paid for her passage to the east with rupees, one of the most valued currencies in those parts. But I'd have taken her on even if she had paid in buckwheat groats. Anna Held was a beautiful woman. She was also strangely familiar and fascinating, though I had never laid eyes on her before.

She spent the night at an inn in the little town of Rinrennen, near where my boat was docked. I first saw her there when I went to get my evening meal. She was at the table eating dock pudding, a stew made of various bits of meat and vegetables, popular in those parts, and poring over a book of maps. Old Teddy Haeten, the innkeeper, served me some of the same, as well as a beer, and pointed at her with his chin.

"That one wants to go downriver a ways. Told her that you were the one to take her—best river runner in these parts."

I took a swallow of beer and studied the woman that Old Teddy had indicated. "She looks sour," I said as I watched her pore over her maps. Indeed she did. Her mouth was pinched and turned down at the corners.

Old Teddy held up a rupee. "She pays well." His eyes crinkled as he smiled.

So after I finished my stew, I took my beer over to the lady's table and nodded to her. "I'm told that you're looking for a way downriver."

She indicated that I should have a seat and shoved a map across the table to me, frowning. "This is where I want to go," she said. "All the way down the Fanfassing to where it spills into the Great Gilead. I'm told that it is a difficult trip, and lengthy. Your backwater little planet doesn't use grav trans, so I have to rely on river travel."

She had not yet looked up at me. She frowned and I studied her face. It was well made, and intelligent—dark hair pulled back absent-mindedly into a rope wound on top of her head. Her eyes were green and her nose evenly shaped. If you took away that frown, I thought, this would be an attractive woman. I was wrong.

I pulled the map away from her to study. Our fingers made contact. She looked up and smiled at me. Her face underwent an amazing transformation. She was not an attractive woman. She was the most breathtakingly beautiful woman I had ever seen. I lost my thoughts, and her expression turned quizzical. I shook my head and smiled back. She paid me and we arranged to meet in the morning on the dock, and start the long trek east.

I walked slowly back to my boat, thinking of Anna Held. Then lay down in my cubby and fell to sleep.

Early in the morning Anna appeared with some cases and her equipment. I rounded up Kip, my oarsman, and we pushed off. We flowed along with the current in the roiling green water while large white birds circled overhead. It was a beautiful day. By the time the sun was high, it grew hot.

Anna sat across from me on a pile of ropes in the stern. Kip brought us both pieces of hot pigeon pie and glasses of strong tea. We ate lunch in a companionable silence, looking out at the water and the steep banks of hilly forest as they rolled by.

Anna broke the silence first. "How far is it to Frethewater?"

"Depends on how fast we move—and that depends on the weather, the wind, and on the strength of our backs."

Anna's eyebrows arched. "The strength of our backs?"

I nodded. "When the wind quits blowing and the current goes around in big lazy circles, we row."

She nodded at my back, bare in the sun from work before lunch. "Well, your back seems strong enough at any rate." She stared at me evenly, without blinking.

I shrugged and turned away, not sure how the remark was meant or how to react. My body had its own reaction that I did my best to ignore. Kip came and took our leftovers from lunch. I went back to work stowing items here and there, getting ready for the ride I knew was coming. Anna wandered the deck looking at things. I heard her ask Kip questions as he swung on the tiller.

Her dark hair was down and the river wind whipped it across her eyes so that she continually had to pull it back. The wind made her cheeks and lips bright red. Her eyes sparkled the same deep green as the river.

By late afternoon we entered a canyon with steep sides carved out of the bloodstone cliffs. Here the river ran deep and wild and demanded all my attention. I put Kip on the bow with a long pole and took the helm. I motioned Anna to one of the masts and told her to hang on to the guy lines.

Then we were in the deep of it and all my attention focused on the river, its patterns, the wind, and its thrust as we flew through the eddies and rapids of the canyon.

Finally as the sun disappeared behind an enormous pink cloud, we came to the slow water of the other side. I had nearly forgotten about Anna, so busy was I with the motion of my skiff. She came up beside me and handed me a glass of hot strong tea, that I took gratefully into my tired hands. Kip went below and started supper while I rested in the last of the day's light.

Anna sat beside me and asked about my life on the river. I told her how I had come to be a river runner. Kip reappeared with thick slabs of roast muskhog on slices of yeasty bread baked by Teddy Haeten's woman early that morning.

The three of us ate supper together as we floated down the lazy river. Later, I tied the boat for the night and went below to sleep.

The next day dawned bright, clear, and warm. Kip and I rowed in the slow water until the wind picked up and filled our sails. The day passed without event—no rough water until we hit Mergen Falls. We got through that gracefully, dancing our way among the rocks with the sun high and full overhead. In the hot afternoon we moored our little boat for about an hour and swam in the warm water.

I watched Anna flipping about in the water with long, graceful strokes, and she made me think of the mythical people said to live below the surface of our great oceans. Back on the boat Kip cleaned some fish he'd caught, while I cast off.

We were on a broad part of the river. So wide was the Fanfassing in some areas that you could not see the shores from the middle. The current here was straight and strong, so I set the tiller for the night and went below after our supper of river fish and ale to fall asleep to the song of the water.

Sometime in the night I was awakened by the touch of a warm body pressing itself to me. Anna had climbed into my bed. It was completely unexpected. Surprised and overjoyed I put my arms around her in welcome.

That was the second time.

•••

The third time was also on Berthehaven. I grew up in a small town near the mouth of the Great Gilead.

I fished. I hunted. I roamed the eastern forests looking for treasure. I discovered it one morning while I was searching for a town that I knew was nearby.

Coming out of the woods, I noticed a small, neat cottage in a meadow just beyond the trees. A woman stood outside, hanging clothes on a line to dry in the morning sun. She faced away from me, and I admired the curve of her body in her long skirts as she stretched to hang something on the line.

A small dog came running from behind the cottage and barked at me. The woman turned and our eyes met. I think we both underwent the shock of recognition at the same time. I looked away, embarrassed by the strong surge of emotion that I felt for this woman I had never before seen.

She called to me cheerfully as is the manner of country people in that part of the world. The little barking dog let me scratch him between the ears, and I advanced.

"Hello," I said. "Your little dog seems to like me."

"Oh, Faci is friendly with everyone. He is not much good as a guard."

"What do you need guarding from?" I asked, trying to make a friendly joke.

"Maybe from you." The smile left her face.

We looked at each other for a long moment, an eternity. "I've been searching for you everywhere," my heart said silently.

I looked away. "I was on my way into Sudbry—" I started.

"Would you like some lunch?" she said at the same time.

I nodded. Hildy fed me barley cakes and stew—thick with carrots and leeks from her garden. We talked as we ate. Her name was Gabriette. I told her about my travels in the eastern forests. She laughed at my silly stories. When I left she invited me to visit again if I chanced by.

I finished my business in town more quickly than I had thought I would. I considered where to go next. I had no obligations, though I had planned to continue on through Sudbry to the north. I wasted time looking in shop windows and chatting with the men who sat outside the pub drinking their various brews.

Late in the afternoon I still hadn't decided what to do.

I could go back the way I came, I thought. Nothing says that I have to go north. I could go back to Gilead and visit my old ma. She would probably like a visit.

I hadn't been to see her for some time. My enthusiasm for this idea grew. I could buy her trinkets, something pretty and useless that I knew she would love. Of course I would have to pass Gabriette's cottage, as well.

It was evening by the time I reached the cottage in the meadow. Wood smoke drifted from the chimney and I could smell meat roasting on a spit. Faci ran out to bark at me, and I greeted him like an old friend. Gabriette came out of the cottage slowly. She looked at me thoughtfully.

"I'm just on my way back to Gilead," I explained.

"Oh, I thought you were heading north."

"Oh . . . yes. Well, you see . . ." I trailed off, at a complete loss for words. It occurred to me that she was not happy to see me again so soon.

"Have you eaten?" she finally asked, possibly to break the long uncomfortable silence.

Say *yes*, I told myself, then move on.

"No, I haven't," I answered.

"Would you like some supper?" Gabriette asked quietly.

I nodded yes. I couldn't speak. My heart was thudding too hard.

"Well, come in then. You can help build the fire up for me."

Gabriette busied herself with the food. She gave me a little dish of tidbits and I took Faci outside where he ate them. We both remained quiet through supper. We drank a bottle of good red wine with our meal. I cleared my throat several times. Gabriette looked up each time, expectantly. But I could think of nothing to say. Our merry chatter of the afternoon was painfully missing.

When we finished eating, I helped clear away the supper dishes, then started to wash them, hoping to put off my departure as long as I could. Gabriette busied herself with other chores. Slowly, I wiped the last plate clean. Then I put my sack over my shoulder.

"Thank you for supper," I said. "I'd better go now."

Gabriette turned from her chores. "Oh, do you have to?" she asked quietly.

I looked at her, not sure I had understood what she meant.

"You could stay tonight," she said, even more softly. I did.

• • •

The fourth time I met Hildy was on the field of battle. I never learned her name. We were on opposing sides in a war that seemed never to end. One morning, as the sun rose, I met her face to face, on the top of a hill.

I saw her, a handsome young man, about my age, with an expression of desperation on his face. His uniform was tattered, and grime crusted his skin. Dirt rimmed his eyes.

Inexplicably, I thought to myself: I would like to be friends with this person. We shouldn't be fighting. We should be comrades, drinking buddies. We should visit women together. I thought about how tired I was, how stupid this war seemed, and I wondered why I was fighting. I opened my mouth to say something when he raised his weapon, glanced away for an instant, then fired.

•••

The fifth time, Hildy and I were traders—part of a small merchant fleet that worked the Galinos Cluster. Merchant fleets are made up mostly of families that have allied themselves in the pursuit of trade. Over time families intermarry and the bonds of association and commerce strengthen. It is rare for an outsider to join a fleet, outside of marriage, but it happens. That is how Hildy joined the Neacahnie Family Fleet.

We had stopped at Robbonan—a small world, rich in a certain type of crystalline silicate that was desirable in the further reaches of the cluster. There had been sickness among us, a virus that came on board during a layover. It had taken several good crewmen. Our ship, *Orial's Hope*, was not hit hard, but our sister ship, the *Goodfellow*, had lost three top crew members to the sickness, as had other ships in the fleet.

So on Robbonan we actively searched for qualified crew. The quals were tight, though, and we didn't expect to fill the complement of all we had lost. Applicants had to have not only an excellent education and grounding in ship basics, they had to have a specialty that we needed. And they had to have, as well, certain less definable traits—a sharp sense of moral uprightness, ingenuity, a sense of aesthetics, and they had to fit in with our group. In other words, most of us had to like them. This is important when you live cheek-to-jowl with someone in a small space for months on end.

Hildy almost didn't make it. She didn't have the specialty training we needed, but in the end she was voted in, along with ten other crew who were spread among our many ships.

Hildy, whose name was Mara, was slated for the *Goodfellow*, but at the last minute was reassigned to

Orial's Hope. For some reason this disturbed me. Something about Hildy disturbed me, but I couldn't put my finger on what it was. It seemed as if I should know her, though of course I didn't. Furthermore, I didn't entirely trust her.

She didn't seem to care for me either. She did her best to avoid me. Our ship was large; we had different duties; and it wasn't hard to stay elsewhere. Still, sometimes at night I thought about her—unwelcome images that I tried, often unsuccessfully, to banish the next morning.

Mara was being trained on logistics and astrogation. Infrequently we pulled duty together. I was her senior officer, but I did my best never to tell her what to do. She accepted correction readily from others but not from me. A black, smoldering look would come into her eye, and though she never disobeyed a direct order from me, she did her best to ignore most of what I said.

In turn, I did my best to ignore her—never easy when she was in close physical proximity. Instead my mind would invent interesting pictures of our bodies twined together in various positions. I coped by staying busy and finding as much to do off the bridge and away from her as I could.

As a strategy it had its merits, but it also had its limitations. One late rotation some of those limitations became extremely clear. Mara was feeding nav figures onto the board to calculate a minor jump due next shift. I checked her data on my own board and discovered a mistake. When I pointed this out, the dark, smoldering look entered her eyes. She justified her figures and calculations.

I suggested she recheck. *Suggested*, not ordered.

I leaned over her to study the board. It was everything I could do not to grab her dark hair in my hands and pull her to me. I wanted the black expression to disappear. I wanted her to gaze at me, the way I must have been gazing at her.

But of course, she didn't. When my thumb accidentally brushed her arm, she arched her eyebrows disdainfully.

So I left the bridge. I went into one of the cold lockers and breathed the icy air. After a while, I judged it safe to return to the bridge.

Something was wrong. I knew it the minute I entered. Mara was desperately pumping numbers into nav. Yellow lights blinked. I grabbed her, pulled her from her seat, and took over.

She tried to explain in garbled sentences what had happened. But I didn't need her words to understand. We were about to hit a mass. My fingers flew over the board, desperately trying to lay in a correction. Part of my mind was disconnected.

I thought to myself, What a shame! What a shame that Mara and I had never become friends. What a shame that my brother and his wife would never have the child they were expecting. I prayed that my sister ship and the rest of the fleet were far enough away so that they would experience minimal damage from the impending explosion.

I downloaded data as rapidly as I could. Comms came in from other ships, but I didn't have time to answer. The yellow lights on the board went red. Alarms sounded. Mara grabbed my arm and I turned. I pulled her into the chair with me and held her tightly.

We made impact.

•••

The sixth time, Hildy and I were twin sisters. She was called Talia and I was called Tamaal. We grew up in a large manse with a courtyard. Our parents were patricians, members of the upper class in our conservative little city.

They loved us, indulged us, and gave us toys to fight over. Talia and I were best friends. We played together, made up stories, and of course we fought—usually over the toys.

One morning I was playing in the courtyard with a toy prancer. It was new, and therefore highly desirable. I rode on it, laughing, and brandishing my little stick. Talia ran out, wiping the last bits of breakfast from her chubby lips, and demanded that I dismount.

The resulting tussle broke one of the prancer's legs. Talia glared at me and said, "I'll tell Mummy. I'll tell Dadda. You broke our prancer. They'll have to get me a new one and *you* won't be able to ride."

This made me angry. I pulled one of her golden curls.

Talia yelled and swung at me.

"Oh yeah," I shouted. "Well, you blew up the starship!"

Talia looked at me. I stared at her, and we both burst out laughing. "You blew up the starship," I said again. We laughed even harder. "What a ninny you are!"

We grabbed each other around the waist and rolled on the ground, we were laughing so hard. "KaBoom!" I said. "KaBoom! We exploded!"

Talia shrieked with laughter. "KaBoom!" we shouted together.

Dadda came into the courtyard to see what all the ruckus was.

"Oh, Dadda," Talia giggled. "I blew up the starship!"

"You girls are so silly," Dadda said. Then he gave us each a big hug and went back into the manse.

"KaBoom," we both cried. We laughed until the tears flowed from our eyes.

• • •

The seventh time, we were part of a large migration to another section of the galaxy. We wanted new lives, new planets for growth and expansion—something not possible in this crowded cluster of stars. I signed on as soon as I heard about it.

Government had become all in the Confederation. There were few acts that weren't legislated. What wasn't dictated by law was dictated by tradition.

I wanted to have children. I wanted to raise them on a frontier world where they would have to work hard and think fast, but where they could prosper from their own sweat. I wanted them to be able to think their own thoughts, not get caught in some endless mumble of meaningless rituals. Most of all, I wanted them to know what freedom was.

I met Hildy soon after I joined up. I noticed him right away—a dark-haired, gray-eyed man. Quiet, but inside it looked like he was laughing.

Jarel was not a large man, but he seemed exactly the right size for me. From the moment I saw him, I knew he was the man I wanted to father my children.

We smiled shyly each time we met, but we never spoke. Then one day Jarel came up, cleared his throat, took my hand, and asked if I would be his partner.

•••

The eighth time, I was the daughter of a Portuguese nobleman. I was sixteen and it was time to marry. Father had someone in mind for me, but I had never met him. I was afraid. My friend Mirabella only last year had been wed to an elderly man, and she was very unhappy. She whispered to me of what he did to her at night, and I rolled my eyes in horror.

I went to my mother for solace. I confessed the things that Mirabella had told me. My mother said it was my duty to do what my husband required, whatever that might be. Then she suggested that we go to church together and pray to the Blessed Virgin for a compassionate man.

Within a ten-day my father told me that I was to meet my lord that evening. I went again to church and prayed to the Blessed Virgin. I asked her to be kind and send me someone whom I could love, and who would love me in return.

That night I met Parobol. His hair was dark and his eyes a bright, piercing blue. He looked stern, and momentarily I felt afraid. But then he smiled and my fear melted, so warm was his expression. And I smiled back, enchanted.

I dreamed of Parobol that night—strange dreams where I was a man and he a woman. I woke up, embarrassed and confused. I went to mass and I prayed.

I saw Parobol often—always in the company of my duenna, of course. It is the duenna's mission to ensure that a young woman of virtue remains virtuous in every way, until she is married.

My duenna was a large and garrulous woman. She liked to eat and she liked to talk. Clothed in black and covered in shawls, she was easy to spot near the pastries, giving her opinions on various subjects to anyone unlucky enough to be in the vicinity. At times like these Parobol and I would wander to the far edge of the room. Sometimes Parobol would touch one of my fingers, and I marveled at the amazing effect that his simple touch could stir within me.

Parobol asked about my life. He wanted to know about my schooling, of which there was little, and he wanted to know my interests, which I scarcely knew myself. Parobol was older than me by about ten years.

He told me of his travels, and I listened in fascination to tales of people in other lands and customs so very different from the ones I had grown up with. He told me of the women in islands far to the south. That they could marry whom they chose was a revolutionary idea, but when he told me of their friendly behavior and what they wore—little more than a skirt and some flowers—I was truly shocked. I know I must have turned bright red, for Parobol looked at me curiously. I could not tell him of my own dreams, where I was with him and wore less than that.

Everyone knew that the Portuguese were the very best sailors. There were few places that Parobol hadn't been, and few things that he hadn't seen. His ideas were far from conventional.

One day he made the strangest remark. We were outside in the early evening. My duenna stood across the garden from us, holding the attention of everyone at the pastry table. Parobol turned to me and he said, "I was so afraid that I wouldn't find you."

I looked at him, unsure how to reply. He continued, almost to himself. "I searched everywhere, and you were none of the places I looked." I thought to myself, with some asperity, that I certainly would not have been on that South Sea Island that he had told me about, but I said nothing; Parobol seemed so serious.

He took my hands, and I glanced over at the duenna to make sure that she was not looking at us. Parobol's hands were so warm. They were not overly large, but well made and strong. I wondered how they would feel on different parts of me, then immediately felt ashamed of my thoughts.

"Do you never think, Francesla, that some of us are fated to love only one other, and that lifetime after life-time, we search for them, and are unhappy without them?" He looked at me so earnestly that I didn't know what to answer. His talk of other lifetimes bothered me.

"I don't know, Parobol. Perhaps." Then the duenna turned her attention to us and I quickly pulled my hands away from Parobol's. I resolved to bring him to mass with me and have him pray.

On our wedding day, I was shy and excited. The mass and the ceremony were a blur. The Monsignor was decked in a long red gown and a golden headdress. He led the benediction and had us exchange vows. The prayers and good wishes were interminable.

My father had invited Maestro Pachobel to play music for us. So, as Lord and Mistress we descended into the courtyard to listen to the music and to receive our guests. I sat there, upright, next to my husband, and we scarcely looked at each other. Then the maestro began to play his music, and the rest of the world dropped away. The music was so exquisitely beautiful that I believe tears must have come into my eyes.

Parobol reached for my hand. Together we listened, entranced. When the canon had ended, I turned to my husband and I said, "Thank you." He lifted his eyebrows in an expression I knew so well. "Thank you for searching," I said.

•••

The ninth time, I was hard at work on a symphony. My health and my hearing were going. I was cantankerous and difficult to get along with, I am sure.

I met Hildy at a recital. A slender woman, her glossy brown hair was wrapped neatly behind her neck. She came up to congratulate me on my splendid music. I studied her and I thought, "She means this. These are not polite, empty words. She understands what I am trying to do." So I let her visit me in my little studio and I played for her often. I let her bring me gifts of food and wine, and I accepted her adoration as if it were my due.

Hildegaard von Ostenhime, Hildy. Her presence was familiar and necessary. Beyond that I never gave it a thought.

Vienna, in those days, was a haven for composers. Music was revered and I kept busy writing for various occasions of state. Often I would work far into the night, a candle burning beside my hand as I wrote out the glorious sounds that I heard inside my head. In the morning I would be tired and disheveled and often irritable. The fire would have burned out hours earlier, unnoticed. Hildy would come, tidy up, and cluck at me to eat some food that she had brought.

Why she stayed with me for so long, I will never know. I was absorbed by my music and my own needs. I subjected her to the worst of my black moods—which were frequent when the music wouldn't come. Yet she continued to visit me daily. She made sure that I had food in my larder, and a fire in the hearth.

I never spoke to her of love. I took her presence for granted. It never occurred to me that a woman of her station and bearing would want a husband and a family, so caught up was I in my sonatas and quartets.

"Listen," I would say as she came in the door. "Listen to this!" And I would play. I would bang on my piano until waves of sound crashed around and through us. Hildy would sit, tears in her eyes, and the expression on her face rapt. Never once did I say, "That was for you." Never once did I say, "Thank you for standing by me and giving me the freedom to make my music."

Then after one particularly black storm in which I raged at her for my lack of genius, she didn't return. I waited, proud, certain that she would come back.

But she did not.

Months went by. I heard that she had married. I wept—great storms of frustration and self-hatred. I played my piano incessantly. Dark, black, brooding music. Around Vienna people whispered that I was like a madman.

Over the years I slowly recovered—not my health or my hearing. They got steadily worse with no one to care if the fire were lit, or to make sure that I had eaten.

But I recovered my joy in the simple things of life: the late afternoon sun pouring in from the west; the light rain in the spring; the irises that grew outside my door, tended by my landlady. I believe that I must have been easier to get along with at this time than at any other point in my life.

Then one early spring morning, a tune started playing through my mind. It was a simple tune. I sang it to myself before I went to sleep at night, and I sang it in the morning when I woke up. I heard it in the great empty caverns of my mind. I read Schiller's poem "Ode to Joy" and I knew what to do with my simple tune.

Illustrated by Eric L. Winter

I wrote a symphony for Hildy, and for the infinite possibilities of our lives. I have not given up hope that we will meet again, some other time, some other place. I am waiting.

VALUABLE ADVICE

Written by
Anne McCaffrey

About the Author

Anne McCaffrey is certainly one of the most successful science fiction authors in the latter half of the twentieth century, and deservedly so. She spins a fine tale, as millions have found out by reading her *Dragon Riders of Pern* series, or her *Killashandra* novels, or her *Pirate Planet* books or any of various other projects.

She has also been a staunch friend to new writers and has been a contest judge for the past fourteen years. In celebration of this, we asked her to write the article that follows.

READ! is my first dictum for those who wish to write. You must know what others have written and how they put the book together.

DON'T GIVE UP THE DAY JOB to concentrate on writing until you earn as much from your backlist as you do from new contracts.

BUY A DICTIONARY and check your spelling. Albeit many computers include a spell checker, but I'm always arguing with mine about the words I invent that are needed in a science fiction story. I also argue the spelling, since I work with the English-Irish, the English-English and the English-American conventions as well as grammar and syntax. And if you think that's funny, it is, but it's true. My American editor once said wistfully, "Anne, your English is too Irish to be American."

LEARN TO USE A THESAURUS to improve your command of synonyms and antonyms. (Some computer programs have them online. Use it.)

Except for the word *said*. There is a sort of virus that affects new writers as they try to prove what a command of the English language they have. They use a new verb for the word *said* each time a character speaks. James Blish, one of the top SF writers of all time, slapped my wrists for "said-bookism" by showing that my character could not have "hissed" that phrase, as it contained no sibilants. Nor could he have growled out a sentence that had no *r*'s or other fricatives. *Said, answered, replied, asked* (a few *queried*'s, maybe even a *stated* if your character is prosaic) are all the speaking verbs you need. Unless you have special need for emphasis. Use the other speaking words sparingly. People can even use whispers, and you can write "he said in a whisper." Any but those four speaking verbs interfere with the reader's progress through your story. You don't want anything to keep him/her from reading on.

When you face that blank sheet of paper or the screen, remember the first and most important task is to TELL A STORY. (By then, of course, you will have had the necessary tools of your trade: grammar, spelling, syntax *and* an idea for a story.) So, TELL IT!

Over the forty-four years since I sold my first story to the late Sam Moskowitz for his magazine *Science Fiction+*, I used that maxim to guide me. I don't do summaries or outlines—because, then, however brief the summary, I *have* already told that story. (There are three outlines in the Del Rey files that have never been written . . . another story took their place when the contract was signed and I was ready to write. Poor Pam Strickler has never forgiven me for not writing the story that was in the outline.) But my perceptions of what would happen, and the emergence of the characters as real "people," took precedence over the sketch I had done to secure the advance. However, most writers don't get away with that. Betty Ballantine, my first editor, understood—she had the outlines for the first two that were never written.

I'll give you another very important tip that I acquired from reading *The Firedrake* by Cecilia Holland. In the sixties when she published her first novel at a mere twenty-one years of age, there was a great revival of thick tomes of historical fiction by Thomas Costain and Sam Shellabarger. Excellent reading, but they went on and on about the details of their historical periods—so that you'd *know* they did their research—until you might start flipping pages to get back to the plot and the interesting parts. Cecilia Holland used only those details that would appear noteworthy or strange to a man living in those times, 1065 in *The Firedrake*. However, because she had been a history major and *knew* her facts, somehow the reader did, too, without all that overwhelming and minute detail.

I thought to myself, what a wonderful way to get a reader into an alien ambience and a strange planet. My deathless first words, using this technique, were "Lessa woke cold." And some two million words later, I haven't stopped writing the Pern Series®.

Gordon R. Dickson, one of my writer role models, said that if the author knew what was in the drawers of the chests in the room he was writing about, what hung in the closet, or lodged in pockets and on shelves, the reader would know, too, without having to be told.

I used that technique as well as another I discovered myself when I wrote *The Ship Who Sang*. If the writer is involved in an emotion, that, too, will be transferred through all the steps it takes to get a story from the mind, through the typescript, to page proofs, to finished edition, to the reader. I have made BBC cameramen weep to hear me read the last four paragraphs of that story. Of course, I'm weeping, too, and barely able to speak. That story came out in 1961: I wrote it as therapy for the grief I felt for the death of my father in 1954.

When readers weep because Moreta, the Dragonlady of Pern, went between on a borrowed dragon, they are not weeping for her. They are actually crying because I was so bereft when I had to put down my gallant grey hunter, Mr. Ed. I gave Master Robinton the kind of death that my brother died in 1988. I've used the anger I've felt, the frustration, the terror, and the humiliation as valid tactics to make my readers feel the emotions of the characters I invent and care what happens to them.

There is no secret way to get published. There is only *one* way—which is hard work, and baring parts of your own soul and life in the process—to get a novel or a story published. You believe in what you're saying and you TELL THE STORY!

AGONY

Written by
Ladonna King

Illustrated by
Sherman McClain

About the Author

Ladonna King grew up in Conway, Arkansas—a three-college town that is a bit weirder than most. There, she found that studying for five years in the drama division of Odyssey of the Mind cured her forever of linear thinking.

In school, she was an editorialist and cartoonist for a school paper, was in the Art Club, and became a National Merit Finalist. After graduation, she moved to Oregon and managed a convenience store in the Portland area, where she found that she got along just fine with the very usual people there.

"Agony" is her first sale.

About the Illustrator

Sherman McClain, a native of Texas, has been studying art for the past several years. He emphasized art and painting in high school, and has since studied fine art at the Glassell School of Art in Houston, Texas, and he has studied visual and graphic art at the Art Institute of Houston.

With a certain kind of reverence, Agony closed the dead man's eyes. A brush of long, pale fingers, delicate as a moth's wing, and those twin mirrors of terror no longer accused the silent room, the smiling woman. In a few more hours, the doctors would come with their pet Arrani healers, but nothing would be left for them to resurrect. The corpse had no soul left.

For a long moment, Agony considered the anonymous hotel room, committing it to memory, at least for a little while. The seconds stretched silently as a plain desk and chair, cheap framed landscapes, and slightly rumpled bed were absorbed into her almost eager mind. No matter that she'd seen this room, or dozens like it, many, many times. Each time was nearly the first. She would have to carefully erase the details from her mind before she left the building, until conviction was all that was left, the face and furnishings equally lost as if unimportant. Back at her employer's office, a petrified Arrani would probe her thoughts to be sure, sweating every tortured minute his mind had to touch hers.

Especially now that she had fed. Dreamily sated, by the fight to take him as much as the taste of his life, she was the epitome of the satisfied beast after the kill, stained and well content. This one had been strong, and strong-willed, the best meal she'd had in a long time. She couldn't even bring herself to think of the danger, that a soul might one day be too large a mouthful to swallow, and drown her in the ecstasy of it. At least she would die happy.

Her lips curved with an echo of menace, and as she spotted an unadorned mirror, she examined the expression with interest. Her pale white hair framed her sharp features like a blizzard's sweep, turning the flat black of her eyes into an exercise in contrast. She'd pulled her clothes on rather loosely, she noticed, and as she straightened the thick, rough cloth over her rangy frame, she studied the feminine curves of her body with surprised detachment. She always forgot she was attractive. She barely remembered she was human.

Sighing, she combed through her hair with her fingers, tired of the black-clad ghost in the mirror. It had nothing to do with her, that woman. Time to go.

Locking the door behind her, she purposefully slid down the hall, thoughts of capture the farthest thing from her mind. No one ever found Agony. She always found them.

She was no one; she had no fingerprints to leave behind, and no one ever quite remembered her face. If presented with a photograph, her closest friend would be hard pressed to claim her as an acquaintance. Minds were her toys; they were soap bubbles a gentle breath could move, and could just as easily be pricked to destruction.

The cab ride was boring, a ritual of punched keys on the dash console before she sat back in silence, waiting for the one-man unit to trundle her off to her destination. Streets blurred past into oblivion, a wash of neon brightness in the corners of her eyes. The speed shuttles whining by failed to distract with their minute vibrations, the hiss and squeal buffered by the cab's thick privacy coating. If she closed her eyes, she could almost imagine she was in her own bedroom, with the world shut out and the heady surge of stolen energy still ricocheting around inside her. . . .

A chime shook her from her reverie, and she looked around to find the forbidding, black Gen-Tech building looming over her suddenly small cab. Opening the door with a quick slide of her credit card, she stepped calmly out onto the bustling sidewalk, a still iceberg in the chaotic flood. Heading unhurriedly for the slick, tinted glass doors, she passed into the featureless lobby and through another set of thick, bulletproof doors where a perfunctory scan found her unarmed.

The receptionist looked up automatically, her metal-capped fingers poised in midair. "Name?" came her emotionless voice. Agony stared at the round, pale face, with its short dark hair and pouting lips, reflex urging her to reach out and claw.

"Agony Zade."

New girl. The fingers danced on an invisible keyboard, and the desk sensors scanned the movements, interpreted them, made them real—unlike this woman; it was a shame to waste a soul on someone so obviously worthless.

The receptionist started, shot the pale woman a peculiar don't-tell-me-I-don't-want-to-know glance, and turned slightly away.

"The Security Director will see you now," she murmured, pretending not see Agony, who smiled in sudden, impulsive cruelty.

"I know," she purred, staring fixedly until the receptionist began to tense and fidget. She walked leisurely away. She would have liked to have torn the little puppet-girl's tiny soul to bits, but Fehrs would never have forgiven her. She almost liked Martin Fehrs; he was very close to her kind of people. He understood her value, accepted her methods, and always played her fairly—all she ever asked and more.

Martin Fehrs had a pristine penthouse office where everything was white, flooded with sunlight. Crystal and glass reflected bright shafts of pure light at her, only to be sucked into the anomaly of her black garb. "Agony," Martin smiled as he stood from his comfortable desk, gesturing her to take a place in one of two pillow chairs ranged before him. As she sank gracefully into one, she smiled back, self-assured as a lioness.

"Did all go well?" he asked, resuming his seat, leaning forward on his elbows with his wide hands clasped before him. Agony caught the amusement in his brown eyes, and shared it herself. Mustn't say "kill," after all.

"Perfectly. Everything went like clockwork."

The Security Director nodded absently even as he pushed a button on his abandoned desk. "Of course. We'll just make sure there are no . . . after-effects, shall we? Routine as usual."

Agony sighed. "As usual." Her dark eyes speared him. His corporate distrust marred him, kept him from being a true friend. The temptation to thrust trust upon him, to change him, was slight, but present. But those damned pet Arrani psions would learn as soon as his next monthly security check, and Agony had no wish to alienate Gen-Tech or Security Director Fehrs. She still needed them.

The Arrani stepped inside then, looking pale and miserable, twisting his long, sticklike fingers absently. His ivory skin was nearly transparent with fear, barring two patches of palest rose on his cheeks, and his stiff mane bristled like the hackles of a terrified hound. Quick and birdlike, he barely reached Agony's shoulder, and she could see the little sparrow bones beneath the thin, snowy skin, as fragile as the composure on his pointed, sparrow's face. In the wildly fluctuating colors of his huge eyes, Agony read his terror. She smiled.

She'd never liked the Arrani, never mind that they were the first space-faring race humanity had met that had not attacked first and asked questions much later, if at all. She despised their hypocritical pacifism, loathed their sneaky mental fingers, their mastery of psionics. Before her, they'd never known a soul-eater, and she enjoyed being a nightmare to the select few the company forced her way.

The Arrani sank stiffly into the second chair, his skin an unhealthy powdery gray, and stared straight ahead. Agony lounged comfortably, completely ignoring the lithe, graceful being beside her, smiling in sheer animal contentment. She loved having these mice under her paw. As the first foggy brush of the Arrani's probe stroked her mind, she closed her eyes in studied unconcern.

A flash of her morning: leaving her dimly detailed apartment. She never let anyone see her home. She'd rather lose its memory entirely than risk her anonymity. She took a cab, but no clue as to where. There was the sensation of the hunt, shadowed, as if seen through the night-eyes of a feline, the gorging on life she enjoyed so much, but not so much as a scrap of wallpaper as evidence. Another cab ride, its origins cloaked in mist, to the streets that led here. Nothing else, no faces, no names, just the smoothly compressed flow of her morning, half of which was blurred beyond recognition. With the skill of a surgeon, she'd operated on her own thoughts, cutting out anything that might incriminate her or the company. There was not one usable shred for the Justice Department psions to work with if she were ever caught.

The Arrani was about to withdraw when Agony tickled his mind with a sharp dagger of thought, heavy enough for him to feel the edge, but not firm enough to cut. *Little man . . . see anything you like?*

She could feel his soul jump and twist to escape in a haze of panic: she slammed a massive paw down on it and flexed her claws only slightly. His soul fluttered like a bird's wing, trapped and terrified, like a maddened heart. Her razored predator's grin filled the Arrani's mental senses and froze him in mesmerized shock. It would be so easy to bite . . . all that energy, hers for the taking.

Agony dropped him as she opened her eyes, confronting Fehrs' worried look with aplomb. "Routine finished. I'm clean. As usual."

With a shriek, the loosed Arrani bolted for the door, clawing it open and rushing into the hall beyond. Laughing in amusement, Agony shook her head, crossing her legs as she reclined fully. They were all so very easy.

Her eyes soaked in Fehrs' expression, his teeth on his lip, his knuckles white. She felt him assess how close he was to receiving the same treatment. She heard him consider her black-clad form in his snowy office, his wanting her pale skin, white, white hair, sprawled just so, delivered from the oppressive darkness she had wrapped herself in, colorless and icy in this godlike white office in the clouds. His fear, when mixed with his desire, was a heady feast.

At last he blinked, looked down. "I have a new job for you. It'll pay triple what you're used to, plus travel expense. It's extremely important . . . and you'll have a partner."

"I don't need a partner," she said with finality.

"His name's Aberlaine," Fehrs continued as if she hadn't spoken, still not looking up. "He's part of your cover. Otherwise, he's yours to do with as you please. All you have to do is drag him around in public."

Agony considered it slowly, not speaking. Hers. They didn't care if she dined on him all at once or nibbled on him for the rest of his life: they didn't care if he died or when. But why the unusual gift? "Where are you sending me, Martin? Not Kansas."

He glanced up, caught her eyes in an intense stare. "Arranis. It's the only way to . . . meet with this client."

A low growl from her made Fehrs shiver, but he didn't drop his eyes. "Are you trying to kill me, Martin?" she purred, eyes glinting dangerously, panther's eyes in the dark. "If I go there—if I even think about doing this job, they'll swarm over me like ants on a grasshopper. I have no wish to be eaten alive."

Ironic, she heard him grumble to himself; he merely smiled.

"That's what Aberlaine is for. You'll be posing as a psychologist, experimental, working on psionic therapy. He's your pet psychopath, and you'll be there to study their methods. They'll attribute random flashes to him. You know they can't male-female differentiate with us, not to mention how 'diffuse' they say we are. The scientific community is very close knit on Arranis—and your client has a thing for human psions."

Agony sighed. They had it all planned out. "A 'thing'? How strong is he?"

"Very. Your . . . settlement would be reward enough without the money, from what we understand. And I mean to say, he finds human psions intellectually enticing. He studies them obsessively. He's been known to go too far, and has been charged with psisexual misconduct a few times, but he's relatively harmless."

She frowned. How disgusting. But if he was as strong as they thought, and with the bonus of Aberlaine thrown in . . . It just might be worth it.

"His name?"

• • •

"Oswis Demarr, at your service," the Arrani bowed, holding Agony's hand loosely as he kissed her finger-tips in the Arrani fashion. "So pleased to make your acquaintance."

She stared unblinkingly at his pure ivory skin, the stiff bone-colored mane that fell past his shoulders. Late middle age, this man, but still in his prime. As Annie Zadek, she'd come all this way for this scientist, this Arrani, a shrink like any other, who dabbled in pharma-ceuticals and molested human psions from time to time. She was not impressed, at least by his appearance.

Beside her, the man the company had given her, Jason Aberlaine, looked about with disarming boredom. When she had met him just before the ride to the shuttle port, he had given her the same look she might have given him were their situation different; this was a man unused to partnership, unsettled and insulted by the whole affair. They had had no time to talk on the ship before they were put in stasis, and had yet to reach a secure environment. She was rather looking forward to the inevitable interview.

Aberlaine didn't seem very impressed by Demarr either, from what she could tell, or by the cacophony of the staff psychologists' meeting room. His eyes flickered over the excessive wall decorations, slid past the crowd of Arrani gathered within, and returned again to the wall just over Demarr's shoulder. He might have been

mute, or dumb, for all the reaction his face showed, but
Agony knew better. She could feel the tension in him,
the listening in his wary stance, the way he had drawn
in on himself almost imperceptibly when they had
entered the high-ceilinged cavern of a staff room.
Perhaps he didn't like Arrani any better than she did, or
perhaps it was the strain of being a killer in a room full
of people who were well aware of it.

"And this is your subject? Quite a specimen, if I may
say so. Would you mind if I—"

She felt the probe coming and raised sudden shields
on Aberlaine, strengthening the "Do Not Touch" sign
that flickered like a halo around his head. "Actually,
mental contact with anyone but me throws him into
uncontrollable fits of violence. He's very hard to work
with after that, so I'd appreciate it if you didn't."

His hesitation was rude, she felt, until he caressed
her shield with his thoughts. It wasn't Aberlaine he was
interested in now. "My, you are strong. I'm sure you can
keep him firmly in line."

A part of her shivered in anticipation of ecstasy. He
was powerful. Consuming his soul would leave her
resonating for a week. She caught the heat in his eyes
and smiled slowly, willing to seduce this creature for the
sake of her own particular appetite.

"I'm quite adept at keeping men in line."

Demarr smiled back, nodding deliberately. "We
must meet again, when we have more time to discuss
method. But I see the liaison coming to drag you away
from me. You will, I trust, have a pleasant stay."

"I will, no doubt of that."

As he left, the staff room of the College of Psychology
struck her with sudden, overwhelming irritation. The
doctors scurried around with total disregard for order

in the huge seatless room, keeping up a constant flow of a hundred discussions at once. If someone had a topic to bring up to the entire group, he made the rounds, and like as not got caught up by a different topic on the way. Introductions by the diplomatic liaison had gone on like they would have at a party, rather than at a meeting of great minds.

"Perhaps you're ready to view your suite, Dr. Zadek? They've opted to put you on college grounds, in the visiting doctors' wing. That way, you won't have to make the trip from the Embassy every day. I do hope this is satisfactory, Dr. Zadek?" He was rather young, good-looking for an Arrani, and his eyes pulsed with shades of enthusiasm and eagerness to please.

She smiled reassuringly, and laughed inwardly at how easy this was going to be. "Of course. I'm honored."

"Please follow me."

The college was huge, when the full scope of buildings could be taken in. There were the actual college classrooms where students learned their mental craft, followed by the huge edifice that housed the doctors' offices. A separate building housed the resident patients, another the non-doctoral staff, and finally a group of apartment-like residences held the psychologists themselves.

The buildings were made of tasteful stone, connected by tree-lined paths and immaculate lawns, with gardens and pools along the way. The atmosphere felt peaceful in the extreme, no doubt from the residue of the students, who practiced at achieving that aura for their future offices. It almost seemed too beautiful a place to study and house the art of madness.

Their suite was on the second floor. The great stone staircase leading up to it was intricately carved with some sort of ivy, and gamboling creatures native to Arranis. Agony assumed that the Arrani's love of ornamentation was world-spanning, which seemed strange to her: all the Arrani at home wore plain clothing and lived in utilitarian houses little better than hotel rooms. It had occurred to her that that was exactly what the rooms on Earth were to the Arrani, who were most often seen dressed for work. The Arrani never stayed very long.

"And here we are," the young liaison bowed her in. Beauty assaulted Agony from all sides.

The sitting room was as verdant and golden as the park outside, and the native flora bloomed madly in every available space, filling the room with the scent of roses. The walls were alive with inlaid carvings and reliefs. Even the furniture was fantastical. Straight ahead stood a sliding glass door, opening onto a balcony above a serene, dark pool; the ironwork enclosing the area was as fine as a pen stroke, infinitely complex.

"I love it," she smiled, barely looking at the beaming liaison. "Thank you."

"It's our pleasure, Doctor. You'll find your stay comfortable, I trust. . . ."

"Of course."

As soon as he left, Agony felt for listeners while the silent Aberlaine checked for mechanical bugs. Satisfied they were left in privacy from psions at least, she watched her so-called partner with interest as he padded around the suite, a pocket-sized machine in his hand.

He really was handsome. Only a little taller than she, with thick brown hair brushed lightly with honey. His powerful body moved with a deadly grace she'd come to recognize. He'd been trained to kill, and well: he was willful enough to make his coming death sweet.

"We're alone, then?" she asked.

He turned slowly to face her, his eyes full of questions, distrust. "Yes. There's nothing here."

She watched him wonder who she was, why she was the one expected to do the job, why he'd been given to her, in more ways than he knew. As the moment stretched and his tension built, she still felt no fear whatsoever from him. Admirable. Deciding suddenly, she melted into the nearest chair and smiled.

"I assume you guessed I'm a psion. You're half right. I have psionic capabilities, but only as they apply to the nature of a soul-eater. When I kill someone, it's final."

His face slowly drained of color when certain things clicked into place. Explanations that had not been forthcoming back home were suddenly unnecessary. In this day and age, when doctors could fix any illness, reverse death, the only thing absolutely required was a soul for the Arrani healers to coax back to the body. That discovery had been a slap in the face to both the atheists and the religious alike, seeing as there actually was such a thing as the immortal spirit, but that mere mortals could manipulate it easily. Memories of an afterlife were little better than dream sequences, the settings predisposed by whatever societal upbringing was at work.

"Why are you here, Aberlaine?" she asked suddenly. Who was he that he could be tossed to her so easily?

His smile was twisted, bitter. "I would have been Security Director, but for two votes. Fehrs hasn't forgotten that." He shook his head almost sadly, and sat down hard.

"I'm your problem now, aren't I? They won't acknowledge me now even if I kill you, will they? I probably can't even kill you." He laughed shortly, interrupting his commentary with a fist punched into the couch. "I should have guessed."

Agony smiled, undisturbed by the train his thoughts had taken. "I don't know what they'll do. But you absolutely are mine, and you couldn't hurt me if you tried. I've seen to that."

His fingers went to his brow as he realized that she'd altered his mind. His wide eyes were full of hurt. His mouth twisted in a mock smile, and he muttered sardonically, "But I don't even know you."

The temptation was a hair too great: reaching out for his strong, stubborn spirit, Agony closed her eyes and sighed. Just a taste.

Cat and mouse, she the lioness, he the small, furred prey as she pounced, holding him down effortlessly. "No," she heard him whisper as if a million miles away, and she brushed him very softly with her mental claws. As his soul writhed in her grip, tormented by the sharpest of feather-touches, she took him in her teeth and stabbed gently down.

Life flooded her as he managed a strangled groan: she didn't drain him swiftly this time, but slowly savored a tiny amount of his bright, golden self. So long as she only took a little, he could regenerate it effortlessly, constantly; she could afford to be patient. He struggled madly, unconsciously, but she could taste the difference. The strange euphoria of being drained was on him, and he didn't want to be held down. He wanted to smother her with life.

She felt hands on her calves, a head pressed help-lessly to her knees, and teased him with a slow, lingering removal of teeth and claws. As she opened her eyes, Aberlaine breathed in deep, shuddering sobs, gulping air like a man who has nearly drowned. He knelt before her, his hands brutally tight, but there was something quite satisfying about his helpless need.

One bite, and he was hooked; he'd beg her to kill him by inches, from now to the end of eternity. Agony's long-fingered, sensitive hands reached out and held his bowed head gently, stroking his silken-soft hair with a proprietary confidence. This would be an enjoyable relationship: he was her kind of people. Killers had to stick together.

•••

The doctors assembled in Demarr's office watched silently with unfeigned interest as he prepared to nudge the sociopath further along the road to normalcy. The sessions had been going on for three months so far, and now that the rapport between doctor and patient had been established, Demarr knew what buttons to push and when.

Agony and Aberlaine sat in the back, with the excuse that it might upset the psychopath to be so close to a psion at work on a fellow patient. Agony watched the session out of curiosity, and to get a better idea of Demarr's power. He was definitely the strongest psion she'd encountered to date. When she'd been younger, psions had occasionally given her trouble; now, so long as she struck first, they were as easy as normal prey.

As she watched the sedated patient's mind being shaped by the doctor's artistic touch, Agony puzzled over the strangeness of her assignment. What was so dangerous about this psychiatrist that Gen-Tech had sent their best operative to kill him—and kill him utterly? What was this man to them? She could understand Fehrs wanting Aberlaine out of the way, but he was still a valuable man. Why throw him away as an incentive? They wanted her here, and strong: they'd given her money, an airtight cover, extra energy, and back-up. Obviously, Gen-Tech expected trouble, but why, and what kind?

Demarr glanced up, caught her eye, and smiled. Smiling back reflexively, Agony watched him behind her pleasant mask. He was dangerous, she could assume that much. Not for the first time, she cursed the pall of corporate secrecy that told her only as much as she absolutely needed to know.

Perhaps, she mused silently, it was time for a new Security Director.

"And there we are. You can feel his violent characteristics have been greatly subdued, and he has been made much more open to positive emotions. In our next session, I will further block those negative reactions, here, and here—" Agony blinked as electric wires of violet snaked through her eyes, radiating from the skull of the patient. "This should increase his tolerance to others, and strengthen his desire to conform to society as a whole. Are there any questions?"

Immediately, the discussion began as the doctors turned to their colleagues and began to hammer out the details of what they'd seen and what it portended toward their craft. The technique was nothing new. It was Demarr's style they were critiquing. They debated how it could be put to better, more efficient use.

Agony caught some talk about using such therapy to alter infants, rendering them unable to become sociopathic, but she dismissed it immediately. Bleeding hearts aside, there were far more children being born every minute than there were psions to repress them, and that was only the first problem.

Demarr sauntered over with a smug grin, his willowy form draped in a gold-embroidered formal suit, extravagantly impractical. "Dr. Zadek. I hope you enjoyed my little demonstration. Perhaps you'd like to step into my office? The debate here will rage on for hours, I'm sure."

"It'd be a pleasure," she smiled. "And call me Annie."

"Charmed—Annie. I am Oswis, to you."

As she followed him back to a closed room beyond the still-oblivious patient, Agony glanced over at Aberlaine. He grinned humorlessly and rolled his eyes at the doctor's back, obviously unimpressed by the Arrani's posturing.

Momentarily at one with Aberlaine, she laid a hand on his arm, giving it a gentle squeeze of agreement. The way he shivered at her touch, a mixture of uncontrollable panic and helpless longing, gave Agony a burst of sheer sensual enjoyment.

The office had a spare beauty far different from the excessive ornamentation she'd seen elsewhere. The severe lines contrasted elegantly with the occasional decorative piece, appearing much more stately than the mad riot of art that other Arrani seemed to favor. "Have a seat, please," Demarr offered, pulling up a third chair from behind his desk for himself. Agony noticed with amusement that he sat quite close to her, closer even than Aberlaine, and wondered if it was from jealousy.

"And what did you think? Is it close to your method, my dear?"

Letting the endearment slide, Agony shrugged. "Close. I've been experimenting with establishing a link between myself and my patients, and converting them to health from the inside out. Rather like leading by example, you might say. It's my opinion that the usual process can lead to emotional scarring. My way should be totally safe."

Demarr nodded, seemingly interested. "It sounds like a good idea, providing the doctor is of strong enough character to resist the negative influence of the patient. But I wouldn't think you'd have that problem." He looked both admiring and acquisitive, and as he laid a hand on her wrist, he snuck a quick feel of her shields and overtones.

Agony smiled as his mind slid across hers, and she reached out to caress him back, without letting him once inside her guard. His eyebrows rose as his soft, warm self met her steely mind, but the sheer power she exuded made him lean forward instinctively. Agony's catlike satisfaction was kept well hidden as she played him on, and his voracious need to get inside her head was a tempting surge. However, this was neither the time nor the place to indulge him, since once she let him truly touch her, she would have to kill him. Drawing back, she snuggled further into her chair and gave him a look that promised.

"We'll have to talk further on the merits of linking. Maybe tomorrow night?" she offered. That should give her time to build up her strength—thank the company for Aberlaine.

"Of course. I can show you around my other projects then, as well," he agreed overeagerly. "For instance, I'm working with pharmaceutical cures for manic depression and schizophrenia, using what I've learned about the mental pathways. It's only a matter of finding the right chemical inhibitor to block those paths, and open the more healthy ones. Once they've been perfected, we can inoculate people for mental illness the same way we can against any other sickness."

Agony's brows rose in surprise. "Then the talk about structuring infants wasn't just talk? What about the so-called moral majority? Won't you have difficulties with them?"

"Perhaps. But they'll see the light eventually. Or maybe we'll just learn to play it covert. Who knows? You'll admit it's far too beneficial to pass up."

Agony nodded hesitantly. If they'd done that to her at birth . . . she shuddered to think of the person she'd be now. "I suppose you're right. I'll certainly watch this closely: if it works here, we might be next." The way he took it, beaming encouragingly, was not at all the way she meant it. Beside her, Aberlaine shuddered.

Someone knocked on the door, causing Demarr to frown. "Yes?"

It opened on one of the other doctors, a lissome woman of early middle age. "Oswis, some of the others want your opinion before Hasen and Crey come to blows. I hope you don't mind."

"Not at all, not at all," he sighed, standing up. "Well, my dear Annie, I suppose we'll have to postpone our talk until tomorrow night. I've got some business to take care of after this, so I'll see you at . . . eight o'clock?"

"Certainly," she smiled, standing as well. "I'm looking forward to it."

Demarr bent over her wrist elegantly, his smile rueful. "Until then," he murmured as he kissed her fingertips.

As Demarr walked out before her, Agony caught the look of pure hate the woman was giving her, and smiled back slowly. Infuriated, the woman doctor spun sharply and marched away, leaving Agony with her amusement. So, Demarr's harem was getting jealous?

"We should go back now," she chuckled to Aberlaine.

"Only too glad," he muttered softly. "These guys give me the creeps."

She made her goodbyes swiftly but comfortably, never slighting anyone but never appearing over-friendly. After the job was done, she'd have to leave in a hurry. She didn't want to be caught in a typical Arrani debate before she made it to the company ship; if that happened, she might never leave.

They walked back in silence, each lost in thought. By habit, they searched the rooms for tampering, but nothing was out of place. Still, it never hurt to be suspicious. Finally, Agony sighed and dropped onto the couch. "Trusting, aren't they? So what do you think?"

"About Demarr? Christ, do him long-distance. There's something about him . . . I dunno, not right." He shook his head, lowering himself gingerly to sit on the far side of the divan, wanting to be close, but not too close. "And the way he looks at you—you'd think he was buying a pet."

Agony laughed. Aberlaine reeked of territorial jealousy. She didn't mind; on the contrary, it was sort of nice. She'd never had anyone want to look out for her before, certainly not someone she was tapping. Speaking of which . . . "What about the drugs?" she asked, purposefully moving to sit beside him. He flinched, but put his arm around her with a sigh.

"Very strange. If it works, then we've got a problem. There's no way it'll stop at curing insanity—it'll be mind control next. Honestly, I can't see why we're not trying to steal the information instead of killing it."

She played with the buttons on his shirt, undoing them one by one. "Well, they'd have no guarantees, would they? It could just as easily be used on them. Probably no antidote, once those pathways get burned out. Me, I'd rather kill it. You?"

"Mmm." His chest was warmer than her hands, hard as rock with tense muscle, nicely tanned. As her lips followed her fingers, he tried gallantly to form a reply. "Must be the reason we're here. In fact, there'll probably be a fire after we're gone. But he's tough, isn't he?" She bit his shoulder, but though he hissed in sudden pain, he refused to be distracted. "That's why I'm with you, to give you the edge."

"Fast learner," she smiled, and attacked.

His spirit fluttered uncertainly, caught between ecstasy and self-preservation. Agony had no intention of killing him: he was far too enjoyable to waste on the spur of the moment. Not that she had any intention of telling him that, either; there was something quite pleasant about the mind of someone who thought he had nothing to lose.

•••

Sleeping like the dead, sprawled across the rumpled bed, Aberlaine's face was remarkably peaceful in dreams. When she ran a sharp fingernail down his chest, he only stirred to curl in close, muttering sleepily, exhausted by the limits to which he'd fed her. Agony smiled, stretching with catlike abandon. She felt as if she could move mountains, brimming with life and fire. Almost, she wanted to wake him, bite down, but she could wait until morning. One more drain, and then, tonight, Demarr. . . .

Frowning slightly, Agony's euphoria faded a little as her thoughts turned to the Arrani doctor. Demarr was strong, easily the strongest psion she had ever tried to tap. In some ways, being near him was like a starving man being chained just out of reach of a magnificent feast; at the same time, he made her skin crawl, and not just because he was Arrani. What would it be like to take hold of that powerful, struggling soul, and try to force it past the jaws of her own voracious need? Would it even *fit*? He might smother her, blow her own soul apart, or swamp her until their edges blended too fuzzily together and she became him. She couldn't know until she tried.

Beside her, Aberlaine suddenly twitched in his sleep, as if flinching away from a slap. Instead of waking, however, he turned toward her, burrowing his face in her neck and throwing one arm across her ribs. Trusting as a babe. And so, she reminded herself, was Demarr.

Watching Aberlaine's sleeping face as she waited for dreams to claim her, Agony chuckled softly. It was going to be nice, having a Security Director foolish enough to trust her.

• • •

"So good to see you again," Demarr smiled. "You left your patient in the suite?"

"Yes. He's relatively harmless when he's alone. Besides, he's totally dependent on me at this point."

Aberlaine had been feeling much better by the time she left to meet with Demarr—still a little washed out, but looking like his old self. She smiled at the memory of the taste of his heart, the feel of him curled sleeping around her. Demarr thought the smile was for him, and took her hand.

"I'm sure that's an easy habit to acquire. Would you like to see my laboratory? I could show you the theory behind what I'm working on. . . ."

"I'd love to," she agreed, and allowed herself to be led away.

From the lobby they took a lift to the third floor, and walked out into a long hallway, lit softly with auxiliary lights. It was obvious that even the janitors were through with this floor for the night. Perversely, Agony felt pleased: Demarr might think he had her where he wanted her, but she was just as glad there'd be no one to interfere, and no witnesses.

As he unlocked his door, the third one in from the lift, he sent out a quick probe that Agony caught neatly. As their minds slid around each other, grappling like lovers, Agony felt the temptation to bite immediately. She wanted to get him inside, however, in among his precious drugs where she could lock the door and leave him for his fellow quacks to discover. She only wished she could blow the lab. She didn't want someone slipping *that* sort of pill to her one day. She couldn't imagine liking the kind of person she would become.

The doctor opened the door but paused with an uncertain look. "It's strange: I can almost imagine your patient is still with us, you feel so much like him."

Agony smiled, inwardly annoyed. "That's just the link. Don't tell me you think I'm a coldblooded killer."

Demarr laughed. "Far from it. Please, come in."

The lab was large, filled with equipment whose purpose Agony could only guess at. Off to one side was a desk and comfortable chair, and a couch like the one the sociopath had reclined upon. So, Demarr was already using his patients as guinea pigs? Maybe Arranis didn't have bleeding hearts, the way Ireland didn't have snakes. Perhaps some self-avowed saint had run them all out, or onto psychiatric couches in hidden labs.

"Please remember, the drug therapy technique is still in the experimental stage. I've synthesized a few prototypes, but there's still no substitute for psionics. Here, have a seat. It's a lengthy explanation," Demarr smiled, gesturing to the couch.

Agony smiled. Here it came. . . .

"We start by establishing a rapport," he began, his mind slipping around hers like an embrace. "We get to know everything about our subjects, from the inside out. We get very personal."

His hands were practiced, but not half as enjoyable as Aberlaine's. She ran her mind along his in a sensuous undulation, darkening his eyes. His thoughts were starting to creep through, and Agony listened out of curiosity.

"Then we shut off certain small parts of the brain, rerouting through more beneficial areas. It's so much easier to just design a drug to do it for us. . . ."

Gods, she feels like heaven, he was thinking. *Even that man's echoes feel good in her. Just a nudge here and there, and she'd be perfect. . . .*

Agony froze inside, although she still played the game. He wanted to change her? Not in a million years. It was time.

His mind lunged into her, dripping desire, shuddering with anticipation. As he began to get his first taste of her real mind, the slaughterhouse fires inside, Agony flexed her claws to strike.

Suddenly, they were not alone. *It's time, Demarr,* someone announced telepathically, distracting them both at the crucial instant.

No! She's mine, get out! he howled, too engrossed in his frustration to realize what he'd seen of her in that brief second.

Agony's eyes narrowed, and she shot out quick probes: at least a dozen Arrani were in the building, and all of them focused on this room, on her. Momentary panic flared up, leaving her shaken with the knowledge that, this time, hunter had turned hunted. They had known she would be here tonight, with Demarr. They had been waiting for her. The only question was how much they knew. *I can't take this many at once*, the thought occurred to her, but caution was drowning in the need to *know*.

You were supposed to wait! Demarr screamed angrily. Agony lashed into him, flaying his thoughts away to reveal the purpose beneath.

Mold her into place. Human psions—they're like children. So pathetic, even this one. We'll train them . . . train them right. A sexual heat, the smell of blood, and Agony's fury rose. *She'll be mine this time. They can't have this one, not her. And she'll bring her fellows to me, once she's been taught how.*

Agony didn't give a damn about his plans of grandeur; she was not about to become a pet psion for some disgusting, demented Arrani or his friends. They thought they could tame her—*her?* Agony Zade was no one's slave. Ever.

With a growl that seemed to shake the heavens, she struck, stripping Demarr's life and soul away mercilessly, eating his screams before they were born. Growing like a nightmare, she harnessed that tremendous power and latched claws of steel into the panicked doctors. The air around her writhed and bubbled as they tried to attack with conflicting talents, but one by one, they dropped and fell, feeding her with an endless waterfall of energy.

She glowed; sparks flew from her hair, her fingers. She clutched the soft cushions beneath her with blind, grasping hands, trying to anchor herself to reality. Roaring through her soundlessly was a wildfire of pure life, sheer being, pulling at her from all sides. She had to absorb it somehow, but there seemed to be no place for it to go. . . .

"Damn you," she hissed, and her breath hung visible in the air, a living aurora. She was the killer here, not them. . . . Screaming at herself in animal frustration, she snapped her jaws closed around it and pulled.

Hidden mouths opened inside her, sucking hungrily at the excess, forming long worm tunnels down into the core of her being that pulsated with life. Agony shivered, watching the change with surprised mental eyes. She'd grown something like storage sites. She'd gone one step further, grown stronger than she'd dreamed she was capable of. If she could drain a dozen men now, how soon until she could take two dozen, fifty, a hundred?

She was still vibrating with the energy inside, humming like a violin string. Trying to stand, she realized she'd never make it back to the suite and onto the waiting cab, not alone.

Aberlaine, help me! she demanded, half a plea, reaching out as unerringly as if there truly were a link between them. She felt him jump, then leave their room at a sprint. Realizing that he was homing in on her by some strange instinct of parasite and host, she fell back with a sigh. Everything was spinning, living things glowing with sickly halos, and her head felt encased by wool. Inside, she was high as a kite, completely smashed. It felt like hell. It was *wonderful*.

The door slammed open, and Agony slitted a cautious eye to find Aberlaine standing in the doorway, dressed to go. He slowly edged toward her, eyes cutting toward the untouched body beside her, then back to her. He could kill her now if he had the strength of will to override her compulsion not to harm her: she doubted

Illustrated by Sherman McClain

she could fit another soul inside at this point. For a long moment, he just stared at her. Then he bent and hauled her to her feet, fitting her into the crook of his arm and supporting her as she tottered with him to the door.

"Did he hurt you?" Aberlaine demanded, worry in his voice.

"No—I killed a dozen of them just now. God, I'm stoned. Too much at once." She snuggled into his side, letting him steer. The cab would be waiting, and then the ship. Aberlaine was coming back with her, something he probably hadn't counted on, and Fehrs was on the endangered list. Everything was beautiful.

"All right," Aberlaine said. They were almost to the cab before he spoke again. "Are you going to kill me?"

Agony looked up at him, drowning him with her black eyes. Unable to stop himself, he buried his face in her snowy hair, then bent to kiss her. Agony smiled, tasting his sadness, his wish to live clashing with his need to die a little at a time. She couldn't believe he'd actually asked her that; she was tremendously impressed.

"No," she chuckled. "I'm going to make you Security Director."

"Damn," Aberlaine muttered, and his cautious relief shone through. As he put her carefully into the preprogrammed cab, Agony grinned evilly.

"And you'd better not give me any assignments like this one, friend. I expect an easy ride from now on."

Aberlaine shrugged. "Anything you want."

Brushing him lightly with mental claws, she watched him shiver, bemusedly. "I know."

METABOLISM

Written by
Scott Nicholson

Illustrated by
Paul Marquis

About the Author

Scott Nicholson began writing seriously in the fall of 1996 after writing constantly as a teenager, then abandoning it for about a decade. During that decade he wrote songs and played bass in several rock bands. When that "career" finally got mothballed, he went back to college and took a couple of writing classes, where he discovered that writing felt like a long-dormant natural calling.

Scott worked daily, three to six hours, and finished his first novel in three months. As he works, he has found that his self-confidence has grown along with his determination.

"Metabolism" is his first fiction sale, but he has recently sold stories to several small magazines, including E-Scape, Xoddity, Blue Murder *and* The Leading Edge.

He says, "I want to thank Orson Scott Card for the best writing advice I've ever heard: 'Just tell your stories.'"

I suspect that Scott will be doing just that for a long time to come.

The city had eyes.

It watched Elise from the glass squares set into its walls, walls that were sheer cliff faces of mortar and brick. She held her breath, waiting for them to blink. No, not eyes, only windows. She kept walking.

And the street was not a tongue, a long black ribbon of asphalt flesh that would roll her into the city's hot jaws at any second. The parking meter poles were not needly teeth, eager to gnash. The city would not swallow her, here in front of everybody. The city kept its secrets.

And the people on the sidewalk—how much did they know? Were they enemy agents or blissful cattle? The man in the charcoal-gray London Fog trench coat, the *Times* tucked under his elbow, dark head down and hands in pockets. A gesture of submission or a crafted stance of neutrality?

The blue-haired lady in the chinchilla wrap, her turquoise eyeliner making her look like a psychedelic raccoon. Was the lady colorblind or had she adopted a clever disguise? And were her mincing high-heeled steps carrying her to a mid-level townhouse or was she on some municipal mission?

That round-faced cabdriver, his black mustache brushing the bleached peg of his cigarette, the tires of his battered yellow cab nudged against the curb. Were his eyes scanning the passersby in hopes of a fare, or was he scouting for plump prey?

Elise tugged on her belt, wrapping her coat more tightly around her waist. The thinner one looked, the better. Not that she had to rely on illusion. Her appetite had been buried with the other things of her old blind life, ordinary pleasures like window shopping and jogging. She had once traveled these streets voluntarily.

Best not to think of the past. Best to pack the pieces of it away like old toys in a closet. Perhaps someday she could open that door, shed some light, blow off the dust, oil the squeaky parts, and resume living. But for now, living must be traded for surviving.

She sucked in her cheeks, hoping she looked as gaunt as she felt. The wisp of breeze that blew up the street, more carbon monoxide than oxygen, was not even strong enough to ruffle the fringe on the awning above that shoeshop. But she felt as if the breeze might sweep her across the broken concrete, sending her tumbling and skittering like a cellophane candy wrapper. Sweeping her toward the city's throat.

She dared a glance up the twenty-story tower of glass to her right. Eyes, eyes, eyes. Show no fear. Stare the monster in the face. It thinks itself invisible.

What a perfectly blatant masquerade. The city was rising from the earth, steel beams and guy wire and cinder block assembling right before their human eyes. Growing bold and hard and reaching for the sky, always bigger, bigger. How could everyone be so easily fooled?

Forget it, Elise. Maybe it reads minds. And you don't want to let it know what you're up to. You can keep a secret as good as it can.

She turned her gaze back down to the tips of her leather shoes. There, just like a good city dweller is supposed to do. Count the cracks. Blend in. Be small.

Ignore the window front of the adult bookstore you pass. Don't see the leather whips, the rude plastic rods

Illustrated by Paul Marquis

that gleam like eager rockets, the burlesque mockery of human flesh displayed on the placards. And the next window, plywooded and barred like an abandoned prison, "Liquor" hand-painted in dull green letters across the dented steel door beside it.

All to keep us drugged, dazed with easy pleasure. Elise knew. If it let us have our little amusements, then we wouldn't flee. We'd stay and graze on lust and drunkenness, growing fat and sleepy and tired and dull.

She flicked her eyes to the sky overhead, ignoring the sharp spears of the building tops, with their antennas for ears. The low red haze meant that night was falling. The city constantly exhaled smog, so thick now that the sun barely peeped down onto the atrocities that were committed under its yellow eye. Even from the vigilant universe, the city kept its secrets.

Elise felt only dimly aware of the traffic that clogged the streets. Not streets. The arteries of the city. The cars rattled past, with raspy breath and an occasional growl of impatience. In the distance, somewhere on the far side of the city, sirens wailed. Sirens, or the screams of victims, face to face with the horrible thing that had crouched around them for years, cold and stone-silent one moment but alive and hungry the next.

Can't waste pity on them. The unwritten code of city life. Inbred indifference. Ignorance is bliss. A natural social instinct developed from decades of being piled atop one another like cold cuts in a grocer's counter. Or was the code taught, learned by rote, instilled upon them by a stern master who had its own best interests at heart?

And what would its heart be like? The sewers, raw black sludge snaking through its veins? The hot coal furnaces that huffed away in basements, leaking steam from corroded pipes? Or the electrical plant, a Gorgon's wig of wire sprouting from its roof, sending its veins into the apartments and office towers and factories so that no part of the city was untouched?

Or was it, as she suspected, heartless? Just a giant meat-eating cement slab of instinct?

She had walked ten blocks now. Not hurriedly, but steadily and with purpose. Perhaps like a thirty-year-old woman out for a leisurely stroll, headed to the park to watch from a bench while the sun set smugly over the jagged skyline. Maybe out to the theatre, for an early seat at a second-rate staging of *Waiting for Godot*. Not like someone who was trying to escape.

No. Don't think about it.

She hadn't meant to, but now that the thought had risen from the murky swamp of subconsciousness, she turned it over in her mind, mentally fingering it like a mechanic checking out a carburetor.

No one escaped. At least no one she knew. They all slid, bloody and soft and bawling, from their mothers' wombs into the arms of the city. Fed on love and hope and dreams. Fed on lies.

She had considered taking a cab, hunching down in the back seat until the city became only a speck in the rearview mirror. But she had seen the faces of the cabbies. They were too robust, too thick-jowled. Such as they should have been taken long ago. No, they were in on it.

And she had shuddered at the thought of stepping onto a city bus, hearing the hissing of the air brakes and the door closing behind her like a squealing mouth. Delivering her not to the outskirts, but to the belly of the beast. They were *city* buses, after all.

Walking was the only way. So she walked. And the night fell around her, in broken scraps at first, furry shadows and gray insubstantial wedges. Lights came on in the buildings around her, soft pale globes and amber specks and opalescent blue stars and yellow-green window squares. Pretty baubles to pacify the masses.

She felt the walls slide toward her, closing in on her under the cloak of darkness. Don't panic, she told herself. Eyes straight ahead. You don't need to look to know the scenery. Sheer concrete, double doors drooling with glass and rubber, geometrical orifices secreting the noxious effluence of consumption.

She thought perhaps she was safe. She was thin. But her sister Leanna had been thin. So thin she had been desired as a model, wearing long sleek gowns and leaning into the greedy eye of the camera, or preening in bathing suits on mock-up beaches in high-rise studios. So wonderfully waifish that she had graced the covers of the magazines that lined the checkout racks. Such a fine sliver of flesh that she had been lured to Los Angeles on the promise of acting work.

They said that she'd hopped on a plane to sunny California, was lounging around swimming pools and getting to know all the right people. Elise had received letters in which Leanna told about the palm trees and open skies, about mountains and moonlit bays. About the bit part she'd gotten in a movie, not much but a start.

Elise had gone to see the movie. She sat in a shabby, gum-tarred seat, the soles of her shoes sticking to the sloping cement floor. There she'd seen Leanna, up on the big screen, walking and talking and doing all the things that she used to do back when she was alive. Leanna, pale and ravishing and now forever young and two-dimensional.

Oh, but putting her in a film could be easily faked, just like the letters. A city that could control and herd a million people would go to such lengths to keep its secrets. All she knew was that Leanna was gone, gobbled up by some manhole or doorway or the hydraulic jaws of a sanitation truck.

And she knew others who had gone missing. Out to the country, they said. Away on vacation. Business trips. Weddings and funerals to attend. But never heard from again. Some of them overweight, some healthy, some muscular, some withered.

So being thin was no guarantee. But she suspected that it helped her chances. If only she was light enough that the sidewalk didn't measure her footsteps.

She'd reached unfamiliar territory now. A strange part of the city. But wasn't it all strange? Alien caves, too precise to be man-made? Elevators, metal boxes dangling at the ends of rusty spiderwebs? Storm grates grinning and leering from street corners? Lampposts bending like alloyed praying mantises?

The faces of the few pedestrians out at that hour were clouded with shadows. Did the white-arrow tips of their eyes flick ever so slightly at her as she passed? Did they sense a traitor in their midst? Were they glaring jealously at her tiny bones, the skin stretched taut around her skull, her meatless appearance?

The smell of donuts wafted across her face, followed by the bittersweet tang of coffee. Her nostrils flared in arousal in spite of herself. She looked into the window of a deli. Couples were huddled at round oak tables, the steam of their drinks rising in front of them like smoke from chemical fires. They were chatting, laughing, eating from loaded plates, reading magazines, acting as if they had all the time in the world. They had tasted the lie, and found it palatable.

She tore her eyes away. They traded pleasure for inevitability. Dinner would one day be served, and they would find themselves on the plate, pale legs splayed indignantly upward, wire mesh at their heads for garnish. Well, she had no tears to spare for them. One chose one's own path.

Her path had started about a year ago, shortly before Leanna left. Not left, was *taken*, she reminded herself. Elise's understanding had started with the television set. The TV stood on a Formica cabinet against the sheetrock wall of her tiny apartment, flashing colorful images at her. Showing her all the things she was being offered. Brand-new sedans. Dental floss and mouthwash. The other white meat. The quicker-picker-upper. The uncola.

The television made things attractive. The angle of the lighting, eye-pleasing color schemes, seductive layouts and product designs. Straight teeth cutting white lines across handsome tan faces. And behind those rigid smiles, she had seen the fear. Fear masquerading as vacuousness. Threatened puppets spouting monologues, the sales pitch of complacency.

She had found other clues. The police, for instance. Never around when one needed them. Delivery vans with unmarked sideboards, prowling at all hours. Limousines, long and dark-glassed, advertisements for conspicuous consumption. Around-the-clock convenience stores and neon billboards. A quiet conspiracy in the streets, unobserved among the bustle and noise of daily life, everyone too busy grabbing merchandise to stop and smell the slag-heap acid of the roses.

But Elise had noticed. Saw how the city grew, stretching obscenely higher, ever thicker and more oppressive and powerful. And she had made the connection. The city fed itself. It was getting bloated on the human hors d'oeuvres that tracked across its tongue like live chocolate-covered ants.

When one knew where to look, one saw signs of its life. The pillars of filthy smoke that marked its exhalations, the iridescent ribbons of its urine that trickled through the gutters, the sweat of the city clinging to moist masonry. The gray snowy ash of its dandruff, the chipped gravel of its sloughed dead skin. The crush of the walls, squeezing in like cobbled teeth, outflanking and surrounding its prey. And all the while spinning its serenade of sonic booms and fire alarms, automobile horns and fast-food speakers, ringing cash registers and clattering jackhammers.

Elise had bided her time, staying cautious, not telling a soul. Whom could she trust? Her neighbors might have an ear pressed to the wall. The city employed thousands.

So she had hid behind her closed door, the TV turned to face the corner. Oh, she had still gone to work, leaving every weekday morning for her post at the bank. It was important to keep up appearances. But, once home, she locked herself in and pulled the window shade. She turned on the radio, just in case the city was using its ears, but she always tuned to commercial-free classical stations. Music to eat sweets by.

Her work mates had expressed concern.

"You're nothing but skin and bones. You feeling okay?"

"You're getting split-ends, girl."

"You look a little pale. Maybe you should go to the doctor, Elise."

As if she were going to listen to them, with their new forty-dollar hairstyles every week and retirement accounts and lawyer husbands and City Council wives and pantyhose and wristwatches and power ties and deodorant. Elise only smiled and shook her head and pretended. Took care of the customers and kept her accounts balanced.

And she had plotted. Steeled herself. Gathered her nerve and slung her handbag over her shoulder and walked out of the bank after work and headed downtown. She kept reminding herself that she had nothing to lose.

And now she was almost free. She could taste the cleaner air, could feel the pressure of the hovering structures ease as she drew nearer to the outskirts. But now darkness descended, and she wasn't sure if that brought the city to keen-edged life or sent it fat and dull into dreamy slumber.

She passed the maw of a subway station. A few people jogged down the steps into the bright throat of the tunnel. She thought of human meat packed into the smooth silver tubes and shot through the intestines of the city.

She walked faster now, gaining confidence and strength as hope spasmed in her chest like a pigeon with a broken wing. She could see the level horizon, a beautiful black flatness only blocks ahead. Buildings skulked here and there, but they were short and squat and clumsy. The road was devoid of traffic, the dead-end arms of the city. The street lights thinned, casting weak cones of light every few hundred feet.

Her footsteps echoed down the empty street, bouncing into the dark canyons of the side alleys. The hollowness of the sound enhanced her sense of isolation. She felt exposed and vulnerable. Easy meat.

Her ears pricked up, tingling.

A noise behind her, out of step with her echo.

Breathing.

The spiteful puff of a forklift, its tines aimed for her back? A fire hydrant, hissing in anger at her audacity? The sputtering gasp of a sinuous power cable?

Footsteps.

A rain of light bulbs, dropping in her wake? The concrete slabs of the sidewalk, folding upon themselves like an accordion, chasing her heels? A street sign hopping after her like a crazed pogo stick?

Not now. Now when she was so close.

But did she really expect that the city would let her simply step out of its garden?

She ducked into an alley, even though walls gathered on three sides. Instinct had driven her into the darkness. But then, why shouldn't it control her instinct? It owned everything else.

And now it moved in for the kill, taking its due. Now she was ripe fruit to be plucked from the chaotic fields the city had sown, a harvest to be reaped by rubber belts and pulleys and metal fins.

She stumbled into a garbage heap, knocking over a trash can in her blindness. She fell face-first into greasy cloth and rotten paper and moldering food scraps. She felt a sting at her knee as she rolled into broken glass.

She turned on her back, resigned to her fate. She would die quietly, but she wanted to see its face. Not the face it showed to human eyes, the one of glass panes and cornerstones and sheet metal. She wanted to see its true face.

She saw a silhouette, a blacker shape against the night. A splinter of silver catching a stray strand of distant street light, flashing at her like a false grin. A featureless machine pressing close, its breath like stale gin and cigarette butts and warm copper.

Its voice fell from out of the thick air, not with the jarring clang of a bulldozer or the sharp rumble of tractor trailer rig, but as a harsh whisper.

"Gimme your money, bitch."

So the city had sent this puny agent after her? With all its great and awesome might, its monumental obelisks, its omnipotent industry, its cast-iron claws, its impregnable asphalt hide, its pressurized fangs, it sent *this?*

The city had a sense of humor. How wonderful!

She thought of that old children's story "The Three Billy Goats Gruff," how the smaller ones offered up the larger ones to slake the evil troll's appetite. She laughed, filling the cramped alley with her cackles. "A skinny thing like me would hardly be a mouthful for you," she said, the words squeezing out between giggles.

She felt the city's knife press against her chest, heard a quick snip, and felt her handbag being lifted from her shoulder. The straps hung like dark spaghetti, and the city tucked the purse against its belly. The city, small and pale and—human. Now she saw it. The human machine had a face the color of bleached rags, greasy gray mop strings dangling down over the hot sparks of eyes. Thin wires sprouted above the coin-slot mouth. Why, he was *young.* The city eats its young.

"You freakin' city folks is all nuts," the machine said, then ran into the street, back under the safe, sane lights. Its words hung over Elise's head, but they were from another world. A world of platinum and fiberglass, loco-motives and razor blades. The real world. Not her world.

And as the real city awoke and busied itself with its commerce and caffeine, it might have seen Elise sprawled among the rubble of a run-down neighborhood, flanked by empty wine bottles and used condoms and milk cartons graced with the photographs of anonymous children. It might have smelled her civet perfume, faint but there, which she had dabbed on her neck in an attempt to smell like everyone else. It might have heard the wind fluttering the collar of her Christian Dior blouse, bought so that she could blend in with the crowd. It might have felt the too-light weight of her frail body, wasted by a steady diet of fear. It might have tasted the human salt where tears of relief had dried on her cheeks.

It might have divined her dreams, intruded on her sleep to find goats at the wheels of steamrollers, corrugated snakes slithering as endlessly as escalators among gelatin hills, caravans of television antennas dancing across flat desert sands, and a flotilla of cellular phones on a windswept ocean of antifreeze, an owl and a pussycat in each.

If the city sensed these things, it remained silent.

The city kept its secrets.

SILENT JUSTICE

Written by
Maureen Jensen

Illustrated by
John Lock

About the Author

As a child, Maureen Jensen was inspired to become a science fiction fan by reading Madeleine L'Engle's A Wrinkle in Time. Shortly afterward, she discovered Heinlein and Asimov, and began to carry their books in her violin case when traveling to and from lessons.

As a sixth-grader, she wrote a short story that got an A+ for her "great imagination." She said it had a good start and nothing more. Thus inspired, she decided to learn how to finish a story.

Maureen now lives in Utah where she belongs to the writing group Xenobia. She works as a medical technologist and has lived in Hawaii, Colorado, and has served as a medical missionary in Ecuador.

"Silent Justice" is her first sale.

emetery Hill spread like a cool green carpet over the Colorado mountainside. The many granite monuments sparkled as the sun touched each one. The cemetery watched over the little town of Crystal Springs like a sheltering wing. It gathered to it the many members of the five original families who had settled the valley, and all the generations thereafter, from the late 1800s, nearly to the year 2000.

Now, at the highest place in the cemetery and visible over the entire valley, a gleaming white marble angel slumped over the granite monument of the latest grave. The angel's wings drooped like those of a broken bird, but it carried a sense of animation. To those in the town, it seemed that a breeze might move the cascade of hair to reveal the hidden features of her face, or a puff of air might part the open robe just a bit more to expose the still-small breasts. One graceful hand touched her throat, reminiscent of how the unfortunate girl buried there had been murdered, her trachea crushed.

The reaction to the monument varied. Since the form and the figure were unmistakably those of Jenny Deyer, the residents of the town found this display intensely disquieting. The news had given Crystal Springs a day of national notoriety when it had displayed a picture of the girl's half-clad body lying amid a scatter of white downy feathers from a torn sleeping bag.

Illustrated by John Lock

•••

Robert Deyer and his wife, Gaylene, sat in on the city council, as quiet as the stone statue they had placed on their daughter's grave. The only movement from the two came from Gaylene as she clenched and unclenched the bedraggled feathers in the pocket of her red blazer. The town, ignorant of the gentle Wiccan arts that she practiced, labeled her a *witch*, for them a negative indictment. And she *could* turn her gentle white magic to dark purposes if she chose. But it was something she had never desired to do—until now.

•••

Molly Bischoff, head of the council, stood and brought the council meeting to order, then turned to the end of the table. "We extend a welcome to Mr. and Mrs. Deyer."

She placed her palms flat to the table and leaned over them. Her nails needed painting; her frizzy red hair needed a touch-up. Next to Gaylene Deyer's polished appearance, she felt dowdy and undone. If she had only colored in her eyebrows. She could look much more intimidating when her eyebrows showed up. She curled her long, thin fingers, letting her stubby nails scratch into the wood. "Before we get to city business, they have requested . . . a word with us." She sat, then lifted her chin.

The Deyers rose. Robert Deyer addressed her: "Mrs. Bischoff, it's been four months since our daughter's murder. In all that time, no one in this town, including Jonathan himself, has come forward with the truth. No one, not even he, will admit to his obsession with

Jennifer. Even after I testified about chasing Jonathan away from my daughter's window, your son has been officially cleared of the charges. Although the search for our daughter's rapist and murderer remains active—*officially*—unofficially it's over. There's no *need* to continue a manhunt, is there? Everyone in this town knows that."

Molly spread her hands over the table and drew her mouth into a frown. She'd been frowning a lot lately. She wondered when she could smile again.

She had adopted a stern expression as Jonathan had vowed he'd been out alone the night of Jenny's murder. He'd sworn he could hardly get near Jenny Deyer. He'd only wanted to talk to her that night when Robert Deyer had chased him away. He'd meant no harm. He'd said that the girl thought she was too good for anyone. Molly had kept her features neutral when the judge had handed down a "not guilty" verdict for lack of substantial evidence or witnesses against her son.

Now, she gave the Deyers a sympathetic yet no-nonsense frown. "I'm sorry," she said sharply, then softened her tone. "We are all sorry for the pain you must be going through. But this meeting isn't a forum for citizens to come and throw around accusations. Especially when a judge—"

"No!" Gaylene snapped, "not *a* judge. Your judge!" Her pale golden hair spilled around her face and into her eyes. She tossed her head, tightening her fist on the feathers until they became a soggy clump. Her growing desire for revenge worked on her, twisting the healing powers she had so carefully nurtured and turning them dark and destructive. She feared that once she used her powers to cause hurt, they would be tainted. Oh, how she resented these people for bringing her to this. The diamond chips in her ears caught the morning light and gave minute blue-and-white flashes like sparks of cold fire. So be it. She would unleash her worst on them if they forced her hand.

Gaylene took a deep breath. "We've come to give you people one more chance. We tried to find a place in this *charming* little town. Family is *everything* here, after all, just the kind of atmosphere we were seeking. Well, the main families of this town are represented at this council—you who run it all. But your loyalties draw you so tightly together . . ."

Her voice faltered and Robert Deyer put his arm around her shoulders. His eyes burned red and dry in his lean, tan face as he gazed at each member of the council one at a time. "Shit, you were all on the jury!" he shouted. "You closed ranks, despite the obvious."

Mayor Joseph Horne, Molly's grandfather, Old Smokey Joe to everyone in town, groped for his breast pocket and the half-empty pack of cigarettes. He gave a phlegmy cough and slapped the table. "You listen here: Johnny says he's innocent. Unless you have—" cough— "proof of some sort—"

Robert slammed his fist on the table and Smokey Joe chomped down on his slightly loose dentures.

Robert Deyer cleared his throat. His hazel eyes narrowed, his mouth going thin and tight. "Jonathan Bischoff was obsessed with our daughter. We had to have our phone number changed. Jenny couldn't step out of our house without Jonathan there, always watching for her. He threatened—he beat up other boys who came too close to her. It was obvious!" He growled, his hands clenching and unclenching. His wife gripped his arm and glared at the council.

• • •

Rebecca Peters cast a pleading look toward Molly, her younger sister. Molly's round, plump face bunched in misery. Why didn't Molly throw the Deyers out? She had the power!

Rebecca wanted to put her hands over her ears. She bent her head and shut her eyes instead, but that didn't help. She couldn't erase that scene from her mind—that day last spring, when Jennifer had disappeared.

Jenny Deyer had been jogging along Rebecca's street. Jonathan had driven slowly behind her, just following along.

Suddenly, Jenny had whirled around, had run to his truck, and jumped right in.

Rebecca had gone to the porch to watch as the two argued. Jennifer had begun pounding on Jonathan with her fists, then turned to jump back out through the open door. She had her leg out, but Johnny appeared to pull her back in and, wheels squealing, just took off with the door partway open and Jennifer still flailing at him.

Rebecca gave her head a shake, but the troublesome images wouldn't leave her in peace. She hadn't spoken to Molly about it because she hadn't been sure if Jenny and Jonathan weren't just having some kind of spat. Nor had she brought it up at the trial.

Her sister, Molly, had been so certain of Jonathan's innocence.

Maybe I should say something now? Rebecca thought.

No. The time to speak about this had passed. Besides, Molly had absolutely stood by Johnny, and he was Rebecca's own nephew, after all. She opened her eyes and kept her attention on her sister, afraid the Deyers might see something in her expression and call on her to speak.

•••

Jed Tuttle, a cousin to Molly's husband, Garth, ran his hand through his thick, black hair. He regretted all the trouble. Gaylene and her husband would likely move now. He gazed steadily at Gaylene Deyer, shifting in his seat. He got a hard-on just thinking about the cleavage that Gaylene usually flashed around town. He'd have had a chance at her. It would have only been a matter of time. That pale, thin husband couldn't have been very satisfying to such a woman.

Jed put his arms up on the table, his short-sleeve shirt revealing the muscular biceps that various women in the town so admired. Too bad about the daughter. She'd been just as fine herself, so slender and agile-looking.

Jed ran his tongue over his lips. Oh, yeah, he was pretty sure that Jonathan had it in him to do the Deyer girl that way, although Jed didn't *know* for sure. Still, he had to wonder because of the day he'd caught Johnny choking the life out of the wild cat out behind the barn. And it wasn't so much that the boy had killed a cat. It was the look on the boy's face, the way his half-closed lids had fluttered, the obvious sexual pleasure he had gotten from it. Not a thing you would report to a mother.

Jed gave an involuntary shudder, then cleared his throat and straightened in his chair. Still, he had to wonder what he'd say if he did actually *know* that Johnny had wrapped those beefy fingers around Jennifer Deyer's long, white throat.

Never mind. That had been up to the judge. It was not his responsibility. Besides, his wife, Phyllis, had warned what she'd do to him if he stuck in his two cents about the cat thing. Phyllis was in the I-Hate-Gaylene Club. Huh! A pack of stiff, rusty women who couldn't keep their own husbands happy.

One thing above all else: he didn't want his own daughters alone with Jonathan Bischoff. He'd given Phyllis strict orders about that.

• • •

Robert Deyer paced angrily, waving his arms as he spoke. "Jonathan harassed our daughter during the whole of the school year, right up until she disappeared last spring. His three-day trial was hardly enough to bring him to a confession. He still has no need to confess." Robert glared at each person at the table. Not one eyeball turned his way—except for Jed Tuttle who drooled at Gaylene. He checked an impulse to leap over the table at the man's throat.

They had moved from Denver to get Gaylene away from the growing jealousy and envy of an active Wiccan society. Her natural talents had far exceeded even the eldest of the practicing witches and sorcerers. Her gifts even exceeded his own meager skills at sorcery. He'd been nothing but proud of her. Now he had to watch her work against her naturally gentle nature.

• • •

Gaylene took a long shuddering breath, avoiding Jed Tuttle's gaze. He thought himself so smooth, so suave. She suppressed a contemptuous smile. Pathetic, bumbling idiot. He presumed the right to any female within his reach. And from what she'd observed, a few weak-minded women in town found his attentions flattering.

She waited another few seconds for a response from the city council. Most of them wore cowboy-country leisure wear. She'd found it quaint at first. Now it represented a closed society of self-righteous, ultra-conservative bigots. Obstinate evasion lay thick over the room like a sulfurous fog.

Gaylene's shoulders dropped, the color of her eyes darkened from light blue to a flat navy. "Our daughter's voice has been silenced forever. She'll never be heard in this town again, but she still cries to us from that grave on your hill. There must be someone willing to speak for her, to bring Jonathan to answer for what he did!"

"That will be just about enough!" Smokey Joe stood and pointed a hesitant finger at them, then wiped his sleeve across his forehead. The odor of old smoke seeped from his plaid western-cut jacket, wafting around him with every halting movement.

Robert Deyer held Gaylene's arm. She shook free and took a step back. Robert touched her, but she remained rigid and unmoving. He nodded and stepped behind her as she spoke.

"This injustice lingers among you, putting a tarnish on this town. You still have it within your power to remove the tarnish yourselves. But, in fact, I'll give you only until this Saturday." Gaylene said, her words like dry ice wrapped in cold, smooth silk. "Many in this town *know* what Jonathan did to our daughter. Enough of you have witnessed the harassments he inflicted on Jennifer."

Gaylene's eyes narrowed. She brought her right fist from her pocket and held it up, her arm coming to the square. "If you choose to remain silent, you'll see us just one more time.

"If you wait too long, your opportunity to speak will come to an end, and it will be too late. By then, only the murderer himself will be able to answer for his deeds. Only he will be able to break the silence!"

She opened her fist and let the damp clump of feathers fall to the floor. Several council members glanced down, then up, dismissing the bit of litter.

• • •

Telephones rang from one ranch to another, and from one end of town to the other as soon as the meeting came to a close. Everyone pretty much agreed that they had no more patience to spare for the Deyers. They expressed open relief among themselves that Robert and Gaylene had stuck a big For Sale sign in front of that naked-fountain-statue-thing where Benjamin Peters used to keep his coral.

• • •

Molly needed groceries for a nice Sunday dinner. She would retain that ritual, along with her especially strict church attendance. Normal routines. She pulled into the parking lot, slammed her door, and started forward, her chin up, always up. Coach Leo Hubbard called to her from his pickup truck. Molly gave him a stiff smile. He hurried over, his face growing alarmingly florid with the effort.

He touched the bill of his baseball cap. "Damn shame what I heard about those Deyers at the council meeting."

"I guess everyone's heard by now." Molly continued forward and the coach fell in step.

"Don't you worry. I won't let it affect Jonathan. He's our star quarterback, after all." He pulled his cap from his bald head and smoothed down nonexistent hair.

The coach held the door for her. Molly hurried through, giving him a nod, and ran into Phyllis Tuttle carrying her sack of groceries.

"Oh, eek, grab that!" Phyllis cried. Leo Hubbard caught some bread that bounced out of her sack. He grinned and packed it back on top of her load.

"Sorry," Molly gave Phyllis a smile that dropped quickly away. "I'm in too much of a hurry."

Several heads turned toward the commotion and the shoppers leaned a bit toward the small group at the door. Molly took a step back, trying to edge away.

Phyllis shifted her groceries and said loudly, "I really feel for Jonathan. He really *liked* Jennifer Deyer. A lot!"

Molly took a deep breath, ready to thank her firmly and leave.

The coach piped up, "Sure he got mad the way the rest of the team, you know, talked about her." He pulled on his ear. "You want *my* opinion, I think that girl bears some of the responsibility."

Phyllis broke in. "Exactly! It's not surprising that the flippy little flirt of a girl came to the end she did. Sooner or later—that's what I say. That Jenny, running wild in those short shorts, teasing the boys like she did. And her own mother letting her. Well, birds of a feather—mother and daughter."

Minister Griffith appeared and everyone fell silent as he held up his hand. "I heard about the council meeting, Molly. I'm not excusing them for saying what they said, but we must remember that grief has deranged them. They have their own—er—spiritual beliefs. Although we don't hold with their strange customs, we can only hope they will find solace in the practice of—whatever they practice. The town is being most charitable to ignore the threatening tone the

Deyers took." He sighed heavily. "Let's try to start the healing process. Put this all behind us, now." He gave them a satisfied smile as they nodded. He moved around them, pushing his cart before him.

As Molly finally moved forward, she heard someone whisper rather loudly about cross-legged meditation and weird religions. The Deyers would never have fit in—even if nothing had happened to Jennifer.

Molly hurried through the aisles. Comments came at her every time she turned. Her cousin passed and murmured regrets. Several neighbors gave her sympathetic smiles. Molly gripped the cart handle and made her features neutral. All the concern and attention, it was wasted energy. There was no basis—no need for it.

She soon finished and joined the line at the cash register. Someone charged forward as if to cut her off. Molly pulled back, irritated, ready to protest.

"Molly!" Her grandmother Horne grabbed her arm. "Joe told me all about the terrible business with the Deyers."

Molly gave her a weak smile. Laughter exploded behind them. She jumped and turned around. Jonathan and his friends, Donald Hubbard and Rocky Tuttle, jostled each other while her son scowled and looked at the floor. The other two boys noticed her and shot looks between themselves, stifling laughs.

"Hello, boys," Molly said, making room for her grandmother. "So, are you ready for the big game?" She forced her gaze away from their chopped-up, ludicrous haircuts.

Jonathan slouched behind Donald and Rocky, keeping his eyes on the tips of his cowboy boots.

"Sure, Mrs. Bischoff," Rocky said. "It'll be a real slaughter." Rocky nudged Jonathan.

Molly flinched but kept her smile in place.

"Yeah, we'll kill 'em," Jonathan said softly as he raised his head. A smirky grin crossed his face. He pulled out the juice container he held, unscrewed the top and took a long drink.

An angry tremor shot through Molly. Jonathan always used that particular expression when he was into something he knew she would not like. She'd hated it the worst when he'd glanced at her that way after the judge had given the "not guilty" verdict.

Donald poked Jonathan in the shoulder. Jonathan shoved back. The others in line moved a few inches.

"Stand up straight, Johnny," Grandmother snapped. "You boys need decent haircuts!" She tugged at Molly's sleeve, pulling her down to speak in her ear. "I always said that Garth should take a stronger hand with the boy. Huh! That obscene little ponytail. And that stupid ear ring! I'd have worked all that out of him on the ranch. Kids just get things handed to them; coming to no good, all of them." She clapped her hands sharply, satisfied that the three boys gave her a startled look.

"Yeah, *Johnny*," Rocky said, his voice high and sing-song. "Get those shoulders back. Suck in that fat gut."

Jonathan's eyes narrowed and he dropped his gaze back to the toes of his boots.

Molly turned around and took a long breath. Another second and *she* would have blurted the same thing, for want of *something* to call her son on. Ignoring them now, she moved up, took the items from the basket and set them on the counter.

Ron, her brother-in-law, began to check them, studiously focusing on his job. He glanced at her once. His face reddened from the neck up. She could just imagine what he was thinking, just like everyone else. Poor Molly, to have a son like Jonathan, accused of such perversions.

Accused, she thought, but not proven. He was a normal teenage boy, a bit obsessed with sex. Gasp! So unlike the *other* boys on the football team. But all *their* sons weren't as pure as a pack of little cherubs. Jonathan had said that every one of them had had an eye on Jenny Deyer—and Jenny had liked it.

Molly handed the check to Ron as she glanced over her shoulder. "See you at home, son. Don't be late for supper."

That nasty little grin of his answered her back. She wanted to shake him, to make him tell her that he'd mashed his car again; hell, maybe he'd stolen some beer—nothing more than that, nothing worse than that.

Grandmother Horne started a running commentary on everything that was wrong with the Deyers. Everyone near enough to hear listened avidly. Molly just wanted the whole subject to go away. She picked up the sacks and stepped out onto the sidewalk, feeling a little rude at leaving her grandmother to babble on. One more word about the Deyers and she felt sure her carefully maintained poise would have cracked, and that wouldn't be pretty.

A large moving van roared by as Molly finished loading the car. The hot dusty wake washed her, making her sneeze. She didn't mark where it turned. She already knew. Only one family was on the move.

She drove too fast, but made it back to the house in good time. She decided that she needed a brisk jog, away from the phone and the house—that should clear her thoughts. Jonathan could return home anytime; she wanted herself centered and calm.

She had to deal with it all, as usual. Her husband kept himself removed from the situation. He refused to discuss any part of this mess, and she couldn't expect more of a response at this late date. She supposed that Garth believed in Jonathan. He probably considered it a waste to give it more attention.

Molly quickly changed into her sweats and left the house. She started on her usual route. Despite the run, her thoughts wound back to Jonathan and the events of the last two months.

The sheriff had been forced to arrest him because of that stupid down sleeping bag. Jonathan had lost track of it! It had been an expensive birthday present from his father. Jonathan had been embarrassed to lose it and hadn't told them, that was all. The only crime he'd committed was irresponsibility. He'd left the sleeping bag behind after one of the spring teenage parties. Bad luck for Jonathan that Jenny had latched on to it somehow. Her body had been found in the trunk of her little red sports car, lying amid a scatter of down feathers from his bag.

Jonathan was so careless with nice things. She wondered if he'd learned *anything* from all this—she doubted it.

From now on, he would get second best. He needed a good lesson.

Molly ran faster and faster, trying to keep pace with the growing whirl of her thoughts. She slowed, gasping for breath. Cemetery Hill lay ahead. She kept her eyes down, avoiding the sight of it and that damned angel monument—the Deyers' condemnation of Crystal Springs. She considered veering at the next street when her sister, Rebecca, drove by, stopped and called to her.

"Molly!" Rebecca pulled up and turned off the engine. "I wanted to tell you. After you left the council meeting today, several of us talked about some regulations for the cemetery."

Molly stopped and jogged in place, a hint to her sister that she was impatient to continue on her way. Rebecca didn't acknowledge hints very well.

"Everyone wants that vulgar statue over the Deyer girl's grave taken down." Rebecca put her plump hand on the open window and rested her chin on it.

"Rebecca, we can't do that."

"But . . ." Her sister sat up and tilted her head in a sympathetic gesture. "Oh, Molly, you're such a good person. How can you worry about the Deyers' feelings? They flaunted themselves at us, and even tried to get some of us interested in that witchcraft stuff. Margie over in the post office told me all about those magazines she put in their box. They didn't so much as attend one Christian church service in this town. Gaylene and Robert didn't even have a decent burial for their daughter."

Molly stopped jogging and stood, her arms hanging loose at her sides.

Rebecca warmed to the subject. "They did some occult mumbo jumbo over the poor thing. One of Jennifer's friends attended and said she got kind of scared. Strangers there put on white robes when they started that ungodly ceremony."

"Ceremony?" Molly said. "Oh, yeah, I did hear a little about that."

"Well, let me tell you! They didn't even have a proper minister! They made a circle around the casket, holding hands and doing some creepy chants."

Molly blinked at Rebecca, imagining a circle of people, clasping hands, playing and chanting ring-around-the-roses, or something of the sort.

"That's not all," Rebecca continued. "Robert and Gaylene threw white feathers all over the casket afterward. The friend—I think it was Phyllis Tuttle's girl—got spooked and ran all the way home to tell her mother."

Molly took a step back. "Feathers?"

"We figured, you know, because of how Jennifer was found in all those feathers from Jonathan's sleeping bag—" Rebecca's face reddened. "Oh. I . . . I'm sorry. I mean . . . Well, anyway, the angel seems like such a statement. It simply has to come down—maybe when they're gone. I can't believe you could care so much about the Deyers' feelings over this matter."

"Rebecca, my caring has nothing to do with moving that statue off Jenny's grave. We can only effect policy on future headstones. Probably." Molly stared at her sister for a moment, then said, "We'll all be more comfortable to have them gone, won't we?" She started jogging in place again. "I'll be in touch."

Rebecca started her car. "See you at the game Saturday! Johnny will give us our first win of the season."

Molly waved at her and started away.

• • •

Rebecca began turning the car, then braked, raising her hand to call Molly back, but changed her mind. Her sister had made it clear that Rebecca had interrupted her. Rebecca had chosen to ignore the obvious hints. She had meant to tell Molly about her latest news touching on Jonathan—obtained only an hour ago. Phyllis had told her that her daughter had seen Jonathan fighting with his own *friend*. Rumor had it that Jennifer Deyer had rejected Jonathan to go out with the friend.

Robert Deyer had been right about Jonathan's violent tendencies.

But what good would it do to bring that up to Molly now? It would only serve to torment her. Molly had enough to deal with. No one really wanted to *know* that Jonathan would commit murder.

The way Rebecca saw it, that Deyer girl and her parents were a one-time circumstance—for Jonathan and for the town. Even if Jonathan *had* done the deed, what good would it do to put him in a jail? He wouldn't repeat it, since—well, the chances of another Jennifer Deyer coming along were very slender.

Rebecca's stomach growled. She chewed on a dry cuticle as she drove, her thick brows drawn tightly together. A cold gust of wind blew through her open window; a large hard bullet of rain smacked her on the cheek. She jumped, quickly rolled up the window and leaned forward to look at the blackening sky. Too soon for winter! They'd had such a chilly, wet spring.

Rebecca had been looking forward to a warm, lingering fall—maybe taking some long walks in the bright fall leaves to get into shape. But things didn't look promising. The leaves would simply turn an ugly brown and drop into soggy piles if it kept getting colder and wetter.

Nothing had seemed quite right from the time the Deyers had moved to Crystal Springs. Besides, didn't the Deyers have some responsibility in this? Why had they chosen to move *here?* When they saw how out of touch they were with everyone, why had they tried to force their way in?

Rebecca nodded, glad she hadn't called Molly back. She'd heard that all the boys had followed that Jennifer around, not just Jonathan. Just because Johnny had been obsessed with the Deyer girl, that was kind of normal for a jealous teenage boy. Jenny had been such a skinny little wisp of a thing. Rebecca had her own theories. She believed that both Gaylene and Jennifer Deyer had been anorexic.

Rebecca looked down at her own thick, round thighs. She'd decided three hours ago to start another diet, and so far she hadn't eaten a thing. But who wanted to look like Gaylene, anyway? If people didn't accept a person for what she was, that was their problem. Being thin wasn't everything, although men seemed to think so. Like Jonathan, who'd gotten all crazy over Jennifer—along with all the other boys—ignoring all the other normal, robust country girls in the high school. Rebecca's own poor daughter cried about her weight all the time.

So Jonathan had started beating other guys off Jennifer. Rebecca's mouth pulled into a frown. He'd gone overboard. It remained to be seen just how far overboard. Rebecca pulled into the Dairy Queen and stopped the car, glad she didn't have to deal with Jonathan.

•••

Molly started forward, running faster than she normally would have. Rebecca seemed to have more on her mind, and Molly didn't want to hear it.

Cemetery Hill loomed ahead, and that accursed statue dragged on her attention. The graveyard had always been such a pleasant goal on her daily jog: the flowering plants, the big shady trees, the ever-cool granite headstones to rest against on a hot summer day. Although, this summer, the grass had been cold and wet, the flowers limp and washed-out looking, the stones chill and damp.

A drop of rain smacked her forehead like a cold, violent kiss. She considered turning back, but picked up her pace instead, looking toward Jenny Deyer's monument. Let it stay. Let the Deyers posture all they wished. She hadn't given life to Jonathan then struggled so hard to put up with him just so he could shame her.

She had to stand up for Jonathan's innocence, because his actions reflected directly on his upbringing—or lack of one. It reflected on Garth, certainly, and his refusal to make his son any part of his life.

She had stepped away, afraid of making Jonathan a mamma's boy. But she'd seen to it that he had every advantage, had everything he wanted or needed. She'd tried. Oh, but that accursed statue, like some lurid whore, had wrapped the town up in a sort of morbid fascination. Well, even if they didn't knock the statue down, the city could certainly plant more trees, clumping them all in one specific place.

•••

The first high-school game of the season kicked off Saturday in the early autumn air. Crystal Springs' supporters crammed the bleachers, everyone dressed in the black and red of Crystal Springs High School colors. Even with—or maybe because of—the Deyers' threats still on most people's minds, the cheers and chants seemed to take on a defiant air. It was time for unity.

•••

Molly took a deep breath as Jonathan ran onto the field, helmet tucked under his arm. Her husband, Garth, stood as she screamed with the rest of the crowd. He clapped and cheered, yet his enthusiasm lacked its usual exuberance. Molly jostled him. He turned to her, a flash of annoyance passing over his face so quickly she nearly missed it. But then he smiled. Never mind. He would get into it when his son ran the first touchdown. Even Judge Wickham, dressed in a red sweat shirt, stomped his foot and roared.

They sat and Molly felt a tug at her sweater. Phyllis Tuttle leaned toward her and cupped her hand to Molly's ear. "Jed only just told me about Robert and Gaylene at the council meeting."

Molly nodded and made a show of looking for Jonathan as the team lined up for the first play.

Phyllis persisted. "I'm so relieved to know they're not going to be here at the game. Can you imagine what Gaylene would wear? You'd think Robert would have had more pride, the way he let both his wife and daughter prance around town in those tiny shorts—I mean the way all the guys stared."

"Oh, Phyllis, surely not *all* the men," Molly said close to Phyllis's ear.

Phyllis drew back, then looked past her toward Garth, one eyebrow raised.

Molly's face tinged pink, but she laughed. "I think a couple of women in town had an eye on Robert Deyer. Understandable, as good-looking and friendly as he is—was. My goodness, even you . . . ?"

Phyllis blanched. "Who's been talking about me? I only spoke to Robert once—twice, maybe. Just being polite!"

It was Molly's turn to raise an eyebrow. Phyllis jounced around to watch the game.

•••

Crystal Valley led by one touchdown at half time. Jonathan had scored it on a quarterback sneak. Garth stomped and called out the cheers with rising enthusiasm. But Molly's first surge of excitement faded as the afternoon sun fell closer to the mountain peaks. The noisy crowd jangled her nerves. The tension in the air seemed to go beyond the immediate game. The band whistled and shrieked through their tunes. Molly put her hands to her ears.

Then the cheers went flat and died. Everyone turned to look toward the enemy goal post. Molly moved slowly to face that way, not surprised to see Robert and Gaylene Deyer hand in hand, looking back at them all. Molly clamped her teeth together so hard that her jaw began to ache. The last band members filed off at the opposite end of the field.

A soft growl gathered in her throat. What more could they hope to accomplish from this display? They had nothing more to say. Even though her son had *not* been in his room the night of the murder the way he'd sworn to the judge, he'd sworn tearfully to *her* that he hadn't hurt the girl. Jonathan had pleaded for Molly to back up his story. Garth had been home all that night, but even *he* had remained silent. He believed his son. Why, then, did she catch Garth, at times, looking at her all full of reproach? He had no right. It made her furious. She and her husband talked even less than usual these days.

The people on the bleachers began to murmur, much to Molly's satisfaction. Soon, the security guard, old man Hawks, limped out to shoo the Deyers away.

Gaylene Deyer met him partway, touched his arm, and leaned toward him, talking earnestly. Molly shifted angrily as Hawks just stood, listening, holding things up. The enthusiasm of the crowd drained away by the second.

Finally Hawks tried to steer Gaylene back toward Robert. Then the Deyers did an odd thing. They cast white feathers into the air. A chill breeze caught the snowy flutter and carried it high to scatter over the center of the field. By the time Molly looked back toward the goal post, the Deyers had gone.

She had a sudden urge to rush out and gather every feather that danced and rolled across the chalk marks. Her husband glowered at the ground. Everyone muttered angrily among themselves. The members of the crowd sat down one by one.

• • •

Crystal Valley High School lost the game by a wide and embarrassing margin. Molly soothed her disappointment with the common consensus that morale for the team and the town had been broken by the little half-time show, courtesy of the Deyers. Still, no one could revile against the Deyers. After all, they had most certainly gone insane with grief.

• • •

Wind gusts pushed Molly along as she took an early jog before Sunday morning church services. The Deyers' moving van turned the corner a block away. She slowed and watched it roll from sight. A shiver trembled just above her stomach as the van seemed to drag a blanket of sullen gray clouds over the town after it.

The green leaves beside the tree-lined walk rattled and slapped together, hurrying her along like an irritable phys. ed. teacher. She picked up her pace, breathing in the faint scent of wood smoke. Just as she began to relax into a pleasant and loose stride, several leaves tore from the boughs above, one catching in her hair. She stumbled, caught her breath, and scraped it out with an impatient huff. Then a small white feather fell from her hair, touched her nose and landed on her chest. She jumped back, brushing frantically at her sweat shirt.

A spear of sunlight sprang between steep white cloud columns. She raised her eyes, following it down. The light splashed over the angel in the cemetery, making it glow. A strong gust of wind blew her hair around her face. Just before she brushed it from her eyes, she thought she saw the glowing statue move; the wings appeared to lift slightly, and flutter in the wind.

Molly stumbled and landed on her knee. She cried out and jumped up, shaking the hair from her face. Nothing. The statue hadn't moved. She became aware of a burning sensation at her knee and touched it gently. Her fingers came away with a trace of blood. "Just great!" she muttered. "Thank you, Gaylene and Robert. Well, you are *not* sucking me into your games." She started walking forward, then picked up her pace. "You're gone and I hope you—"

Her words died as she now noticed a movement near the statue. A bulky figure came from behind the monument and her mouth went dry. The clouds moved, dimming the beam of light. She squinted, trying to identify the person: a man certainly, all hunched over and skulking like a thief. Then she recoiled in disgust. He appeared to be running his hands over the marble, caressing the stone.

Okay, no more of this nonsense with that statue! It had to go if it inspired such indecency. Removing it would be less of a desecration. She looked up and down the street, hoping someone else saw this lurid display. All she really needed was one witness.

Robert's deep voice penetrated into her thoughts. "All we really need is one witness."

"No! It's *not* Jonathan," she cried aloud. She whirled back to the statue just as the sun winked out. The figure writhed against the statue. Gaylene's voice came to her now. ". . . bring Jonathan to answer . . ."

"No proof—no witnesses," Molly whispered hoarsely. She continued to stare at the dark figure, almost mesmerized, not knowing that she shook her head slowly back and forth. But even from this distance, she recognized Jonathan's black jacket with the red-and-gold dragon emblazoned on the back—the expensive jacket he had begged her to buy. Finally he disengaged from the weeping angel and started away in a lumbering run. She had told Jonathan *not* to slouch like that.

No, *not* like that! Similar—a person with another jacket like the one she'd given Jonathan. Maybe he'd lost it, like he had lost his sleeping bag. Nevertheless, she felt the determined grip she had on Jonathan's innocence slip.

She cast her eyes about the neighborhood, wondering who else might have taken interest in that dirty little act that the heavens chose to spotlight.

Okay. So what if it had been Jonathan up there mauling that stupid angel. *That* kind of "art" would incite the active imagination of any normally over-sexed teenage boy. But that indecent statue being placed over the site of a rape victim—the Deyers were sending their perverse message to the town, and she didn't care to waste any more energy worrying about it. Anyway, it wasn't a problem. If she couldn't positively identify the man in the graveyard at this distance—except for the jacket—then no one else could either. So—still, no witnesses.

Molly decided to cut her run short. The shifting clouds strobed sunlight over Cemetery Hill, just as she started to turn. Again the wings of the angel seemed to rise and spread. She growled, rubbing hard at her eyes. When she looked again, a few white flecks swirled around the angel statue, settling over the green carpet of grass. The clouds overcame the sun, and all the brightness left the day. Of course the statue stood as ever, wings fallen and draped over the gray granite stone. She turned and fled toward home.

"Jonathan?" Molly called sharply, as she came through the front door. Just this once she hoped to find him lounging in his room, his headphones on, his body twitching to the music that blasted into his ears. She went quickly up the stairs and pushed through his door. The usual array of dirty clothing and football paraphernalia spilled over the unmade bed and the unused desk, but Jonathan was not a part of the mess.

Molly's face heated with anger. It was Sunday and by damn if he wouldn't attend church! She would drag him there by that idiotic ponytail. . . .

The shower started up across the hall. She huffed and turned to go out, when something slipped from under a wadded-up T-shirt on the small bedside stand and spun to the floor. A photograph. Molly jumped, snorted at herself, and went to pick it up.

As she raised it, the hair on the back of her neck prickled. The photo was of a very thin girl. She was leaning forward and her hair fell in a golden curtain over her shoulder, obscuring her features. Unaware that she held her breath, Molly picked up the T-shirt between two fingers and a cascade of photos showered off the stand and fell around her feet.

Then, one white feather detached from the shirt and twirled lightly down to rest on one of the photographs. Molly let the air go from her lungs in a low moan.

She found herself loath to touch the feather and bent to brush it out of sight under the bed. As if in a dream, she gathered the photos. Every shot showed Jennifer Deyer, all candid. One photo had something scrawled right over the picture. She read: "'If I can't have you, then no one . . .'" The writing went off the edge of the photo.

"Then no one will." Molly's lips moved involuntarily, finishing the phrase. Another photo had a ring drawn around Jennifer and a line through it. The image of the marble statue—Jenny Deyer with the limp wings—filled her head.

The room seemed to spin. Her stomach gave a sick lurch. Her fingers tightened on the photos as she saw herself handing them over—to the sheriff, or to the Deyers. So, here it was, confirmation of her fears, of what her head—her soul—already knew: her son's involvement, his obsession with Jennifer Deyer, now underscored with scrawled threats across her picture.

She crumpled the photo in her fist. If she had known this then . . . for *sure*.

She could still wring a confession from Jonathan. If Gaylene and Robert had just given her more time—maybe until *next* weekend. . . .

Until now, how could she have condemned her own son without something concrete—like this? If she had seen these photos even just a few days ago, why, yes, she *would* have taken them straight to . . .

Molly gave herself a shake and her vision cleared. How could she tell what she'd have done—say, if she'd even found these last spring? She had no idea. She did not have the energy or desire to speculate.

She gathered every photo and walked determinedly from the room. What would Jonathan say to his missing collection? Ha! Like he would dare ask. She slammed the door on the musky odor of stale sheets and sweaty socks. The water stopped in the shower. She waited a few seconds, but the door to the bathroom remained closed. Fine!

"Honey?" Garth called sleepily from the bedroom.

Molly stared down at the images of Jennifer Deyer in her hand, took a step toward the bedroom, but stopped, a bitter smile twisting her mouth out of shape. She imagined flinging them over the bed just to watch Garth shrug, avert his eyes, mumble ineffectually, and make his way from the room, avoiding any responsibility for his own son.

Instead, she stomped downstairs, grabbing some sheets of newspaper along the way. She started to crush Jennifer's images together with the paper, then stopped to stare at the pictures. A pretty girl, too young to be in a grave. The death of the girl hit her for the first time like a jab to her stomach. She'd been so immersed in concern over Jonathan and his—his innocence—his pledge of disinterest in the girl.

But whose fault was it, really, for the tragic end to Jennifer's life? A product of her mother's liberal ways and her father's indulgent permissiveness. The Deyers had made a victim of Jonathan, also, by allowing their daughter to become such a wild little thing, then putting her in his path—in the paths of all those boys who were in the middle of their teenage hormonal frenzy. She threw the photos into the fireplace, then crushed the newspaper and pitched it in after, setting a match to it all. She stepped back to watch the black smoke curl up the chimney.

Suddenly she wished she'd buried the photos. Somehow the smoke seemed to be a beacon, rising up through the chimney, the black particles signaling to the town, alerting everyone to what she had done—what she knew.

She imagined asking Johnny about these, and knew his head would just swing back and forth like a dazed bull as he denied everything. Oh, but even now she wanted those denials. She returned to her room, passing the open bathroom door. She glanced toward Jonathan's closed door, chewing on her fingernail. If he would burst from his room, angrily demanding those photos, wouldn't that show something? Guilt liked to hide and pretend to its own innocence.

Jonathan's door remained closed. She banged once on it. "Church in an hour," she said, her sharp tone daring him to argue. By damn, if either one of the men in this house even dared show the least reluctance . . .

She silently led the way through a cold breakfast, then marched the two in front of her, out the door to the car. They were early. Molly drove, found a place right out front and parked. She directed her two men into the church and right toward the forward pews. There would be no slinking about somewhere in the back of the chapel.

Jonathan hunched over and shoved his fists into his pockets. Molly repressed the urge to grab his hair and pull him up straight. His expression appeared lumpy-looking with repressed wrath. Ah yes, she thought, aren't you ready to explode about the loss of your precious photos? Why don't you confront me for invading your room? Please do. She gave him a steady glare and he bunched his shoulders together around his thick neck—pulling his head down between them. She was in control now. And all without a word, he would do exactly as she wished for the rest of his life.

•••

Jonathan Bischoff had visited the Jenny angel three times in the three weeks since its placement over her grave. It felt to him like a sort of worship, but with a lot more impact than sitting in this stupid church where his ass went numb and the pastor's drone anesthetized his brain.

But here he had to sit, glued to this hard bench, stiff with fury and fear at his own mother. Sneaking bitch! She hadn't said a word to him all morning, and he hadn't encouraged her to. She'd had no right prying into his private room, his personal business. Who else would swipe his pictures? And he had to take it without a word. Just like his father did. She'd whipped any manhood out of her own husband with her orders and demands. And he never stood up to her, not even once!

Had his mother shown those photos to his father? He hated the thought. His mother had mostly quit getting on his father to "spend a little time with the boy." That had been painful for them both, since his dad had never had two words to say to him.

When his mother did force them together, his dad's face would get flushed and damp with sweat, and he would stammer about the weather or how much more fertilizer or seed he'd been selling this season than last. All Jonathan could do was shrug and nod and hate his mother.

He shrank at the idea of his father actually asking him about his pictures of Jennifer. No, his dad would choke before he could get two words out about it. But the look on his face, the sadness and the disappointment— his mother had better not bring *that* on. Jonathan scowled and started to shift, got a sharp fingernail in his side, and remained rigid, his butt aching. The pastor moaned and whined about forgiving and throwing stones.

Yeah, he'd thrown a couple of stones, right through his so-called friend's car window, for going after *his* Jenny. Rocky had known that Jonathan had staked his claim on her. Jenny had brought everything on herself by going out with him and almost ruining herself. Hell, everyone knew that Rocky scored with all his girl-friends if they went out with him very long.

Jonathan's eyes misted and he squeezed them tightly together, mortified that someone might see him bawling here in church next to his mom, as if he were being punished like a two-year-old.

He flexed his hands, and again felt Jennifer's velvet-soft throat against his fingers. If she had just realized how devoted he'd been to her, how much he'd wanted her, she'd never have screamed at him or fought so hard to get away. She'd at least have given him a chance—gone out with him even one damned time.

The image came to him again of Jennifer's thin, bare legs flashing in the sun. His Sunday slacks strained slightly at the groin and he broke into a light sweat. It took all his concentration to remain motionless. He fixed his thoughts on Jennifer, still wondering what had gotten into him that day he'd called out to her.

She'd appeared only a little annoyed, but had come over to his truck—and, miracle, had gotten in.

Jonathan's lower lip curled down at the memory. She'd given him about two seconds of blinding joy, bouncing up onto the seat. Then she'd turned and yelled at him to stop following her! He'd grabbed her arm before she could get out, and he'd slammed his foot hard onto the gas pedal, going straight up behind the cemetery.

A vision of feathers cluttered his head, Jennifer's quiet little body lying among them like a broken swan. She'd had a burst of strength during his struggle to keep her quiet. Her shoe had ripped his sleeping bag and spilled the contents over the grass. He'd gathered up most of the feathers. All he could see right now were those damned feathers rolling all over the place. It had seemed important to retrieve them. He couldn't get them all, though, because of the little breeze that had sprung up and scattered them, teasing him as he ran after those stupid, damned feathers.

He'd waited until dark and found Jennifer's car and laid her gently in her trunk over his torn sleeping bag as comfortably as he could manage. It hadn't occurred to him how much trouble that stupid bag would get him into. But he'd *had* to put something under Jennifer.

It was no one's business—including his mom's— what he did with his stuff. He thought he'd been pretty smart, claiming he'd left the bag at the spring camp-out and insisting that it had ended up in Jennifer Deyer's trunk.

Well, she *could* have picked it up. He'd kept track of her. She'd spent time on *several* different guys' sleeping bags that night—not just his.

But the bag almost got him blamed for her death. Which would have been unfair, because no one would have stopped long enough to listen about why it had all had to happen this way. No one would have cared about everything he'd gone through. Even his own mother and father. All they would have cared about was that HE DID IT. Period.

His fingers curled and he ground his right fist into the palm of his left hand. He wanted to slam into something. His body twitched involuntarily. Again, another sharp fingernail went into his side. Jonathan ground his fist into his palm.

Jennifer lay safe now, tucked away and out of reach from all the hands that would have been pawing at her. He'd done it for her. She knew that now, of course, and she had to be grateful that he'd kept her from hurting herself—from being less than perfect. No one could touch her now.

Jonathan took a long, careful breath and straightened. So what if he had pictures of Jennifer? It wasn't like he'd taken a picture of her actual dead body.

He had to stifle a snicker. His mother didn't *know* anything. All she really cared about was her standing in the town and how embarrassing it would be to have a murderer for a son.

So she had to protect him for her own sake—not because she really cared about him. Even now she was just working herself up to scream at him after church, same as she did over any and every tiny little thing—like that lost down sleeping bag. Hell, she'd been so pissed off at him. Joke, he hadn't lost it. But would she care about *his* concerns and the loving use he'd put it to? Nooo.

•••

Molly sat between Garth and Jonathan, barely restraining herself from slapping them both, but she knew that if she started, she wouldn't be able to quit. All she could see when she closed her eyes for prayer was Jonathan writhing against that statue, and all those photographs falling to the floor of his room.

Molly glanced around the chapel. No one met her eyes. In fact, it seemed that everyone studiously avoided looking her way. Her face heated in anger. How dare they judge! They had no right to shun her. No one knew what she was going through! No one had to deal with a husband or son like hers. No one had to carry the kind of burden she would bear for the rest of her life. If anything, she deserved a little sympathy. Never mind. Time would take care of it all.

The meeting finally concluded in an almost unnatural silence. Everyone quickly jostled into the aisle. Even Minister Griffith closed his bible and left the pulpit without another look at the congregation. Belatedly, Molly realized that she couldn't recall a single word of the sermon.

She shrugged and waited belligerently for Garth to lead the way, which meant they had to sit there until most everyone else had made it to the door. Garth tilted his head idiotically, giving her a questioning look, then stood. Jonathan followed, pouting.

The rest of the day passed in silence. Jonathan slipped out before dinner and stayed away, even after Molly and Garth went to bed.

Molly lay awake waiting. She rehearsed all the new rules. Jonathan would not make a complete escape from his actions. Her son would agree to her heavy restrictions—or he'd starve. There would be some changes around here for everyone.

Jonathan had known it was coming and would try to escape. Sorry, kid, but you're stuck. Low average grades, no ambition—you wouldn't last three days on your own. You'll have to stick around here for a while—on *my* terms. She drifted into an uneasy dream, running through a blizzard, her nose and throat clogged with snow.

She woke gasping, feeling as if someone held her down and smothered her face in a heavy blanket. Someone pounded on the west window. But no, she thought sluggishly, surely just the tall maple outside. One of the limbs Garth had neglected to trim. She struggled to sit up, thick-headed, fighting to draw air into her lungs. Pieces of moonlight pushed through the leaves of the tree; the white flutter of the light danced over the room and the bed like a shower of white feathers.

No! *Not* feathers! Molly tried to cry out at the absurdity of it. The sound stuck in her throat. Another blow struck the window and made her start, then a strong wind whipped the branches into a frenzy. The leaves caught the moonlight and seemed to turn into a thousand shimmering wings.

The front door squeaked open. Jonathan—finally coming home. She pushed at her husband, still half-captured in a dream. Something soft caressed her cheek, then moved down over her neck, tickling as it went. The feather-touch lingered at her neck, then tightened, crushing her throat with steady pressure. She fell back on the bed thrashing, trying to scream. She could make no sound at all.

"Stop it," Garth grumbled. "Ow, you're hurting . . ." he bellowed, then gagged and kicked Molly from the bed as he clawed at his neck.

Molly pushed herself up from the floor, hands fluttering. She calmed somewhat as she realized that some air still made it through the tight passage in her throat.

Garth kneeled on the bed, the faint light from the street lamp showing him in outline, grasping the blanket to his chest.

She stumbled to the light switch and flipped it on. White feathers lay scattered over the quilts and carpeting. Her husband's mouth stretched wide as he tried to howl. His only sound was the harsh panting breaths he took.

He remained kneeled, rubbing his throat and gave her a pleading look, as if imploring her to explain. Molly could only shake her head and kick at the feathers under her feet. A siren started in the direction of the hospital. A nearby police car started its own siren wailing into the night.

Several feathers dislodged from Molly's hair and fell softly over her nose and cheeks. Several thumps and a strangled groan came from the stairway. Molly ran from the bedroom.

• • •

Jonathan staggered to his feet and threw himself up the dark stairs. He tried again to scream at his mother to come out and fix this, but he could only make a wet gurgle. Damn, his throat hurt *bad*. He stumbled twice, putting dents in his shins as he went.

Finally, she appeared, coming at him without a word, her mouth all thin and twisted up in that nasty frown of hers.

She's not yelling? She thinks she's going to beat on me instead?

He gawked at her as she lunged forward, then made a grab as she got near, tearing the sleeve of her nightgown. She pushed at him, then began hitting his chest with her fists! What the hell was *this?* His father came out and leaned heavily against the door frame, his shoulders sagging. At least *he* looked as if he might say something, but he just gave Jonathan a pathetic, whiny sound.

Jonathan's eyes bulged and his mouth gaped wide. He wasn't breathing! The curse had him. He grabbed at his mother; she was breathing well enough.

•••

Molly twisted away and the material of her gown ripped. This was Jonathan's fault, the curse, all of this. Her sight dissolved in a red haze and her fists began to ache.

A numbing calm settled around Molly, permeating her brain. Comfortable reality, her wall against insanity, shifted off center. That vile statue, that angel of death over Jennifer's grave, symbolized it all. Had the Deyers endowed the marble angel with a demon spirit? Had they called their daughter back from the dead and stuck her in that winged thing so she could seek her own vengeance?

They certainly made it appear that the Jenny angel was coming after them—coming after every voice who could have spoken against Jonathan. Molly stooped and picked up a feather, rolling it between her finger and thumb. Garth lurched into the hall and Molly held the feather out to Garth. Didn't he *see?*

Her husband held up his hands and backed away. Ah, so he did see—or he just thought she had lost her mind. She turned and walked up to her son, bringing the bit of white up to his face. She cocked her head and stared at the piece of feather, wondering what friends and family were also not saying to each other. A sudden urge to giggle rose in her chest, then silent, maniacal laughter tore at her throat.

•••

Jonathan knocked his mother's fists away, horrified at the wide-open rictus that stretched her mouth into noiseless laughter. Why didn't either one of them at least *say* something, swear at him, ground him for a year? Anything! Shit, his throat felt like it had been put in a vise.

They had to *do* something. He pointed at his throat, stomping his feet. Several white feathers shook loose from his shoulder and sleeve. He stared at them, then lifted his head, puzzled at first, then understanding: his own parents—*they* had done this to him—set something up at the front door—what—to punish him? They knew he'd killed Jenny, and they were going to torture him!

He fell back against the wall, unable to comprehend the vacuous expression on his mother's face. The dumb, impotent misery of his father hadn't changed much. But he knew one thing: he couldn't count on either one of them. They didn't believe in his innocence—his vow that he wouldn't *hurt* Jennifer.

He had done it to save her, not hurt her. Her death *saved* her. *They* would never comprehend that, he could see that now. His mother could still only guess. No one would ever know the real truth of it.

He rubbed at his throat, trying to make one last mute appeal. His parents just mocked him with repulsive gurgling squawks.

Jonathan gave his mother another shove, then whirled and drove his fist into the wall, feeling a couple of bones give in his fingers. He was on his own. He opened his mouth to howl, and choked instead. Forget them—forget everyone! He ran back out into the night, his feet pointing him toward the cemetery.

•••

Molly stumbled back from the hard push Jonathan had given her. She watched him bolt back downstairs and out the front door. She batted away Garth's hand and went into the bathroom. Purple-black ovals, like heavy thumbprints, marred her throat. She made a dry squawk, feeling that her voice had been taken from her, crushed and silenced—maybe forever.

Acid horror began eating away at her defensive wall as an image of Jenny Deyer came to mind. Molly wheezed out a laugh, then slammed the flat of her palm against the mirror, and went back into the hall. Garth grabbed her, and Molly kicked away from him. This was his fault for not taking Jonathan in hand. It was the Deyers' fault for letting their wild little slut daughter entice teenage boys.

Jonathan! He'd bolted from the house, and she suddenly knew where he'd gone. Jennifer Deyer still enticed him, called him to her, even in death.

It was true then, about Gaylene and her witchcraft. She'd thought the woman insane or playing stupid games for attention—a bored, rich housewife. But wouldn't it be more insane to take *seriously* some kind of occult vengeance—to believe that the Deyers could possibly lay a curse?

Cold conviction grew, making her tremble. "Gaylene!" Molly's mouth moved as she silently screamed the woman's name. She ran to the front door and out onto the dark lawn, unheeding that she wore only her thin nightgown. She took several strides toward the sidewalk, then stopped as fragments of Gaylene's bitter curse came into her mind: "If you choose to remain silent . . . your opportunity to speak is coming swiftly to an end. . . ."

Molly shuddered as her bare feet sank into the cool, damp lawn. Several neighbors ran mute through the streets, their arms flapping wildly. A car careened by, narrowly missing one of them.

Through it all, Molly stood silent and rigid, her bare toes clenching blades of grass. Another siren started up near the hospital. A baby's cry came through an open window next door. She realized that the only voices left to the town would be those of the very young children, and any others who might be innocent—untouched by any knowledge of Jonathan.

Phyllis Tuttle burst through her front door in silent panic, arms out, robe flapping, making her look like a clumsy goose as she headed down the street.

Fools! Molly regarded Phyllis with contempt. Another thought struck her. The Deyers had somehow suggested all this—had hypnotized them in some way. They had induced mass hallucination, group hysteria. Nothing supernatural about it. A cold breeze molded her nightgown against her body. She shivered and looked up as clouds shredded away from the impassive moon.

That winged obscenity up in the graveyard; it stood like an indictment over the town. And with Robert and Gaylene coming to the council meeting, muttering their curses, throwing those stupid white feathers at the game when we were all primed for it—of course! We've all been suckered right into this.

Well, not *me*. She swallowed against the dry raw ache in her throat. Fury bloomed in her chest, heating her from the inside out. So, then, she would have to see to this manipulation herself. As she'd had to see to everything all along, to Jonathan, to Garth—to the whole damned helpless town.

It all centered on that wicked angel. She would yank Jonathan *off* that evil thing and topple it with her bare hands. That would shatter the hypnotic grip the Deyers seemed to hold over them.

She began jogging toward the graveyard, oblivious of the rocks that cut her feet. She had to dodge those who recognized her and tried to clutch at her, gurgling for help. Others veered around her, going from door to door, banging and ringing doorbells. Why didn't they just pick up the phone? Her eyes widened. A hard grin stretched her mouth. She wheezed and wheezed and wondered if she would laugh like that all the rest of her life.

She reached the street that inclined toward the cemetery, looking up toward her destination as she went. The moon's full, white death-head face glared at her now, its chill light glinting over the rows of stones.

Despite herself, fear closed around her heart like icy stone fingers. She searched out that one shrine that stood higher than all the rest, that angel from hell itself. She couldn't see it! But it had to be there! She hadn't *honestly* believed in a curse, or a piece of rock that could come to life. But doubt, like a breath of frigid air, flowed through her bones, and cooled the hot rage in her gut.

The moonlight faded as another gust of wind hit her in the back. She glanced up as a large shape fluttered overhead, completely obliterating the heavens, then it was gone and the moon appeared again, making her blink against the light. Now she searched the cemetery with fierce intent.

There! she thought triumphantly, spotting Jennifer Deyer's monument.

Molly slowed and stopped. The angel seemed to be moving—like it had earlier that day. Its wings spread high and wide, but there was more. The statue had changed in some fundamental way: two distinct shapes now appeared under the extended wings, both rimmed in white pasty moonlight.

The hair rose on the back of Molly's neck. She started forward at full speed.

Molly slowed at the low fence and walked through the open gate, her arms down now and dangling by her sides. She continued steadily forward, stopping finally in front of the Jennifer angel. She reached out to touch Jonathan as he hung, secured at the neck by the cold marble hands of the statue. Molly looked to the angel's face; a strand of flowing marble hair settled and froze on the bare shoulder; marble eyelids closed and opened once and the head tilted ever so slightly toward Molly. Then the eyes remained open.

The delicate lips smiled gently down at her.

Molly felt the burn in her throat cease. A low keen issued from vocal cords that no longer felt crushed, were no longer injured beyond repair.

Gaylene's voice whispered over the grass and around the gravestones, ". . . only the murderer himself can answer for his deeds. Only he will be able to break the silence."

Molly raised her head to the moon, opened her mouth, and screamed.

OUR MISSION TO DREAM

Written by
Vincent Di Fate

About the Author

Vincent Di Fate has worked in animation and as a science fiction illustrator. He has won the Hugo Award for best professional artist, and I could go on to mention other awards and honors. But I think that the quality of his work shows in the fact that, as you read the biographies of artists in this and other volumes of **Writers of the Future**, *today's emerging illustrators routinely cite Di Fate as one of the modern masters who most influence their work.*

Nuff said.

In addition to providing us with his own art, Di Fate has written numerous articles on the topic. Most recently he has authored a book, Infinite Worlds: The Fantastic Vision of Science Fiction Art, *in which Di Fate collects works from many of the modern masters into a fine volume and discusses the significance of each artist.*

Here, he gives a little personal advice for new illustrators.

've been asked to provide some practical advice to aspiring illustrators of the fantastic for this current volume of *Writers of the Future*, and I'm both pleased and honored to do so. I should point out that I've been doing just that—illustrating the fantastic—for the past thirty years. I've been prolific at it, too, having produced somewhere between eighty and a hundred images per year for commercial publication for most of that time. I've also authored and edited a survey history of the genre's artwork (*Infinite Worlds: The Fantastic Visions of Science Fiction Art*—Penguin Studio Books, 1997), have taught my illustration specialty on both the college undergraduate and graduate levels, and have recently completed two terms as president of the Society of Illustrators. But while all of that might appear to give me impeccable credentials, I'm probably the last person to be giving advice on how to get started in the field.

For one thing, the field of fantastic literature has grown enormously over the last thirty years and it's changed considerably in the process; and for another, the competition has become so fierce during that time that I can scarcely begin to imagine what it must take to get established nowadays. Add to that the ever-increasing impact of computer technology on the arts, the breathless pace at which marketing strategies change in modern publishing, and the chaos of recent mergers, and one immediately appreciates how much more uncertain the future appears compared to those simpler times when publishing was considered a helplessly quaint and antiquated cottage industry.

The fact is that few of us are any good at all at predicting the future, and to give any reasonable counsel to young artists about what lies ahead for them requires greater prescience than I or anyone else possess. If it's any consolation to you, for as long as there has been a field of illustration, artists have always mistakenly believed the sky was falling. While overseeing a recent survey of the membership of the Society of Illustrators, I uncovered records of several earlier Society surveys dating from 1901 to 1955—during a time now affectionately known as illustration's "Golden Age"—only to discover that artists were plagued by the same troubles then as now and that the prevailing sentiment was that the field of illustration was doomed. Illustration had been alternately expected to meet its demise from the intrusion of photography, the airbrush, stock image sources and the computer. Over the decades publishing, almost certainly the largest consumer of illustrative art, was also thought to be doomed—by radio, by motion pictures, by the manufacturing of inexpensive paperback books, by television and by the Internet.

To be sure, the publishing field has taken some major hits. The entrenchment of television in popular culture did take a terrible toll in the magazine field, dealing it a near fatal blow in the mid-to-late 1950s— and today we see a steady and seemingly irreversible decline in both magazine and book sales, which has in turn been blamed on growing illiteracy, intense competition with other forms of entertainment, and the seductive attraction of the Internet with its multiplicity of charms and vices.

Somehow through it all, artists have persevered. The world seems to need at least *some* of us to do its dreaming for it. There will always be a need for us, albeit an ever changing one. And the same is probably true of writers, poets, fine artists, musicians and those in all the other disciplines that comprise the communication arts. We provide a mirror of the human soul, a record of the human experience, and we present important speculation about where our species has come from and where it may be headed. We provide a means by which people can more clearly comprehend what they feel inside; by which they can measure themselves against others; by which they can better discern the limitations of self and physical being from the universe around them. And in the process the arts constantly clarify, preserve, refine and disseminate our cultural values.

So, bearing in mind that all things in a progressive, technological society are in a constant state of flux, allow me to offer you advice about what I know to be true of this highly specialized field and what is likely *not* to change anytime soon.

Fantastic literature is about ideas and things that lie beyond the common frame of reference. For "traditional" illustrators—and here, let me define an illustration as a picture that specifically tells a story—the process involves assembling the appropriate references and interpreting and recreating those elements in a picture that evokes the spirit of the accompanying text. No doubt creating a painting depicting the hardships of General George Washington and his troops at Valley Forge, for instance, poses unique challenges for the artist in terms of researching historical details and tracking down appropriate costumes and props. And a really good artist can do far more than merely regurgitate the research; he or she can infuse the painting with an atmosphere that brings the experience to life for the reader by recreating a palpable sense of that historical time period and a vivid impression of the immense hardships those valiant soldiers faced.

With the fantastic, however, there *is* no reference—or rather, no reference beyond what we already know, or think we know, about present-day reality. But those real-world elements are never the central focus of this kind of art. In an historical work, where the parameters are assumed to be fixed in time, we have some sense of the clothing people might have worn or the implements they may have used. Not so with stories set in the future, or in imagined realms. Thus, the artist presents the viewer with some elements that will be familiar and others that are entirely novel, and in so doing helps the viewer to accept the painting as a whole. The trick lies in how well the artist can integrate the known elements with those that have been invented to follow the story, and in hiding the seams between what is real and what is imagined.

It seems to me, given this fact, that the artist must have some grasp of how fantastic literature is different from other kinds of fiction and must also have some understanding of the ideas that underlie these stories. He or she must also understand how the various forms of fantastic fiction are different from one another—say, science fiction from fantasy or supernatural horror. One must also have some sense of the iconography of these subgenres: to know the revered symbols that instantly identify and set apart one subgenre from another. Thus a painting of a spaceship or a robot is likely to have been done for a science fiction story, whereas an image of a dragon or a unicorn suggests an association with fantasy. Sometimes a subtle manipulation of color scheme might differentiate between light fantasy and supernatural horror, inasmuch as these subgenres often share common elements (for example, dragons and witches can turn up in both types of stories, and even on rare occasions they can appear in science fiction, too. Anne McCaffrey's popular Pern novels are good examples of how works of fantastic fiction can blur the distinctions between subgenres).

So, my first item of advice is that the illustrator of the fantastic must have an understanding of the subject matter and must know the icons that identify it. For most of you who already know and love fantastic literature, that's the easy part. For those of you who don't *read* in the genre and only know it from the things you've seen on TV or in the movies, be warned that SF and fantasy in the electronic and film media are not quite the same as on the written page.

Item #2: While the stereotype of the starving artist is as inaccurate as most other overstated characterizations, working in the arts should not be about money. That is not to say that making a decent living as an illustrator is impossible, but few of us become obscenely wealthy in this line of work—and I've probably made as much money as anyone doing it. Our society has put far too much emphasis on material wealth as a measure of success and if making a large income is high on your list of career goals, you might want to consider other vocational options. Working in the arts should be about functioning in a craft you find pleasurable and having the unique opportunity to connect with a large audience with which you can communicate ideas that are important to you.

Item #3: There is no substitute for hard, honest work and perseverance. While most of what makes us artists comes from our genes and our environment, what we do with it is up to us. The energy, concentration and dedication to become a good artist is easily equivalent to what it takes to be a research chemist, a theoretical physicist or a neurosurgeon. If you're not utterly consumed by your passion to pursue art, you should do something else—it probably pays better! If it doesn't hurt, you just aren't doing it right.

Item #4: Maybe you were drawn to art in the first place because you have a poor self-image and this was the one way in which you were most successful at expressing yourself. Understand that about yourself and embrace it. Art is about the ceaseless quest for the perfect vision. If you feel you've achieved that already, you have an immense problem with self-delusion and ought to be far more insecure than you are. For me, the last thirty years have been a constant, brutalizing confrontation with my inadequacies. I'm happy in a way to be so flawed and forever obsessed with the quest for greater perfection. As good as you are, or imagine yourself to be, never start believing you couldn't be better—or that someone else, somewhere, isn't already! Having low self-esteem in itself isn't a problem; surrendering to it is.

Item, the last (there are easily 500 of these little pointers that I feel are of equal importance, so we'll let this be the end of it): Fantastic literature is an enterprise with a mission and its mission is about our survival as a species and about utilizing our potential. Early in the twentieth century physicists such as Niels Bohr and Werner Heisenberg, confronted by the puzzling nature of the subatomic universe and its apparent immunity to the principles that govern larger bodies, reasoned that the observer of an object on the subatomic level has a direct influence on the nature of the object being observed. Bohr further advanced the idea that subatomic matter does not exist independently of our ability to observe it, or if it does, its indeterminate nature makes it pointless to consider its characteristics and properties, since those factors are decided by the particular attributes we choose to look at. The implications of this idea have, over time, brought together the elements of mind and matter in the fields of science and in the arts to produce a broader understanding of the nature of the universe.

In more recent times, Dr. Montague Ullman (founder of the Dream Laboratory at the Maimonides Medical Center) and other researchers have suggested that some aspects of the "free" associations we make when we're asleep and dreaming, and of our creative processes when we're awake and hard at work, are analogous to the quantum wave of subatomic physics. Whatever that means (and I'm told the implications of it are potentially staggering), recent studies on the nature of the human mind have strongly hinted at the importance of dreaming and of fantasizing, not only for the sake of our individual well-being, but for the very survival of our species. Artists and storytellers, since the days that humans first gathered into tribes for their mutual protection, have been the dreamers, the idea makers and the trendsetters for the rest of civilization.

When the camera came into practical use in the middle of the last century, for instance, artists, who traditionally believed their main function was to create a precise visual record of the people and objects they painted, suddenly found that this new device could do nearly the same thing more quickly and economically. This recognition, while frightening at first, was ultimately liberating, for artists were suddenly free to experiment with color and form in applications that went beyond mere literal representation. Their paintings could effectively capture the mood of a particular place, or the inner character of a human subject, and were evocative in ways that extended beyond the qualities that the camera could record. And in these respects, this new art—what we now call Modern Art—created a more complete view of reality than could ever have been achieved through the limitations of both photography and pictorial academic realism.

Art does far more than just strive to produce pictures that look pretty. At its best it reminds us of the beauty of the world around us, or of the ugliness we can sometimes bring to it. It can reveal to us our dark side, but it can also show us the beauty that lies within us through visions that dwell in the heart and mind beyond a normal lifetime, surviving the passage of centuries and transcending the barriers of language and culture and race.

When I was a youngster I was drawn to science fiction because it showed me a universe full of wonder, in which virtually anything was possible and which was bounded only by the limits of my own imagination. Our culture seems at times to flounder, without focus or direction. By being the public dreamers for our species, we give life meaning beyond the mundane matters of work and responsibility. We keep a vision of a better world and a better life acute in the universal consciousness. We point to the infinite potentials that lie within us and to the limitless frontiers that lie among the stars, and all the while we remind ourselves that as good as it gets, it could always be better.

CYCLOPS IN B MINOR

Written by
Jayme Lynn Blaschke

Illustrated by
John Lock

About the Author

Jayme Lynn Blaschke has been seriously pursuing short story fiction for the past ten years, and has had two stories—"Project Timespan" and "The Dust"—appear in the British magazine Interzone. *In addition to various short stories, he is currently at work on two novels, tentatively titled* Maelstrom *and* Nexorcist.

He graduated from Texas A&M University in 1992 with a B.A. in journalism. He then worked for six years as a sports reporter, covering high-school sports, college football and minor league hockey. He currently works in the public affairs department of a large regional hospital.

While at Texas A&M, Jayme helped run AggieCon, the largest and oldest student-run science fiction and fantasy convention in the United States.

Charles de Lint has had a particularly strong influence on his writing, as have Lillian Stewart Carl and Steve Gould. Jayme's web site can be found at http://www.vvm.com/~caius.

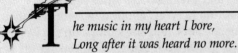

The music in my heart I bore,
Long after it was heard no more.
—William Wordsworth, from "The Solitary Reaper"

It's not easy, you know, hiking through the swamp, even when it's dry like it is now, on account of the spring drought. Gina, though, she don't give it no nevermind. She's been this way many a time before, or at least one way like it. She's gonna go this way many a time again. 'Course, that's just the way she is.

The backpack she's carrying, one of those green, army surplus things, it's damn near big as she is. No surprise, though. She's just barely five foot high—and that's on a good day. She's one of them perfect proportion people. Might as well be seven feet tall. Can't tell, 'less she's standing next to someone, that Gina Davis.

Yeah, Gina Davis. Like the movie actress. That's her name, for sure. God's honest truth. Not her fault, though. Used to be Gina Ceballos, and that suits her just fine. But then, these things, they're gonna happen.

She stops a minute, looks for landmarks. There ain't none. Never is. Nothing ever looks familiar out here, yet she always manages to find her way. Funny that.

It's hot out, don't you know, and she's sweating something awful. Mosquitos buzzing pretty bad too. She swats one on her arm, leaving a bloody splatter on cinnamon skin. She wrinkles her nose and wipes at the blood. Little nose, she has. Like a squirrel's. Little eyes, too. Dark, and set wide apart in a baby-doll face. She's a real cutie, all right. Looks closer to thirteen than thirty, but that's what she is.

There's the shack. She catches sight of the tin roof, rusty and all, and breathes this little sigh. Relief. She always gets a little nervous about now, worried about being lost. But she ain't, and she stomps up the warped plywood steps to the front porch, mud flaking off her boots and jeans. Yeah, the swamp looks dry, but then the swamp's funny that way.

A chain of catfish dangle from the overhang. Four thirty-pounders or so, from the look of it. They're dripping on the porch, *plop, plop*.

Gina knocks on the door, all covered up with tar paper. The Cyclops opens it, 'cause that's who lives here. He's nine foot three, one big green eye in the middle of his forehead. He's got a head of yellow hair and beard, and is barefoot. He's got this red bandanna sticking out of his bib overalls.

"Gina," he says, voice all rumbly and stopped-up sounding, 'cause his skull's built different from normal folks, and he got bad sinus problems, you know. "C-Come in! Come in! I was about to s-start d-dinner. Corn bread and c-catfish." He stutters, too. Just a little.

She smiles, teeth all pretty and white. The inside's pretty much like the out. Tar paper stapled to the walls, the ceiling bare rafters. There's a bunch of one-by-sixes nailed up to the wall to make shelves, all cluttered up with cans and stuff. Some got books on them. Old paperbacks, yellow and mildewy. Herman Melville. Victor Hugo. Homer. No fluff reader, this Daniel. In one corner there's these two cots stuck end-to-end. The

Illustrated by John Lock

other, there's this big, old wood-burning stove, what was fancy stuff ninety years ago.

"Thanks for the offer, Daniel, but I can't stay. Todd's expecting me home. I only dropped in for a little bit."

"Oh," he says, disappointed. There's this little diamond ring on her left hand that says she's someone else's. Daniel don't make passes at married women. That ain't right. "You d-don't come around enough anymore. We're losing t-touch."

"Well, I'm sorry, Daniel," she says, uncomfortable-like. "I try my best. You know you're my best friend. I've just had a lot of personal things going on lately."

"Oh," he says. Personal stuff ain't none of his business, but he can guess.

"Oh, quit worrying about me, " Gina says, reaching up on her tiptoes to slug him in the arm. "I got something for you." She unslings her pack. She pulls out some D-size batteries for his radio. She always brings those. Then she pulls out this box, two foot long, one wide. Flattish. Red- and blue-striped paper. She shoves it at him.

"F-For me? But, but I didn't g-get you anything," he says, blushing all red.

"You're not supposed to, you goof. It's your birthday present. Open it."

"B-But . . . I don't *have* a birthday."

"Of course you do. Everyone does. We just don't know when yours is. So today's it. Come on, open up."

Super-careful, Daniel is, peeling off the paper, prying open the cardboard flaps on the end. He looks in, scrunching up his brow, all puzzled. He slides it out, and that Daniel don't know what to make of it. It looks like this skinny wooden triangle, two foot long, with all these pegs nailed in the long sides, strung down to the short side. In the middle, there's this hole, and a pretty green and purple thistle cutout over the top of it. There's this curved wooden bow, too. It falls out of the box onto the floor, and Daniel grabs it up, quick.

"It's a bowed psaltery," Gina says, excited. Her eyes, they twinkle. "There's an instruction book in the box, too. Now you can play music."

"But my fingers . . ." He flexes them, big meaty things, each bigger than Gina's wrist.

She shakes her head. "There's no fingering with this. I guarantee you can play this psaltery." She takes his arms, shows him how to hold it across his lap. Gina does it from the side, 'cause he's too big to do it from behind.

He smells her, all sweet and sweaty, and has to concentrate to keep his mind on the psaltery. She takes his hand, and draws the bow across the lowest string. A sweet note sings out, pure, like a fiddle, or *violin* if you're city folk. Daniel, oh boy, do Daniel's eye get real big then. And that's really something, considering it about as big as a baseball, normally.

"It's a t-triangle fiddle. I can p-play this!" he says, mouth all hanging open like a hound dog. "I can play this!" He snatches her up in a big old bear hug, Gina's boots dangling about four foot off the ground.

"I'm glad you like it," she laughs. He sets her back.

"Good gosh. G-Good gosh. I can play m-music." He paws the instruction book out of the box, burying his face in it. "I c-can see music, you know. Other people only h-hear it, but I see it. Up here." Daniel taps his head with one of those meaty fingers.

"I know. You've told me. I'm glad you like it, but Daniel," she takes his hand, getting serious, "I've seen others get this excited. It doesn't come easy. Music takes a lot of hard work. Practice every day. You won't be able to play Beethoven in a day. Not in a year. Don't be discouraged. It takes time."

He grins at her, big and goofy. If you ain't never seen a Cyclops grin, well, there just ain't no straight way to describe it. "Maybe . . . maybe when I g-get g-good enough, we could play together? Something easy?"

It's like a shadow goes over her face. She's still smiling, but it's like he reminded her of something bad. Sad. She looks at her watch. "That sounds like an idea, Daniel. I've got to get going now. You practice on that, and I promise the next time I come out here, I'll give you a real lesson."

"So, when's that going to be?"

"I don't know, Daniel." She looks even sadder. "I wish I did."

•••

Gina coaxes her VW bug up into the gravel driveway. Transmission's about to go. Her man's Ford pickup is already there. She don't look at it. She grabs an armload of groceries from the passenger seat—paper, 'cause they was out of plastic—and kicks the bug's door shut.

Her house is big and white, but needs a new coat of paint. New roof, too. Todd says he's going to get around to it, but ain't. Least not yet.

She goes in, sets the grocery bags on the kitchen table. Todd, he's down the hall. Bathroom door open, drawers down around his ankles, he's peeing. Real loud. He's got a tattoo of a naked lady on his right shoulder, skull and rose on his left. Both turning green and smearing. "That you, Gina?" he hollers.

Gina, she grunts something, and keeps putting away the groceries. Milk. Macaroni. Eggs. Ground meat. Bread.

Todd, he comes strolling in wearing a dirty old tee shirt and boxers, his thing flopping out of the pee-hole. That Todd, he mighty proud of his thing. Want to show it to as many women as he can. "You remember to get me my Budweiser?"

"There wasn't enough money," she answers, not looking up. Green beans. Hominy.

"God damn. Shit." Todd, he's not happy. "I said *shit*, Gina. What am I going to do with you? I give you one simple thing to do, and you can't even do that right."

"There wasn't enough money, Todd. I had to buy us food."

"Well, you tell me where the hell all this money's going to. I always had enough before I married you. You think you got to work, fine, but that don't give you leave to go off blowing it all the time."

Gina, she gives him a tired look. They done gone through this a million time before. He goes on bitching about her working, but they ain't never seen a dime from his paycheck—not that they ever gonna get rich with him sacking gravel at the gravel pits. Too much booze and cards and craps on his part. But you know he don't see it that way.

"Don't you look at me that way, woman. I know what you're thinking. Don't think I don't." Todd, he gets worked up, easy. He's that kind of fellow. That little greasy mustache that he think looks all good and cool scrunches up, wrinkly-like. "I bust my ass out there in the hot sun all day. Don't you dare say I don't deserve a night out every so often."

"No, dear. I wasn't going to say that." She looks at him, trying to remind herself how much she loves him. It sure ain't his looks. He about as butt-ugly as they come. Oh yeah.

"I didn't think you were." He pushes past her, grabs up a six-pack of Bud out of the fridge. Only there's just four left. It dangles from his fingers by the plastic rings.

Her heart, now, it can still get fluttery looking at him, just the way it did in high school when she decided she wanted him. He was cool then. Always had the snappy line. Varsity receiver. More cheerleaders wanted him than the quarterback. Prom night, oh, that Todd, he come up with a case of Milwaukee's Best and talked her into skipping the dance. They spent the night in the back of his truck on a levee in the swamp. She couldn't sit for a week after that, what with all the mosquito bites, you know. But she was happy. She knew she'd done got him hooked. He was still there in Cottonwood when she got out of college, waiting on her. Got drunk one night, and puked in her living room. Then asked her to marry him. Yeah, Todd's the old smoothie.

He shuffles out the kitchen and flops down on the couch in the living room. There's a mess of beer stains, and worse, all over the rug. They've even got some little mouse turds in the corner. Gina, she sweeps them up, but they're back the next day. On the other wall they've got a piano. Big, upright one. Hundred years old. Still sounds good. Got holes on the front though, from when Todd came home drunk and tried playing darts on it.

Todd, he plays with his thing a few minutes, then tucks it back in his shorts. He clicks on the remote, which is broke and only sets the TV on channel three. It don't matter, though, 'cause the cable's done been cut off, and channel three's the only one they can get. He cusses the cable company for cutting them off, then cusses Gina for not paying the bill. Gina, though, she gave him the money to pay the bill. He bet Donny Miles down at Poor Boy's, though, that he could get this fat blonde to show him her tits by midnight. Old Todd lost. He don't remember that, though.

"We need to get rid of that damn old piano," he says sudden-like, then takes a big swallow of beer.

Gina, she freezes up real quick at that. Her face, looking all tired, gets stony all of the sudden. "What did you say?" she asks, coming into the living room.

"I said we ought to get rid of that piano. Takes up too damn much room. You don't never use it, anyway. Junk dealer over in Sheridan said he'd give me fifty bucks for it. Sure could use that money."

"We're not selling the piano."

"It ain't doing us no good now."

"I only play it when you're not here." Gina, her voice is all icy. "You told me you don't like me to play when you're here."

"That's 'cause you can't play worth shit."

"We're not selling the piano. You hear me, Todd? Don't you even think about it."

"Yeah, fine. Whatever." Todd, he glares at Gina. When she turns back into the kitchen, he shakes his thing at her. That Todd.

●●●

Gina, she's hiking through the swamp again. It done rained the other day, finally, don't you know, so it's all wet everywhere. Nothing looks familiar, for sure.

Everything's looking powerful green. Ferns and bushes and weeds, all around the big puddles and pools. Water's still dripping from big, hairy Spanish mosses hanging off the post oaks. It looks pretty much like the first time she done gone out into the swamp, the time she went and found old Daniel.

That'd be two years ago, give or take. Some weird-sounding noise woke her up, 'cause she'd gone to bed early on account it was Thursday and she had school the next day. Todd, he weren't there, you know, 'cause it was payday, and he had to go out to Poor Boy's and drink up his check, see?

Anyway, this noise goes and wakes Gina up, and she gets all nervous, since it's already one o'clock in the a.m. So she sneaks all careful to the living room, where the noise is coming from. There's old Todd, don't you know. Drunk as the skunk. He's got Lucy Lopez on the couch, skirt hitched up, legs in the air. Todd, he's going after her something fierce, and don't you know he's having the time of his life. Todd, he goes for them Mexican girls. Yeah, and with his wife just down the hall.

Now Gina, maybe she suspected on him before, maybe not. She's sure a smart one, so you gotta think, yeah, she knows. This, though, this is too much for her to take. She scoots out the back door and drives that little bug of hers out to the swamp. Her papa, he used to take her out there fishing before he died, see? To Gina, it's like her happy place. So she parks on this levee, and starts walking. She don't know where she's going. She don't care. She's too busy crying. She tells herself she don't love Todd no more, for sure. She can't leave him, though. She Catholic, see. Her mama and papa, they teach her good. Marriage is forever, for her.

So Gina, all crying, she starts thinking she's lost. Then she hears this music, far off. She follows it, and before long she can make it out, you know? It's that Fogerty boy, and he's singing "Born on the Bayou." Funny that. It's coming from the radio sitting on Daniel's porch. He's up laying on the roof, just a-staring at the moon.

There you go.

Gina, now, she hears music again. This time it ain't Fogerty. It ain't no radio, either. Gina, she's real curious, so she runs up to the shack and throws open the door. That Gina, she get herself a real surprise.

There sits Daniel on his cot, fiddling away at his triangle fiddle. And the music he's making, it's pretty. Mighty pretty. He's playing like some kind of old pro.

But that's only half the surprise. The other half, that'd be the man sitting across from him. That guy, he done struck Gina as some kind of Indian. Or Native American. Whatever you want to call it—don't make him no never-mind. This guy, his skin's red. You know, really red. Rust-like. His hair, black, you know, it's braided in these long braids with feathers and coins and little woven wool dolls mixed in. He's got this big old hump on his back, like he's hiding a basketball, or something. His tee shirt, jeans and boots, they all splattered with mud, just like Gina. And he's playing this flute, one of those big cedarwood things, with the end carved out to look like some bird or hawk. Or something. His fingers, they're like old dried-up beef jerky, and his fingernails, they're these bony shells capping the fingertips.

Anyway, they're both playing real pretty, this kind of melody that ain't really a melody, but you can only tell that if you concentrate, see? Anyway, they both stop when Gina, she busts in.

"G-Gina," Daniel says, jumping up. "D-Did you hear? Did you hear me playing?"

She nods, not taking her eyes off the other guy. He looks back at her, grinning. Uh-oh looking. Wanting to find some kind of trouble to get into.

"Oh," says Daniel. "M-My manners. Gina, this is Kokopelli. He's a friend of mine. Not like you, b-but he's a friend."

Gina, she nods again. His eyes, they're hot and steamy. This guy's up to no good, for sure. "Nice to meet you, Mr. Kokopelli. I'm Gina. Gina Davis." She holds out her hand.

Now Kokopelli, he's a scoundrel. He reaches out for her hand, all innocent-like, but he pretends to slip, and his hand jerks out to touch her boob. Gina, though, she seen this coming in his eyes, and she jumps back, slapping his hand away.

"Ow. You hurt me," Kokopelli says, then he falls onto the floor, laughing like he just made some kind of super-funny joke.

"Koko, stop," Daniel says. His face, it turns all bright red, so he and Kokopelli, they look like twins. Excepting for the eye, of course. "Gina's a g-good friend. Be nice a-around her. She's n-not like th-that."

Kokopelli, he stops laughing a minute, and he gives Gina this wink, just a-shaking his head at Daniel. "How you know what she's like? You ever try and find out for yourself?"

Daniel, if anything, he turns redder. He's about to die of embarrassment, for sure. "Koko, she's *married*."

"Married girls, now they're the best kind," Kokopelli goes and says, giving Gina another wink. "At least, those whose husbands are no-good skirt chasers. They go and spend themselves on other sweet things, and they ain't got nothing good left for their own. Isn't that not so, Gina?"

Gina, she opens her mouth, then shuts it again, looking like some kind of stranded fish. Daniel, he just sits back there making some strangling noises.

Kokopelli, he looks at Gina real close, then shrugs his shoulders. "Aw, she doesn't look like she's in the mood. Just my luck. Well, maybe next time, you think?"

Gina, she's still sort of befuddled by this guy, so she gives this little half-nod. That gets Kokopelli smiling. Oh yeah, he's sure happy now.

"I knew it," he says laughing, then grabs up his flute again. "Ready to go? You lead, or me?" This he says to Daniel.

"What? You're playing again, just like that?" Gina, she's real confused now. That Kokopelli, he's mighty tough to keep up with.

"Yes. Why shouldn't we? Since you don't want to do anything more interesting"—he goes and laughs when Daniel, he grimaces—"we play. Every second we waste, that's just one more song that goes by, unplayed. You should know that. You going to play?"

"I—I haven't brought an instrument."

Kokopelli, he shakes his head, making this *tsk-tsk* sound. "How can you go anywhere not ready to make music? I tell you, I've traveled all over, longer than I can remember, and I've never been without my flute. Or at least a drum. How some people get along without never learning to play, I won't ever understand." He looks at her different this time, not sexy-like, but like she disappoints him somehow. Like he expects more from her, or something. "You listen, then. Me and old Daniel here are going to play. You tell us what you think."

Kokopelli, he don't give her no more room to talk. He sticks his flute up to his mouth, and he starts blowing. Daniel, too, he picks up his triangle fiddle and comes in following. Gina, she just sits herself right down there on the floor, leaning back up against the door frame.

Kokopelli, his flute music, it reaches out to her, and it wraps around her. Gina, she knows he's trying to seduce her again, this time with music. If she didn't know better, it might sometimes work. But Gina knows better. Old Kokopelli, he gives up on this real quick and he backs off. He had to give it just one more try, you know. On account of that's who he is.

Now the music, it's what Kokopelli really wants to play. It flows from his flute, a slow, lazy river of sound. Sad, in its own way, and maybe a little sleepy, but full of life. Lots of life, you'd be surprised. It slows time, because that kind of music can do that, and Gina, she closes her eyes. That music, it picks her up, and it carries her off. She could be in West Texas, maybe Arizona. Maybe someplace what never been. She feels the heat of the desert at sunset, the ground itself warming the air. There's this flapping in the air, around these desert flowers. But these flowers are on stalks way up above the ground. They're in clusters up there. Some kind of yucca plant, you know. This flapping, though, it's bats, you see. They're flapping around the flowers. Like butterflies. Or hummingbirds, only they ain't humming. Gina, she hears them. Smells the pollen, too, what they knock loose.

She hears Coyote far off, yipping his fool head off like there ain't no tomorrow. She hears the little kangaroo rats hopping out onto the sand. A snake slide across the rock—those scales, they scrape real soft, see?

Gina, she sees all this, then sees something else, too. Daniel, that triangle fiddle of his, it's been going right along with the flute, drifting in between the notes, the little waves and currents and eddies in that music river. Now Daniel, he takes over the flow, channels that river into the desert.

Flowers, they bloom real sudden, and them cactus, they grow into trees. Daniel, though, he don't stop there. No sir. Them trees keep growing, sweeping up higher and higher, until they're not no trees no more. They look like polished marble, but they not, 'cause this stuff is living stuff. You just know stuff like that. These things, they weave themselves together, all the time they're throwing off the most wildest sparks you ever seen. They go flashing in all the colors that ever was, and in some that never was. Maybe they're colors only Daniel can see with that one eye of his.

Those colors, they flash brighter and brighter, and Gina, she's close to one of them marble tree things, and she sees these long, smooth grooves in it. She settles into it, see, just sliding along, and the walls of it, they rise up above her, close over her head. It's real dark now, and Gina, she don't know when she stops sliding. All she knows is that there are stars around her now. You know, *stars*. Billions of them. Trillions. Maybe more. Yeah, lots more. Gina, she knows she's at the center of it all.

Gina opens up her eyes. "That was beautiful. Jesus, that was so very beautiful. Daniel, you . . . you were amazing."

Daniel, he gets all embarrassed again, and it don't look like that Cyclops is ever going to be nothing but red ever again.

"Mister Kokopelli, I think I owe you an apology," Gina says. You know when Gina is impressed, and boy, is the girl impressed. "I don't know how you did it, but thank you for teaching Daniel to play that way. I never could've done it."

"Bah," Kokopelli goes, wrinkling up his nose. "I didn't teach him nothing. I'm not a teacher. No patience. No, everything you heard from Daniel came from in here." He leans over and thumps Daniel in the chest. "This boy got the music in him. Deep inside him. He just let it out is all."

"That's impossible, unless Daniel's some kind of savant. I've taught for close to seven years—"

"Impossible, my left nut. You heard him. You *heard* him. You could do the same thing, if you wanted. Yeah, there's the music inside you, all right. You just never let it out. Not right to keep something bottled up like that."

"You're wrong. I play almost every—" Gina, her mouth falls open. See, she just notices the window, and it's dark out. It's night, and it was just three-thirty or so when she got there. "Oh, shit. How long have I been sitting here?" She feels her butt's asleep now, and her legs, they're all stiff.

Kokopelli shrugs. "What's it matter? You heard the music. That's all that counts."

"I'll tell you what it matters—Todd's going to have a cow, that's what it matters." She scrambles up to her feet. "Sorry, Daniel, but I've got to run."

"It's okay, Gina. Th-Thanks for listening. I a-appreciate the compliments."

"I really enjoyed it, Daniel, but Todd's going to be *furious*."

"You ever think a man that gets mad at you about music might not be the man for you?" Kokopelli says, pretending to examine the little rawhide ties on his flute. "How many songs have you not played because of him?"

Gina, then, she just freezes half out the door, and she gives Kokopelli the absolute *meanest* stare there ever was. Old Kokopelli, he's sure lucky he not made of wood, 'cause he'd done be catching fire, you know. So Gina, then, she slams the door, and she's gone. Kokopelli, he don't look after her. He just turns to Daniel, and says, "Ready to go again?"

Oh, that Kokopelli.

• • •

"Thank you for seeing me, Father Michael," Gina says. She's got this nervous look about her, which is not too normal for her.

"Any time, Gina. You know you're always welcome to come by with your problems," Father Michael answers. Now, Father Michael, he's sure not everybody's idea of a priest. First of all, he's big. Real big. Could of been one of those wrestlers on TV, if he'd only wanted. Works out a lot. He also keeps his hair cut short to this little black stubble on the top of his head, and he's got this mustache and goatee that makes him look like some biker dude. Which really ain't too far from the truth, since he's got an old Harley he tinkers with and takes out riding on the weekends when he's not being a priest. He's wearing this raggedy old pair of jeans, and this white pullover shirt, with a little golden fish symbol stitched over the breast.

Gina, she's sitting on a frayed wicker chair in his tiny living room, and there he is, sitting on the couch not an arm's reach off. They both got tall glasses of ice tea sitting between them, just sweating away, because the church, it can't afford to run the air conditioner. She shifts in her seat. She wants to run away more than anything. Father Michael, he's too close. The walls are too close. She feels trapped. But Gina, she realizes that's how she always feels.

"It's my marriage. It's . . . in trouble," she says, finally, and lets out a big breath. She ain't never said it before, at least not to anyone but Todd, and he don't count, 'cause he either laughs at her or cusses her out.

Father Michael just closes his eyes and clasps his hands. He's been afraid of this. Every time he sees Gina, he's afraid this is coming up. And he just don't know what to say. He knows all about Todd. There ain't no

way he couldn't know—not in a town as small as
Cottonwood. He wants to tell her to leave that sorry no-
good, but he can't, because he's a priest, see? That's not
allowed. So he finally just decides to play it safe, and
says, "I see."

"I've tried to be a good wife. I've really tried, but
Todd . . . nothing I ever do seems to satisfy him.
Nothing." Gina, she's surprised. It's coming easier now,
like the dam done finally burst, and all the bad stuff
built up behind it comes pouring through. "We've been
married five years, but . . . he's a stranger to me. He used
to bring me flowers, and tell me how much he loved me,
how beautiful I was. He doesn't do that anymore.
That's—Father, am *I* wrong? Am I being selfish,
worrying what he does *for me?*"

"No, Gina. Don't second-guess yourself. Talk to me
first, and we'll sort out what's what later."

"Well, okay. If you're sure. It's just that I don't want
you to think I don't love him. Because I don't. No, wait,
I didn't say that. I mean I did, but I didn't mean it. I
mean . . . oh, shit."

Father Michael smiles at her. Sympathetic, see? "It's
all right, Gina. Why don't you calm down and start
over."

Gina, she nods, takes a big swallow of tea. "He's still
my husband. I still love him, but when he drinks . . .
when he drinks he's different. He changes. I mean, he
drank in high school, but it made him exciting then.
Now he just gets mean."

Father Michael's eyes, they get real big.

"No, no, no," Gina says quick, reaching out to put a
hand on his shoulder. "Not like that. He doesn't hit me,
if that's what you think. But—you promise to keep this
confidential? Todd, he yells at me. And sleeps around."

FREE

Send in this card and you'll receive a FREE POSTER while supplies last. No order required for this Special Offer! Mail your card today!

☐ Please send me a FREE poster.

☐ Please send me information about other books by L. Ron Hubbard.

ORDERS SHIPPED WITHIN 24 HRS OF RECEIPT

NEW RELEASE!

___ Ai! Pedrito! When Intelligence Goes Wrong hardcover	$25.00	___
___ Ai! Pedrito! When Intelligence Goes Wrong audio	$25.00	___

SCIENCE FICTION/FANTASY:

___ Battlefield Earth paperback	$7.99	___
___ Battlefield Earth audio	$29.95	___
MISSION EARTH® series (10 volumes)		
___ paperbacks (specify volumes:_____)(each) $5.99		___
___ audio (specify volumes:_____)(each) $15.95		___
___ Final Blackout paperback	$6.99	___
___ Final Blackout audio **SPECIAL**	$11.95	___
___ Fear paperback	$6.99	___
___ Fear audio **SPECIAL**	$9.95	___
___ Slaves of Sleep & The Masters of Sleep hardcover	$19.95	___
___ Slaves of Sleep & The Masters of Sleep audio	$19.95	___
___ Typewriter in the Sky hardcover (Fantasy)	$16.95	___
___ Typewriter in the Sky audio	$16.95	___
___ Ole Doc Methuselah hardcover	$18.95	___
___ Ole Doc Methuselah audio	$24.95	___

___ L. RON HUBBARD PRESENTS WRITERS OF THE FUTURE® Volumes: (paperback)

☐ Vol IV $4.95 ☐ Vol V $4.95 ☐ Vol IX $5.99
☐ Vol X $6.99 ☐ Vol XI $6.99 ☐ Vol XII $6.99
☐ Vol XIII $6.99 ___

CHECK AS APPLICABLE:

TAX*: ___

TOTAL: ___

☐ Check/Money Order enclosed.
(Use an envelope please)

☐ American Express ☐ Visa ☐ MasterCard ☐ Discover

★ California residents add 8.25% sales tax.

Card#:_____

Exp. Date:_____Signature:_____

Credit Card Billing Address Zip Code :_____

NAME:_____

ADDRESS:_____

CITY:_____ STATE:_____ ZIP:_____

PHONE#:_____

Call us now with your Order 1-800-722-1733
http://www.bridgepub.com

Name: _____

Address: _____

City: _____ State: _____ Zip: _____

Gina pulls back, glancing back and forth like she's done something wrong. She chews her bottom lip. Father Michael, he don't say nothing. He just sits there with a neutral look on his face, wondering how any man in his right mind could treat such a good woman so wrong.

"I don't know how long it's been going on. No, that's a lie. Back in high school, he and Brenda . . . Well, I guess I let it happen. I thought, you know, he'd settle down once we were married, right? And he did, sort of. But when he starts drinking, he doesn't think. He doesn't remember things," she says, voice wavering. "He's drinking more and more. Lord knows how many women he's been with. What if he gives me some kind of disease?"

So what do you say to something like that, Father Michael, he wonders. Anything he says, it's going to sound real stupid. "And have you discussed these concerns with him? Counseling? He has a problem, obviously." Yeah, real stupid.

"Discuss? According to him, there's nothing to discuss. He swears he's never done anything. I even caught him once. *In the act.* He made up some stupid story about how her legs'd cramped up and he was just being a good Samaritan. Can you believe that? I could smell the liquor across the room. Maybe he really doesn't remember. I don't know, but I can't keep taking it." Gina, she's really cooking now. She's getting pretty mad, but it feels good. "All Todd ever does is complain. Me, the house, our money, his beer. He complains all the time about my music. Father Michael, I don't even play the piano when he's home, and he still fusses about it."

Gina, she's so wound up, she stands and starts pacing the floor. "My music, and my job. He wants me to quit my job! He's getting worse and worse about it. How can I do that? We can't survive as it is, now. He blows his check the day he gets it, then he screams at me when the water gets cut off. He spends more money on his slut girlfriends than on his own marriage!" She stops pacing and looks down at her hands. She fidgets with her thumbs some. "The school superintendent, he called me out of class yesterday. He said Werner Schultz was retiring at the end of the year. He said they wanted me to have his job. Can you believe it? Me, band director at the high school. Do you know what that would mean to me? No more second-graders singing *Robin laid an egg* during 'Jingle Bells.' No more plastic recorders. No more sixth-graders hammering drums and blaring trombones, just to see who can be loudest. I could direct a real band for once. Make real music."

"So what are you waiting for? Tell them yes," Father Michael says.

Gina, she laughs, real bitter. "Yeah. Right. Todd would scream bloody murder. He'd never stand for his wife making more than him. All he wants is for me to stay home and make—"

"Make? Make what, Gina?"

"Make babies," she says, real soft-like.

"Is that a problem?" Michael asks gently.

Gina nods. Oh, this sure is a sore spot. 'Cause Gina, she wants babies, wants them bad. She even got pregnant, after about a year. It didn't last though. In the hospital, Todd, he started talking about trying again right away. Yeah, with Gina lying there, all cramped up with tubes sticking out of her. Gina, you won't be surprised, she wasn't ready for that, so she gets with her doctor and goes on the pill. Been ever since. Oh, she wants babies, sure enough, but the only time Todd touches her is when he's drunk. That's not the way she wants a baby to happen.

Poor thing, Father Michael, he thinks, guessing wrong, but close enough. But you know he can't say that out loud. "These are some very serious concerns," he says instead, because the church, it don't like birth control, so he just plays dumb. "It takes a lot of thought and prayer before committing yourself to bringing a new life into this world. If everyone showed as much thought as you, our families wouldn't be in such trouble."

"But Father Michael, I can't live like this anymore."

"Are you . . . leaving him?"

"Leave? I can't leave him. Todd can't take care of himself. The bills, his drinking . . . He wouldn't last a week. He wouldn't know where to start. He can't even put the damn toilet seat down, much less wash his clothes. If I left, he'd self-destruct. I can't do that to him. I can't let him do that to himself."

Poor Father Michael, this is what he was afraid of. He don't think anything he can tell her will be helpful, and anything helpful, he can't tell. "Marriages are not easy to maintain. It takes a lot of work, from all parties. God wants your marriage to work. He will help you through this difficult time. I can set aside some time each week for you to come in for counseling—"

"Todd will never agree to that."

Of course Father Michael knows this is probably true. That Todd, he don't even come to Sunday church. "Then you come. One person working to save a marriage has a better chance than none."

"But I've tried for *five years*." Gina, she's almost crying now. "It's only gotten worse."

"Gina, you're in a difficult situation. I'm not denying that. But your life isn't going to get any better until you stop feeling so sorry for yourself and start cleaning up the mess you've gotten into."

Gina reels back. Father Michael's words, they're like a slap across her face. She stares at him, in shock, you know.

"I'm not saying Todd's treating you right," Father Michael says, a little gentler. "He's wrong. But you're partly to blame. You've known what's happening, and you allowed it to happen. In that, you've done him a disservice. You've allowed him to hurt you, your marriage, and himself. Listening to you talk, I still don't know what you want. The church doesn't call down miracles from heaven to make bad situations better, Gina. You've got to understand that. God helps those who help themselves. Take control of your life, Gina. You're a strong person. I know it won't be easy, but you've got to."

Gina, she wipes her eyes and thanks Father Michael for seeing her, but she's got to go now and start fixing Todd his dinner, or he'll be mighty upset when he gets home and it ain't ready.

"You'll talk to him about counseling? He's a sick man. He needs help," Father Michael, he says, wondering if she's heard anything he's told her. "I do want to help you. Call me any time you need to talk."

"Yes, I'll ask him. But don't get your hopes up," she says, then she shuts the door behind her.

Father Michael, he watches her walk across the yard to her old bug. He can't help it. He has to get his hopes up. That's his job, you know.

• • •

It's a clarinet Gina's got in her pack the next time she visits Daniel. At school, they have a work day for the teachers, so she gets off after lunch and has the rest of the day to spend with Daniel.

"I was a-afraid you wouldn't come back after last t-time," Daniel says. He's sitting on his cot, and has that triangle fiddle on his lap. He's putting rosin on the bow, getting ready to play with Gina. "I'm s-sorry Koko got out of line. He's not like n-normal people." Daniel, he taps at his forehead.

"You goof. Of course I'm going to come back. It's not like *you* were pawing at me," Gina says, sitting in that old wicker chair. She checks the reed, and it's cracked, so she gets a new one.

There's no rush. Gina's feeling pretty confident now, after the big blow-up with Todd. She poured out his beer, and Todd, he weren't none too happy about that. Gina, though, she none too happy, either. She lays it on the line to Todd, and boy, does he get the look of surprise when she lays into him. Gina never really ripped him a new one like that, you know? So old Todd, he backs down. Says, sure, he'll go to counseling. Sure, he'll stop the drinking. Didn't have no idea she was so unhappy. That Todd, he done got plumb scared.

"Besides," Gina says to Daniel, "I can handle guys like him that come on like a herd of elephants. It's the sneaky ones that get me."

Daniel, he don't know how to answer to that, so he just nods.

"I've been really looking forward to playing with you. Or, rather, hearing you play again," she says, fingering her valves. "So tell me, how'd he teach you to play like that? I know the psaltery's easy, but I just barely got through 'Mary Had a Little Lamb' before I wrapped it up for you."

"He d-didn't teach me. He says he c-can't p-play it. Too c-complicated."

Gina raises her eyebrows.

"I taught myself. It took m-me a couple hours to get all the n-notes down. I practiced every d-day after that, like you told me to. Koko, he showed up j-just b-before you did. He said it was about time I'd started playing. He's stopped in before, b-but never s-stayed that long."

"So where's he from? What does a dirty old man like that do?"

"He plays music, mostly. At least, that's w-what he tells me. Claims he doesn't live a-anywhere. J-Just travels, playing his flute."

"Sounds like fun. So what are we going to play?"

"D-Do you know 'The Devil Went Down to Georgia'?"

"What? The Charlie Daniels song?" Gina shakes her head. "No, I don't. I'm more of a classical person. Especially not with a clarinet. I take it you do?"

Daniel smiles, nodding. "I listened to KKYX all week just to hear it. They don't p-play it much anymore."

"So quit teasing me. Let's hear it."

And Daniel, he puts that bow to the strings and takes out after it. He don't sing none, but it don't matter any. That triangle fiddle sings. He beats his fingers on the side for the drum-time in a couple of fiddle breaks he throws in for effect. When he gets to that part—you know, where the Devil plays—well, his hand, it *flies*, and it sounds like he's playing on some electronic gizmo. When the Johnny part comes up, he's really cooking. It's like every country fiddle-player that ever picked up a bow is playing right there, and old Charlie Daniels himself would've cried if he'd been there to hear it.

Gina, she just about falls off that wicker chair when Daniel finishes, she's clapping so hard. "My God, Daniel. That was fabulous!"

"Thanks, Gina. That means a lot, c-coming from you. I didn't think it was that good, because I only heard it once. If I c-could listen a few more t-times, I think I could get it perfect. It's harder for me to play songs that are already out there."

"So you're saying you're a jazz musician, then?" Gina grins at him. "Okay, Mister Improvisation, let's jam. Be gentle with me, please, if I can't keep up."

Daniel laughs, setting bow to string. He starts softly this time, almost like he's testing the waters. Not like before, when he jumped right in. He plays simple, slow, so Gina can join in. She puts that clarinet to her lips, and she slips right along with the notes in that lazy old song Daniel is making up.

All of a sudden, Daniel, he makes this unexpected turn. His music, it jumps up an octave, and goes staccato. Gina, she almost misses the change. If she'd been sleeping, she's sure wide awake now.

Daniel, he don't slow down none. The changes come faster now, sweeping in some big musical loop-de-loop, dipping down to the lower reaches of his instrument. And Daniel, he starts playing both sides of his triangle fiddle against the other, setting up his own melody, and the melody to counter it. He's playing as hard as he did with that Devil song, harder even, but this is all his own. It's all coming out through his heart, or his eye, on account he can see the music, but this music, it's downright personal.

Gina, she struggles real hard at first. The music he played the first time she heard him with Kokopelli, well, that was just kiddie stuff. She knows that now. What could old Daniel do with another week of practice, she starts to think, but can't, 'cause she's got to concentrate not to mess up his music.

And then it's not so hard no more. Those key changes, they come easier, and her fingers, they go when they're supposed to and she don't have to tell them. Instead of chasing around after Daniel, she's right there with him, laying down this pretty background that kind of dances around what Daniel's doing, see? Gina, she starts listening to what they're playing, and she just about falls out of that chair all over again.

She ain't *never* played music like this before. And she feels it waking up inside of her. It's something that's been there all along, she knows, but she ain't let it out in a long, long time.

Gina, she throws her clarinet down on the floor, and Daniel, he jumps at that. And Gina starts bawling. Bawling like she's a little baby. All that time in school where she worried about structure and technique, instead of the music itself. All those instruments she can play, but she never really played *any* of them. All that time she didn't play what she wanted to, *needed* to, just because someone like Todd or somebody didn't want her to. That part of her's been hurting all this time, just she wouldn't see it, like she wouldn't see what Todd's been up to. But now she knows. She knows how much she's hurting.

Poor Daniel, he don't know what to think. When she throws down that clarinet, he thinks he's done something wrong.

But he's heard her play. He knows she could feel it. He could *see* that music she was making, with that one big eye he's got. So he takes her in his arms, and he hugs her, cradling her, rocking her back and forth.

Gina, she keeps on crying. Her nose gets all runny and her eyes turn red and puffy. She cries so hard her throat goes all dry and scratchy, and she nearly coughs herself to death there for a time. Daniel, he strokes her hair.

"It was killing me," Gina says finally. "I didn't know. How could I not know? God, Daniel, how did I get myself into this?"

She looks up at him, her cheeks all wet and eyes big and scared, and she looks more like a little girl than ever. Daniel, he wants to keep her and protect her. He wants to kiss her. More than anything, that's what he wants to do. But Daniel, he's no dummy. He's got that big brain in that big head, see? He knows he not anyone's Prince Charming. He's the hunchback, and Gina, she's Esmeralda. He's that rock that gives her support when she needs it. She sure does need it now. And Daniel, he's okay with that. She gives him stuff, too. Maybe not what he wants, but what he needs. 'Cause Daniel, he don't got too many friends. Most folks that come around, they run off screaming when they catch sight of him. Gina, she didn't even jump.

"You didn't get yourself into anything," he says. "Don't blame yourself. Everything will work out. It always does. You're a good person. You'll make it through this. And I'll always be here for you." And that Daniel, he don't stutter once.

Gina, she looks at him a second with those puffy eyes of hers, then she throws her arms around that big old neck of his, and gives him a kiss on a hairy cheek. "Thank you, Daniel. Thank you."

"So, Gina. Are you g-going to be okay?"

"I think so. Todd and I had a talk. Everything's out in the open. For the first time in a long time, I think things are going to be better tomorrow than they were today."

And Daniel, at that he smiles.

•••

Todd's family, his relatives, they're all in the front yard when Gina pulls up. She has to park the bug in the street, 'cause the driveway's all full of cars and trucks.

Gina, she gets this sinking feeling. She gets out of her car, and right away she sees two of Todd's brothers. They're sitting on the front porch—on two of the good dining room chairs—with this big old beer keg between them. Six kids or so, grimy from head to toe, they're chasing each other around the yard, throwing rocks that hit each other almost as often as the house and cars. They're making a godawful racket too, don't you know. Todd's sister, or maybe cousin, she comes out of the house, all pregnant, just puffing away on a cigarette. And they all know how Gina hates smoke. She's got one of Gina's bedroom pillows under one arm. She drops it onto the front steps, then flops her own self down. Then she hollers at one of them kids to get her a beer.

Todd, he there in the middle of it, cooking something like hamburgers on their little rusty barbecue pit. He's smoking, too, balancing the cigarette with a big old mug of beer in one hand. And the pit, well, that smoke's just about everywhere.

"Where the hell you been, girl?" he hollers when he sees her. "There's people to feed. What am I ever going to do with you? Get on in there and help Momma with the potato salad. She don't need to be doing all that work herself. Bring us out some more plates, too. These burgers are just about done."

"Todd, what is going on here?" she asks. Her voice, it's cool and even.

"Well, what the hell's it look like? We're having a family barbecue." His eyes, they're kinda wet and glassy, and she smells the Jack underneath the beer.

"Todd, what about our talk? I thought we had an understanding."

He looks at her directly, taking a deliberate swallow. She pinches the bridge of her nose between thumb and forefinger.

"Where did you get the money? A couple of days ago, we didn't have enough to cover the water bill."

"Hell, Gina. I sold that old piano, like we talked about doing." He belches.

"You sold my piano?"

"Shit, yeah. That fellow from Sheridan, he offered fifty, like I told you before, but I talked him up to seventy-five. Hey, where you going, woman?"

Gina walks up the steps, into the house. She stands there in the living room, looking at the empty space where her piano used to be. Her beautiful piano. She starts for the phone, then stops. She knows this Sheridan man. He runs this antique store, and Gina knows he's got her piano marked up for fifteen hundred dollars, if not more. He's a bastard, all right. She ain't getting the piano back, at least not with no phone call.

Gina, she sits down on the couch, staring at her hands, staring at the floor. Her piano is gone. Her papa gave her that piano. He would sing, and she would play.

Her marriage is gone. That hits her. Todd, he ain't never going to change. He don't want to. Maybe it's her fault, for letting him go on so long. Maybe not. Don't matter no more. He'll only change when he wants to, and right now it's pretty plain to Gina he loves his bottle more than her.

Todd's mamma, this big fat lady with a mustache as big as Todd's, she finds Gina there. And she lays into Gina. She tells her how having a job just ain't right, according to the Bible, and that God's punishing her for that by keeping her from having babies. That and the stress of work. Either one, makes no difference. The point is, Gina ain't no good as a wife. Not for poor old Todd, who's just out there every day working himself to the bone with no thanks whatsoever.

Gina, she's hearing all this, but she don't listen, you know? See, there's this roach crawling in and out under the couch, and she just sits there watching it. Not one of those big ones, but a little one without wings. And Gina remembers a time where she wouldn't have any bugs at all in her house. And here, there's bugs everywhere. All the time.

She squashes it with her heel, and it makes this little black stain on the rug. One little stain to go along with all the others. And she looks at the couch. It's stained too. From what, she don't know. Maybe all the girls Todd brought home. And then, things get real clear for Gina.

She gets up and just walks off, right in the middle of Todd's mamma's speech. Boy, the look on that fat lady's face, it's truly something!

See, Gina done got it all figured out. She's been playing by the rules. Everybody's been making up rules for her to follow, and she's been following them. Where there weren't rules already, she'd make some up. Hiding behind them. Trouble is, nobody else's been following those rules. They been doing what they please, and mostly doing it to her.

Not no more. No sirree. From now on Gina makes her own rules, and rule number one is she ain't going to let anyone keep hurting her like Todd's been doing. Rule two is that no one's going to keep her from her music. And rule three . . . well, that Gina, her rule three is that she won't be like these people that break the rules on her.

Todd, he's screaming at her something awful as she gets in her car, but she don't hear him no more. His words, they stopped hurting.

That air-cooled VW engine, it turns over *rat-a-tat-tat*. She pulls out into the street and leaves Todd and everything else behind her.

She's driving to the courthouse, she thinks. She's not quite sure. Maybe she'll figure out how to file for divorce. She feels guilty at that, like she's giving up. She'll talk to Father Michael later.

He'll understand, she hopes. Then she'll call the superintendent, and take that band director job.

And after that? Who knows. Maybe she'll change her name back to Ceballos. That would be nice. Get her piano back. Oh, yes.

She smiles, thinking how soon Todd'll get evicted to the street, maybe end up in jail. She feels guilty at that, too, a little. But she don't want to take care of him no more. She really don't know why she ever did.

The only thing she knows for sure, that Gina, is that she's going back out to the swamp, to Daniel's shack.

They make beautiful music together, don't you know.

BROKEN MIRROR

Written by
David Masters

Illustrated by
John Philo

About the Author

David Masters was born under an assumed name and raised in the small town of Bluewater Village, New Mexico. It was a town surrounded by sagebrush, canyons and a whole lot of nothing—but it proved to be fertile ground for the imagination.

Through a book-by-mail library program, he learned to love science fiction even before he knew what it was.

David graduated from Brigham Young University with a degree in statistics/computer science as his major and English as his minor. He is currently working on a Master's Degree in communications while he runs his own software firm, providing academic software for schools.

And now, David is also an author.

About the Illustrator

John Philo was born in Anchorage, Alaska, and moved to Michigan as a child. From there, he became a traveling salesman and eventually joined the army. It wasn't until he was twenty-seven that he realized that he wanted to do something with his artistic talent.

John is self-taught as an artist. He enjoys doing portraits, but is currently studying how to tell a story through his illustration.

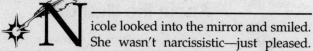icole looked into the mirror and smiled. She wasn't narcissistic—just pleased.

She closed her eyes and splashed two handfuls of water. The droplets slid away. Off of her eyebrows. Down her cheek to her chin. With that one little bead hanging on the tip of her nose. She shook her face and the bead dropped into the sink.

She smiled again, emphasizing her smile lines. Which is, of course, what they were. Not wrinkles. Just a small echo of the laughs that she'd had over the years. The grinning face in the mirror agreed with her. She was still attractive. Not bad for forty-something.

She stretched to take the kinks out. She waited for the satisfying pops. One. Two. She twisted her neck. There, that got it. Ah, to wake up in the morning to . . .

And then she saw him. Over her left shoulder, back in the bedroom. From the reflection, she could see that he had his back to her. Without taking her eyes off of him, her hand searched the countertop, closing around the first object that felt right. The grip of the curling iron felt natural, at least. It gave her the confidence she needed to speak.

"Hello."

The word echoed in the small bathroom. The man took no notice. He bent down a little, then straightened up.

"Hello!" Nicole repeated firmly. "I see you."

As if to mock her, the reflection disappeared for a moment. Then the man reappeared, back still towards her. He bent again, and straightened. He was making her bed!

"Look, mister, I don't know who you are or what you think you're doing here . . ."

The man started to turn around.

"But I'll have you know that I . . ."

She spun around and stood face to face with . . . nobody. He just wasn't there anymore.

Nicole stepped through her walk-through closet and into the bedroom. Curtains still closed. Lamp turned on. Bed still unmade. And no man.

The bedroom door was closed; the one that always creaked when you opened it. He couldn't have left that way. She slipped quietly up to the bed, then dropped to her knees. In a flash, she peered under the bed, straight into the eyes of . . . nobody.

Nicole giggled nervously. Whether at her fear of looking under the bed, or her courage in actually doing it, she wasn't sure. She stood and looked around. The room was large, but not *that* big. Not big enough to hold an extra man.

She peeked into the laundry basket. Nobody there. Nicole walked to her dresser and carefully opened a drawer. Then her eyes caught her reflection in the dresser mirror—boldly looking into her sock drawer, a curling iron clenched in her upraised hand, the cord dragging helplessly behind. She had to laugh.

Nicole walked back to the bathroom to finish her morning routine. Just in case, she stood on tiptoes and looked over her reflection's shoulder. Nobody else was there. Just a grinning young woman (much younger than her forty-something years) whose mind was playing tricks on her.

She tried not to let that bother her. Stuff like that happens on occasion. It was imagination, not senility. *If* it had really happened anyway. It's not like she had really seen anything. Probably just a blur. A shadow. A cloud that had passed by outside, and she turned it into a man. She had been listening to her mother for too long.

Nicole was *not* an old maid. She just didn't have a husband. It was her own choice. And her mind had no right to sneak in suggestions like that. Besides, she had to get ready to go to work. She didn't have time to worry about little things. She was too busy.

•••

"So, dear, are you seeing anyone?" Nicole's mother asked over the phone.

"Well, Mother," Nicole began, "I don't exactly think you could call it that. . . ."

"Oh, I'm so happy for you, dear. Is it that John fellow? John was such a nice man. Not that I didn't like Tom, of course. Or should I call him Thomas? He had such a nice smile. Either John or Thomas. Either one. Or maybe it's someone new. Oh, I do hope that's it. John really wasn't right for you. And Thomas . . . well, you know, a mother can sort of sense these things. I bet it's that nice man from the company social. What was his name again?"

"No, Mother, its nothing like that. It's nobody."

"But I thought you just said . . ."

"I know. It—it's nothing. Just forget I said anything."

"Oh. I'm sorry. . . . Did I say something wrong?"

"No, Mother. It's not something you said."

"Then what is it, darling? You know how I worry about you. All alone in that big house. Maybe you should come up and visit us more often."

"No, Mother. Everything is fine. I'll . . . I'll see you next Sunday for dinner. I have to go now."

"Are you sure you can't come *this* Sunday? Your father would love to see you."

"No, next Sunday will be fine. I really have to go now."

"Well, okay. Will you be bringing someone? It's not any trouble. I could just set an extra plate on. We always have enough food. And we'd love to meet him. I mean, not that we would bother him, or anything. You don't have to worry about me, dear. But still, I'm sure your father would enjoy talking with him. He sure does like to talk these days. . . ."

"Good-bye, Mother, I've got to go. I'll see you next Sunday, and I *won't* be bringing anyone."

"Okay. But I'll set that extra place anyway. I mean, you never know, do you?"

"Whoops," Nicole said suddenly. "Someone's on the other line; could be a guy. Catch you later."

"Oh, well, then. Don't just keep talking to me. Good-bye, dear."

Nicole set down the receiver. She really didn't like lying to her mother. But, for all her babbling, Mom was still a pretty sharp old lady. She probably wasn't fooled by her clicking the line to imitate call waiting. It didn't count as a lie if the other person didn't believe what you said.

But what about the lies you tell to yourself? she wondered.

● ● ●

He was back. She knew he would be. He couldn't stay away, and she couldn't keep him away. Or didn't want to.

She'd seen him four times since that first day. Sometimes making the bed. Sometimes just walking by. She only had a small window of opportunity to see him, because it was always from the bathroom mirror. Never from the mirror on her dresser. Or the guest bathroom. Or anywhere else in the house. She had a feeling that he was still there—somewhere—all of the time. Or most of it, at least. He was walking just out of sight; but still in mind.

At times she thought of ripping the bathroom mirror off the wall and dragging it into the kitchen. Ridiculous, of course, but she wondered what he liked to eat. At other times she would walk into the bathroom without turning on the light, just to avoid the reflection.

This wasn't one of those mornings.

He stood in the background, making the bed. Which was strange, since she had purposely made the bed herself just as soon as she got up. He seemed like such a nice man; she really wanted to get to know him better.

Nicole had seen his face. Several times. He wasn't something to swoon over, but neither was he unattractive. His face was just . . . there. Friendly, helpful . . . probably courteous, kind, cheerful and whatever else a Boy Scout would be. But older, of course. Not too old; just old enough.

The room brightened in the background as a beam of light sliced across the bed. He must have opened the curtains. It was so like him. He himself was a ray of sunshine in her world—something she had been missing, but never noticed. She felt as if he had belonged there all along.

Nicole wasn't depressed or lonely—at least, she didn't think so. But she did miss him. Whoever he was. This reflection of a man that she should know.

He looked her way and smiled. Nicole smiled back. She raised her hand and wiggled her fingers in a wave. He laughed and waved back.

He was so close, yet only a distant echo. If only she could touch him. She stretched her fingers, ever so cautiously, not wanting to disturb the dream. If that's what it was. Almost within reach.

She turned . . . and he was gone.

•••

"Nicole, darling, eat some more potatoes. Really, dear, you're looking so thin."

"No, thank you, I've had enough."

"Don't you think she's too thin, Henry?"

Nicole's father shrugged and took another helping of mashed potatoes. "So, tell me more about this dream man of yours. Is he somebody you know?"

"No, he's nobody. It's just, you know, kind of an imaginary friend. Didn't I have one when I was growing up?"

"No," her father said. "You were always down-to-earth."

"Until she decided not to get married," Nicole's mother snapped in. Her father shrugged and went back to his roast beef.

"I didn't *decide* not to get married, Mother. It's just that—I don't know—it seems like I just didn't."

"Well, you *should* have. You knew plenty of nice young men. You should have one of them in your life right now. Remember Charles? He runs an accounting firm. Well, maybe he doesn't run it. But he's right up there near the top.

"And Walter. Walter Piggins. You used to call him 'Piggin-toed.' He married Julia. And right now they're off touring Europe together."

"Yes, Mother. I know. And I'm happy for them." She pushed her fork around on her plate. "Mmmm. Good peas."

"No, you're not happy," her mother insisted. "That's what this is all about. Somewhere deep inside, you really want to get married. Or think you should have. And that's why you invented this man."

"I didn't invent him, Mother. He's—*it's*—just some sort of reflection. Probably just a warp in the mirror or something."

"But that only shows what you're thinking. Remember: 'The mirror is the window to your soul.'"

"That's *eyes*, Mother. The *eyes* are supposed to be the window to the soul."

Nicole's mother said, "Don't contradict your mother, young lady. Tell her, Henry: tell her what you know about mirrors."

"Well," her father smiled, "I knew an Apache shaman once. Didn't believe in mirrors, but he did believe in reflections. He had a sacred pool that he would visit to seek counsel. Funny thing, though: he believes that the other side is real, and we're just the reflections. So, when your reflection walks away, you cease to exist."

"Kind of like the tree in the forest," Nicole put in. "If it falls, and nobody hears it, did it make a sound?"

"Exactly." Henry was warming to his subject. "But suppose that, on the other side of the mirror, they can't see you. Do you still exist?"

"Of course not." Nicole smiled, joining into the spirit of it. "Because you can't exist if you're not there."

"Right. But what happens if the person on the other side used to be able to see you and now can't anymore? Do you stop existing? Or does it mean that you *never* existed? And does the world have to correct for the fact that you never existed?"

"Oh, Henry! Don't go filling your daughter's head with such nonsense. I swear, I don't know what to do with either of you. Now hush up and eat your dinner."

Nicole and her father shared a secret smile. "Yes, Mother," they said.

• • •

Nicole had been standing in front of the mirror for thirty-five minutes. Her hair was done up, with a slight twist to one side. She had makeup on just right. She wore a daring dash of *rum raisin* lipstick. She had slipped out of her pj's and into the slinkiest nightgown she had. It wouldn't do for a honeymoon, but it was the best she could come up with on short notice.

She waited patiently by the mirror. She caught a glimpse of him as he entered the room and walked past her field of vision. His tie dropped to the floor. A moment later he picked it up and hung it across a hook in the closet. But then he turned, walked back out and sat on the bed.

Nicole watched him remove his shoes, then slide them under the bed. She wanted to go to him. Sit by

Illustrated by John Philo

him. Touch him on the shoulder. Just let him know that she cared. But she was trapped. Stuck inside the bathroom, with only a distant image of the man she thought she loved.

He looked up now, and smiled. He looked weary. She could tell that he had had a long day. But he smiled nonetheless.

Nicole smiled back. Not a cautious, friendly smile. But the most sultry look she could imagine. She didn't wave. With her right index finger, she beckoned. Simple, yet understandable.

He rose quickly. Much of the weariness left his face. His smile changed too. He walked slowly toward her, then stopped at the entry of the closet. He raised an eyebrow, then winked.

Nicole had to laugh. But she quickly dropped back into her "come hither" mode. She blew him a quiet kiss across the mirror and winked back.

He stepped into the closet. He was right there. Just behind her. Three feet away. She turned slowly and faced . . . nothing.

Her smile disappeared as an anguished moan came from her throat. She slammed the bathroom door. And locked it.

• • •

"Nicole, dear, I don't see him," Nicole's mother called.

"Mother!" Nicole rushed into the bathroom. "What are you doing in here?"

"You said I could use the bathroom. You didn't say which one."

"This is *my* bathroom. The guest bathroom is down the hall."

"Oh, silly me," her mother said slyly. "But, since I'm here anyway . . . "

"Oh, all right. Go ahead and look!" Nicole fumed as she stormed from the room.

Out in the living room she sat on the couch. She wasn't really mad. Her mother knew that, too. It was just a little act that she had to put up. She actually felt kind of glad that her mother was snooping. She had known that she would. Which was why she let her mother invite herself over for dinner.

She hoped that her mother would find something. That way, Nicole would know that she wasn't going crazy. Or at least know that it ran in the family. Whichever would be fine.

After several minutes, her mother came back out. "I couldn't see him, dear. I'm sorry. I even tried to look to see if the mirror was warped, but I couldn't really see anything major. . . ."

"Oh, it was just a joke anyway," Nicole said. "Like I said, my imagination. Of course you couldn't see him. He's *my* dream man." Her laugh sounded empty.

"Look, dear. Perhaps you should talk to a therapist. I can call Dr. Weyland tomorrow. She's very nice, and I'm sure she can help."

"No, Mother, I'm fine. I . . . I had better go wash up before dinner."

Nicole walked down the hall. She purposely walked past the guest bathroom. She could have washed up there and avoided having to face the mirror. But she was not going to become a prisoner in her own house. At least, not while her mother was here.

She stepped into her bathroom and turned on the light. She washed her hands without looking up. She turned and dried them on the towel. She would not look into the mirror. She would not. No matter how curious she felt, she would *not* look into the mirror.

She turned and looked.

He wasn't there. Just the closet. And the bedroom in the background. And . . .

A flicker of motion caught her eye. The toe from a single argyle sock peeked into view. He must be taking a nap. She smiled. She turned off the light and walked quietly from the room.

•••

Nicole sighed as she stood at her bathroom sink. The dinner had gone well. Her mother had been . . . well . . . a mother. But Nicole had managed to steer the conversation from *him* to safe topics: her job, food, the latest TV shows. She started to wonder if forty-something really was getting old when she liked the same TV shows as her mother.

But now Nicole noticed her counter space. It was cluttered, but not as cluttered as it appeared in the mirror. Something was out of sync.

Slowly she began removing items and setting them on the toilet seat. Some of her lipsticks, first: primrose, cocoa cherry and nutmeg. The moisturizer—both bottles; she probably should keep just one, but they both had looked so good in the ads. And, of course, her curling iron and hair dryer. Those took up a lot of space.

The reflection still didn't look right, and she wasn't sure why.

Her toothbrush, of course. In the commemorative cartoon glass. The best-selling *Diet in 3 Easy Steps with No Pain*. The cotton balls. Her hand started to shake. The tube of coverup. Her compact.

She couldn't take the pressure anymore. She closed her eyes and swept her arm across the counter. Bottles and tubes scattered onto the floor. Her fine-bristled brush banged against the shower door. The bar of soap shot out into her closet. The rattles and tinkles died down. Finally, it fell quiet.

Nicole opened her eyes and looked up. The counter was cleaned. Empty. Nothing on it.

In the mirror, she saw what remained. A razor. A bottle of shaving cream. A blue toothbrush with bent and worn bristles. A dog-eared issue of a hot-rod magazine.

She sighed and smiled a nervous smile. Then she bent and began picking up her things. As she placed each item down, she looked into the mirror. Making sure that she left space for *his* stuff.

●●●

Nicole looked at herself in the mirror. The stress was beginning to show. She still looked attractive. She knew that. But she also knew that, in addition to smile lines, she had some genuine wrinkles.

She still saw him. *Him.*

And she loved him. She knew that now. Not a puppy love, or just a fascination with the unknown. But a real love that had been there for years.

And she feared him. No, not him; but she felt afraid. She feared the fact of him being there, but not. Somehow just out of her reach. A reflection. A memory. And out of touch.

Her shoulders sagged. She needed something— someone—to support her. To tell her it was okay. That everything would be all right. She needed *him*.

Nicole almost felt him. Almost. She knew he was there. She looked up and saw his reflection. Standing by her, his arm on her shoulder. His lips moved, but she couldn't hear the words. Probably something like, "What is wrong, honey?"

She shrugged.

Nicole glanced to her sides, looked down, and then up. His reflection was there. But, of course, he wasn't. A single tear trickled down her cheek.

He bent over to kiss her neck. She arched her head slightly to allow it. Oh, to actually feel the touch. The warmth. To know that he was more than just a reflection.

He kissed again, then nuzzled up close to her. His smile was comforting and sincere. He turned his head and looked into the mirror. And froze.

A chill shot through Nicole's body. He was looking at her now. But not directly. He stared several inches to the side. He was looking at himself. Where he was. Where he *should* have been. He was looking out from the mirror—and he couldn't see himself either!

His jaw dropped. In the mirror, the arm slipped from Nicole's shoulder. He waved his hand and stared ahead blankly. Then the reflection reached forward and touched the mirror. His lips slowly mouthed the words *"Where am I?"*

Nicole ran screaming from the room.

• • •

On the other side, Raymond blinked his eyes. For a moment, he thought that he hadn't seen his reflection. But now the image shone back. He fingered the mirror again, his real finger touching the copy. He feinted left, then right. His double followed his moves to perfection.

Maybe insanity was hereditary—you caught it from your wife. She had been acting a bit peculiar lately. Like those funny little waves she'd been giving him from the bathroom. Or seducing him, then slamming the door in his face.

And, each time, she had absolutely no explanation why she had done it. Worse yet, she was telling the truth. After twenty years of marriage, you get to know someone. And she was beginning to become someone that he didn't know. Or that, sometimes, didn't know him.

"Honey, are you coming?" Nicole called.

"Yes, dear." Raymond shook his head. She wouldn't even know why she had run away screaming. If she remembered it at all.

Maybe it was the bathroom. Paint fumes, or something. He took a large sniff, then looked in the mirror. He was still there. Both of him. Real and reflection. It couldn't be that, could it? Unless it was from prolonged exposure to . . . whatever.

Maybe he should call in a doctor to check it out. Or a technician. Or both. In the meantime, he was getting a whopper of a headache.

Now, where had Nicole hidden those aspirin?

•••

"Is she all right, Dr. Weyland?"

"I'm fine." Nicole sat up in bed. "Really, Mother, you didn't have to drive all this way."

"I'm your mother, dear. That's my job."

"What did you tell Dad?"

"Oh, I just said it was 'female stuff.'" She smiled. "Don't worry, you couldn't drag him here with a monster truck now that he thinks that's what's going on."

"Thanks."

"You're welcome, dear. Now, what does the good doctor say?"

"I really don't know," Dr. Weyland said. "Please, Miss Glenn, how do *you* feel about it?"

"It's . . . well . . . "

"Don't worry," the doctor coaxed. "We're friends here."

"It's like I said. I've been seeing this man—not dating, just seeing him in my mirror. He's nice. I like him. I even think . . . I love him. But he's only in the mirror. He's not really there."

"He must be somewhere, Nicole. Where do you think he is?"

"I didn't make him up!" Nicole snapped. She bit her lip as the other two women waited patiently. "I'm . . . I'm sorry."

"That's understandable," Dr. Weyland said. "Please. Continue. Is that what is bothering you?"

"Yes. And no. Or, at least, not all. This morning I saw him. Up close. And he saw me. But he couldn't see himself. What does that mean?"

"It means you should get rid of that nasty old mirror," her mother said. "Smash it. Bust it. Whatever. No piece of glass is going to hurt my little angel."

"But what happens to *them?*" Nicole asked.

"Who are *they?*" The doctor looked puzzled.

"The images, or people . . . or whatever. On the other side. They'll be trapped."

"Oh, that's just nonsense," her mom cut in. "Probably something your father told you. Don't mind him. Tell her, Doctor. Tell her that nothing will happen."

"I can't."

"Come on, Doctor. Surely . . . surely *you* don't think that's real?"

"It doesn't matter what *I* think. That's not reality. Reality for Nicole is what she perceives it to be. Now perhaps you can go into the other room while Nicole and I discuss some things."

Nicole watched her mother leave.

Forty-something, and here I am, being treated like a small child. The problem was that she actually still felt like one.

Dr. Weyland stayed with her for more than an hour—letting her talk.

Nicole let out her feelings as well as her memories. Of *him*. And some were even memories that she didn't even remember knowing. Of times together. The way he ate his corn with a knife by squishing it into his mashed potatoes. How he made machine-gun noises at cars that cut him off on the freeway. The gentle passion of his kisses . . .

She finally let it all out. Not all the memories—those were starting to come in a flood. But at least the admission of memories. She felt drained, but relaxed.

"Are you feeling better now?"

"Yes, Doctor. Thanks."

"You understand that it's not over yet, don't you? You still have to confront these feelings, one way or another; it's your choice how. Until you get these conflicts resolved, you will still see *him*."

"Yes, Doctor. I understand. Thank you."

Nicole heard the doctor walk down the hall and talk to her mother at the door.

"She's all better now, isn't she?"

"She's doing fine, Mrs. Glenn. But she isn't *all* better."

"What's wrong with her?"

"It's a question of something missing in her life. Something she knows she needs—and even truly believes that she had once. Something such as this can really alter someone's perspective of reality."

"I knew it all along. She's just lonely. Why, if she had grabbed up Charles or John or Thomas, this never would have happened. A mother's always right on these things. She just needs a man. I'm right, aren't I?"

"Maybe," Dr. Weyland corrected, "she already *has* a man. The only problem is . . . he's on the other side of the mirror."

• • •

It was a dream. Nicole knew that.

The images flowed like a newsreel. The wedding. The reception. Forest-green colors. A stunning black tuxedo for him with the dazzling white gown for her. She even knew the corner in the attic where the gown was stored, and the can beside it with a piece of cake.

But that corner now held an old desk that she had bought when she had tried to start her own business a few years back.

And the honeymoon. Tahiti. The glorious weather. The sounds of the birds. The lush green growth mixed in with the colorful flowers. The five rolls of film that she had taken of the island, an island where she had never been.

Nicole rolled over in bed. She stared at the blank wall. She was still dreaming.

Their first apartment. Hardly big enough for one, yet it held them both. She had worked at the grocery store while he finished college. Times were tough and quarters cramped, but they made it through.

The condo came next. Rented, at first. Then the owner let them buy it. They had to tighten their budget to afford the payments, but it was worth it. Not long after, real estate prices doubled. The equity alone enabled them to move up to a house within three years.

And, finally, to this house. *Their* house. They'd built it; designed it, at least. With the extra bedrooms and the three bathrooms. The third bathroom. In the fourth bedroom. Nicole wondered why she would need a house that big. And why the house needed the bathroom that she had never even remembered.

Nicole turned over again. The far wall stared back at her. She was still dreaming. Even though her eyes remained open, and she was wide awake, she knew that she was dreaming.

And the children. Who could forget them? The children she'd never had?

Roger was first. Twelve hours of labor, but a labor of love. The diapers, the skinned knees, the wrecked car. He was in college now, on a scholastic scholarship. His father had always wanted him to play basketball, but Roger had never cared for the sport. His father cheered him on anyway.

Susan came next. Or *Suzanne*, as she now liked to be called. It was a high-school thing. She hung around with the "older" girls, pretending that Melissa—her little sister—didn't exist. But, now, neither of them existed.

And neither did William or Joshua. They had never existed. And neither had the years it had taken to raise them. Nor the expenses, or the pain. Or the love. Especially the love. It had never existed.

A tear slipped down Nicole's cheek as she faded off to sleep.

"Honey, what did you do?" Nicole asked.

"I cut myself shaving, dear." His face was covered in bandages. Only his eyes and mouth had patches that showed skin. Even his nose was covered over.

"How did it happen?" Nicole asked.

"Oh, you know. The usual. I was shaving when the mirror went out. I couldn't see myself anymore. One thing led to another and, well, this happened."

"I'm sorry, dear," Nicole muttered in her sleep. "So sorry."

• • •

Nicole waited outside the bathroom. He was in there now, on the other side of the mirror. Shaving. A good coat of lather covered his face, and the blade slid easily down to his chin. Which meant he could see himself.

She hid in the closet. An old winter coat covered her fairly well. It was last year's fashion, and she'd have to get rid of it. But it served a purpose now. The bathroom light was on and the closet light off. That, and the fact that he wasn't really looking for her, concealed her from his view.

He seemed the same as usual. Maybe a little worried. His brow furrowed slightly—perhaps because he was intent on shaving.

He could see himself and she could see his reflection. So why couldn't she see him?

Maybe this time she'd find out. While he looked right at himself, she would just jump out. If he was concentrating on seeing himself, and she concentrated hard enough, he would appear. Maybe. At least, that was her theory.

But what should she say? "Hello, I am in love with you?" "Who are you?" "What are you doing in my bathroom?" or even, "Why *aren't* you in my bathroom?"

Nicole tensed. She felt like a little girl, waiting to scare her brother. Her heart beat fast and loud. She felt almost sure that he could hear it, even on the other side of the mirror. It was now or never. She didn't know what she'd say, but she felt sure it would come.

Suddenly she leapt into the bathroom and put her arms around where he should be. "Boo!"

He looked up in shock, razor poised against his cheek. His eyes went blank. Where they had once focused straight forward, they now saw only emptiness. The image was jostled and surprised by the reflected Nicole that now held him tight.

His hand slipped. The blade slid sideways across his cheek. It was only an inch, but it was enough. A drop of blood spun through the air and hit the mirror with a silent splat! The reflected droplet slid down the mirror, tracing its path as it went.

Nicole fell to the floor in a dead faint.

• • •

Raymond hovered above the doctor. He unconsciously fingered the bandage on his cheek. "Well, Dr. Fuller? Do you have it?"

"Patience," the doctor said.

"Is it a virus? Or worse?"

"Just one more moment." The doctor let out a couple of grunts as he fiddled around with his tools. "There. Got it." He triumphantly held up a sliver of glass with his forceps. The image inside bounced around frantically.

"That's it?"

"Yup. Apparently the mirror was injured sometime in the last few weeks. It got this image trapped inside. Yours, I believe."

"But then," Raymond persisted, "how come I could see myself when she wasn't there?"

"The mirror probably tried to compensate. When nobody else was around, it just warped some lines through. But when somebody else came in—poof! you're gone! How is your wife doing, by the way?"

"Oh, she's fine. I think. As long as this is fixed. I called the technician before I called you. It took a while to realize that this might be causing her anxiety. And she still doesn't know why she ran screaming from the bathroom the other day."

Raymond paused, then continued, "Is it possible . . . you know . . . that something on the other side caused this? Is there a chance that we might have caused some changes over there?"

"No, I wouldn't worry about *that*," Dr. Fuller said in a reassuring tone. "Stories of the 'other side' are probably just old wives' tales meant to scare small children."

"I can tell you, it sure scared me. Will you be able to heal it?"

Dr. Fuller fiddled with his instruments a little more as he planted a device through the edge of the lens. "Well, these things take about seven years to heal. Naturally. But science has made some giant leaps in the last few years. I've installed a splint that should serve as a work-around until the wound mends. Let's see if the mirror still works."

The two men stood and stared into the mirror. Both images gazed back. "It looks good to me," the doctor commented. "At least, it's better than when I first got here. Although I can't explain that bluish blur off to the right. . . ."

"Oh, don't worry about that; it's just a stain. Melissa and William did a Science Fair project last month. Something about combining makeup with rocket fuel."

"Kids," Dr. Fuller laughed. "I saw them playing outside when I came in. You gotta love 'em. So, is this good enough for you?"

"It works for me. But I want her to try it."

"Good idea."

"Nicole, honey," Raymond called back into the bedroom. "It's healed now. Are you feeling up to trying it?"

The men shifted on their feet, but waited patiently. After several minutes, Nicole appeared. She walked cautiously towards the bathroom, her eyes glazed over, but pointing at the floor. In her right hand she had a hammer.

Both men held their breath. Nicole slowly looked up, straight into the mirror. She breathed a sigh of relief, and the two men joined in. Her hand dropped to her side and the hammer clattered to the floor.

"See, honey, it's all better now. There's me," he waved, "Dr. Fuller," the doctor waved, "and you."

Nicole smiled. She waved at herself and laughed at the reflection. Yes, it was nice to see the faces. *All* of them.

"Well, I'd best be going," the doctor commented. "Plenty of house calls to make. But, before I go, would you like me to heal the creaking in your bedroom door?"

"How much extra would that cost?"

"No charge. I'm already here. And I have a bottle of door plasma that'll expire in a couple of weeks if I don't use it."

"That would be great, Doc. Thanks a lot."

"Yes," Nicole added with a smile. "Thank you very much."

"So," Raymond continued, "how much do we owe you for the visit?"

Dr. Fuller pulled out his calculator and punched in a couple of figures. "Basic visit," he mumbled as he worked. "Diagnosis, labor and parts for the splint." He punched a couple more keys, and the total appeared.

"$125."

RED TIDE, WHITE TIDE

Written by
T. M. Spell

Illustrated by
Eric L. Winter

About the Author

T. M. Spell is a native Floridian. She graduated from high school at the age of sixteen, and while waiting to go to college, she took up writing with an eye toward becoming a professional SF writer.

She graduated from Flagler College with a major in English literature and a minor in journalism. She has since worked as a reporter both in Florida and in Washington, D. C. She has continued her education, taking writing courses at the graduate level, and is currently studying at Clarion East, a high-level writing workshop whose graduates now include many professional writers of science fiction and fantasy.

"Red Tide, White Tide" is her first professional sale, but will surely not be her last.

I think you should sleep with Brooks," Etienne told his wife over breakfast. He didn't bother to look up from the *Smithsonian* article he was reading.

"Jeffrey Brooks?" Julia D'Anjou hesitated with a forkful of *huevos rancheros* partway to her open mouth. "Your lab assistant?" To her, Jeffrey was just one of several tight-lipped, power-suited men who spent most of their time hunched over computer terminals in the laboratory behind the house. What, precisely, any of Etienne's assistants did for him, Julia had never been told nor encouraged to find out. Etienne's days of confiding in her about his research into immune system theories, or anything else, were long gone.

Etienne nodded. "Lab assistant, chauffeur, bodyguard, whatever. A man of many talents. Why not?" He took a sip of orange juice and returned his glass to the table, still without looking up.

"How about because I'm your wife?" Julia asked.

"You don't think he's attractive?"

"No!" Julia dropped her fork onto her plate with a loud *clank* and bits of egg flew across the table, spattering onto Etienne's article. "The man's forty years old!"

"Thirty-eight," Etienne corrected. With a frown, he flicked egg off of the page he was reading. It left a small grease stain which he ignored. "You're nearly thirty."

"I'm twenty-seven," Julia said, her voice suddenly small and wounded. "As of two months ago. That's not nearly thirty at all."

Etienne finally looked up at his wife, his dark sapphire-blue eyes as emotionally flat and hard as the gemstones they resembled. "And thirty-eight isn't nearly forty, either, is it?"

"That's not the point," Julia said, her voice regaining strength from the anger that began to surge through her. "There's an eleven-year difference between us, and I don't find him the least bit attractive." After a pause, she added, "You think I'm too old?"

Etienne shook his head. "Not at all. You brought up the subject of age. I only said I think you should sleep with Jeffrey Brooks."

"But—why?" Julia asked. "Don't you love me anymore?"

"No." Etienne closed the magazine and stood to finish his juice. His eggs, cottage fries and chicken sausage links lay nearly untouched. "Not for some time." The sound of his glass clinking on the green-and-gold patterned tiles of the table was cold, empty. Sunlight, from a sky etched red at the bottom and brilliant blue above that, streamed through the mullioned bay windows and suffused the day room with bleak, wan light.

Julia appeared corpse-white in that light and her gray eyes gleamed like gravestone marble. "What did I do?"

"Nothing," Etienne said. "It's not your fault. It's mine, really. But it's not something either of us can change . . . not just by wanting to."

"*Do* you want to?" Julia asked.

"More than you can imagine," Etienne said, but his voice remained as flat and unmoved as a man quoting stock prices.

"You're in love with someone else, aren't you?"

"No, Julia, there's no one else. Sometimes it's just over."

Etienne moved away from the table, toward the door that led out onto the back porch and the grounds beyond. "I'll be in the laboratory for the rest of the day."

"Do you want a divorce?" Julia's voice caught him before he could leave.

"No." Etienne looked over his shoulder. "No. I want you to sleep with Jeffrey Brooks."

Julia shook her head. "I won't."

"Well, then," Etienne said, "that's that." He didn't slam the door behind him, but shut it softly, as obscenely polite as he had been hideously courteous throughout their breakup.

Julia realized that that was exactly what had just happened. She and her husband had broken up. But he didn't want a divorce, and he didn't love her, and there wasn't another woman, and she believed him about that, which was crazy, but then the whole conversation had been crazy—and—and he wanted her to sleep with another man.

"Jeffrey?" She shook her head in disbelief at her husband's deserted plate of congealing food. "*Jeffrey?*"

"Oh, he's been in the lab since before daylight, Mrs. D'Anjou," said Grace, cook and maid to the D'Anjous, stepping in from the kitchen. A big, dark-haired woman of Puerto Rican descent with fifty-two years' worth of laugh lines on her face, and hips broadened by giving birth to seven children, she had heard Etienne close the side door and stepped promptly through the kitchen's swinging doors to start removing dirty dishes. How much, if any, of the conversation she had heard, she didn't let on. "Would you like me to clear these away?"

Julia nodded. "Thank you."

Grace paused, studying the nearly full plates she was carrying. "Was everything okay this morning?"

"Oh, yes," Julia said. "Everything was excellently prepared. As always."

"Okay," Grace said, "I'll just dump these then." She sighed and shook her head over good cooking gone to waste. "I'm sure you two will have a big appetite by this afternoon."

"As a matter of fact," Julia said on an impulse, "I'm going to be out all day. And Mr. D'Anjou will be working until at least dinner time. Why don't you just take the day off?"

When Grace brightened but still hesitated, Julia added, "With pay, of course."

"You're sure everything is okay, Mrs. D'Anjou?" Grace asked, obviously meaning more than just the food.

Julia managed to smile at Grace and give a convincing nod. "Absolutely. Have a good time. I'm going to."

"Okay. If you're sure." Grace stopped at the swinging doors and glanced back at Julia. "You're going shopping, Mrs. D'Anjou? I could call over to the lab and have Jeffrey get the car ready for you."

"Actually," Julia said, "I'm going to be driving myself today."

• • •

Although it took Julia less than a quarter of an hour to freshen her make-up, smooth out the lines of her simple black bouclé dress, check the contents of her purse for keys, cash and credit cards, and make a quick phone call to her best friend, Sandy, to set up a *my-life-is-ending-what-do-I-do-about-it?* lunch date, by the time she stepped into the garage, Jeffrey had arrived. He had already opened one of the four garage doors. The engine of the powder-blue Mercedes hummed quietly while Jeffrey stood patiently near the rear passenger-side door.

Julia caught herself shaking her head, partly with disbelief, but mostly with disapproval, at the sight of Jeffrey Brooks hovering about her favorite car. She pressed her lips together until they turned white around the edges with growing anger, desperately repressed.

"Grace must have misunderstood me," Julia said, walking around to the driver's side of the Mercedes. "I'm going to drive myself today."

Faster than a cockroach, Jeffrey scuttled around and got his hand on the driver's-side door handle before she could. "Yes, ma'am," he said, pretending not to notice the adversarial glare she gave him, "Grace said you'd indicated you didn't want a driver today. But Mr. D'Anjou thought you'd be safer with me along. After all, I am trained in the martial arts and licensed to carry a handgun."

Julia put one hand on her hip and gave Jeffrey a sweeping glance up and down. He was an inch or so shorter than she—a thin, unimposing, narrow-faced, dark-haired man in a three-piece charcoal-gray suit. He had big, liquid-black eyes like a cartoon dog's, and they studied her nervously during this scrutiny.

"I'm sure you're trained in a great many arts, Jeffrey," she said, finally, "but I'm just going to the shopping mall, not a Tyson-Holyfield rematch. And I'm going to be meeting a friend, so I'll be perfectly safe."

"Yes, ma'am," Jeffrey said, "I'm sure you will be once you're inside the mall. But it's while you're entering and exiting the vehicle that you're the most vulnerable to attack."

"Jeffrey—" she began.

"It's just not a sane world out there, anymore, Mrs. D'Anjou," Jeffrey interjected.

"It's not a sane world in here, either," Julia said.

Jeffrey hesitated, either unsure of her meaning, or unwilling to pursue the topic, then continued doggedly. "I strongly recommend that you allow me to escort you, Mrs. D'Anjou."

"*You* recommend?" Julia realized that Jeffrey was asserting his own reasoned judgment in place of her husband's authority, a tactic she found somewhat disarming.

"Yes, ma'am, I do," Jeffrey said, keeping his black eyes steadily fixed on her face.

After a long, considering pause, Julia said, "You're probably right." And he was. The world she had grown up in wasn't very safe anymore for a woman alone. Rape had become the most commonly committed crime against women, and serial killers were working over-time to meet an escalating quota in human butchery. During previous decades, such hyper-caution would have been paranoid. These days . . . these days it was just common sense.

Without further comment, Julia turned and moved to open the rear door. Again, Jeffrey darted around her and got his hand on the door handle first. Silently, Julia allowed herself to be handed into the rear seat of the Mercedes like the pampered though good-natured preppie that she was. For the first time, she noticed how Jeffrey's hand felt against her own bare palm. His grip was firm, solid, but never too tight, the fingers long and slightly calloused. Against her will, Julia imagined how it would feel to have Jeffrey's hands on her body.

When Jeffrey released her and shut the door, Julia leaned back against the seat, closed her eyes and sighed with frustration. Even if her husband didn't love her and didn't want to sleep with her anymore, there was still no reason why he had to go putting weird ideas into her head about who *he* thought she ought to sleep with.

• • •

In the squat, two-story red brick building where Etienne conducted his own privately funded research, Jeffrey's corner office faced the main house rather than the lake. The picture window behind his desk was made of two-way mirrored glass that could be shielded at night by black vertical blinds, which were now drawn back. Jeffrey stood at the window and watched the house, his dark eyes fixed on a light that burned in an upper window. Julia's suite.

The last bloody tinge of sunset had faded, leaving the sky a pallid, crepuscular gray. The elegantly land-scaped lawn faded slowly from sight as the world darkened, until only the vaguest outline of trees and rosebushes remained visible, but the light shining through the cross-woven Jacquard lace curtains in Julia's room blazed ever more clearly.

"You blew it." Etienne stepped through the open door of Jeffrey's office and moved across the room until he stood just behind Jeffrey, but to one side so that he also had a clear view of the house.

Jeffrey glanced without undue concern at Etienne's reflection in the glass. "How so?" His stance, tone of voice and manner were that of someone addressing an equal.

"I just got a call from Stuart," Etienne said, naming the director of a private investigative firm he retained to keep an eye on his wife. "Julia has been leaving the house without telling us. She was seen having dinner at *Le Pavillon* yesterday evening with Daniel Whittington."

Jeffrey shook his head and frowned at Etienne's reflection. "I'm not familiar with that name."

"Daniel and I were roommates in college," Etienne said. "Best friends."

"I see. Maybe she just needed to talk to someone who knows you both from . . . back when."

"You know better than that. If my wife needs a shoulder to cry on, she's got girlfriends. Or she can go to her shrink. If she's dating my old college buddies—and that's what it was, a date—then she's got more on her mind than a friendly chat about old times."

"All right," Jeffrey said. "I admit you're probably right. Can you blame her?"

"No. We haven't been in bed together for over a year. I haven't even slept in the house for two weeks now, not since I moved into the lab." Etienne's blue eyes glittered with arctic clarity as he spoke. "I've made it plain that she and I don't have any kind of a future to look forward to, so, no, I don't blame her for trying to salvage what she can of her life . . . and her self-respect. But I sure as hell *will* blame Daniel Whittington. If he fucks my wife, I'll kill him." He spoke with no trace of anger in his voice, as if he were merely swearing to perform a duty he no longer felt one way or another about.

Jeffrey started slightly, but managed to keep a calm expression on his face as he turned to look directly at Etienne. "Him, but not me?"

"If it's Daniel, I get absolutely nothing out of it," Etienne said. "Except betrayal. I've lost everything else. I will *not* lose this."

"And you see any involvement between Julia and myself as being no threat whatsoever to your hopes of salvaging your marriage once you've regained your emotional equilibrium?" Jeffrey asked.

"I'm ready to consider it a calculated risk," Etienne said.

"Well, factor this into your calculations while you're at it, Etienne," Jeffrey said. "Julia has no sexual interest in me whatsoever. In fact, she probably considers me somewhat . . . ridiculous. Certainly, she thinks I'm beneath her, although I doubt she'd ever actually say so."

"And your point is?"

"Basically, it's that what you're asking me to do isn't just a moral outrage, it's also going to be damned hard to pull off."

Etienne shrugged, as if his partner's objections centered around trivial concerns. "The woman's not made out of stone, Jeffrey. She has needs. And the fact that she's not strongly attracted to you may even be a plus for her in the long run. She can have sex with you without feeling that she's emotionally breaking faith with me in the process of fulfilling her own physical needs."

"And you think that she'd be willing to settle for that?" Jeffrey asked, letting the fact that he'd just been insulted on several different levels pass without comment. "Sex without love?"

"She still loves me," Etienne said. "Probably as much as you love her. It's entirely likely that if you can establish a sexual relationship with Julia, she'll develop affectionate feelings toward you, but nothing that would threaten our marriage."

"You do hear yourself, don't you?" Jeffrey asked.

Etienne nodded. "Yes, I know. Coldblooded as hell. We're working on correcting that, aren't we?"

"Overtime," Jeffrey said.

"But in the interim, my marriage is falling apart," Etienne said. "Truthfully, it was falling apart before we ever stopped sleeping together. Julia didn't know what was wrong, exactly, just that some part of me was . . . missing. The sex was better than ever, but she was starving to death emotionally. I know how she felt."

"Yes," Jeffrey said quietly. He studied Etienne's impassive face, in which only the eyes still seemed alive. "I guess you do."

"So I withdrew all physical contact as well," Etienne said. "Just like we agreed. Until we were sure that she was ready to accept a surrogate."

Jeffrey suddenly couldn't meet Etienne's gaze. He turned back to the window and stared out through the darkness, at the bright, curtained square on the second floor of the house. He and Etienne *had* agreed on this plan over a year ago, each out of his own desperate need. But now that it came down to the actual seduction of Julia, he wasn't sure he wanted to . . . wasn't even sure he *could* go through with it. Adultery was bad enough. But what they had planned went beyond that into a realm of depravity that might well shatter Julia emotionally if she ever learned the truth.

"We all win out of this," Etienne insisted. "You get to make love to Julia. She gets to feel the fulfillment of being loved. And *I* get to feed."

When Jeffrey didn't respond, Etienne moved a step closer. "Jeffrey, if I don't get an outlet soon, I'm not going to be responsible for what happens."

Jeffrey looked at Etienne's reflection. "Oh, you'll be responsible, all right."

"Okay," Etienne said. "But I guarantee you, I won't be alone. When the shit hits the fan, Jeffrey, you'll be standing right beside me."

• • •

A loud crash downstairs caused Julia to stiffen and look up in alarm from her hardcover copy of Dean Koontz's *Watchers*. She had just finished reading a scene in which a psychotic hit man had beaten one of his female victims to death with a hammer. However, as she closed the book, laid it aside and slid quietly out of bed, she wasn't thinking about psychotic hit men. As near as Julia could judge, the sound had come from the back of the house. Close to Etienne's study.

Julia descended the main staircase, a long, straight flight made of pink Italian marble, flanked on one side by a wall and on the other by a sturdy mahogany rail that she gripped lightly on the way down. Her bare feet moved silently across the chill marble floor of the foyer and equally silently on the thickly carpeted hallway leading to the study. The door was open and the light on when she reached it. Julia glanced into the room, saw that Etienne's oxblood leather chair had been wheeled away from his desk a few paces, and his Acer computer monitor had fallen heavily onto the carpeted floor where it lay in a black heap of twisted metal speakers, split plastic casing and shattered glass screen. The room was empty now, so Julia glanced up and down the hallway, straining her eyes and ears for any sign of the much-longed-for figure of her husband.

"Etienne?" she called.

The clinking of glass bottles being shifted about in the bathroom at the far end of the hall caught her attention. Looking more closely, Julia realized that a weak beam of light from the cracked bathroom door illuminated a sliver of carpet. She walked over to the door, tapped twice and pushed it slowly open, peering around the edge as she did so. The figure she saw rummaging around in the bathroom cabinet was not Etienne.

"Jeffrey?" When he turned toward her, Julia saw that Jeffrey's hand was dripping blood.

"Sorry to disturb you at this hour, Mrs. D'Anjou," Jeffrey said, cradling the injured hand with his good one. His lean, taut-featured face was pale and he was shaking.

"Oh, God, Jeffrey," Julia exclaimed, "what happened?" With a few quick strides she stood directly in front of him. Instinctively, she reached out and took his bloodied hand in both of hers, a move that he submitted to without protest. She saw a long, thin gash had been sliced into the upper part of his palm, and the pads of two of his fingers had been cut deeply enough to bleed, not copiously, but seriously enough to bespatter the tiles at their feet and the white ceramic sinktop with numerous dark red drops. Julia realized belatedly she was actually standing in Jeffrey's blood. She felt her scalp creep with alarm for his sake.

"It was really quite stupid of me," Jeffrey said, his voice steady and clear despite the pallor of his face. "Earlier this afternoon, Mr. D'Anjou asked me to move some of his computer equipment from his office here, into the laboratory. I just managed to get around to it this evening. I didn't want to disturb you, so I let myself in with Mr. D'Anjou's keys."

Julia shot Jeffrey a stricken glance—though she didn't release his hand—at the mention of her husband removing more of his personal belongings from the house.

"I must have tripped on a ruck in the carpet," Jeffrey said, apparently oblivious to the impact his previous statement had had on her. "I probably could've won an Olympic medal for the distance I threw Mr. D'Anjou's monitor. You wouldn't believe how aerodynamic Acers are once they're airborne. They don't touch down well, though. I was picking up a few shards from the screen— its remains, in any case—when I cut myself. As you can see."

Julia nodded. The damage was plain. "Do you think this is going to need stitches?"

"This?" Jeffrey said, as if referring to a paper cut. "I don't think it's nearly deep enough for that. I was just looking for some iodine and gauze, to keep it clean and dry until it can heal on its own."

"You're such a stoic, Jeffrey," Julia scolded him gently, but she smiled as she spoke. "Here, why don't you sit on the edge of the bathtub while I find the first-aid kit?"

Jeffrey sat. While Julia rifled the cabinets, he turned on the tub's cold water tap. He put his hand under the running water until all of the blood washed away and only the clean white lines on either side of the deep cut and the angry inner pink of sliced flesh remained visible.

In the cabinet under the sink Julia found a first-aid kit with a blue cross on the lid, opened it and sat next to Jeffrey.

"This is very kind of you," Jeffrey said as Julia daubed at his injured palm with the iodine dropper. "You really don't have to do this."

"Oh, yes I do," Julia said quietly, painting the pads of the two cut fingers a jaundiced orange. When Jeffrey winced at the sting, she leaned forward and blew on the iodine to cool the wounds. She had absolutely no idea of the lightning streak of heat that flashed through Jeffrey's body when she did this, though his fingers were certainly cool enough. "I take care of my friends, Jeffrey."

"Thank you," Jeffrey said, as much because she had called him a friend as because she was tending to his injured hand.

Julia smiled at him, her gray eyes warm as summer rain, as she began to wind his hand in a gauze strip. "You're welcome."

"That was a very expensive monitor I broke," Jeffrey said in worried tones. "I hope he doesn't take it out of my pay."

"Oh, I'm sure he won't," Julia said quickly. "It was an accident. Besides, everything in this house is insured against breakage, theft, fire, flood, lightning, hurricane force winds and various other acts of God, so-called. Don't worry about it."

With his free hand, Jeffrey reached out and fingered a loose strand of gleaming auburn hair that lay against Julia's cheek. "You have an incredibly generous spirit."

Startled, Julia glanced up and and met Jeffrey's jet-black eyes—and found such approval, affection and undisguised admiration that she actually had to resist an unexpected urge to lean forward and kiss him. It had been such a long time since any man had gazed at her like that, or spoken to her in that soothingly intimate tone. She forced herself to look down, concentrate on securing the bandage with metal clips. Jeffrey withdrew the caressing hand from her cheek slowly, as if underscoring the fact that he wasn't embarrassed by the contact he'd initiated or her reaction to it.

Silently, she applied two strip bandages to Jeffrey's fingers and closed the first-aid kit. "All better," she said.

Jeffrey nodded. "Yes."

Julia felt her cheeks start to burn with more than simple embarrassment as she rose and put the first-aid kit away. She heard Jeffrey turn on the tap again. When she turned back around he was holding out a washcloth he'd taken from the nearby guest rack.

"You may want to wash that off," he said, with a glance at her feet, "before you go back into the hallway."

Examining the sole of one foot, Julia realized that she had picked up quite a bit of Jeffrey's blood where it had hit the tiles. It was drying on her skin in ugly stains. She accepted the washcloth, placed it under the tap until it was soaked, wrung it out slightly and then sat down to scrub the blood away. When Jeffrey leaned past her to turn the tap off, she felt acutely aware of his arm brushing against her back. The emerald-green silk teddy she wore accentuated the pleasant sensation this brief, accidental contact provoked in her. When the cold washcloth touched her foot, Julia shivered.

Jeffrey noticed and rubbed her back gently with his good hand. "You must be freezing," he said. "Here, take my jacket."

Before Julia could find the words to form a polite protest, Jeffrey removed his pinstriped, slate-gray jacket and draped it over her shoulders. Once her feet were scrubbed pinkly clean, Julia put the washcloth aside and drew the jacket close around her. It smelled strongly of cologne—Calvin Klein's *Obsession* for men, she guessed. It made her senses swim pleasantly.

After a moment of companionable silence, she asked, "Would you care for a cup of coffee, or a beer, Jeffrey?"

Jeffrey nodded. "Yes, ma'am, I would."

Slowly, like the sun breaking free of a storm cloud, Julia smiled at him.

•••

In a coffin-like tube that had once been a tanning bed, but which had since been equipped for other uses, Etienne D'Anjou lay open-eyed and alert. A ventilation system near Etienne's head filled the pitch-dark tube with a faint white-noise roar, like the ocean heard from a distance. After a while, his mind ceased to notice the sound, and in the absence of light or other sensory input, Etienne experienced the hallucinogenic rush of sensory deprivation.

In his case, the reaction was rather extreme, due to the fact that he also suffered from a damaged endocrine system which rendered him incapable of experiencing any emotion. Fear, love, hate, pity—these existed in Etienne's mind, but did not have the power to touch his body through the tide of such hormones as cortisol and adrenaline, which fuel the adrenal glands during times of stress and fear; or cholecystokinin, which tells the body it's just enjoyed a satisfying meal; or any of the other peptides, neurotransmitters, growth factors and lymphokines that control the human ability to fully experience the entire range of human emotions.

As Etienne allowed his external senses to be severed from him as thoroughly as his internal ones were, his mind seemed to implode in a blinding white burst of energy as cold and silent as the vacuum of space. He reached out with his mind, searching, probing through the darkness that stretched between the lab and the house, until he found his target. He entered easily, unobtrusively, into the mind of Jeffrey Brooks, like a man slipping into a familiar suit. Which indeed it was. The two of them had done this often, though never with the purpose they shared tonight.

Etienne kept a respectful distance from Jeffrey's thoughts, which were like a faint and unintelligible murmur in the background of Etienne's mind. Etienne had his own thoughts, he hardly needed Jeffrey's. But now Etienne also had complete access to the sensory input flooding, effortlessly and almost unheeded, through Jeffrey's body. *That* he needed. Desperately. Etienne felt like a man stretching his muscles after spending a week strapped into a straitjacket.

Jeffrey sat at the kitchen table. One hand, bandaged from a recent cut, rested on his leg, the other rested on the oak tabletop. He had a clear view of Julia, who stood peering into the oversized chef's refrigerator at a selection of beers, domestic and foreign. She had Jeffrey's coat draped across her shoulders and not much else that Etienne could see.

Congratulations, you bastard, Etienne thought with a faint smile, though the expression was invisible in the darkness and Jeffrey couldn't hear Etienne's thoughts anymore than Etienne could hear Jeffrey's. *I knew you had it in you. And I'll bet you did, too.*

The sight of her like that sent wave after wave of warmth and desire though Jeffrey. The burning in his loins was the least of the sensations she aroused. There was such a crowding in Jeffrey's chest that, under other circumstances, he might have suspected indigestion or some other oncoming physical illness. It was the sort of feeling that allowed men to spout the persuasive, poetic bullshit women responded to so well.

"How about a *Tsing Tao?*" Julia asked, pronouncing it *chin dow*.

"What's that?" Jeffrey asked.

"Chinese beer." Julia looked at Jeffrey and grinned. "Tastes better than it sounds."

"I'd love one," Jeffrey said.

As Jeffrey reached to take the long-neck bottle Julia held out to him, Etienne felt a slight . . . *shift* in Jeffrey's perceptions, as he became consciously aware of Etienne's presence. With a suddenness equivalent to a hard physical blow delivered without warning, Etienne was flung out of Jeffrey's mind and back into the claustrophobic darkness of the sensory deprivation chamber.

The drop from a body overflowing with emotional input back into the emotionally voided shell that Etienne inhabited was like crashing from a strong drug. The need for hormonal release assaulted him with a black-salt hunger so ravenous it was only by a great effort of the will that he managed to force himself to breathe deeply and empty his mind of frustration and rage. His body had no mechanism whereby he could release such emotions anymore. They were devoured almost instantly by a host of biomechanical parasites of his own design that targeted many of the hormones found in his bloodstream or vital organs.

Originally, the parasites had been intended to regulate only the ACTH hormone produced by the pituitary gland, to lessen stress and prevent the diseases associated with it. It had worked well on several chimps, who would live significantly increased life spans as a result. In his own body, however, the regulating cells that attached to the parasites quickly mutated and began to suppress other hormonal activity with equal precision.

This caused an emotional shutdown, a state of being that Etienne D'Anjou frantically desired to escape.

Etienne strained forward with his mind, desperately seeking to regain a foothold in Jeffrey's perceptions. Human minds typically resisted such intrusion. Forcefully. Jeffrey's was the only one that he had ever successfully inhabited for longer than a few minutes. Now, Etienne thought, if he could just get back *in*.

The silent implosion of contact and entry was so sudden this time that Jeffrey's head swam with vertigo for a moment before host and "observer" reoriented themselves.

"Are you all right?" Julia asked.

When the dizziness passed, Jeffrey smiled slightly and nodded toward the partly drained beer at his elbow. "I'm not used to alcohol," he said. "It makes me lightheaded."

"God, Jeffrey," Julia said, "you're white as a sheet."

"Probably just stress," Jeffrey said. "My blood sugar drops sometimes."

"Can I get you anything?" she asked.

"No, I'll be fine. Really." He took a sip of the *Tsing Tao*. "I'm sorry, my attention wandered. What were we talking about?"

"How you ever ended up working here," Julia prompted.

Jeffrey hesitated. "It's a long story."

"I've got time," Julia said, then added gently, "or we can talk about something else."

"Oh, I don't mind talking about myself," Jeffrey said. "It's just that . . ."

Don't you dare, Etienne thought fiercely. *Lie, make something up, but don't even think about—*

"I was in a car accident," Jeffrey said.

—*son of a bitch!*

"It was broad daylight. I was sober, the other driver was sober, but . . . it was rush hour and he decided to race the stoplight at an intersection. I'd say the stoplight won and that the two of us decidedly lost."

"Were you badly hurt?"

"I was in a coma for six days. The other driver didn't even make it to the hospital. Dead on arrival."

Julia sat in stunned silence.

"Road rage, they call it," Jeffrey said. "Kills about 28,000 people a year. A really stupid way to die, in my opinion."

Julia nodded, her luminous gray eyes fixed with awe on Jeffrey as if she were staring at someone who'd returned from the dead. "Was there anyone else in the car with you?"

"No. I was on my way home from work."

"To Mrs. Brooks?"

"To the *ex*–Mrs. Brooks."

"She must've been happy when you finally woke up."

Jeffrey paused, took another pull on his beer. "Not so happy that she didn't file for a divorce two months later." A dark, bitter spasm of humiliation flashed through Jeffrey as he spoke.

"I'm sorry," Julia said. "It must have been a rough time for you."

"Comas can be very difficult to recuperate from," Jeffrey said, "especially when they stretch beyond the thirty-six-hour mark, which mine certainly did. There was no brain damage, and no irreparable physical damage. It was mostly broken bones and dislocated ribs. But it still took several months before I could walk ten steps unassisted without falling over or collapsing from exhaustion. I'm sure it was hard on her—on Madison—the waiting, the uncertainty."

He spoke his ex-wife's name with a great deal more difficulty than he spoke of his broken bones or physical debilitation, indicating that the unendurable pain had not been caused by the injuries to his body.

"I hope I don't sound too bitter," Jeffrey said.

Julia shook her head. "Not at all. I understand."

"It's just that . . . I loved her, " Jeffrey said. "More than my own life. And I know, beyond any doubt, that I never could have done that to her. *Never*."

Instantly, Julia leaned across the table and gently clasped Jeffrey's free hand, the bandaged one. "I'm sorry, Jeffrey."

A warm rush of tenderness quickly supplanted the bitterness and Jeffrey gratefully stroked his thumb across the knuckles of Julia's hand. "Thank you." When Jeffrey's ebony eyes locked with Julia's, a silent and intimate signal passed between them, each one giving and receiving more than a friendly gesture of sympathy.

Etienne basked in the moment, even as a small ember of resentment burned in the back of his mind because another man, any man, could so quickly forge an emotional bond with his wife. She was his. He hated sharing Julia, hated—*almost* hated—Jeffrey for being the one he had to share her with. He wanted to hate her, too, for needing anyone else, even though he had deserted her—hell, practically flung her into Jeffrey's arms. But once upon a time, before he had destroyed himself, Etienne D'Anjou had been a fair-minded and compassionate man. A residue of empathy for others remained in his mind, enough that he could recognize his own selfish impulses for what they were—and reject them.

Before the physical contact could become too intimate, or either of them could grow uncomfortable with it, Julia withdrew her hand and leaned back in her chair again. She still wore Jeffrey's coat, though Etienne could see the shimmering green of her teddy between the gray lapels.

"I met Mr. D'Anjou while I was recuperating," Jeffrey said. "He had a . . . scientific interest in the recuperative processes associated with coma. We hit it off. And when I was well again, and all of my . . . domestic problems were settled, he offered me a position working with him."

Nice save, Etienne thought with genuine admiration. It was the cleanest non-lying evasion he had ever heard, glossing over the fact that the two men had met while Etienne was probing the mind of the comatose Jeffrey, trying to determine if he could take possession of what seemed to be a deserted shell. Instead, Jeffrey's instinctive subconscious resistance to having his body thus invaded and controlled had driven him out of the coma into full consciousness.

Even without emotional cues to guide his behavior, Etienne realized that he had been caught doing the psychic equivalent of peeking under someone's skirt while they were unaware. Unable to blush, Etienne had simply introduced himself, explained his "problem," and done his best to win Jeffrey's support and friendship. It was an odd, complicated, frustrating relationship for both of them.

"As a lab assistant," Julia said.

"I do computer research into Mr. D'Anjou's field of study," Jeffrey said. "I compile data on the latest studies in psychoneuroimmunology, organize it, and so forth."

You breach computer firewalls and steal corporate secrets for me that might help me cure myself, is what you mean to say, Etienne thought, the equivalent of a mental snicker echoing through his mind.

"The mind-body connection," Julia said, using the lay term for psychoneuroimmunology. "That's a pretty broad field to cover."

"It is." Jeffrey nodded. "It embraces psychology, biology, genetics, chemistry, pharmacology, a dozen or more other branches of the medical sciences, and it doesn't hurt to understand the latest developments in computer science, either."

"Etienne told me once," Julia said, "that he wanted to find a cure for aging."

"Don't we all?"

"I really think Etienne could, though—if anyone could. He said he was on the right track a few years ago, right after he got out of grad school. He was working for a company called the Zakarian Research Institute, said he was making real headway, but then they cut his funding and shunted him off on a side project."

"How did he take it?" Jeffrey asked.

"Not too well," Julia said. "He resigned. He said he could do his own research with his own money, or find investors who had a little imagination and the . . . um, the *guts* to take a calculated risk. But it's been—I don't know—he just—he hasn't been the same since then."

"And your marriage?" Jeffrey asked.

Julia avoided Jeffrey's gaze for a few moments, and there was nothing practiced in the desolate expression on her face as she considered the question. "Nothing's been the same," she said in a low voice. She sounded ashamed, as if she were the one who had failed Etienne, rather then the other way around.

"Not that I'm complaining," she added.

"I know," Jeffrey said.

Etienne stared through Jeffrey's eyes as Julia looked up at him and again found the approval, desire and admiration that she had been without for so long. Etienne realized with genuine shock just how worthless and unattractive he had made Julia feel with his seeming rejection, how starved for human warmth he had had to render her before she stumbled in her resolve to be faithful to him. Too late, it occurred to him that he should have told her the truth.

"It's after ten, isn't it?" she asked.

Jeffrey glanced at his watch and nodded. "Half-past."

"He's not expecting you back tonight, is he?" Julia asked.

"No," Jeffrey said. "In fact, I think he's already retired for the evening."

"I should, too," Julia said, though she didn't move from her chair.

Jeffrey waited.

"Would you mind escorting me to my room, Jeffrey?" she asked.

"I'd be happy to," he said.

Their chairs scraped the tiles as they both stood and left the drained beer bottles behind them. Jeffrey placed one hand in the small of Julia's back as they walked up the grand marble staircase together and he kept it there until they reached the door of the master bedroom suite.

It was while he was gently removing his coat from her shoulders that Julia put her arms around Jeffrey's neck. He let the coat fall to the floor and leaned forward into a kiss that sent wave after wave of fire and ice through his body. The fire was his compelling sexual need; the ice, the silent, secret fear that he would do something wrong, ruin the moment, botch the act and leave Julia unsatisfied and loathing him, or in some other way prove himself not man enough for the woman he wanted so badly.

As Jeffrey's lips moved from Julia's mouth down to her neck and the soft hollow of her throat, Etienne heard Julia's breathing quicken but realized that Jeffrey's did not, even though the sound of Julia's soft panting gasps caused his pulse to race. The man was consciously controlling his breathing, Etienne realized, and thus his own sexual pace. This would not be some quick and sloppy encounter with an inexperienced or selfish lover. Jeffrey had been waiting for this for quite a while and, whether there was a second time or not, he meant to make the most of what he had been given.

When his tongue darted into the hollow of Julia's neck, she dug her fingers into his shoulders and arched toward him. With the realization that she greatly enjoyed being nibbled and licked, Jeffrey slowly drew her into a tighter embrace and proceeded to do just that, nuzzling his way up from her neck to her left ear and back down to the side of her mouth, just brushed her parted lips, kissed the other side of her mouth and began another downward exploration of her neck. After several minutes of this methodical, leisurely teasing of her body, Julia went limp in Jeffrey's arms, eyes closed, head tilted back. The only signs that she was still fully aware were her rapid breathing and the intensity with which she dug her beautifully manicured nails into his shoulders. Otherwise, she completely surrendered to whatever Jeffrey did to her.

With deft hands, Jeffrey slid the silk teddy from Julia's shoulders and let it slither into a shimmering green coil around her feet. He admired the slender, unblemished lines of her body, the full, high breasts with their large, pale-pink nipples, the ivory-white and marble-smooth expanse of her flat belly, and the exotic russet foliage that formed an inverted triangle between her thighs. All of this was Julia, but Julia was far more than merely this, and despite his aroused state Jeffrey took the time to look, to appreciate the body with which he was about to become intimately acquainted.

Julia opened her eyes, glazed now with desire and need, and when she saw the expression on Jeffrey's face she smiled tenderly and moved her hand to caress the strong tendons at the back of his neck. Jeffrey reached around her and opened the door to the master bedroom. With their eyes still locked together, he picked her up. If she had weighed two hundred fifty pounds he would have picked her up, would have tried to, but she weighed less than half that amount and Jeffrey hid a deceptively wiry and athletically fit body beneath his dull gray suits. He carried her through the door, nudged it shut with his foot, and carried her to the bed, a massive four-poster on which she looked small, fragile and vulnerable when he laid her down.

Jeffrey removed his clothes, neither quickly nor as if he were putting on a show, and let her examine him as he had examined her. Fire and ice ran through him, fire and ice, until she sat up and placed exploratory hands on his chest. When he felt her lips against the pebbled surface of one of his nipples, he cradled the back of her neck with his bandaged hand and kissed the top of her head gently, not as if he were burning and aching to plunge himself into her, but as if the act had already been completed and this was just a leisurely gesture of affection indulged in afterward. A deep and persistent trembling shook him, though, and the only word he could say was her name, in a loving whisper.

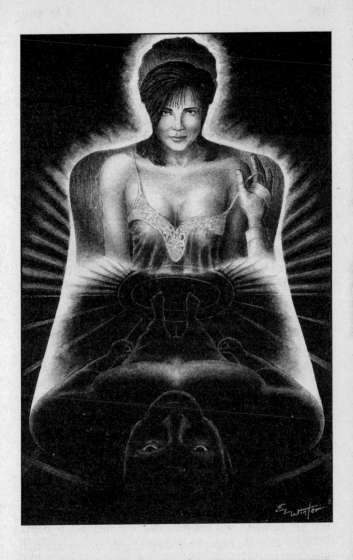

Illustrated by Eric L. Winter

A tide of hormones surged through Jeffrey, and Etienne flowed with the current, as Julia laid back and invited Jeffrey to make love to her in the unspoken language that passes between people at such times.

Jeffrey lowered himself onto the bed next to Julia and began to do to her body what he had done to her face and neck earlier. He explored, caressed, teased, massaged, nibbled and licked from shoulder to inner thigh until Julia's hands were clenching and unclenching into his shoulder blades.

"Jeffrey, please," she said. "Please."

Stretching out beside her, Jeffrey placed one hand against the side of her face, holding her gaze as he slid himself into the tight, molten depths of her body. Her legs locked around him, as if she were afraid he'd change his mind and try to escape. There was no chance of that.

He kissed one side of Julia's mouth and then the other as he began a slow, steady stroking that tried to match the rhythm of her own instinctive pelvic gyrations. If she slowed, he slowed; if she sped up, so did he. He let his kisses grow deep and gentle as their love-making continued. Once or twice his breathing grew as ragged and frantic as Julia's, but as soon as he realized it, Jeffrey would smooth it out again, pacing, controlling himself without dominating the woman who embraced him.

Iron-willed bastard, Etienne thought, as he felt through Jeffrey the tensing in Julia's hips when she stopped gyrating and simply lay with her pelvis thrust upward, not yet fulfilled but approaching the meltdown point.

Julia's whole body shuddered with an orgasm that Jeffrey felt pulse through her abdomen, while her soft recesses seemed to blossom around him. Her beautiful face twisted as if she were in the most exquisite agony, her back arched and she rocked with her breasts upthrust against Jeffrey's smooth chest, twice, three times, and then she fell back, limp, jeweled in sweat and shaking. As if she had given him permission and he couldn't wait to obey, Jeffrey released himself inside her with a deep groan that carried her name on it.

Etienne felt himself slipping out of Jeffrey at just this moment. Terror, stark and overwhelming, seemed to swallow him in a darkness blacker than the interior of the sensory deprivation chamber in which his abandoned shell now lay. This extreme reaction took Etienne by surprise. There was no fear-supporting adrenaline to fuel his body as his mind confronted the need to fight or flee. In the blank space between his body and Jeffrey's, Etienne discovered that some needs existed in the mind before they ever touched the glands.

He wasn't afraid of losing the physical pleasure of afterglow, or of missing whatever trivial pillow talk, if any, might follow the physical bonding between Jeffrey and Julia. His fear revolved around sinking back into the cold depths of unfeeling, unloving, unending loneliness.

The world, his world, was flesh and blood, and Julia was that world. Without her, without the ability to receive her love with appreciation or to give her the genuine, unaffected warmth she needed in return, he had no life, just a body that he hated, and a mind that he hated still more for its arrogance—the arrogance that had made him believe he could wrest from a jealous God with ease what other, better men would have approached with caution and humility, asking first, not *Is this possible?* but *Is this right?*

Jeffrey, intensely focused on the woman whose body was twined around him, was so filled with his own thoughts and feelings, his own spirit so securely settled into his body, that Etienne was simply being crowded out. As if clawing to scale a cliff that dropped away beneath him, Etienne fought against the return to his own body.

His mind surged toward Jeffrey, frantic, full of horror at the emptiness waiting for him back in the sensory deprivation chamber, more horrified than he would have been by his own death; for ex–altar boy and lapsed Catholic though he was, he didn't believe death would be the end of him or that purgatory would hold him forever. In death, at least, he would feel the love of God as his sins (*my most grievous sins . . .*) were purged from him. But here, outside of Jeffrey, separated by a chasm from Julia and all that was worth living for, he was like the rich man who lifted up his eyes in hell and looked at Lazarus at rest in a place of peace and comfort where he could never again tread.

As Etienne pressed forward into Jeffrey's resisting mind, and his deserted body drew him inexorably back toward living damnation, there was a silent yet distinctly perceptible *rip* that Etienne recognized as the severing of some psychic fabric.

Etienne felt sickeningly afraid that he had somehow damaged Jeffrey's hold on his body, afraid that he had injured the soul of a man who had given him far more than any human being had a right to ask of another. Then, smoothly and solidly, with an easy familiarity he had never experienced in any body other than his own, Etienne slid deep into Jeffrey's mind, and was enveloped in Jeffrey's sensations to an even greater degree than before.

At the moment, those sensations centered mostly around nausea, and Jeffrey rolled away from Julia and put a shaking hand over his eyes.

Julia turned on her side and laid a concerned hand against Jeffrey's cheek. "What?" she asked simply.

"I'm not sure," Jeffrey said. "I think the beer—and then—my stomach's just a little . . . uneasy."

"Tsing Tao not good to drink before make love, handsome sailor," Julia murmured in mock-oriental cadence. "Next time, wait till after maybe?"

Her tone was light, but when Jeffrey drew his hand away from his face, her gray eyes looked dark with concern. She leaned forward and gave him an affectionate kiss on the forehead.

"I could get you an Alka-Seltzer," she offered.

"I'll be okay," Jeffrey said, turning his head to plant a kiss into the palm resting against his cheek. "Besides, you've already had to be my nurse once tonight." He held up the bandaged hand.

"And you got to play doctor," Julia said provocatively. "It's my turn again."

"I think I just need a drink of water," Jeffrey said. When Julia turned to slide off the bed, Jeffrey sat up and put a gentle hand on her shoulder. "No, it's all right. I'll get it."

She settled back on the bed and watched him move toward the bathroom.

At the open bathroom door Jeffrey stopped and turned toward her. "I'll be right back," he said, obviously anxious to know if he would be welcome when he returned.

Julia bobbed playfully on the bed and patted the empty space beside her. "I'll be waiting."

In the privacy of the bathroom, Jeffrey did in fact rinse his mouth out at the sink tap and wash his ashenly pallid face. As he dried his face on one of Etienne's monogrammed bath towels, he looked at himself in the mirror.

"You're here to stay, aren't you?" he asked, speaking at a whisper so as not to be heard beyond the closed door. "I had a feeling . . . you didn't even know it your-self, did you? Too hard to go back to nothing, when everything that matters is right here. Believe me, I know."

Etienne felt like a man trapped with his hand in a cookie jar that had been clearly marked Thou Shalt *Not*.

"And what am I going to find when I go out to the lab and open the chamber? An empty body in an irre-versible coma? Or just a corpse in a steel coffin? Won't that be dandy? We won't even have to buy you a casket."

Jeffrey studied his reflection, which Etienne now realized was his own, and sighed with resignation. "I owe you my life. I know that. Without you, I probably wouldn't have come out of that coma before Madison or some other concerned party got to worrying that my quality of life had dipped too low and that it was time for my organs to be redistributed. You've got a piece of my soul, now. Don't ever say I don't pay my debts."

I won't.

"Oh, Jesus," Jeffrey's whisper grew hoarse. "I heard that. Can you hear my thoughts, too?"

No, Etienne said mentally, as stunned as Jeffrey that he was now an *articulate* resident in Jeffrey's mind and body. *And I won't ever try to.*

After that sank in, Jeffrey took several deep, calming breaths. "Okay, then. How does this work, now? Do we take turns, or just continue to—to share?"

I think sharing is our only option right now, Etienne said. *If that changes, I'm sure we can work something out.*

Jeffrey gazed carefully at his reflection as if he were searching for a glimpse of Etienne staring back—which he was, but without the ability to control Jeffrey's motor system. Nor did he want that control . . . or if he did, even secretly, he vowed to himself that he would never seek to gain it. He and Jeffrey were closer than brothers, closer even than lovers. Etienne could not imagine betraying him, would not let himself imagine it. He had been spared the worst pain there was, he would do nothing else to deserve more of it.

"All right," Jeffrey said. "We'll play it like it lays. And good luck to us both."

When Jeffrey returned to bed, Julia had slipped a tape into the VCR and was propped up on pillows watching *It's a Wonderful Life* on the big-screen television across the room. She muted the sound when he slid onto the bed beside her and laid his head on her chest, just above her bare breasts. He rested his bandaged hand on her flat belly, stroked the soft, transparent hairs there with one thumb.

"My favorite movie," he said.

"The colorized or black-and-white version?" she asked, turning up the sound a few notches.

"Black-and-white of course," Jeffrey said. "Colorization is a plot by extraterrestrial computer technicians who want to turn our brains into canned Spam."

"Yuck," Julia said. "Why would they want to do that?"

"I think Ted Turner owns a controlling interest in the Hormel meat packing corporation," Jeffrey speculated. He heard Julia snicker and felt her hand winding its way through the hair at the nape of his neck.

He lay still and listened to a black-and-white Jimmy Stewart and Donna Reed sing *"Buffalo gal, can't you come out tonight and . . . dance by the light of the moo-oo-oon,"* with one ear, and to the fierce, steady rhythm of Julia's heart with the other.

"You really like those, don't you?" Julia asked.

Jeffrey raised his head and looked at her. "What?"

"Those," Julia said, with a glance at her breasts.

Solemnly, Jeffrey nodded. "They are impressive," he said. "But if you were to lose them tomorrow, it wouldn't change anything."

A shocked look passed over her face and Jeffrey was certain for one split second that he had just said something disastrous. She dropped the remote control and reached out to stroke his face. Jeffrey blinked at the contact, surprised when she didn't slap him silly for saying something so outrageous.

"I love you, Jeffrey," she said, her eyes large and filled with the knowledge of how much pain loving another man was likely to cost her.

"I love you, too, Julia," Jeffrey said, as naturally as if he said the words every day and never meant them any less. He turned and laid his head against her chest again, calmed by her avowal of love, determined to deserve it, and equally determined to make her believe in his love for her.

Etienne let his mind drift lazily in private, shielded circles that wouldn't disturb Jeffrey's peace. He regretted Julia's inevitable grief at his seeming death but was mightily glad that, come tomorrow morning, she would be free of the need to pick between them, happier still that he wouldn't have to be the one to push her away yet again into another man's arms—though another man's arms were now his as well. He had a distinct feeling that she would appreciate the discovery that Jeffrey was a successful computer scientist with a small fortune of his own and had been Etienne's silent (*very* silent) business partner, rather than a lab assistant, chauffeur, bodyguard, whatever. Not that Julia was a snob, but . . . it would just make things easier, for both of them. He also had a feeling that Julia wasn't going to have any trouble staying in love with Jeffrey Brooks, even if he lacked the Kennedy-ish physical charms of one Etienne D'Anjou.

How Jeffrey was going to explain Etienne's dead (or possibly comatose) body to the police was another issue entirely. Etienne realized that they would have to allow public disclosure of the illegal experiments he had performed on himself while at the Zakarian Research Institute and that he would also end up shouldering the blame for everything quasi-legal and outright illegal that had followed. He didn't mind. Scandal couldn't hurt a dead man, even if he wasn't exactly dead, and the law couldn't punish a corpse. He and Jeffrey would work something out and Julia would be protected.

Etienne sank gratefully with Jeffrey into the blissful sleep of one who has not only made physical love with ardor, but has given his heart to love and, however undeserving, received the heart of another in exchange.

ON WRITING
SCIENCE FICTION

Written by
Eric Kotani

About the Author

Eric Kotani is a master of many arts. Among other things, he is a fifth-degree black belt in judo and a sixth-degree black belt in aikido, and has taught a martial arts class in Columbia for twenty years.

He has a Ph.D. in astrophysics and headed the astrophysics laboratory at the Johnson Space Center during the Apollo and Skylab Missions. For fifteen years, he was director of the NASA International Ultraviolet Explorer (IUE) satellite observatory.

His research interests have encompassed everything from interacting binary stars, the local interstellar medium, and active galactic nuclei to relativistic astrophysics. He has published over three hundred scientific papers and is editor of eleven scientific volumes, the last of which is "Examining the Big Bang."

Among the professional honors he has received are the Federal Design Achievement Award, which was issued in conjunction with the U.S. Presidential Award for Design

Excellence in IUE; the NASA Medal for Exceptional Scientific Achievement and the National Space Club Science Award.

*And by the way, he writes science fiction. Eric Kotani has published five novels: four with John Maddox Roberts—*Act of God, The Island Worlds, Between the Stars *and* Delta Pavonis—*and one with Robert MacBride Allen,* Supernova. *He also edited* Requiem: New Collected Works of Robert A. Heinlein and Tributes to the Grand Master, *a national bestseller. He has just written his sixth novel, a Star Trek Voyager book entitled* Death of a Neutron Star. *And in collaboration with John Maddox Roberts, he will soon complete his seventh novel,* The Legacy of Prometheus.

Here, he gives a little advice to new writers.

Robert A. Heinlein preferred to call science fiction *speculative fiction*. It is a good name and has the advantage of encompassing fantasy that is not always easily discernible from science fiction. It may also be argued that all fiction is speculative in one sense or another. Be that as it may, the term *science fiction* is likely to stay with us for the foreseeable future. Let me then try to define it in some rational fashion.

Science fiction must be based on science and technology as we understand it here and now. To be more accurate, a science fiction story is usually based on some form of speculative extrapolation from our present scientific knowledge. There is a great deal that we do not know about the universe; hence, we have plenty of room for speculation.

I am aware that some scientists believe that we already know as much about the physical world as we ever will. Many scientists in the nineteenth century felt that way too. One famous "philosopher" of science of the last century commented that all the important laws of nature had been discovered and that the remaining task for the scientists of the future would be to push the decimal place a step further. That sort of thinking is clearly wrong-headed in view of our current state of ignorance.

To make matters more interesting, some aspects of our present scientific knowledge are not too well established either. In popular publications, as well as in professional ones, firmly established scientific knowledge and borderline ideas are often presented with equal emphasis. This can make it difficult to tell the two types apart.

Nevertheless, if you are a serious science fiction writer, you must make efforts to learn the difference. That task is not always easy, even for professional scientists. If you take occasional missteps as a writer, be consoled that it is a hazard also shared by professional scientists.

All in all, as a writer you have unlimited opportunities for speculation—with the whole universe as your playground. You don't need to ignore well-tested scientific principles and write defective non-science fiction.

So, if you want your story to be science fiction, here are the basic guidelines that good science fiction stories should abide by:

(A) Do *not* violate firmly established laws (knowledge) of science. Let me give an example. Recently, two novels were published about a little black hole orbiting around Earth. The first book, which was written by a professor of astronomy at the University of Texas, was honest-to-goodness science fiction, but the latter was definitely not. The author of the latter book gave the semi-major axis and the period for the black hole's orbit; the two figures were inconsistent with well-tested laws of celestial mechanics that have been known since the seventeenth century. The second book wasn't even fantasy—it was simply in error. Had its author asked a typical student of astronomy at a nearby university, he would have been able to get that part of the science right.

(B) If your story requires you to contravene some well-established law of science, you must provide plausible scientific explanations for it. Actually, this process works in real-life scientific research too. Scientists often develop theories that, under certain circumstances, contravene conventional wisdom. For example, the Michelson-Morley experiment refuted the hypothetical existence of ether as a medium for the propagation of light; this discovery moved Einstein to develop his special theory of relativity.

(C) You *can* speculate as much as you like in the gray area of science. The use of hyperspace for traveling between stars would fall under this category. We do not know how hyperspace might work or even if it exists. Hence, it is fair game.

(D) Your speculations need not be limited to "hard" science, such as physics, biology, or astronomy. Good science fiction has been written based on "soft" science, such as sociology, cultural anthropology, economics, politics, and so on. Consider such novels as *1984* and *Animal Farm*. These are first-rate science fiction novels by any standard. However, we must be aware that the laws tend to be even less tractable in soft science.

But you might ask, "What about stories that are full of technobabble?" Does mere use of technical jargon, such as "blaster" and "hyperspace drive," qualify a story as science fiction? Not always. Many stories that look like science fiction are merely adventure tales dressed up to look like science fiction. These are called "space operas," and they are not very different from adventure stories of bygone years (such as the "Captain Horatio Hornblower" tales). The only difference is that the hero in a space opera uses a ray gun (instead of a pistol) and may travel between stars in a space cruiser (rather than in a ship that sails over the ocean).

We are in murky waters here. It is not always easy to make a clear distinction between authentic science fiction stories and space operas, since expressions that sound like technobabble turn up in all sorts of science fiction. The real issue is whether the story contains genuine scientific elements—not whether one finds certain types of neologisms in the story.

A discerning reader could perhaps tell the difference between the two kinds of fiction, even if the writer is not sure.

In the final analysis, it may not be important to you whether your story is space opera or genuine science fiction. The most important thing about any fiction— be it science fiction, fantasy, or any other genre—is that the story be entertaining and emotionally engrossing to both the reader and the writer.

LITERACY

Written by
Stefano Donati

Illustrated by
Dionisios Fragias

About the Author

Stefano Donati's introduction to science fiction came with an early edition of **The Hugo Winners,** *edited by Isaac Asimov. It contained Harlan Ellison's "'Repent, Harlequin,' said the Ticktockman." After that, Stefano was hooked.*

His heroes include columnist Nat Hentoff, songwriter Morrissey and new horror writer Suzanne Donahue.

He has been writing for a couple of years, and though he says he has had some recent success, he has also gotten enough rejection slips to wallpaper his apartment. So it was especially gratifying when his story "Literacy" took first place in the first quarter of the contest.

About the Illustrator

Dionisios Fragias was born on the island of Kefalonia in Greece, and moved to the United States as a child. He was fascinated with science, and worked as a child at combining his love of science with art.

But it wasn't until he got into high school that he began to develop his own style, looking for inspiration to Renaissance masters such as Michelangelo and Vermeer, and to contemporary masters like Salvador Dali, Frank Frazetta and Vincent Di Fate.

Now in college, where he is a sophomore at the Fashion Institute of Technology, Dionisios has begun writing as a complement to his art.

After they've voyaged inside my father, some people whisper to me grotesque details about him. They say his left thigh bears a snake-shaped tattoo, and that on his wedding night he lay trembling beside my mother, impotent from fear.

And then they taunt me for not even knowing if they're lying.

Today, while sitting across from me in science, Queen Francine flicks a note onto my desk. *About your dad*, it says in graceful cursive, *he's having a decent morning. I'm reading him right now and he's connected to the world today.*

When I come home I discover that Queen Francine has lied. My father is in the bathroom, peering at the sink, and it takes him one full minute to realize I'm nearby, another to realize who I am. Neither of us dares mention what we both know: that he's completely forgotten why he's in there. A quick pee, nail clippers, a brush, it could be anything.

"Eleira," he says, awed that he can still recognize his daughter.

"Where's Mom?" I ask.

"At . . . the store." Which could mean the grocery store, the drugstore, or the bookstore. Or maybe just out for a walk.

Days like this are frequent now.

Illustrated by Dionisios Fragias

Finally I hear the front door click and then my mother clattering toward us. Her glittering blue eyes let me know she's started reading him again. I envy her. As she reaches fully inside his brain, her lips make smacking noises, the kind they make before she dives into a hot fudge sundae. No doubt others are reading along with her, from elsewhere in the city, but hers is the phase that's just beginning. She won't speak his thoughts, and I despise her for excluding me.

So I guess at the mental dialogue between them. Maybe he's vaguely remembering some love-struck gaze she once warmed him with, and she's feeding his nostalgia by sending him the distant aroma of the first loaf of bread he ever baked her. Or maybe they're firing silent insults through the air.

But my guesses don't satisfy me. "Say it, Mom. Tell me."

She loves me just enough to at least report her own share of the dialogue aloud: "Perry . . . No, I'm your wife, Katrina, and this isn't your niece . . . No, no, it's your daughter, Eleira . . . Perry, you don't have a tree-house . . . Summer job? Oh, Perry, you're much too old to want a summer job!" She draws him to her, hugs him carefully, as if he'll break. The kiss she gives him startles him, confuses him. My mother starts to sob, and then she whirls on me: "Goddammit, Eleira, I can't take care of him all by myself. Why can't you read him? It isn't that hard!"

I'm his daughter. It's impossible.

As impossible as watching him slowly die.

•••

"Someday they'll read you, too."

The first time my father told me this, on my twelfth birthday, we believed he was still well.

"It's in my family blood," he said. "We all get read; it'll start happening to you, Eleira, in just two or three more years."

He blushed the color of the red bicycle I was gripping in the driveway mud. "For me, it started with that little jerk Joe Gant. I still remember the message in my brain: *Miss Keeley would never date you.* I'd never, ever talked about Miss Keeley, but he told everyone just what dreams I'd had the night before. Even told Miss Keeley. Poor woman, she didn't need to hear that kind of stuff. If I'd been her, I would have flunked me."

My father was already rambling, beginning to be robbed of clarity; he was partly with me, partly back with Joe Gant and Miss Keeley—a *young* Miss Keeley— partly with all the people and years in between. But I was only twelve. I didn't understand.

"They'll crave their phases of reading you," he said. "Even after two or three days straight, they won't like to stop."

My mother touched his arm. "Don't scare her."

"She has to know."

"Not yet."

"You crave it, too, don't you, Katrina? When you go even a month without reading me, it's like withdrawal."

"We can't help ourselves," she said.

"And we can't either. We can't help the thoughts we have; we can't censor them completely." He stared at me intently, a stare I'd seen reserved for grown-ups, and I no longer wanted to be all adult. "Eleira, if you're dreaming of the perfect crime, dream it now. Dredge up any thought that's remotely sinful, then get it the hell out of your system. And, later, start to practice censoring your mind as best you can."

"How?"

"Self-discipline. My own father gave me the same advice, and I thought, well, I have a whole couple of years to practice. But I put it off, and by the time they started reading me, I was too goddamn used to thinking freely."

"Perry, shush. You're—"

"She *needs* to be scared."

And I still am. Two years of discipline have not made my thoughts any more wholesome. Soon everybody will be taking turns learning which movie actors arouse me, and that I bloat up after my period and not before, and how much I wish someone would really talk to me about Dad.

•••

When Kinloch returns my arachnids exam with its fat, red 37, I worry that it's already begun. Maybe with Kinloch himself. He's reading how afraid I've been each day this spring, afraid to run home to find my father even worse. Already Kinloch has said, "I'm not going to pass you just because you're daddy's sick."

I've never asked him to. *Stupid bastard*, I think toward him. Anger doesn't come over him; I'm still safe. So I think it again. *Stupid bastard, stupid bastard*, over and over.

"Hey." In a whisper hoarse from cigarettes, Queen Francine says, "I'm picking up the junk mail in your father's brain."

"Yesterday you told me he was doing well."

She shrugs. I guess she thinks she'll never die. "Today he isn't doing well at all. But don't worry. Me and plenty of other people are in him, especially this carpenter downtown and some housewife on Ellis Street. We're watching over him."

"You're a liar, Queenie."

"Maybe. Maybe not."

I fire my pen at her. Green ink splatters her blonde tresses and trickles down her jumpsuit. I yank on Don Talvey's hair, savoring each rendition of "Ouch!" performed one octave higher than the last. I yell several names at Kinloch, urging him to attempt acts even a biology teacher would find impossible.

And then I calmly fold my hands upon the desk.

Everybody stares at me, Kinloch included. Clearly they've foreseen no portion of my outburst. So for now, at least, my mind is still safe from all of them.

The discovery is worth the walk to the principal's office.

• • •

"But why do you treat me like a child?"

My mother gives Dad a mournful stare. "Because, at times, you are a child."

Quietly I close the front door behind me.

"But there are other times, Katrina—times I'm lucid."

"Not enough of them."

If either of them has to go, it should be her. She isn't the one who clutched my hand when I was five and helped me sketch the willow tree in our backyard. She isn't the one who drew paintings, just for me, of candy canes sledding down a mountainside or of sunlight melting the chocolate insides of the Easter Bunny.

They notice me. My father says, "Let's not fight in front of Eleira."

My mother sighs. "Don't worry about Eleira."

"Mom's right." Instantly I regret my words. I shouldn't challenge him. I need to defend him against her.

"You're my daughter; I'll be worrying about you until the end."

My mother says, "He could beat this if he tried." Abruptly she leaves the kitchen for another angry walk.

"More spaghetti for us, then." He grins at me, that dorky grin I actually used to make fun of, with my friends.

But later, as I ladle the spaghetti onto our plates, he coughs—his way of broaching something serious. We sit at the dinette, and he says, "Eleira, your mother's right. You deserve to know: your old man isn't what he used to be." He intends for this to gently surprise me; he can't imagine that for all the denial around me, I might actually know what's going on. Even though I still can't read him, I can tell: mixed with everything else he's wishing for but has lost forever is the naive child I once was.

But I ask what he means. I can't let him think it's obvious.

"I'm not absolutely sure," he says. "I never will be, not completely, and nobody else will either until the autopsy."

So I let him tell me. I let him tell me how he wakes up crying, frightened by the strange bed he's in, asking my mother where his mommy and daddy are. How just last week one of his old painting students stopped him on the street, asked how he's been doing, and he muddled through as best he could, did not let on that the student was like an alien to him.

I let him tell me about his Alzheimer's.

It might not be so bad, but twice I have to remind him what he's talking about.

"Eleira, there's a way you can help me—if you want to."

"How, Dad? Suicide?"

He lowers his head. I shouldn't have asked. Maybe he hasn't realized how much agony I'm in because of him. Not enough to really want him dead; but awful agony. Maybe he hasn't realized.

"Not suicide," he says. "But you can help by reading me."

"Dad. Dad, I'm your daughter. I'm going to be a readable, not a reader. It's in our blood, remember?"

"You're wrong."

"You've said so yourself. All down your family line, we're readables, not readers. I'll never get inside your mind."

The dazed look comes over him, the look I dread the most.

"If you concentrate, you can do it," he says, yearning to place the power in me. With his deterioration, maybe he's forgotten. I'm just his daughter; not his wife, and not some ancient friend. When he's with me, his thoughts will always return to him, unread.

"No. If helping you means reading you . . . I can't do it."

He shuts his eyes. "Just being alive, Eleira, you're a help to me."

But not enough. I know it.

•••

"You're the one whose father people read," Jason says, as April sunlight streaks through his hair. Jason is the new boy, and it's me he's walking with. Not Queen Francine or Karen Treemont; me. We clutch our textbooks and move along the sidelines of the athletic field.

"Have you read him yet?" I ask.

"I've never read anybody." He gazes shyly toward the fog beyond the mountains. For him to be my age and inexperienced is hardly unusual, I've heard, but certainly confessing to it is unusual.

"Someday, Eleira . . . I *will* read your dad. And I'll read you. Even if I don't want to—I mean, you deserve your privacy."

So many people have said that lately, as if to seek my assurance that I won't resent them. But Jason's tone is genuine. "Don't feel guilty," I say. "I just hope it won't bother you if we're not brilliant. I know how some people hate it when the readable's retarded or dying or even just sad."

"I'm not that picky. Besides, I can already tell you're brilliant."

And so was my father once, I want to say—even as I hope Jason doesn't suddenly start reading me, for my thrilled reaction to his praise is way too scary for him to know about.

To try to ease the atmosphere, he says, "So, I hear your presentation is going to be on telepathy."

"Wanted to know what I'd be going through, I guess. Get ready, Jason; people are going to blush. I'm going to refer to it as 'Snaring the Medulla,' 'Cerebellating,' *and* 'Kissing the Cortex.'"

"Kinloch will be incensed. Great."

From behind us, Coach Harris shouts tips on archery. Luckily we're much too clumsy for him to note our absence. "You know what I hate remembering?" I say. "Being a little kid. We'd be in a crowd someplace, there'd be all those grown-ups looming over me, and someone would just say my father's thoughts out loud."

The way my mother does sometimes.

"I thought that was magic," I say. "It never occurred to me how humiliating it must have been for him."

"Maybe . . . maybe when they start reading you, Eleira, you can humiliate them back. Throw them off. Say something like, 'You must have misread me. That wasn't what I was thinking at all!'"

I laugh. It's been so long. Jason's brown eyes glance at me. He takes my hand and the world vanishes.

"Eleira . . . I've heard about your father. How ill he is."

I'd almost forgotten. For moments at a time, I almost can. This has been so perfect, this walk with Jason, that I can't be mad at him for mentioning Dad.

He says, "If I can help . . ."

And then Coach Harris blows his whistle, and we scurry back to our locker rooms, and Jason can't see how much he's done for me.

•••

Today is good. Today my father lets my mother bathe him, then lies in bed and curls his knees against his chest. No moaning. Maybe his are pleasant dreams, today.

While my father sleeps, I work on my class presentation for Kinloch. I burrow deep inside back disks of *Mindmonthly*. There's an item on speculative history proposing that maybe Henry V slaughtered the French at Agincourt only because a crucial commander was readable or reading, and maybe Archduke Ferdinand's being readable led to his murder and the beginning of the Great War. People weren't always so vulgarly open about reading, and who was doing it and when.

A second item says Alzheimer's strikes readables at four times the rate that it strikes readers. In fifty years I might be like my father. I'll remember him only dimly, and as I grow unable to count on a single cogent evening, my friends will shy away.

But maybe Jason won't.

Two hours of articles like "How to Teach Your Kids to Keep Their Reads to Themselves" and "When Your Child Insists People Can Read Him" is plenty. I'd rather be with Jason.

How can I even think of Jason when my father's dying?

I come back over and over to my father's insistence that I can somehow read. Is that really possible?

I'm clutching at anything now.

I'm going to try to read. Somehow. I'm going to get to know him, thoroughly, before he goes.

•••

Silent concerts are disgusting.

As Jason and I settle into our seats, I pray the McGarrigle Sisters will instead perform aloud. Any readable can memorize *The March of the Capulets* or recall the voice of Sinatra, then let the lucky readers in the audience cull the music from their brain.

Soon the McGarrigles emerge onstage and reassure me. Kate plays the baby grand aloud, and Anna's actual voice fills the hall with "Kitty Come Home."

For a few happy listeners this must be *déjà entendu:* they can foretell the playlist, the jokey exchanges between songs, the angle at which Kate's head will hunch over the piano. But as the sisters segue from "Dancer With Bruised Knees" to *"Perrine Était Servante,"* Jason and I revel in the surprise. Even when Kate's voice cracks, we're spared having to read her reaction. A lyric altered, a fiddle crescendo . . . each variation from the recordings thrills us only as it happens, not before.

But then it starts. Sweatdrops pour from me. My arms shake, the whole hall tilts, it's like a thousand beehives swarming at me. A thousand sunlights. The noise imposes a pounding migraine. I swear I'm screaming. . . .

I've begun. I've begun to read. And it isn't just the sisters onstage. I'm reading everyone.

Even Jason. Even distantly my father. He was right. He's sleeping now, but he was right.

Yet even readers can't read this much.

The entire city swoops in on me, sixty thousand people with all their smells and passions blending, hues I've never glimpsed before, muscles I've never felt the ache of. Like sixty thousand radio stations all at once, each with bursts of crackle, broadcasting in languages I can barely understand.

A deaf person, on gaining hearing, can't distinguish details.

Three songs later, though, I've begun to. The minds on the city's fringes remain murky, but those nearer are becoming distinct. There are mix-ups: at first the music is pouring forth from the Maine-born, forty-year-old dentist in the fifth row, and the silently bickering family on Stoddard Street is Kate at the piano. But secrets leap at me: what it's like to be eighty-nine, a baby, a surgeon, self-confident; the miracle of Medjugorje; the somber lingering over a dead child's photos . . . everything is open to me now, and if I'm too wanton I'll absorb it all. I try to banish all the minds, but the best I can manage is to subdue them. On the sisters' dolorous humming, *"À Boire"* ends, and beneath the applause I say to Jason, "I'm reading."

"What do you mean?"

"I mean I'm reading."

Frantically, he says, "But you're a readable. You—"

"I don't understand it, either. Maybe I'm adopted." Maybe that's what my father meant to imply. But how can I be reading *everyone*? "I'm really reading, Jason."

His face tightens in amazement, and then he thinks he understands. He doesn't know I'm reading more than just the sisters and my father. I begin to cry, for me because I don't want to read him, for him because he doesn't know I can.

His hand moves to my arm, in fits. He frightens me, for being someone I so hate to hurt. And I'm hurting him right now, by going through this pain he can't understand. All he says is, "It's okay, El." *Déjà entendu*. But I can't convey it, how this isn't even normal reading, the thrill I've heard that most people get their first time inside another mind.

I'm still sorting through the crush of lives inside me: the frail survivor of long-ago prison-camp starvation; the bashful, pudgy scholar's absolute command of algebra; the prostitute near the harbor and the awful things she does with men. . . .

I can't tell Jason about this. Not yet. What would he think?

But how will I manage to not slip up? To not refer, someday, to some truth about him which he's never shared? His mind keeps buzzing at me, engulfing me, and I almost shriek at him. Too much, at once. Jason, you never told me about the street gang that killed your cousin. Or that you like my dimples. You can't really sense, for all your efforts, what it's like to watch a father worsen. I try to stop, to preserve his privacy and keep my obscene gift from drowning me. I want to shut this off, but don't know how.

"What's it like?" he asks, happy for me, envious. His mind is the same pitch as his voice, only fainter.

"It's . . . good, I guess. It will be when I get used to it."

"This shouldn't be happening to you. Not to a readable."

More *déjà entendu*. Speech is maddeningly slow now.

"I'm adopted. I must be." But that explains just part of it, I think. Somehow I can read the city, and I'll have to get used to that. Or else I'll grow insane. I know it.

Has this power everyone else possesses been crouching inside me, gorging itself, poised to erupt and overflow, to spill through my mind? Drive me mad?

I can't go mad. Not until my father no longer needs me.

"What song will they play next?"

I try to focus on just the sisters, but other minds still swarm at me. Jason's most strongly. "'Heart Like a Wheel.' Silent version."

This is the one song they will perform only for those who are in phase. I can read Jason's frustration; why should only readers get to savor this perfect rendering, unmarred by acoustics problems or a sudden sharp? He clasps my hand, sits patiently as they move through it. At the finish, the lovely finish, the other readers "clap" by whooshing their hands past each other in silent tribute. I don't join them.

Jason deserved to hear this.

Why is this strange power mine?

A spinal birthmark I've never glimpsed firsteye. The stammer in his parents' voices when they told him about his cousin.

Forget. Forget these details.

And Jason, good old Jason, oblivious to what I'm doing to him, simply says, "Hey, El; you can read your dad now."

•••

Even before I come downstairs, I hear the dishes slam onto the floor. "You don't care!" he yells at her. "Every day you go off for hours, and you never tell me where you are!"

"Perry. I go to work."

His fury and her fear accost me, squelching every other mind in town. My father has never slapped my mother, but he slaps her now, hard across the cheek. I rush between them, pry his hands off her, and glare at each of them—at her for not grasping that what just hit her isn't *him*, and at him for not beating his disease. I'm being unfair, but this once I allow myself that.

"Go to work, Mom."

"He's going to need round-the-clock care now." She won't say it, but she's thinking it: Soon we're going to have to put him in diapers.

"I'll stay with him," I say.

"I don't pity him, not one bit. Not after how he hit me."

He seldom knows what pity is. But I don't point that out; she wouldn't care, and he'd not want to be discussed as if he weren't here.

She does pity him. Reaching far inside her, I detect it. But for all the reading I can do, I can't fathom why she thinks concealing her sorrow from him will protect him.

When she's out of the house, her mind recedes, and it's as if my brain's lost thirty pounds.

The day comes into focus for him. "I slapped your mother just now, didn't I?"

"She understands."

"No, she doesn't. She's a frightened woman. I should have been more gentle with her."

"You've been gentle with her your whole life. You . . ." Not too much; don't make him think about too much. That faraway look has come over him. I read him and confirm that he's no longer certain who we are.

"Dad, I can help you now." Only by invading him. I venture into his mind, to orient him. I patch his fractured thoughts together, can almost feel the synapses reconnect. Soon they'll dissolve into randomness again, but for a while I win him partly back.

Venturing, I stumble upon the knowledge that I was not adopted. I do have his genes. He even remembers coaching my mother through the delivery. I exit him, as gingerly as I can, before I have to glimpse the bloody specifics.

But I say again, "I can help you."

"You're reading?"

"Way too much."

He squints at me. He's never been brought back this much or this fast, not even by my mother. "How long?"

"Since last night."

"Reading other people?"

"Everyone."

It rushes at me, like a gestalt: once, he could read them too.

"Answer out loud," I say. "Please, Dad." I want something to be like how it always was.

"I could read them all," he says, "just like you can now. Every readable can, at first. Terrific, isn't it?" He's truly remembering it that way. The immense power of being a teenaged boy able to spy on the minds of wiser elders, or to learn that big, bad Chester Engam can't decode a word of printed text. It was terrific, my father recalls with guilt, to know each question Mr. Gullogh planned to put on the history exam.

"It only lasts a week or so, Eleira. At least for me, and for my sister and my father."

"Just a week?"

"More or less. All at once it dies."

"Then what?"

"Then it's their turn."

I remember from the autobiographies. The first classmate to prove he's reading you gets a party thrown for him.

"But why don't they know we've read them?" I could root out the answer, but I want him to tell me. He's always loved teaching me: how to hold a paintbrush, or tie my sneakers, or build a snowman. This past year he's taught me such things again, and I've pretended to be his little grade-schooler. I want my father, one last time, to teach me something I don't already know.

"There's a tiny corner of our minds," he says. "One part that readers never seem to get access to. And that's

where we store our memories of reading *them*." He
smiles, not the confused smile I've seen too much of
lately. "I guess that tiny corner is our compensation for
the privacy they rip from us."

"Why haven't you told them?"

"Why haven't you? Too dangerous. I would never
even tell your mom." Both his mind and voice ooze
bitterness. "It's okay for them to read us, since there are
so few of us. But if they found out we'd ever read them,
even for just a week when we were teenagers, they'd
destroy us. It'd be like our facing down a bully who
would just hit harder later. Some of the readers mean
well, but some of them are just bloodthirsty hypocrites.
They'd kill us if they learned that our power is anything
like theirs. There's a city full of them, Eleira; there are
just the two of us. Soon there'll just be you."

I read my father's hope that I won't pity him. He's
only aiming to tell me what I need to know.

"Can I at least tell Jason?"

"Who?"

"A friend."

"I hope he's friend enough to put up with
knowing that all your thoughts, including the ones
about him, will be open to the outside world. Do you
realize your mother was the only girl who ever dated
me?"

I give him a bemused grin, try to act surprised.

Jason is the only boy who'll ever date me. But he's
enough. I almost saunter into him right now, just a
quick mind-peek.

No.

"Don't tell your friend anything. I'd hate to see some
reader hurt you."

"Jason would keep the secret."

"Do you already know him that well?"

My father wonders if I've kissed my friend. He wants to meet him, but he's afraid of embarrassing me, of warning Jason that I'm some impostor, and his real daughter is only eight years old.

Yearning.

Yearning dominates. Jason is pushed aside; my father's brain surges into me, sordid truths seep from it. I learn much about my father—some things I'd just as soon not know, and some I'll never tell. But mainly I detect his yearning for release from sickness. Permanent release. He won't seek it when he's clear-minded; there's a sort of pleasure in those times, and he makes himself forget how much he wants to die. And wants my help.

"I can't give it."

He doesn't fully understand what I'm objecting to. Already the synapses are loosening. What focusing his brain can manage is on this: the painting he's been working on for a month, during his stable hours—a painting of an orange sunset and, superimposed over a hillside of lush green grass, a kind and matronly face. An angel calling him home?

Last night, while I slept and couldn't read him, he moved toward that painting, grabbed an Exacto knife, and slashed the canvas into tatters.

He's a tolerant husband, an approachable father, and one of the few people who don't grow boring once they start families. This little weakness in his last stages is not shameful.

But I think to him that the help he seeks sounds a lot like suicide, the thing he promised it wouldn't be. Or a mercy killing, which I think to him I don't believe in. This brings him partly around. I can read his insistence that there will be more mercy in this than killing. And—almost offending me with his arrogance, but this arrogance is new so it's not really his—he thinks I'm too young to grasp how life can lose its meaning.

Wrong; I'm reading you, and there is meaning in you.

Barely; next time I'm not lucid, Eleira, get me killed. Please.

•••

Over the blanket on the riverbank Jason and I spread the deli sandwiches, the orange soda, and the cherry brownies my father has baked for us. I see everything Jason sees: me, the maples behind me, the patch around them still damp from spring's slow meltings.

"Was your dad any better this morning?"

"Quite a bit." Seeing him briskly stir the brownie mix, then paint and hum during the baking, had almost brought me back to eight or nine years old. So long as there are still stretches like that, I'll refuse to let him succumb.

One stretch of not dwelling on my father. Just one.

"Jason. I can read you."

"What?"

My father deserves to not have him learn too much, but he deserves to learn a little. "I can practically read the blue jay over there. You, you're coming in loud and clear."

Jason stops chewing his roast-beef sandwich. "Since when?"

"Since the concert."

"How? Even if you are adopted, even if you are a reader, how can you be reading me? I don't have a readable gene in my body."

"Not just you—everybody. I can't explain it. I guess I'm just some kind of freak."

He wants desperately not to think of me that way. But he sits on his knees, and his view of the maples behind me tilts slightly. "What's in my mind now?"

Be discrete, I urge myself. Be discreet, but still persuade him. "You're thinking that I must be mistaken. But also that I'm not. And you wish I'd told you right away."

I hesitate; I can read him, but can't yet predict him. I'll learn, now, if he'll be willing to endure me. "Your favorite color is a sort of light maroon. Your favorite pie is rhubarb, and—"

I stop. His mind is trying to suppress something: his desire to stroke my hair. He wants and doesn't want me to know.

"Jason. When I read you, I can get very far in."

"How far?" he asks.

"Far enough."

He looks away. Before long, my own desires will reach his mind. And later, if later comes, he'll know precisely how to satisfy me. I think I'd prefer some mystery.

I hope what I say next doesn't betray my father too much. "I'm not adopted, Jason; I do have readable genes. And before long you'll start reading me, and so will everybody else. They'll know everything I think about you."

So much for him to absorb.

"Everything, Jason; any quarrel we might have, or secret you tell me." This shouldn't shame me; it's not my fault.

"Even how I kiss?"

He means it. He wants the two of us to learn right now how well or poorly we both kiss. But he's as afraid as I am.

"Yes," I say. "Even how you kiss. Can you put up with a girl that the city knows everything about?"

After a long while, he murmurs his answer. And I wish I couldn't read it first.

"I don't care what the city knows. I'm with you forever."

Timidly he strokes my hair, and timidly I stroke his. The touch thrills us yet embarrasses us, and awkwardly we each retreat. "Your father makes great brownies."

"He wants to die, Jason. He wants me to help him die."

My boyfriend looks at me in a way I can't describe. It makes me wish we'd both been born a few years earlier, and begun our romance in time for him to meet the man my father once was.

"Will you . . . will you help him, do you think?"

"All I know is that I don't want to."

I lift a piece of brownie into Jason's mouth.

"What's that for?"

"Being afraid *for* me and not of me."

•••

Monday morning, Queen Francine says for all to hear, "Come on, Jason. Just one detail about Eleira. Tell the world one detail about Eleira you could only learn by reading her father."

He stays silent. From the seat in front of him and across from me, she says, "Jesus, Jason; my baby sister's going to start reading before you do."

I glare at her. "Francine, your baby sister's going to grow up before *you* do."

My brain calls out to my father. I think, *Tell me how the morning's been.*

Nothing.

I try again, harder: *Tell me how the morning's been.*

Eleira, he thinks. Eleira. He can't form an ordered image. But what he does think answers me. Fragmented memories. Finding china in the garbage . . . green paint blotches on the kitchen wall . . . two or three weeping spells . . . and, within the hour—I deduce it by the smells in his brain—soiling his pajamas.

I try to reconnect his synapses long-distance. If he can just recapture some of himself, he may get oriented enough so that I don't have to lose him yet.

But this is Alzheimer's. He'll never get oriented for long.

He needs to die today.

But when they all start reading me, I'll need him there to help me.

No. He needs to die today.

Jason shuts his eyes for me. Maybe he can't read me, but he can read my face.

Change your clothes, I send to my father. *Put those soiled pajamas where Mom . . . your wife . . . Katrina . . . the one who yells . . . will find them. Now, put on something else. Yes, those tan slacks are fine, and so is the green shirt. Quickly, please.* When he has finished changing, I send, *Now walk outside.*

My mother's voice says, *Perry, don't let her do this.*

I almost turn and look for her, but the tone is too faint; she's in her business meeting downtown, pointing to a poster board of graphs and giving a presentation to trustees. She's also begun her latest phase of reading him.

And, reading him, she knows I'm in there too. She can't imagine how, but in her frenzy she doesn't ask.

Perry, don't let her send you outside. You'll get hurt.

Her voice alarms him. That voice he's loved, the voice that's always soothed him, God knows how, suddenly sounds so frantic. He wants so very much to understand.

I keep my instructions simple:

Now, walk out of the house.

Barely, his mind calls up his memory of asking me to someday command him; confused but pliant, he walks out of the house.

Kinloch enters the classroom. I hardly notice until he says, "Speech time. Eleira?" He shuffles through his papers, pretends to be uncertain as he says, "Telepathy's your topic, right?"

Giggles ripple through the room like gunfire. Except for Jason, no one knows I've joined those who've read. No one knows how *much* I've joined them.

My mother intrudes again. *For twenty-three years, Perry, you've been the most important person in my life. Don't ever let her take you from me.*

If I stay matter-of-fact, maybe he won't be so afraid.

Now, onto the curb. My father walks onto the curb. Traffic soars past him.

"Eleira, get in front of the classroom. Give your speech."

Into the street, now.

My father walks into the street.

"Give your speech, or get a zero and flunk this class."

Reading you, Dad, I can see that there's an orange van approaching. Walk in front of the van.

No, Perry, don't listen to her. She's just being selfish.

He walks in front of the van, then wavers.

Let it hit you, Dad.

Perry, no!

Pull out, lady, he thinks to her, not sure who she is. And then he thinks the same plea to me: *You, too, girl; pull out.*

He doesn't know me. And whatever I'm doing for him or to him, he's just lucid enough to not want me with him in his truly final instant.

Brakes screech, a horn blares, screams erupt from him and others, metal pelts him, crushes him, he tumbles, darkness.

I almost glimpse where he goes next.

My mother drops her pointer. The trustees hear her curse me, but they don't know why.

Kinloch says, "That's it, Eleira. You've failed!"

Queen Francine cackles. The next speech starts. Pedestrians hurry toward my father, much too late. An ambulance is called. And Jason holds me.

THE DRAGON AND THE LORELEI

Written by
Carla Montgomery

Illustrated by
Christopher Jouan

About the Author

Though Carla Montgomery currently lives in North Carolina, she was raised in New Mexico and finds that her childhood exposure to various cultures and to unmarred wilderness is the driving force behind her writing.

She earned her B.A. at the University of Texas in Austin in biology and her M.A. at Duke in philosophy and the history of science.

She has worked as a museum instructor, research specialist, science reporter and as a freelance technical writer—combining her love of science and writing in each of her career choices. Recently, she has turned to writing science fiction and fantasy (quite eloquently, I might add) with the result that her first story, "Thiefs's Flight" was recently published in the anthology Magic: The Gathering, Tapestries. *A second story "Leeward of Broken Jerusalem" will appear in the anthology* Armageddon, *edited by David Drake and Billy Mosiman.*

Currently, Carla is working on a historical novel with speculative aspects set in the early nineteenth-century America.

About the Illustrator

Christopher Jouan began his artistic career on the walls of his parents' home . . . and on the windowsills, doors, trim . . .

Though he loved art, he spent much of his schooling studying music and wanted to be an aerospace engineer. But one semester in college studying engineering convinced him that he should quickly return to art. When problems at his university in California necessitated cutbacks, the university cut the illustration program.

Cast onto the streets, Christopher went into the wide world of freelance, where he has worked on a number of projects in illustration—in newspapers, illustrating a children's book, doing cartoons and so on. Along the way, he has learned much that isn't taught in college.

To pay the bills, he works at the Chula Vista Public Library in California, and with the help of his fiancé, Charlette, he is working hard to get his work discovered.

enya faced into the ocean wind as the breakers crashed around her, sending white plumes of spray into the air. She perched on the edge of a slippery, jagged-edged jumble of rock clinging to the cliffs of the island, her pale legs curled beneath her slight form. Delicate hands wrapped around her knees like starfish, the rose-colored webbing between the two smallest fingers bedewed with evening mist. Slowly she lifted sightless eyes, like luminous pearls, toward the approaching banks of fog. An ethereal sound, lonely and haunting as the keening call of a lost gull, rose above the hiss of the surf to mingle with the swirling, gray vapors gathering overhead.

Renya, the lorelei, was singing.

She had been a child the first time she felt her way to the wave-etched rocks piled outside the hidden sea entrance to the dragon's cave. The rushing voices of wind and wave had led her to the place where her song could join with theirs, a place where a small part of herself could be lifted free of the island and borne away.

That was long ago. Renya's body had grown tall and curved and strikingly beautiful in the years that followed, and she had lost count long ago of the times she had climbed her rocks to sing her evening songs of memory and longing. Only faintly now could she recall the richness of a song that was not sung alone. Yet it was that dim memory, the tenuous hope that a voice might someday rise above the waves in answer and lead her homeward, which brought her back to her rocks dusk after dusk.

The shock of icy water in her lap stopped Renya in the middle of a lyrical phrase. The sun had set and it was growing cold. Gracefully, she stretched her long legs, then realized that the black band she wore on her upper arm was tingling. With slender fingers she touched the polished obsidian armband and cleared her mind.

"If you have any interest in learning the tragic end to the Lady of Vortha, I suggest you quit your crooning and come in, Renya. You may just miss your chance to hear how I ate her."

Renya smiled a little as the dragon's molten purr washed over her. Irritable and vain as he was, she could not have borne life on the island without Qual.

"I am coming, O Terrible One," she sent back sarcastically. *"Try not to scorch the wartlefish tonight."*

Silently, she slipped into the waves and swam the short distance back to the sea cave. The fog drifted in behind her as she climbed from the water and followed the narrow tunnel up to the dragon's cavern lair.

●●●

Out at sea, a lone man started as if suddenly waking and nearly dropped his oar overboard. He raised a shaking, calloused hand to his forehead for a moment, then ran his fingers through the snarls of his unbound hair.

"You've been paddling so long, Skandir, you're starting to do it in your sleep," he mumbled gruffly, peering into the featureless gray that surrounded his small boat and the empty coracle he towed behind him. "There's no way to tell where you've gotten yourself to, either."

He gave a frustrated snort and clenched the oar tightly. If he ever made it back to Wallinma, he'd find the hag who'd cackled on about the island "dripping with gold and named for the dragon that dwelt there" and he'd slit her tip to tail. He had boasted to everyone in the mead hall that he would find the legendary monster, Qual—who had burned their homeland like chaff in a furnace when his great-grandsire was a babe—and slay it on its stolen treasure heap. Then, with a set of dragon's teeth around his neck and a dragon's hoard in his hall, he would become thane at last. His people would regain their former greatness.

He had been a fool. Island and dragon were nothing more than a beggarwoman's tale told to frighten children and impress drunkards. He had followed the crone's star north across the waves for nearly a fortnight now and found nothing. He was lost.

Skandir rolled his shoulders to ease the iron-tight muscles and listened in the muffled grayness that was rapidly turning to the darkness of night. Silence, except for the steady lapping of the waves against the boat he sat in and the second, empty one that he towed in hopes of bounty.

Yet, he *had* heard a voice, hadn't he? A faint, otherworldly song drifting over the waves that had pierced his chest like a harpoon—a wordless call so full of longing and loneliness that he had felt the barbs of it tear at his very soul. The strains had flowed into him, filling him with a need of such terrible power that he must find its maker or perish.

He had followed it, stroking forward like a madman. Then suddenly the fog had closed in around him and the beautiful voice had disappeared with the setting sun.

"Nothing like a lone voyage to start a man believing his dreams are real," Skandir derided himself. "Time for a little company."

The warrior reached under his weathered cloak and pulled out an object hanging from a leather thong around his neck. It was a spiraled shell, its mottled green surface carved with spidery symbols. He gripped it tightly and barked a series of guttural words.

The water off the prow flattened like glass, then churned and bubbled into a man-sized vortex. Salty foam became flowing hair and beard. Rippling waves formed into supple limbs as the water spirit rose from the depths.

"Twice more, and the shell is mine," the being gurgled, its watery visage shifting from that of an old merman to the likeness of a pouting child.

"Yes, but until then you are mine to command," Skandir snapped. He wasn't in the mood for the water spirit's whining. The hag hadn't told him that the creature would be so tiresome when he had bought the amulet from her. Another reason to wring her scrawny neck when he got back.

"Get me out of this devil's breath and to the nearest land—" he ordered, "or else."

He held the shell higher, tightening his fingers around it to make his point.

The creature's child face gave him a pleading look, then it was replaced with the grimace of an enormous eel. A thick, liquid coil formed and looped around the prow. Without warning, the boat lurched forward. Skandir was thrown back, banging his head on the bottom with a loud *thunk*. He rubbed at the sore spot, cursing all old women, as the elemental pulled him into the night. Then, exhausted, he let himself drift into a sleep where a dream voice called to him still.

•••

Morning. Renya could always tell by the way Qual's breathing shifted as she lay with her head against his great chest. Gradually, the basso snore would grow to the roar of a hundred stampeding centaurs as his ancient lungs worked like bellows, stoking the embers that burned in his belly into flame. Each day it seemed to take a bit longer, but eventually twin tendrils of thick, black smoke would rise from the dragon's nostrils, followed by a tremendous cough that filled the cavern with a cloud of soot. Awake at last, Qual would shake his broad head with a clatter of horned ridges and scales, smack his lips, and crane his serpentine neck around to rouse her.

There were definite advantages to living with a dragon, Renya sighed to herself. She snuggled farther into the warming crook of the dragon's foreleg and pretended to sleep.

It was Qual who, years ago, that first morning after the disaster, had found her sprawled on the beach in a tangle of dark hair and seaweed. His fire had burned brighter in those days, and he had still hauled his grating bones and whitening scales out the large inland mouth of his cave and down to the shore each morning to discover what delectables—of both the sparkling *and* the edible kind—the tide had left behind. Renya often wondered why he hadn't eaten her for breakfast right then and there. Once she had asked him, but he had only rumbled in his you-are-trying-my-infinite-patience tone and stated, "There wasn't enough of you to sink my teeth into."

It was true enough. Born blind and frail, Renya had relied on her sisters to help her navigate the unpredictable currents of the great river Tynlos, in the roaring estuary that was their home. More amphibious than their merfolk cousins, the lorelei spent their days plying the dancing shallows along its banks, herding their schools of fish like shepherds, their calls to each other bouncing shore to shore in echoing song. When the wild taste of the ocean grew too strong in the waters, they turned back upriver. And each twilight, they curled together in warm eddies or draped themselves on sun-heated stones and raised a lilting chorus to snare the unwary with its beauty.

Nothing could have prepared her for the day the late afternoon sunshine was snuffed out like a candle as she played with her sisters where the Tynlos met the tides of the Northern Sea. A strange, smothering silence had descended. Her sister's hand had clasped hers painfully as the river actually paused, then began to reverse its ancient course. Ponderously, the mighty river had pulled itself backward up the valley like an enormous snail into its shell, leaving the sisters floundering in a thick slurry of river-bottom sludge, along with hundreds of flapping fish.

"Tynlos has heard the Chanter," Unya had cried in fear, speaking of the great wizardess who lived in the mountains. "We must reach the bank before the river is freed again!"

But the world had split in a deafening roar. The ground had swelled beneath Renya, then fallen away into nothing. And a towering wall of water had broken down upon them, ripping Renya from Unya's grasp and sweeping her out into the open sea. Flipped and tossed until she lost all sense of direction, Renya had struggled in the darkness, engulfed in a vast and heaving ocean. She had awakened to the acrid tang of brimstone, the metallic rattle of scaly plates, and an immense presence that blocked the warmth of the sun with its bulk.

Perhaps if Renya had been able to see the dragon's serrated smile, his age-yellowed but meticulously sharpened talons, she would have chosen to flee back into the hateful emptiness of the ocean waves. As it was, she had been strangely comforted by Qual's dry, sulphurous breath and his gently growled words. Like a living furnace, the nearness of his massive body had warmed the sand and her cold blood. When next she woke, she was in his lair.

"Wake up, little bird," Qual said in his golden voice, nudging Renya out of her reverie with his nose. "My stomach wants breakfast, and then my ears want to hear the 'King's List of Zanzir' *and* the 'Battle of Arnoth'—to make sure you still haven't got them confused— especially the part where I come in."

Renya stretched languidly, turning sightless eyes toward the dragon.

"The only reason I get the details of *your* part mixed up is because it's always the same," she countered. "You arrive in a cloud of flame, torch the countryside, eat a few nobles, and take all their treasure."

Great sinews popped, joints creaked, and Qual's muscular tail twitched as he rose, dumping Renya unceremoniously on the ground.

"Obviously, you don't appreciate the importance of the history I'm teaching you," he said, towering over her. One claw clicked impatiently on the stone floor.

"I can't change the fact that I played a part in pivotal events over the centuries, or that I acted like a rabid hellcat when the greed-fire raged in my younger days," he rumbled, then sighed. "It was all very long ago now, Renya. But I do know that *someone* must learn my story so that the elder days will live on. And maybe the mistakes we made . . . I made . . . won't get made again."

He turned with a rasping of scales along the floor and started toward his treasure den at the back of the cave. Chagrined, Renya reached out to touch her mentor's knobby hide.

"I'm sorry, Qual," she whispered. "I was only trying to make a joke."

Above her, the dragon paused for a long moment, blowing a cloud of sulphur and steam.

"I suppose you might make it up to me with those seaweed-and-turtle-egg omelets you promised," he said, his voice growing warm and gentle again.

Renya smiled with pearly, pointed teeth.

"Maybe I can call up a couple of rays as well," she said, padding gracefully on webbed tiptoe to her passage that led to the sea. "I'll be back before you finish sharpening your claws."

She ducked through her doorway. Behind her, Qual's leathery wings slumped as he moved stiffly to the back of the cave.

The rising sun was lifting the veil of mist that surrounded the island. Renya reveled in the warmth of the shallows and hummed a bit to herself as she swam effortlessly through a liquid world of blue and green. She headed toward the strand she called Muse Lagoon, where the turtles came on moonlit nights to dig their nests in the fine sand and weep melancholy tears. Yet somehow it was not a morning for sadness. The sea rippled with teasing secrets, dancing around her in giddy pulses, while schools of tiny fish fluttered against her skin like butterflies.

Something had happened, the sea said. Something was different. She felt light, effervescent, as she passed the coral tower that marked the entrance to the lagoon. She surfaced in a splash of foam and laughter.

Then she heard it, a low grating against the beach and the slap of water against something hollow. Curious, she swam cautiously toward the alien noise. She drew close. Her nostrils flared at the smell of salt-soaked wood and a strange, oily musk emanating from it. Tentatively, she reached out and ran her fingers along wood planks, worn sensuously smooth. Her hand slipped over the rim of the boat, brushing against something soft and warm. A face.

Full of wonder, Renya let her fingers trace the line of brow, the curve of a cheekbone, drawing a sharp breath when they touched something like moss that covered the angle of jaw.

Suddenly, an enormous hand grabbed hers. Renya cried out in surprise as she was half lifted out of the water. Throaty words pelted her. The heady perfume of oiled leathers and honeyed mead enveloped her as she was brought nose to nose with her captor. Something sharp pressed against her ribs.

•••

Skandir had heard the musical laughter as he lay dozing in the bottom of his boat. He thought it best to lie in wait. With bated breath, he had endured the inquisitive touch of cold, wet fingers, then grabbed with a fighter's speed, yelling, "Friend or foe?" as his dagger flashed in the sunlight.

The utter beauty of the face that turned up to meet his struck him like a blow. A dripping cascade of blue-black hair, iridescent as a raven's wing, framed features so finely wrought that they shone like starlight. Her lips, full and silky, were the shade of red coral. She wore a gleaming band of black stone on one arm, and her womanly body was draped in cloth of gold that clung to skin white as milk. Skandir stared, paralyzed, into angled mother-of-pearl eyes that looked through him and beyond.

"What place is this?" he asked. "Who are you?"

He eyed the obsidian armband. Faintly scratched onto its surface was a single word: Qual.

The woman's brows drew together in a silent query. Her free hand reached toward him. Then her mouth opened, and the air shimmered with sound. It began as a staccato dolphin's whistle that melted into the tumbling music of a high meadow brook. Her song fell about him like rain, and echoed in his head like pebbles in a well. Gradually, the music shifted in strength and tone, growing louder, more insistent, until it washed over him in a roaring waterfall of music, exhilarated, overflowing, asking only for him to join with it in voice and limb.

It was too much. Skandir put his hands to his ringing ears. He staggered back as his knees buckled and the boat rocked wildly.

The woman of the waves disappeared with a splash—and was gone.

•••

Renya sped in confused terror into the labyrinthine reef that encircled the cove. Fish darted in panic as she plunged through familiar sapphire hallways, searching for a way to hide her anguish in the depths.

Was this not the companion she had called for on countless nights? If he had come at last, why hadn't he leapt into the surf and joined in her song, in her arms?

Could it be that he did not understand the tongue of the lorelei? A thought struck her like an icy current as she fled. Had her song been too simple or ungainly? She had not sung to another in her speech for so long, perhaps all her proper words had washed away. Worse still, was it because he had seen her poor sightless eyes?

Renya cringed as she swam deep into waters grown suddenly sullen and cold.

It was well after noon when she approached the cave with only an undersized wartlefish and an armful of kelp to show for her long absence. The catch had been an afterthought and, even then, her song of summoning had been halfhearted and poorly sung.

She could have sent to Qual and told him of the stranger. He had given her the armband so that they could always speak. Yet to tell him would mean to reveal the depth of her loneliness, the secret sadness she kept locked far away. She could not bear to hurt her teacher and friend. Her heart hung in her chest like a stone.

Renya felt Qual's steady gaze on her as they ate their paltry meal in silence. Twice, he cleared his throat as if to say something, then swallowed and remained silent. Renya's food stuck in her mouth along with her words.

"I suppose we should get started if you're going to make it through those blasted ballads before midnight," the dragon grumbled afterward, a shadow creeping into his gilded voice. "Unless there is something you would rather do instead?"

"Of course not," she answered quickly. Too quickly. Her heart fluttered wretchedly against her ribs. Miserable, she wondered if lies could be seen.

For the second time that day, Qual turned his back on her. A tinkling shower of coins struck the floor as the dragon clambered atop his treasure heap with a groan and coiled his tail about his sinuous body. His horned head dipped to rest on armored forelegs. Rings of dark smoke circled it, wafting slowly up to the ceiling.

"Very well," he sighed heavily. "Begin."

So she did. But it was not of great battles and warrior queens that she sang. Instead, for the first time Renya's song to him was one of her own making. Fluidly, her dulcet voice wove a musical tapestry that told of a lost child and a great friend, of the terror of an ocean of emptiness and the warmth of another in the darkness. She sang a gift song to ease the hurt in life-worn dragon bones and her own guilty longing for a companion. With heart full to bursting, the lorelei poured herself outward until cavern walls hummed with the purity of her song.

Stretched upon his precious bed, Qual nodded and drifted into a sleep of profound serenity that the pain caused by centuries of living could not broach. Renya sat quietly for some time, still hearing the quavering refrains of her song long after it had ended. She felt clear, strong. Quietly, she padded out of the dragon's chamber. It did not matter if the stranger thought her a fool, if he could not bear to look at her. She would speak to him in all the tongues Qual had taught her, if she had to. But she *would* face him and learn, for good or ill, if this was the one she had sought.

•••

Darkness cloaked the island as Skandir made his final preparations for battle. Flickering light from a small fire on the beach played across polished shield, shining mail and sharp features set in a grim line. He finished tightening the leather straps of his battleworn greaves and stood noisily to pull fingered gauntlets over eager hands.

Excitement flashed through him like lightning. The dragon existed! He had lived for the day when Fate would tap him on the shoulder. Now that it had come at last, he could scarcely believe his good fortune. By his hands, the great Qual would fall. He, Skandir, called the Dragonbane, would return his people to their former glory. And he would sit at their head with a mysterious, dark-haired queen by his side.

He had followed her voice when it started singing again, wary now that the dragon might be using his captive sorceress to try and enchant him. Her voice had led him inland along a winding, overgrown trail to a gaping cave gouged into the mountainside. There was no mistaking the smoke-stained stone of the maw-like opening, the fragments of old bone and shed scales that littered the ground, or the sulphurous stench of dragon-fire that permeated the place.

Almost, Skandir had fallen under the beautiful woman's spell of sleeping there. Velvet tones had wrapped around him like a blanket as he huddled behind thorn bushes, planning his attack. His eyelids drew closed. Head grew heavy, breathing slowed. But just as he was about to embrace the warm cocoon of sleep, it was ripped away. The song suddenly ended and he had found himself standing bolt upright in the rays of the westering sun. Out of the darkened depths before him there had risen a low, resonating snore.

Skandir patted the heavy scabbard at his side. The dragon *was* here; at least the hag at Wallinma had gotten that part right. And now, Skandir felt ready. One well-aimed thrust of his longsword and the legendary beast would die as it slept.

A slight movement in the darkness near his boats caught his eye. He turned toward it, drawing his sword.

Out of the curl of the next wave stepped the dark-haired woman. She was so hauntingly lovely, her alabaster skin bronzed by the red-gold light of the fire, every wet curve revealed by the chill night air. Despite his wariness, Skandir felt his pulse quicken as her unsettling beauty called to him again with a pull as old as the sea. He longed to bury his face in that black hair, press his lips against that perfect red mouth, feel those fluid, graceful limbs wrap around his hardened body. Cautiously, he stepped toward her. She did not move. He watched, fascinated, as her chest rose and fell with each breath. She was trembling slightly. Yet she stood her ground, her strange, glowing eyes fixed intently upon him.

"Try no tricks on the dragon's behalf," he said, taking another step toward her. "I'm quite good with this sword."

Arched eyebrows drew together in concentration. After a long silence she spoke.

"Y . . . you come to Renya?" she asked.

She spoke in the Old Wallenden speech, the tongue his people used only in the ancient rites and ballads. But it was her voice that was unsettling. The way she struck each syllable like a bell; too clear, too precise, to be human, and then the words would open up, roll outward like the ripples from a strummed harp to set the inside of his head, his chest, tingling with alien vibrations. The word that must have been her name sounded like the play of a fountain on a hot summer day. Suddenly, Skandir felt thirsty.

This time she was the one who walked, almost floated, toward him.

"You know why I'm here," Skandir replied, glancing into the darkness around him for signs of danger. "The question is, will you help me slay your captor, or will you hinder me?"

She paused. He watched the emotions play across her flawless face. They stood scant inches from each other now. The air felt hot, electrified, as if he had a fever that only the touch of her cool skin could quench. He stared, mesmerized by the black lashes that fluttered over her blind eyes as she closed them and shook her head in confusion.

"Renya sang, you come," she whispered, voice quiet, probing, like a reed pipe. "You come not *to* Renya, not to sing as one?"

Skandir's free hand shot forward like a striking snake and grabbed the black ring of stone on her upper arm.

"I came here to kill the dragon and set you free," he said, shaking her arm for emphasis. "It doesn't have anything to do with singing. Will you help me!"

Something dimmed in the eyes that were turned toward him. His words found their mark. Hope melted into horror that transformed again into a mixture of denial and fear. "Na!" she shrieked with a sound that split the night like a lightning bolt.

Skandir dropped his sword, clapping his hands to his head in pain as she backed away from him into the waves.

"Don't go!" he called after her, but in an instant, she was gone.

Quickly, Skandir grabbed the shell amulet at his neck, speaking words of command. A rippling figure formed to stand in the shallows, complete with flowing armor that imitated his own.

"Follow the dragon's prisoner, and keep her from warning it that I'm coming," he said, stepping nose to nose with the water spirit. "If I succeed tonight, the shell is yours. Is that clear?"

In answer, all semblance of color drained from the creature, leaving it as transparent and rigid as ice. It held up one finger, as if to say, "One more time."

Skandir ignored it, donning his horned helm. He slung his shield over his shoulder and grabbed his sword out of the sand, swinging it in a whistling arc. The figure in the waves mimicked his actions, drawing an icy blade.

"Death to Qual!" Skandir shouted, raising his sword in salute. He turned and sprinted across the sand toward the inland trail.

Behind him, the water spirit plunged back into the sea.

●●●

Renya's webbed fingers clenched into fists as the meaning of the stranger's guttural words sorted themselves out in her mind. A crushing, sinking feeling settled in her stomach. The heavy clinking of his armored movements, the aggressive edge in his throaty voice, the hunger in his grip, all made sudden, terrible sense as she swam with silent speed across the lagoon. His accent was murky and much of what he'd said remained unclear. Yet two words rang again and again in her ears: *kill* and *dragon*. This man was no companion; he was an assassin. Qual was in grave danger.

Shakily, she started a sending.

"Qual, wake!—" she blurted, but her message broke off. Something was in the water with her. A presence. It prodded the darkened waves, searching for her. Panic seized her. She had to reach the sea passage. She had to warn Qual. In silent dread she swam on.

It came at her from behind as she passed the coral tower at the edge of the lagoon. Fast as a dolphin, it nudged her firmly in the side, deflecting her from her path, prodding her repeatedly toward the open sea. Then it seemed to disappear, to melt into the chill waters around her. Shakily, Renya took a breath and sped forward again. She felt it coalesce beside her as she swam.

"Qual, wake up! There is a stranger," she sent desperately. *"Hurry, he is coming for you!"*

This time, it circled her like a shark. She could sense it pulling back, predatory and unswerving. It struck then, with a blow to her stomach that sent her careening into a jagged wall. Coral spires bit into pale skin, and fire shot up her back. Again the thing withdrew. Renya tasted blood seeping into the water around her. Somewhere in the maze of stone and reef it was lurking. She spun around, cursing eyes that could not see. Her groping fingers clasped a spike of dead coral and she snapped it off.

Holding it like a dagger before her, Renya plunged ahead.

Watery hands gripped her ankles. She twisted and jabbed with her makeshift dagger. Then she was rolling over and over in a frothing cloud with an adversary that shifted and churned and would not let go. Snaky tentacles sprouted and wrapped around her legs and torso, pulling her downward as she struggled. With all the nightmarish slowness of the sea, octopus arms pinned her shoulders to the rocky bottom. The creature held her fast, bearing her down with its fluid weight. Horribly, she felt the pulsing rush pressing against her flesh as it transformed yet again. Suddenly, it was the stranger that held her in rippling arms. Clammy lips brushed hers.

Renya screamed in fury.

The sonic blast that emanated from her mind and out through her throat tore the waters about her into fragments. For an instant the being above her quivered, arching its back as if speared on a trident. Then it blew apart in a roaring explosion of bubbles and sound.

Renya shuddered in revulsion as the sea trembled and stilled about her. This was no time to be sick. She could not fail Qual. Resolutely, she clamped one hand onto the obsidian armband and lashed toward her hidden cave, even as the thing in the water began to draw itself together again.

"Qual!" she sent. All her fear flew before her to the dragon's mind. This time, she knew that he woke.

●●●

Sweat trickled down the back of Skandir's neck as he inched down the widening cavern corridor. He had spent his life preparing for the decisive event that would forge him into a great leader. The moment was here at last. The walls and floor of the cave vibrated with the monster's breathing as he neared its den. The air felt thick with its heat, reeked of its foul, hellfire fumes.

Heart pounding, Skandir flattened himself against the stone, tightened his fingers on the pommel of his sword, and peered into the dragon's lair.

The dragon was massive, yet somehow smaller than he'd expected, long and lean as a coursing hound, sprawled on a mountain of gold. Its skin, stretched taut over wide ribs and ridged backbone, was not the vivid yellow-green of a poisonous serpent that he had imagined, but more like horny plates of steely-gray armor streaked with a dull verdigris that spoke of countless years. Great leathery wings lay folded along its back, and wickedly sharp talons clutched the dazzling heap of gold and jewels that was its bed.

The dragon's body twitched convulsively. The thick tail flicked, claws snatched, and its heavy head turned with a jerk.

Skandir pulled back around the doorway, his heart leaping in his chest. Had he been seen? Slowly the monster quieted. Skandir looked upon it again. No, it slept still. Almost, he thought he could see its pulse beating in the thin-skinned hollow of its temples. There was the weak spot. Plunge his sword in to the hilt and the thing would die without ever knowing what struck it.

Skandir took a deep breath and grasped his sword in both hands. Then, with deadly speed, he dashed into the dragon's den.

He was halfway across the chamber when the horned head shot up and a yellow, reptilian glare stunned him motionless with its gaze.

"Ahhh, so here is the reason for Renya's odd behavior," purred a deep voice that was all honey and fire. "It's only a matter of time before the vermin track you down."

Skandir's sword wavered a bit.

"What, surprised are you?" the dragon asked, sardonically. "Didn't know I could speak, little man?"

Fangs gleamed as Qual flashed a perilous smile.

"I-I c-came here of my own will, monster," Skandir stammered, eyeing the tensing muscles in the dragon's limbs. "To reclaim the wealth you've stolen from my people."

"Oh, this?" Qual snarled. He rose languidly, swiping at the heap with his foreleg and sending a spray of gold ricocheting off Skandir's shield.

"Believe me, human, it's worthless," he said in disgust.

Skandir watched, riveted, as the dragon wearily shook its head. Something was happening. Its silvery belly was pumping in and out, in and out, and its bitter, acrid breath was growing more sulphurous with each passing moment.

The room began heating, filling with angry fumes. Beneath his armor, Skandir was drenched with sweat.

Warily, he raised his sword to strike. The massive head whipped around to face him.

"You don't understand, do you?" Qual hissed in a cloud of acid and steam. "I didn't either when I was young. But perhaps, if riches were all you were after, human, I would let you have them and be done with it. But that isn't *all*, is it?"

Yellow eyes glowed with inner fire. Dark vapors curled from the corners of the dragon's mouth. The air pulsed with waves of heat.

Skandir took a step backward.

"No, it never changes," Qual rumbled as if to himself. "The gold is just an excuse. What you truly crave is to become a god by writing your name in the blood of your foes. I knew that hunger once, believe me, and I slaughtered your ancestors like sheep to feed it."

The dragon's eyes narrowed and it brought its head closer.

"My name will be remembered, but for what? There are other paths to glory, human."

"If there are, I do not know them," Skandir said. "Your words change nothing. You are still the monster that killed my people. They *will* be avenged!"

He steadied his sword and stepped forward.

Illustrated by Christopher Jouan

"And so the wheel continues to spin," the dragon sighed. "So be it, warrior. I am old, but I am far from dead yet."

Qual reared to his full height. Black wingtips brushed against the ceiling, throwing Skandir into shadow.

Skandir dodged and rolled to the side, barely escaping the orange geyser of flame that poured from the dragon's throat. Sulphur and ozone burned in his lungs. He leapt to his feet, raising his shield above his head, and gave the battle cry of his fathers as he charged.

• • •

Rocks tumbled and the ground shook beneath her as Renya fought her way up the passage. She yelled to Qual that she was coming, but the thunderous bellows and clanging din of the fight in the mountain above her drowned it out. Her foot twisted on fallen rock and she went down hard. The ankle throbbed as she pulled herself to her feet. Desperately, she sang a thin phrase of strength through gritted teeth as she hobbled onward.

She made it to the den just as something metal struck the wall with a jarring *clang* and slid groaning to the floor. The cavern reeked of rotten eggs and sweat, singed hair and blood, lots of blood. Wheezing with effort, Qual dragged himself on three legs to where the man lay.

"Do you see now?" he rasped, talons gripping mail shirt and crumpling it like paper.

Skandir struggled for breath, one hand pawing at his throat.

"I see that we shall die together," he choked out in a hoarse whisper. "But at least the woman will be free of you."

The dragon's yellow eyes winced shut as if he had been struck in the face. In that instant the man clutched the shell in his hand and yelled his summons.

Years peeled away as Renya heard the terrifying crescendo of an unleashed power crashing up from the sea passage below. Again, she was a child filled with the dreadful knowledge of impending destruction. Chunks of ceiling cracked and fell around her, the ground ripped and tore as she ran toward Qual. The wounded dragon was rearing, preparing to unleash his last reserve of fire and incinerate the warrior who struggled weakly in his grasp. He roared. She heard herself scream for them to stop. And the sea burst into the cave like a giant hand, transforming it in an instant into a seething cauldron.

The tempest crashed into Renya, knocking her off her feet. She heard Qual howl, then a deafening hiss as the cold water struck him. A cloud of steam filled the room and she was sucked under. She felt a sundering tear as the bond between dragon and lorelei stretched and frayed. Then she felt no more.

•••

She woke to the sound of draining water. Disoriented, she raised her head, then sat up gingerly. The air was sticky and heavy with warm vapors. Dripping sounds echoed everywhere.

Something bumped into her knee, pulled there by the receding waters. Renya picked it up—a conical shell dangling from a leather thong. The thinning waters stirred around her. Before she could react, she sensed the presence of the water spirit before her.

This time it did not attack. Instead, it placed liquid fingers around hers in a humble, childlike plea. Strangely,

Renya recognized the gentle touch. It felt just a little like her sister's.

The being sought understanding, its grasp told her. It had not acted of its own volition, but had been commanded by another's will. Slowly, she released the amulet into the waiting hand. It squeezed hers once, then was gone, carrying the shell with it back to the sea.

She found Qual lying against the back wall. His breathing was labored and ragged, and he bled from a dozen wounds. With a gasp, she fell to her knees and wrapped her arms around his drooping neck. A thick cloud of sludgy ash fell from his scales, coating her and setting her coughing. The sudden immersion in cold water had been the final blow, dousing his ancient fire, turning the brimstone in his belly into lead. The dragon was cooling, stiffening. Qual, who had seen whole forests grow from seedlings, vast empires rise and fall, and witnessed the birth of the second moon, was dying.

Great pearly tears swelled up in Renya's eyes, spilling onto his hoary face. Qual's eyes opened.

"Are you safe, little one?" asked the golden voice.

"Yes," she said, biting her lip to keep from sobbing aloud. "Oh, Qual, forgive me. I didn't know the stranger meant you harm."

"It is I who must ask forgiveness, Renya," he murmured. "For me and for the man who came here. It seems neither of us could hear anything besides ourselves."

With trembling fingers, Renya touched the horned ridges of his great brow. The dragon coughed a slurry of wet coal dust and continued.

"He thought he was saving you. And I, well, I've been too busy teaching you about my life to let you have

one of your own. I never meant for you to be lonely . . .
to live with an old dragon against your will."

He coughed again.

"I didn't stay here because you forced it upon me,
my teacher," Renya said. The tears flowed freely now. "I
stayed because I loved you."

The dragon sighed.

"In all my centuries, you are the first to tell me so,
little bird," he rumbled. His great head lowered to rest
upon his forelegs. "I will die content. Journey well,
Renya."

"Journey well, Qual."

She felt the last fire in his eyes flicker out, and he was
gone.

For long hours, there was only rocking and weeping
as the warmth slowly faded from the dragon's still
form. Only gradually did Renya become aware of the
moans of the man. Woodenly, she rose and crossed to
the place where he lay in a small pile of gold debris—all
that remained of the dragon's hoard.

She meant to scream her grief over him, to rupture
his eardrums with her voice, or send him toppling over
the edge into madness. She had the power, yet she
could not use it. Burned and bleeding, he seemed so
small, this man she had hoped would share her world
and who had destroyed it. She could not forgive him
that. But Qual had said he had fought thinking to help
her. She could not just let him die.

It was, perhaps, the hardest thing she had ever done.
Haltingly, she let her anger drain away with the last of
the retreating waters. Then, though a part of her ranted
at the thought, Renya hummed a low song of healing
over the wounded man until he quieted and she knew
he would live.

She staggered slightly as she returned to Qual's side, noticing for the first time that the armband he had given her now dangled at her wrist. He was cold, turned to stone. An iron and obsidian statue, frozen beneath the mountain for all time in sleep. Gingerly, she stroked the place between his horns that had always wanted scratching. Then with great reverence, she placed the band he had carved for her upon his brow like a wreath and kissed him farewell.

• • •

The twin moons hung full and low over the horizon. They mirrored the pearls of her upturned eyes as Renya leaned back against the worn wood of the stranger's spare boat. She had found it drifting against her singing rocks, a parting gift from the water spirit. Exhausted, she had crawled inside. By dawn, the island would be far behind.

She felt tired beyond measure; yet, deep within, a new lightness was gathering. She felt no fear, only a certainty that she could find her own way, that she would someday sing again with the lorelei. And she knew that she would carry Qual with her wherever she chose to go.

The double moons spilled a quicksilver path over the indigo sea as the boat moved onward through the night. It glided like a leaf over the gentle waves, as if propelled by an unseen hand. And from the coracle arose a sparkling, crystalline song that floated higher and higher, upward to the lightening heavens to shine among the myriad stars.

Renya, the lorelei, was singing.

RED MOON

Written by
Scott M. Azmus

Illustrated by
Rob Hassan

About the Author

Scott Azmus is a part-time teacher and general contractor who hopes soon to open a specialty bookstore, Full Circle Books, which will specialize in first-edition books.

As a naval officer, he earned the rank of lieutenant commander and worked as a navigator, operations officer, and executive officer. In addition, he has been an observatory manager, a cashier, a marine outfitter, a bank "gofer," an electrician, a field gemologist, and a few other things.

He gained his teaching certificate at Oregon State University, his gemologist training certificate at the Gemological Institute of America, and he has received advanced training in a number of military schools.

His finalist story, "Reflections in Period Glass," was published in Volume XII of this anthology, and he has also published or soon will be published in Space and Time, Galaxy, *and* Little Green Men #5.

Scott is working in several different styles and seems willing to take on just about any writing challenge. The fact that I've published him twice now suggests to me that he shows some very great potential.

About the Illustrator

Rob Hassan has divided his life between Chicago and New York. Born in New York, he moved to Chicago as an early teen, but returned to study at the School of Visual Arts in New York.

He has long been influenced by artists such as Moebius, Frazetta, Eisner, Kirby, Vallejo, and others. He prefers to work in pencil, scan his work into a computer, and then render the work in a graphic arts program. Currently, he freelances for several small-press comic companies while he continues his education in 3-D animation. Along with his wife, he is also raising two daughters.

Cheating was bad. Bad, bad, bad. *Really* bad. Marky didn't like to cheat on the tests, but high scores seemed to make everyone *so* happy. Especially Doctor Pat and his friend, Doctor Harkness. And Trisa. It made Trisa happy, too.

"Yes, Marky," she sent over their private carrier. "Now move the little black pieces into place. One by one. Do you see what they make?"

Marky moved the first little black piece. Trisa was nice to help him. She was his little sister. She lived far away in a dome on the other side of Kibero Patera. Two generations advanced, Doctor Harkness said she was a better "total-concept model" than he. Intelligent. More reliable. Better suited to the harsh realities of surface life on Io.

His gill rakers flattened. He was *proud* to have such a smart sister!

"Thank you, Marky. Now try the second piece, please. You're doing very well."

He pulled another black piece from the Lego bag and pressed it into position between the yellow triangles. He stared. It made an eye. Was it a cat's eye?

He looked over the whole picture and grinned. Yes, the picture was a cat! A cat!

"Press the buttons, Marky."

He had made a cat. Just like Doctor Pat made things. Alive things. Marky hugged the keyboard. He carefully pressed *C* and *A* and, finally, *T*.

The little green light strobed. Food, waxy nuggets of clear eso-three, clattered into his bin. They smelled wonderful. They tasted better. He even liked how they felt against his minutely scaled skin.

Trisa's voice came to him, once again. "In the mouth, please, dear. You've made everyone very happy."

Marky looked out his window and nibbled the pungent eso-three. Doctor Harkness certainly looked happy. She smiled as she flashed a sheaf of freshly extruded Mylex at Doctor Pat. "Unbelievable," she said. "Simply unbelievable. Look at this. I know he'll never be brilliant again, but he is improving. Two weeks ago we voted to put him down and now, just look at his scores!"

Doctor Pat frowned. He didn't look so happy. The way he looked into Marky's special room made Marky feel bad inside. Like he knew Marky was a cheater. Nothing but a big, fat cheater.

"It's all right, Marky," Trisa whispered into his thoughts. "There's no way Doctor Pattison can tell. Not with that equipment set up. Not for certain. The frequency's all wrong."

Marky sent a spike of frustration at her. How could she tell from so far away? He might get in trouble. Why was she—

"You won't get into trouble. If they ever do figure out that our comm bands overlap, they'll probably be thrilled. They'll celebrate by writing a joint paper or something. Yeah, with a title like 'Interference and Resonance of Organic Interpersonal Communications Bands between Mode One and Mode Three Ionians.' Earth will love it. Probably bring more fear. More riots. Escalate the fighting."

She paused. Her transmission became more soothing. "Besides, I didn't help you all that much, big brother. You're a lot smarter than they think."

Marky sat a little straighter. He grinned at Doctor Pat. All he wanted was to make Doctor Pat happy. He loved Doctor Pat.

• • •

Trisa was still sleeping when Doctor Pat came to visit Marky. It was early in the Ionian morning. Doctor Pat's hair was messy. It stood up funny behind his headset. He pressed his palm to the thick Perspex barrier and clicked his talk button. "Rise and shine, Marky-boy. We've got a big day ahead of us."

Marky stretched and splayed a wide palm over Doctor Pat's. He had eight fingers. Doctor Pat had five. Later, suited and on the surface, they might wrestle and hug. If it was Saturday. And *if* he did well on his tests. But other than the accidental "containment breach" Marky caused way back before Doctor Pat made Trisa and his other brothers and sisters, he and Doctor Pat had never touched. Not actually. Not for real.

Sulfur sand rained from Marky's gill rakers as he yawned. He pressed his face to the barrier. Whenever they were close like this, Marky tried to remember how hot Doctor Pat's skin had felt. How smooth and damp. How sharp his true voice had been when they were both frightened. How the air smelled bad. How Earth humans looked when they were doing important things like saving Marky.

Doctor Pat said he almost died that day. Having been eso-two deprived, he might never get back to being as smart as he was supposed to be. Might not live up to his potential. Meet the model projections. Whatever that meant. All Marky knew was that he'd been very sick. And for a long time. Doctor Pat had saved him.

When he was okay again, Doctor Pat told him it was bad to cut the barrier. Very bad. No matter how much he wanted to be with Doctor Pat, Marky promised never to cut the barrier again.

He splayed his feet and pushed his legs against his bed. He scratched a hard, yellow crust from his rakers.

"Stretch and grow, Marky-boy," said Doctor Pat. "Stretch and grow."

Marky smiled. He flexed his muscles. That's what Doctor Pat always said. Every morning. Just like sometimes, at night, he warned Marky about bed bugs.

Imaginary bed bugs.

Bugs that didn't bite.

Bugs that were *not* for real.

Marky liked it better when Doctor Pat turned off the day light and said, "See you later, alligator."

Marky was supposed to send, "After a while, crocodile!" but he sometimes forgot. And sometimes he didn't try hard enough and Doctor Pat's radio couldn't hear him.

It was funny to call Doctor Pat "crocodile." It was a game. His touchscreen tutor once showed him a vid of real crocodiles. And real alligators. They couldn't live on Io. Or Jupiter. They had cold blood. Which was a good thing because if they ever came, they might try and eat Doctor Pat. They couldn't eat Marky, though! Or Trisa. Doctor Harkness said not to worry. She said Ionians had their own special chemistry.

Marky liked that. Being special.

Doctor Pat checked his watch. "Listen, Marky. You're probably going to have some visitors later this morning."

"Friends?"

"Yes. Friends. Probably friends. After you went to sleep last night, Ra station picked up the inbound track. The plasma signature is one we recognize. It's an Earth patrol, probably sent to check our progress. Nothing to worry about, I'm sure. They're mostly interested in your brothers and sisters."

Marky's head tilted to the side almost all by itself. Doctor Pat sounded funny. Like when he said Marky's booster shots wouldn't hurt. Marky knew it wasn't a lie—Doctor Pat never lied—but the shots always hurt. Always.

"Will they hurt me?" Marky sent.

Doctor Pat pressed his head, the shiny part where his hair had fallen out, to the barrier. He clicked his transmit button a couple times before his words finally came. "No, Marky, I won't let them hurt you. Or your brothers and sisters."

Marky's cutting nails scissored out without him really wanting them to, but he did not cut the barrier.

"You're a brave boy, Marky. If anyone comes here, they may want to ask you a few questions or play some games. That's all. Just do what they say. Keep your claws sheathed and they'll probably like you just fine."

Marky concentrated and sent, "If I do good on their tests, will they wrestle with me?"

Doctor Pat stared at him. He looked sad. After a while, he shook his head and said, "I'd better get a move on, Marky. There is a great deal of work to assign before the landing. Back soon."

He began to unclip his headset, but before he did, Marky called, "See you later, alligator!"

Doctor Pat held the microphone bead to his lips, but didn't answer right away. "It is," he finally whispered, "and always has been, my fondest wish that as soon as everyone sees how downright human—childlike, really—you and your poor misused brothers and sisters actually are, they'll all love you, too. As much as I do. I pray that humanity isn't so far gone in their nightmare propaganda that that day has not passed us by. Good luck, my buddy."

He clicked off before Marky had a chance to answer.

• • •

Marky was sniffing the crack beneath the door that sometimes opened to the outside when Trisa's voice came to him. "Marky! Wake up, Marky!"

He was already awake. Trisa sounded scared. Why did Trisa sound scared? Trisa was brave.

"You're brave, too, Marky. That's why we need your help. Now, before it's too late."

His help? Did Trisa have to take a test? Marky wasn't sure if he could help Trisa with one of her tests. Her tests were hard. Complicated. Building things out of wires and modules. Digging trenches. Tracking spaceships. Loading weapons. She never made cats. Never played with Lego.

"Marky! Pay attention. Some Earth people are coming here. The ones who *paid* for us, Marky. They'll probably hit you first and then come here."

Marky felt smart. He already knew about the visitors. Friends, he thought. Doctor Pat said they were friends. "Probably friends," he said. They wouldn't hurt him if he kept his claws put away and answered their questions.

In his head, Trisa's voice took on a renewed urgency. "They are *not* friends, Marky. They are not ordinary people from Earth. People who might like you. These people are coming to hurt you. They cut your program a long time ago. Long before they forced Doctor Pattison and Doctor Harkness to make us.

"You've got to warn Doctor Pattison. The Earth people are frightened by what these bad people have told them. This is their last chance to gain control. Tell Doctor Pattison not to—"

Trisa's voice cut out. A chaos of mixed perceptions swept Marky's mind. Images of Jupiter, dark spacecraft, bright weapons, schematics, stars, moons . . .

He was still trying to sort it out when something awful happened.

The day lights flared and failed and every surface shimmered in a luminous, auroral haze. The air smelled strange, almost burnt, and the shimmering sank right into everything. The gene sequencer's tiny diagnostic lights flared. Small bulbs popped and sprayed. Threads of blue lights erupted from the big LASK computer where Marky's tutor lived. The lights rolled from control panel to control panel. Then, for a fraction of a second, even the chirp and warble of Jupiter's great voice fell from Marky's thoughts.

It was a quiet unlike any he had ever known. He stood at the center of his room, frozen in mid-panic, listening. Where was Jupiter? Where was Trisa?

Sparks flew from a bank of computer displays. A column of spotlights burst. Bright shards scattered.

Only when a string of brown and black bubbles rippled across his sealed keyboard, did Marky react. His cat was in trouble. He grabbed the Lego and screamed as it, too, shattered. His claws flashed in and out. His gill rakers pumped and pumped. His big tail sweeps slapped wildly until a familiar darkness caught his eye.

His nails peeled curls of bright foam steel from the floor as he forced himself under his bed.

•••

An oval flashed on Marky's wall, brightened as it shrank to a circle, and disappeared as the light beam probed his room. Someone, a regular human like Doctor Pat, peered through the barrier. Marky's heart throbbed anxiously. His tiny eyelids quickly nictitated. This was not Doctor Pat. Though suited for surface exposure, this person was smaller. More compact. Armed.

The light flashed past Marky's eyes, paused, returned. A red line briefly joined it, then veered farther under the bed. When Marky followed it, he found a small red dot. It was moving. Tracing the curve of his gill rakers. Marky tried to cover it, but every time he thought he had it, the red dot jumped to the back of his hand.

Was it a new game? Like scissors, rock, paper? Or leapfrog? What did Doctor Pat call the game where they slapped hands, one atop the other?

Marky paused at an unfamiliar burst of modulation. A man's voice came to him. Strange words rolled into his awareness. "Colonel Blaton? Greeley reporting, sir."

A brief chop of static, then: "Blaton."

"I am in lab five, sir. Crèche level on our maps. Orange zone. Got a live one here. A mode."

Marky blinked at the light. He could not hear Trisa. He could not hear Jupiter. Why could he hear this man talk?

"You don't say. A friggin' mode? Specify."

Greeley's light flickered over the walls. It stopped beside the outer lock door. "Io stock," he read. "Mode 4, mark 1 humanoid. Sulfur dioxide breather. Sulfur trioxide slash sulfur metabolism."

Marky recognized the words "sulfur dioxide" and "sulfur trioxide." Doctor Pat said them a lot. They meant eso-two and eso-three. Air and food. He didn't know what the last word meant.

"So flush the friggin' thing," Blaton said. "Toss him out on the surface with the rest of Pattison's unauthorized freak show."

Marky pressed himself into the darkness. The light hurt his eyes. And calling him a "mode" wasn't very nice, either. Doctor Pat said all humans were brothers. The people of Earth and his New Jovians. Didn't they share the same genes? The same past? Part of the same future?

As always, the thought made him feel all warm inside. He was the same as the people on Earth, her moon and even Mars. Brothers and sisters, all. Just as he was with Trisa and Doctor Pat's other made people on Callisto, Ganymede, and Europa.

The light beam dropped to his gill rakers. Lingering crystals shot back a fine, monochromatic yellow. Greeley said, "Begging your pardon, Colonel, but this one's different from all the holos the boys down in Intel showed us. Bigger for one thing."

"Dangerous? Threatening?"

"Only through sheer ugliness, I suppose. It's hiding under some kind of nest."

"Freaking modes," Colonel Blaton said. "Damnedest waste of Defense Department funds I've ever seen. But, shit, I suppose I'd best drop in for a look-see. Comm says the ionosphere's a bit more frazzed than we anticipated, anyway. Something to do with Io's Jupiter connection, I assume. So there's plenty of time before lift. Stand by."

Colonel Blaton's voice came back just a few seconds later. "Damn modes. All right, second squad has already taken Pattison into custody. Looks like you've found the only mode to survive our EMP. Leastwise, 'round here. On my way."

•••

Except for the picture on his chest, Colonel Blaton's surface suit was the same as Doctor Pat's. Instead of the tree and the snakes and the wings, though, there was a fist and shield. The shield had some kind of twisted ladder. And there were words, too. Three hard words and one easy word. "Earthforce Corps of Bioengineers."

Blaton pulled a sheet of warped Mylex from Doctor Harkness's clipboard. He shook his head and crumpled the Mylex in his fist. When he got to the barrier, he pushed Greeley's weapon aside and said, "Marky? Is that your name? Is that what Pattison called you?"

Marky did not answer. Both men were staring right at him. They were not smiling. Doctor Pat always smiled when he talked. Almost always.

"It is *all right,* Marky. We will *not* hurt you. I understand that you are a smart fellow. That you like to make things."

Marky smiled and edged closer. He thought hard and broadcast a hopeful "I like games. Can we play the red light game some more? I almost caught the dot!"

Greeley went rigid. He pivoted toward Colonel Blaton. "Did you hear that, sir?"

"Of course I heard it. And it can hear us, too. Can't you, Marky? What is your favorite game?"

Marky swung his sweeps out from under the bed so he could hear better. "My most favorite is wrestling. Do you like to wrestle? Doctor Pat does. Where's Doctor Pat?"

"They did it," Greeley said. "First Ganymede, then Callisto and Europa, and now here. Pattison really did it!"

Marky was glad that Greeley liked Doctor Pat. Why did Trisa think these were bad men? That they were not his friends?

"Yeah," Blaton said. To Marky, it sounded like when Doctor Harkness was being "sarcastic." "Who would have thunk it. Actually, Lieutenant, if this is the mode I'm thinking of, he used to be quite the junior genius. A hell of a lot more impressive. Heard he bought it in some kind of lab accident. A decompression."

Blaton shook his head. "What else can you do, Marky?"

Marky held out what was left of his cat. One of its eyes gleamed in the light. "I made a cat."

"Yes, I see. That looks like a very fine cat. Ever handle any weapons?"

Marky knew his cat wasn't a very fine cat. Not like it was before all the bad lights came. He crawled out from under his bed and began gathering the loose pieces into a pile. "Trisa sometimes makes weapons. Only sometimes. She doesn't like it. Weapons are com . . . comp —hard to make."

"Trisa?" said Greeley.

"Third generation mode, most likely," Blaton said. "Part of tomorrow's catch. Pattison may once have housed all his modes together."

Marky flexed his hands. He looked at the pieces. He cocked his head to the side, as a tingle of raw anxiety ran through him. Where should he start? Which piece went first? There were so many. What size? What color?

Blaton turned away from the barrier. "Useless. Worse than useless. Hard to believe he used to be Pattison's top comm designer. Of all Pattison's freaking modes, the most promising. Flush him out onto the surface."

"But he could live out there. Might actually survive."

"And I suppose you think it's some kind of threat?"

"No, sir. But the general's going to have our heads if he learns we—"

"Just do it, Lieutenant. If we bring this mockery of humanity home, word will eventually leak. And despite this guy's nasty looks, nobody who talks to him or, God forbid, *hears* him on the freaking public service band or something as they tool through the morning traffic is going to stay scared for long. Frightened and on *our* side.

"Right now nobody knows Pattison pulled this one out of the hat. If they did, they might think that Pattison was right about tailoring DNA to fit the ecology rather than the other way around. Giving the other side hope is just going to prolong the uprising."

"I don't know, Colonel . . ."

"The only way the general's going to learn about this is if you or I spill our guts. Why make life so hard? We've already arrested Pattison and all his flunkies. After we pick up all the military modes, we take them home for exhibition. Believe me, they are ten times as scary looking as this poor mark 1, here. And from what Intel I've seen, *they* don't have a friggin' positive thought in their souls.

"We run through what's definitely going to be the circus trial of the millennium—and I do mean *circus*— and once the convictions are handed down, the uprising's over. We release the conscripts and you non-career types and the solar system gets back to normal. We terraform Io and move on. Follow?

"Yessir."

"Flush him."

•••

Marky ran. Although the gravity was similar, his gait barely resembled the bunny-hopping that Luna's first visitors used to scout the shores of Mare Tranquillitatis or to scale the Apennine foothills. With each step, Marky's webbed feet splayed out in front of him and gently cupped the Ionian surface. As he moved forward, each foot scissored until, altogether, sixteen toes bit into the soil. His tail sweeps rocked for balance. His rakers pumped with each push. At nearly 25 klicks per hour, he almost flew across the surface.

He liked the way the eso-two hissed as he rushed through it. The way the loose Ionian soil rasped his pads, his toes.

Doctor Pat sometimes played a tickle game with Marky's toes. He grabbed each claw one by one and counted. "This little piggy went to market. This little piggy stayed home. This little piggy ate frost and this little piggy had none. This little piggy took a nap and this little piggy stayed up. This little piggy had a sulfur bath and *this* little piggy . . . went *wee-wee-wee*, all the way home!"

When he reached the *"wee-wee-wee"* part, he tickled Marky all over.

That was so fun! He'd grab one of Doctor Pat's legs and hug for all he was worth. Lately, he'd almost been able to lift Doctor Pat off the ground!

"Yes, Marky," Doctor Pat would sometimes say. "You're very strong. You're getting to be a very big boy. Soon you'll be all grown up."

Marky liked showing Doctor Pat his muscles. The big ones on his legs. The even bigger ones at the base of his twin sweep tails.

"Careful with those," Doctor Pat would say. And then he would grab one of the sweeps and pretend it had whipped him across the chest. He would tumble over backward and the bright Ionian soil would fly!

The first time Dr. Pattison had done it, Marky cried because he thought he'd really hurt Doctor Pat. But it was just a game. Better than tickling. Better than running. Almost as good as wrestling.

"Slow down, Marky. Tricky ground ahead," Trisa said.

Marky smiled as he skirted the east ridge of Kibero Patera's irregular caldera. He was glad Trisa's voice had come back in his head. Without her, he would not have known which direction to go. He would have been afraid. He would not have climbed the big volcano.

He was still afraid. Like Loki to the northwest and Pele behind him, Kibero would one day send its plume jetting toward Jupiter. Resembling geysers more than volcanic eruptions, the plumes regularly spewed forth ejecta at nearly a klick per second. Faster than Marky could run. Way faster. And never stopping, not for months at a time.

"It's all right, Marky. Relax. Concentrate on your feet. Kibero's sulfur chamber is still filling. The main feeder's too busy pumping silicates. Watch your footing and you've nothing to worry about."

A flash of lurid red caught Marky's eye. The silicate flows stayed way down in the cracks, red- or white-hot.

Doctor Pat once told Marky that they came from somewhere way deep. That the other moons and Jupiter made the heat.

Marky smiled. The glass flows were fun. He, Doctor Pat, and Doctor Harkness once spent an entire day learning to blow obsidian bubbles from the melt. They came out black and green and sometimes blue. Very pretty, but also delicate and hard for Marky to hold in his slender fingers.

He rounded a recent flow and leaped a two-meter crevasse. The soil that met his landing was brittle with cold. The crust broke into perfect footprints with every stride.

That reminded him of something else Doctor Pat did.

Ochre dirt spewed into the sky and both his tails whipped around as Marky skidded to a halt. He dropped and, frowning so that he could think hard, scrawled his name in the sulfur sand. The *R* was backwards. And the *Y* was too small, but he liked the way the far sun reflected off the edges of the big *M*. *M* for Marky.

Doctor Pat said, in another life, he'd had a little boy named Marky. That's where it came from. Doctor Pat's other life.

"Hurry up, please, Marky. No time for games, dear. Doctor Pattison's going to be long gone if you don't get moving. So will I."

Marky carefully scrubbed his name from the ochre soil. How did Trisa know about Doctor Pat? Where he was? What was going to happen to him?

"Listen carefully, Marky."

Something broke from the camouflage of Jupiter's dekameter radio emission. Some faint tingling in the electromagnetic spectrum.

Illustrated by Rob Hassan

Listen, listen, listen, he told himself. He swung his sweeps at the western horizon.

There. Very faint. The buzz of a regular human's voice. The stuttering half-phase encryption of a secure military frequency.

"That's where Doctor Pattison is," sent Trisa.

Where? All around?

"I will teach you something. Something Doctor Pattison never thought of. Is that all right, Marky?"

Something Doctor Pat never thought of? Impossible.

"Ask yourself, 'Where is the signal strongest?' Listen, Marky. Listen and point. Draw an arrow in the sand."

Keep talking, Marky thought at the signal, but not so loud as to interrupt it. He swung his sweeps at the horizon. The voices were the loudest almost in line with Ra Patera.

"Good. Good. Draw an arrow to the west and run a little way to your left. Downhill, Marky."

Several hundred meters to the south, Marky could barely hear the signal. At Trisa's direction, he faced west and rocked gently from side to side.

There. Again, very faint. The word "Tiercel." A lot of numbers. The second arrow pointed more toward Loki's towering, mushroom-shaped plume.

"Very nicely done, Marky. That word precedes almost every new break in the carrier. It is the name of Colonel Blaton's spaceship. That is where Doctor Pattison is. Inside *Tiercel*. Remember the angle of your first two lines and move farther south."

Marky trotted another thousand yards and scanned the sky. Good. There was the word "Tiercel" again. And a garbled voice and more numbers. A lot of big numbers, but getting smaller. Falling by multiples of one hundred.

Marky liked counting by eights. Tens and hundreds were harder.

He studied the horizon. The last arrow pointed almost directly at Loki.

"Cross all three lines of bearing in your head. Do you see where they come together, Marky? It won't be a single point because *Tiercel* is moving."

Marky imagined a tiny triangle. In his head it looked like it was very far away.

"You are very smart, big brother. That's where *Tiercel* is. Where the bad men have Doctor Pattison. Now run. They're only a few minutes from touching down. You must hurry."

Fear clenched Marky's ribs. His rakers trembled. His sweeps followed *Tiercel*'s descent, but he still didn't see where it was going to land. Where he could find Doctor Pat.

"You already know where it is," Trisa sent. "Do you remember your Io globe? How we used to look at it when we talked to one another? *Tiercel* is coming to the small supply station on the other side of Kibero Patera. That's where I live, too."

How far?

"Seventy klicks. Three hours, if you run hard. If you find food on the way, and avoid the cold."

Marky ran.

• • •

Jupiter looked like it turned about three times an Ionian day. But that was a trick. Something Doctor Pat called an "illusion." The gas giant really "rotated" a little more than four times for each of Io's times around. And because Io spent part of the time *behind* Jupiter, and sometimes faced Jupiter's light and *not* the sun's, a lot of Doctor Pat's assistants couldn't get used to the "local clock." Especially when part of the "night" was a heck of a lot brighter than the part of the "day" when the sun went behind Jupiter.

But it wasn't something Marky could easily forget. He'd been born with the rhythms of his home neatly wired into his reflexes and so it surprised him when the cold started to come early. But it did.

At Trisa's bidding, he had stopped for a quick, surprisingly urgent meal on the shallow slope of Kibero's west flank. *Tiercel* had landed and Colonel Blaton was busy putting Trisa and his other brothers and sisters "through their paces." Doctor Pat was still inside *Tiercel* and because Colonel Blaton was having almost everything from the dome put inside with him, she figured Marky had enough time to eat. Or, as Trisa sent, "Gas up."

Marky munched one velvet frond while he scouted the slope for more. Doctor Pat called the eso-three plants "skunk cabbage," but Marky didn't think the plants looked like skunks. Not at all. Besides, they smelled good. Skunks smelled bad. His touchscreen tutor had told him so.

His tutor also said the plants grew near Io's rare oxygen seeps. That they used light from the sun to catch the oxygen.

Maybe, Marky thought, it was like Lieutenant Greeley's red dot game. He smiled. That was fun.

He chewed the last frond. Somewhere inside, the plants used the oxygen to change eso-two to eso-three. Doctor Harkness said that when the eso-three mixed with the sulfur retained by Marky's gill rakers, it gave him energy.

Which seemed pretty neat, when he thought about it. After all, it was Doctor Pat's idea, wasn't it? Somewhere inside him—a place that *growled* when he was hungry—a solid meal was usually enough to get Marky through an entire day.

But not this time. Not after all the excitement and not after the long run. Marky munched the last frond only to find his belly groaning for more. He could eat the roots, but Doctor Pat said that was bad. The roots were fragile and there wouldn't be any more skunk cabbage if Marky ate the roots.

He found more eso-three at the bottom of a high cliff. Doctor Pat called the encrusted pools there "hot springs" even though they were not very hot. One of the pools, perhaps heated from below, was large enough to attract Marky's attention. Rafts of bright sulfur drifted over its surface. Interlocking sprays of finer crystals lined the shore.

"Very good," Trisa sent. "Somewhere in the melt, eso-two may have picked up the oxygen left behind as the pure sulfur crusts formed. If so, you're sure to find eso-three."

Even though Marky felt good that Trisa thought he was smart, he tried not to show it. It wasn't like he knew how the springs made food. It just felt *right* to him, somehow. It smelled good. It tasted better.

"Throw in a few copper sulfides for flavor," Trisa sent, "and *voilà* . . . a feast."

He was still drinking when he noticed that his pool was shrinking. It was getting shallower and shallower. Some of the others nearby were gone entirely!

Was he drinking that much?

He studied the surface and trembled as a portion congealed, grew glossy-bright, and sank.

Ice, he thought. Bad ice. Dangerous.

"Get out of there, Marky! You're still pretty high up. The cold's going to come on *fast!*"

Trisa was right. Marky had been climbing most of the day. The air he needed to breathe was beginning to freeze out of the sky. It happened at the poles all the time and almost everywhere except the equator at night. Doctor Pat had once warned him to be afraid of such things. His tutors had even told him that it was the same near the Martian polar caps, except with carbon dioxide.

Only hardly anyone *breathed* carbon dioxide. Did they?

But, for now, Marky's thoughts were not registering such things. Along with Trisa's warning, he had caught several images. *Tiercel* had landed. His brothers and sisters were carrying crates and bins to her cargo bay. And a lot of Earth people were around Trisa. They were all suited up. Some Earth people pointed weapons.

Was Trisa all right? They wouldn't hurt her, would they? Would Doctor Pat let them hurt Trisa?

"Doctor Pattison doesn't have a lot to say in this, brother of mine. Not without a little help from his friends back on Earth. Now get out of there. Run if you can. Dig in, if you can't. Look for somewhere to—"

Trisa's voice cut out, but not before Marky caught the image of a weapon's butt jammed into her face. His fingers clenched into a tight ball. His claws sprang out. He rolled to his feet and looked upslope. Especially in the shadows, a new white frost was closing in on him.

His heart raced. He was in trouble. He quickly checked the positions of Europa, Callisto, and Gany-mede. Jupiter itself was the size of Doctor Pat's gloved fist held at arm's length. The dark drew very near its edge. No matter how much he wanted to, he wasn't going to make it to *Tiercel*. To Doctor Pat. To Trisa. Not today. Maybe not *any* day. Without Trisa's help, what would he do?

Like finding the springs, the answer seemed to come from somewhere inside him. As if he had been through this all before, Marky suddenly knew just what to do. He needed a cave. A place to hibernate through the night. It would be like camping with Doctor Pat.

His cutting claws were still out and, without thinking, he began carving the scarp wall. Undercut by the springs, the frozen sands gave easily. Marky pulled what debris he could in after him and settled in to wait out the cold.

He rolled into a ball. He hoped Trisa would be all right. And Doctor Pat, too.

He said his prayers, "Now I lay me down to sleep. I pray the Lord my human soul to keep," and he slept.

He dreamed of wrestling. Blowing glass bubbles. And, most of all, hugging Doctor Pat.

•••

Tiercel stood alongside the supply depot's big launch rails. White except for her orange-dusted landing cone, she reminded Marky of one of the soft-boiled eggs Doctor Harkness ate. Her cargo ramp door was closed. None of his brothers or sisters were out on the surface. A stream of vapor trailed from her plasma vents.

The supply station was exactly the same size as Doctor Pat's dome. It had the same triangle facets that made circles and diamonds, depending on how Marky looked at it, and the same three doors. Big doors, one every third of the way around.

"Hide, Marky," Trisa sent. "I think we're about to lift, so don't let anyone see you. They might try taking a shot or two as we pass. Head for the dome or the launch rails. Try to blend in."

Marky shook his head. Doctor Pat had once said that Marky had the most marvelous orange skin he had ever seen. It made it easy for him to hide. He always won at hide-and-go-seek. But not now. Now, he did not want to hide. He wanted to save Trisa. He wanted to stop Colonel Blaton. He wanted to find Doctor Pat and ask him why he was letting all this happen. Why he hadn't stopped it before it all began.

He wondered if Trisa was with Doctor Pat.

"None of us saw him leave the ship," Trisa sent. "They herded us in here pretty fast, though."

Marky stared at the white egg. When Trisa spoke, a sudden darkness cloaked his vision. The air smelled oddly metallic. Around him, he seemed to sense the heartbeats and mental signatures of all his siblings.

"Yes, big brother. This is as close as we—you and I, you and we—have ever been. Now you see what the Earth people fear. Not our looks. Not our military capabilities. Not even our differences, but our closeness. Something they crave and fear at the same time. It may have been an undesired consequence of some other genetic modification, but somehow Doctor Pattison bonded us each to one another. Everything that happens to one of us is known to the others. Every time you and I have talked, the others have been with me."

That made Marky afraid, too. Did all of his brothers know he was a cheater? Did his sisters know he was secretly afraid of bed bugs? Of crocodiles? That, deep down, he knew that he used to be smart like they were? That he hurt himself just so he could touch Doctor Pat? Once, for real?

A multitude of voices swelled into his personal carrier. Even though the other voices seemed equally earnest, Trisa's voice was still the clearest, "We love you, Marky. You've been alone for a long time. We know why you're afraid. We know that breaking the barrier wasn't really your fault. We know you love Doctor Pat. We know you love us."

He crawled to the launch rail's sunward side. When his sweeps rasped a patch of corrosion, Jupiter's usual radio noise suddenly magnified. The background clicks and pops and whistles he'd heard and ignored all his life seemed suddenly foreboding. The looming planet, a danger.

"Don't be silly," Trisa sent. "Being afraid of Jupiter would be like an Earth human being afraid of the sun. Without Jupiter, more than half the day would be dark. Why, without its magnetic field continually sweeping our ionosphere, we couldn't even speak!"

That was true. Doctor Pat had told him so. It used to make Marky feel good to be part of something so big. So strong. Now, though, it only made him feel helpless and small.

The ground around *Tiercel*'s vents began to melt and steam.

Trisa sent, "Good-bye, big brother. If you still want to try talking to Doctor Pattison, get into the dome. We left behind as many electronic modules as we could find. I'll try to help you put things together, but I don't know how long we can hold out. They'll probably throw us into cryosleep once we're in flight, but I'll help as much as I can."

Like the tests, Marky thought. He felt horrible for being afraid. Hadn't Trisa always helped him? With the tests? With his cat? By telling how to find Doctor Pat?

He pumped his scales to full extension, pushed from the launch rail, and chased his shadow downslope.

He was still more than a klick distant when the launch blast threw him to the ground. He rolled across a patch of eso-two frost and watched *Tiercel* rise.

"Come back," he broadcast at the ship. "Come back, Trisa! Doctor Pat! I need you, Doctor Pat!"

Tiercel dwindled to a bright dot. After a while, she was just another pinpoint in the heavens, almost lost in Jupiter's flushed face.

"I love you, Doctor Pat. Please come back. Please?"

No word, other than something resembling a chill, low groan, came from the darkness. Except for Jupiter's background hiss—quieter now that he was away from the launch rail—he heard almost no sound. No sound beside his breathing and the few sobs he couldn't quite hold back.

Finally, when he lost *Tiercel* completely, he forced an urgent calmness upon himself. Doctor Pat didn't like it when he cried. Neither did Trisa. Wasn't he a special boy? Hadn't Doctor Pat told him so almost every day of his life?

Yes, he was. He was Doctor Pat's best buddy. And while he felt a rough tightness in his throat and a sting along his eye ducts, he knew he was too old to cry. He would think of something. He would find a way to tell Doctor Pat that he loved him. To tell his brothers and sisters that he loved them back even though he'd forgotten to say so.

He turned to the dome. He would think of something.

• • •

Sometimes, Marky had to sit for a long time before he imagined Trisa's voice coming to him. "Now for the last few components," she might have said. He wasn't sure. Her voice was hard to pick out of the background noise.

He thought back to when she helped him make his cat. And his rat, before that. And his hat and his mat. "You're doing very well," she would say.

And what else?

He thought hard until her voice seemed to return. "Good, Marky. Now, can you find a silver rectifier module for Trisa?"

Marky smiled. Still packaged for shipment, the spare circuit modules seemed to have survived *Tiercel*'s preemptive pulse. In addition to a handful of specialty modules, he still had ten green power blocks, four red resistor packs, several dozen optronic connectors and field modifiers, and another dozen blue capacitance transformers. The colors were pretty, but the labels were hard to read.

He searched the pile. Where was that rectifier?

His subconscious hopes of finding an intact transmitter had failed the instant he opened one of the circuit panels. The odor was horribly familiar. A condition one of Doctor Pat's technicians had once described as "fried."

Not such a bad smell, Marky thought, but each new exposure recalled the sparks and the white currents that ran through Doctor Pat's dome just before *Tiercel* set down. On top of that, the circuits, not expected to have to endure Io's harsh atmosphere, were never hardened against corrosion. Every time he pulled a panel from its protective sheath, the bright paths connecting one chip to another glazed with darkness.

No wonder the automated pods weren't climbing the acceleration rail. No wonder Trisa's dome was still cooling.

His fingers closed on the silver module almost of their own accord. He slid it into place. "Good, good, very good," he said, echoing distant Trisa.

When her voice stopped coming from *Tiercel*, he'd had to make an imaginary Trisa in his head. She wasn't as smart as the real Trisa, but she knew a lot that he didn't. Or maybe she just remembered a lot that he had lost in the accident.

"Almost there," she seemed to say. "Now, be careful. The next stage has a lot of juice running through it. You'll have to couple it directly to the broadcast channel. . . ."

Finally, with nearly all the parts used up, one last connection brought Jupiter's faint hiss into the room. Though scaled on a different frequency, the gliding resonance of pops and tones were the same as those in Marky's head.

He moved the modules to the dome's front door.

It was getting late. Sulfur loess coated every bright surface. A growing rime of bright eso-two frost allowed no sharp angle. His gill rakers fluttered as they struggled to draw eso-two from the dome's deepening chill. He had better hurry. It wouldn't be long before there wasn't enough pressure to breathe.

When he pressed the transmit key and spoke, his own voice pushed Jupiter's to the background. "Doctor Pat? Can you hear me? It's me, Marky. If you can hear me, would you please answer?"

Jupiter's noise poured back through the speaker module. Only the faintest countermodulation seemed in any way different from what he heard outside the receiving circuit.

"Doctor Pat? Where are the bad men taking you? I thought that maybe your other made people on Ganymede or Callisto or Europa might need you, but why didn't you say good-bye? Why did you take Trisa and all the others? Are you taking them to show the Earth people? To stop the fighting?"

Jupiter crackled. A pulsing tone climbed in frequency and died.

"I'm tired of being alone, Doctor Pat. I miss you. I wish you would make the bad men bring you back. Doctor Pat, why won't you answer? Where have you gone? I need you, Doctor Pat."

Marky listened to Jupiter for the next four hours.

"Nothing," Trisa finally seemed to say. "I'm sorry, Marky."

Marky nodded. He was sorry, too. Sorry he was not smart enough to build a better radio. Sorry he didn't know what else to do. Sorry he was so stupid, stupid, *stupid!*

"That's not true, Marky, and you know it. You're a lot smarter than you think."

Marky pulled the power blocks from the rest of the modules. He didn't know what else to do. He felt sorry he had let Trisa down. Sorry he forgot to say he loved her.

"That's all right, Marky. I know. And I know something else, too."

Marky flexed his legs. He was cold. When he rubbed his face, eso-two crystals broke away. They dropped and shattered against the floor. Did Trisa know how to get warm?

"Yes, Marky, and so do you. Same as you know what people used before chips and wafers and modules."

Earth people? Marky did not know what people used before they had chips and wafers and modules. What else could there have been?

"Great big things called transistors, capacitors, resistors, and diodes. And wires, Marky. You know what wires are, don't you?"

Marky rubbed his chest. Doctor Harkness hooked him to lots of colored wires before some of her tests. Sometimes she used little glue globs to hold the pickups under his scales. The wires were pretty, but sometimes they hurt when they came off.

"Well, we don't have any of the right stuff to throw together any transistors, but before they came along, people used something even more primitive."

Wires, Marky thought hopefully. Did they use wires?

"Sort of, big brother. They put wires in bottles of metal and glass. They called them grids and filaments and tubes. The more wires, the more powerful the tubes. We are going to make a tube."

With lots of wires?

"Many, many wires, Marky."

Won't the air eat the wires? Turn them black?

"Many wires and many small chambers. Get moving. When we're done, everyone will hear us. Everyone!"

● ● ●

Marky blinked tears and pulled back from the rushing magma. The heat had dried his face and cracked his scales. White blisters marched along the tender inner joints of both arms. His fingers shook from remembered pain and his gill rakers, their scales puckered against the heat, rasped and stabbed with every taste of the vent's harsh exhaust.

Only two shells looked worth keeping. Two. Only *two* out of a dozen attempts. And in neither case had he managed to press the wires through in time. The wires had gone black and crumbled too quickly.

He wrapped his arms around his legs, pressed his face to his knees, and rocked gently back and forth. What was he doing wrong? Doctor Pat never broke so many bubbles. Maybe Marky had made a mistake. Maybe this was the wrong way to build the parts he needed. Maybe he was on the wrong track, altogether?

"Cheer up, Marky. If anything has a chance to work, this does. Why, even before Earth people started going into space, they listened to Jupiter. Even back then, Io modulated Jupiter's long wavelength radio-noise storms. All we have to do is establish a working cross shear along the . . ."

Marky stopped listening. He could barely hear Trisa. If it even was Trisa. He couldn't tell if she was real. Maybe she lived in his head the way his tutors lived inside the big LASK computers. Not that it mattered. He didn't understand what she was saying, anyway. Amidst the pain—the burns were deep and *oh*, how he *missed* Trisa and Doctor Pat!—words like "kilovolt drop across Io's diameter" and "magnetic flux tube" and "synchronous modulation" were meaningless.

Ignoring the voice in his head, Marky gathered his tools. The probe pipe and the air pack from the dome. The tongs and the rolls of gold tape. The carefully wrapped wires—with shapes like coiled snakes and kites—that he'd fought the cold and the air to bend. He made sure he wasn't going to drop anything, and then climbed back into the vent.

He knelt on the overhang and shielded his face as the magma rushed downslope. A few meters farther up, the magma was too well mixed for his needs. A few meters downslope the obsidian already piled up in what looked like crags of morning frost.

"One more try, Marky. Careful not to lean out too far."

Marky nodded. He already knew that. The melt sometimes splashed the ledge and the sides were too hot and jagged to offer a good handhold. If he slipped, the ledge could take his fingers off in mid-grasp.

One meter, then two, he pushed the probe pipe over the edge. He had to be careful though, to keep the pipe turning. It was really a length of old wave guide and so might bend and snap if he left it on one side too long. When he had it suspended over the middle of the flow, he let it fall.

It didn't splash, but it didn't bounce either. The tip hit and just sort of *eased* its way in.

Marky braced himself. The tip was clearing the outer sheath that formed wherever the magma cooled. When it pushed through to the real current—

The pipe jerked hard into his chest, but he was ready for it. It wasn't going to knock him off his feet like the first time Doctor Pat showed him how to blow bubbles. No way. Still turning the pipe, Marky locked it in the notch he'd cut before his first attempt. He pushed the pipe deep and then threw all his weight on it.

Lift, he thought at the end. "Lift!" he shouted.

The pipe broke free and levered up at him. The bright glob on its end was bigger than he'd hoped for, but cooling fast.

Hand over hand, he brought it in. It was very hot, but not so hot that he could afford the time to worry about it. If it cooled too far, he would have to start all the way over with another glob.

He coupled the air pack to the pipe and vented a short burst. Turn, turn, turn . . . vent. Turn, turn, turn . . . vent.

A bubble formed. Flame swept its interior as it grew.

Marky braced the pipe and pulled the first wire pack halfway from its sheath. Immediately, darkness began to glaze its surface.

Not this time, he thought.

He pressed the wires to the glass. The bubble bent, compressed, and finally gave without popping or shattering. Perfect timing.

Marky grabbed the tongs and pinched the bubble closed around the wires.

Turn, turn, turn . . . vent. Another bubble began to form. He added more wires and then flipped the pipe overhead so the glass began to spread out with the spin. When the bowl spread back and the darkening, cooling lip had radiated out far enough, Marky snapped the whole thing back down to the rushing magma. The bowl pinched into a flower-bud shape, forming a new sphere around the first bubble.

It was time to seal the first and second bubbles and gather a second glob right on top of them.

Marky hesitated. Too early in the process and the whole thing would return to the melt. Too late and the bubbles would shatter and drag off the end of the pipe.

"Cross your fingers," Trisa seemed to say.

Too busy, Marky thought. He watched the color deepen and, just when the glass began to gleam, he threw all his weight on the pipe. It hesitated at the magma's surface, then plunged through.

One alligator, he thought as his muscles trembled. Two alligator. He twisted the pipe. Three alligator! Lift!

Three times before, he'd come this far only to have the pipe break from the surface perfectly clean. No bubbles. No blob of hot melt. No wires.

This time, it came away from the surface with a sucking sound. The end was hot and red and the glass was sagging as he dragged the pipe back toward him. He connected the air pack and swung the pipe straight down between his legs to let the new glob lengthen into a tube.

Time seemed to fly as he wrestled the glass into shape. He added a wire here, a bank of heating meshes there. A coating of gold ribbon and a wrapping of fine wire. Then another coat of glass and another series of tong sculpting. A long, helical cavity. More wire. More gold. Glass, coils, anodes, cathodes, supports, contacts, more filaments and grids. . . .

Marky finished wrapping a focusing coil around the drift space between two cavities and stopped. Simply, stopped. He was done. It wasn't pretty. Nor was it like anything he had ever seen. Except that was, for the picture in his head, which Trisa must have sent him.

Her voice seemed to come somewhere deep inside him. "No, Marky. This is yours. All yours. I always said you were smarter than you thought."

Marky wasted no time connecting his new tube, still hot from its genesis, to the circuits he had already prepared. Though heavily modified, it was basically the same design as the one he had tried earlier. He connected the last power pack and a luminous iridescence swirled through the glass. A band of orange light sizzled into shape along the helical tube. As Marky adjusted the voltage, dark nodes swept up and down its length.

The orange light pinched into eight separate lenses and then snapped into one brilliant arc. It went red. Red like Jupiter's Great Spot. A standing wave formed between the first contacts and the last. The air around Marky seemed to stand still. The whole world seemed brittle and electric at the same time.

Trembling with excitement, he took a strand of insulated wire and walked the length of the launch rail. Though half hidden by a fresh coat of sulfur dust, it wasn't difficult to find the same corroded patch he had touched before *Tiercel's* launch. Dull where it had once been bright, the exposed metal couldn't have been corroding for long. After a while, Marky knew, nothing would be left but the rail's hard duraplast exoskeleton.

"Cut in until you find bright metal. There, where the covering has broken away. Now press one sweep to the acceleration ramp. The metal will feel cold, but it won't hurt you."

Marky slashed the ramp until bright metal flashed. He pressed a sweep to make contact. Jupiter's voice boomed through him.

He swung his other sweep to his new tube. He felt an almost overwhelming tickle as the current rushed through his sweeps.

What do I do?

"Talk, Marky. Don't move and just talk. Tell Doctor Pat how much you miss him. How much you need him. Tell everyone, Marky. Tell everyone."

"Hello? Doctor Pat?"

Marky rocked back on his haunches and gazed upward. When he spoke, all of Jupiter trembled with his voice. It sounded so loud in his head that, for a moment, he thought *God* must be talking.

"Talk, Marky! Talk."

He cleared his rakers. "Doctor Pat? This is Marky. It seems like a long time since the bad men took you away.

I don't know if you can ever come back, but I wish you would. I miss you. And I miss Trisa and all the others.

"Even if you can't come back, you need to make sure they can. This is where they live. It will hurt them to live somewhere else. Especially on Earth where people are afraid of us because we know how to love each other. To be the same and to share everything deep inside."

Marky paused. Jupiter didn't *look* any different. The clouds were still sliding along like they always did. The bright storm centers were still swirling. "I wish I was smart enough to figure out why the bad men took you away," he said. "Why they couldn't just leave everything alone. Why they took Trisa and the others.

"Trisa, she always said I was smart. She helped me make this thing to talk to you. At least I think she did. Like she's always helped me. Even if it sometimes made me feel bad, it wasn't her fault I cheated on your tests. I'm real real sorry about that. I hope that's not why the bad men took you away. It wasn't Trisa's fault if they did. Just my fault. I wanted to look smart. I wanted to make you happy. Everyone happy.

"Just like the time I wanted to touch you, I did something bad. Real bad.

"And I wanted to make a cat. Like you make things, Doctor Pat. Alive things. Beautiful, alive things. People. Real people. Like you. Like me and Trisa.

"Do you remember my cat? The one I made with Lego? With the yellow eyes? Someday, can we make a real cat? One to be my friend?"

The night began to settle into Marky's bones. But even as first one limb and then another began to numb, Jupiter's immense radio aura continued to boom. Marky's voice continued to cut through the night.

"I know you will remember me, Doctor Pat. Just like you remembered the other Marky from your other life. I'm getting cold, but Trisa said to talk, so I'm going to talk.

"Remember how you used to tickle my toes? This little piggy went to market. This little piggy stayed home. This little piggy ate frost and this little piggy . . ."

•••

The splash of plasma jets warmed Marky and sent a gust of freshly sublimated sulfur dioxide across his rakers. He startled awake and instantly felt horrible. Sick with guilt. Angry with frustration. He had stopped talking! His sweeps were off the launch rail. Off the transmitter. Sometime during the night he'd given up and crawled off to find warmth.

He heard a noise. The clatter of locking struts. The grind of ramp pushers.

His heart beat wildly. He backpedaled into a pocket of darkness still untouched by the rising sun.

A lone figure stood atop *Tiercel*'s ramp. One hand lifted. "Rise and shine, Marky-boy. Rise and shine!"

Marky ran toward Doctor Pat. He caught him in his arms and flung him around in sheer joy. "Doctor Pat, Doctor Pat! It's really you! You came back!"

Doctor Pat's voice came into Marky's head. "Thanks to you, Marky-boy. Thanks to you."

"And Trisa," Marky sent. "Thanks to Trisa, too. She helped."

Doctor Pat laughed. "No, Marky. Nobody helped you. Trisa's been out cold—literally, since we're talking cryosleep—since we left Io. Same with your brothers and sisters. Anything you did was on your own."

Marky's rakers drooped open. He stared until Doctor Pat gripped his hand.

"You did good, Marky. You got the word out. They heard you first on Europa. Then on Ganymede and Callisto. We heard you after that. Then the belt and Mars. When the people of Earth heard your voice, they knew they'd made a mistake."

Marky pressed his face to Doctor's Pat's chest.

"They turned us around, Marky. Colonel Blaton's finished. The fighting's not over yet, but you've made a good start at changing people's perceptions of what we've been doing out here. Now that Earth, the whole world and the whole solar system, knows you're human, we're free. You're free, too. Same for Trisa and your brothers and sisters. Thanks to you, we're all free to live how we want and explore this new world of yours."

Marky grinned. He was glad Doctor Pat was back. Glad that he'd done something smart. Glad there would not be any more bad men coming to take Doctor Pat and Trisa away.

Doctor Pat hugged him. "I'm proud of you, son. Seriously proud."

THE THIRD AGENDA

Written by
Michael A. Stackpole

About the Author

For those of you who haven't had a chance to read Stackpole's work yet, I (Dave Wolverton) highly recommend it. Stackpole came to my attention a few years ago when I heard some fans describe him as "the Tolkien of military science fiction." I think it an apt description, but Stackpole's talents far exceed military fiction and spill into other areas. I particularly like his fantasy.

Michael A. Stackpole is an award-winning game designer, computer game designer, and writer who has had twenty-seven novels published since 1988. His best-known work has been in the Star Wars universe and includes the first four New York Times *best-selling X-Wing novels and the stand-alone novel I, Jedi. His fantasy novels include* Once a Hero *and* Talion: Revenant. *He is currently working on* The Dark Glory War, *the first novel in an epic fantasy series called the DragonCrown War.*

There is always a lot of very good advice that is given to beginning writers, and most all of it is true. Most all of it also generally pertains to writing itself. The emphasis on that area makes sense because without addressing the fundamentals of writing, it's difficult for someone to get to the point where other concerns come into play. I agree with that idea in general, but pointing out how publishing has changed over the last twenty years, and helping writers call into question certain assumptions that no longer hold true, provides a way for writers to anticipate new problems and set themselves up to deal with them.

It used to be that someone wanting a career as a writer really only needed to master two areas of work. One was writing, which seems rather obvious. The other was learning the ins and outs of running a small business. This aspect is still very important because of a myriad of tax laws and the like which can cause stresses that interfere with writing. If a writer wants a *career* in writing, getting the business aspect down is vital.

This focus on *career*, I think, is very important because, unlike years past, the way the market has shifted makes new demands on writers. Time once was that having a publisher who would nurture a writer and build his audience meant that if you got published and worked hard, you were in great career shape. Poul Anderson told Roger Zelazny, on the advent of Roger's twentieth novel seeing print, that Roger was set. Now having twenty novels in print means nothing—most writers are a sales disaster away from working at McDonald's. Careers have to be built and pursued with perseverance and intelligence.

This requires the writer to address what I term the third agenda: understanding the business of publishing. There are many who would suggest that "the business of publishing" is an oxymoron because publishing is seldom run in a very businesslike manner. For example, there is no demographic study that shows which authors sell, beyond the survey conducted at the checkout counter. The problem with this is that such a lack allows trends to drive the market. The cyberpunk phenomena, the horror market and the current hunger for epic fantasies are all examples of publishers choosing works based on subject and with little regard to a particular author's ability to actually carry the work off. A simple canvassing of used bookstores and comparing the number of books by an author there with the numbers of copies printed would indicate if the author has any reader loyalty. If a book sold lots and very few copies are in the resale market, the author produces books that are "keepers." Conversely, a book that printed low numbers that shows up in used bookstores in droves means the author failed to deliver and probably is not a safe bet for future work.

One thing that I encourage in writers at all stages of development is to read in the field where they want to write, and to read critically. For beginners, especially the young, I suggest they read a book and, at the end of each chapter, just jot down notes concerning what they liked in the chapter, what they hated, whether or not the ending of the chapter made them want to read further, and so on. After they've finished the book, I ask them to go back through the chapters and study those elements they liked to try to learn how the author accomplished that effect. The good things they should learn to incorporate into their own work, and they should learn to avoid the things they don't like.

For example, a lot of my readers have told me they keep coming to the end of a chapter and I hit them with something that forces them to keep reading. I refer to that end-of-chapter bombshell as a "button." The technique for doing that is fairly simple, and you can see it if you study a bunch of the buttons. It all comes down to having a character reveal an important factoid the reader knows nothing about. "Very well," said Percival, "but the aliens have melted New York!" might not be the best example, but you can see the elements there. Drop that sort of button at the end of your chapters and readers will race through your books.

Critical reading of work in your field will also, I hope, produce another revelation: regardless of the trappings of the tale being told, good stories focus on characters, how they change and how they grow. I believe it is very important to provide the reader with at least one character who is "normal." This character provides a touchstone for the reader, a way to calibrate himself to what is expected and considered usual in this world and time. Other characters can and probably should range all over the place, but without a safe haven the reader will be lost and may set the book down, never to pick it up again.

Characters should also provoke reactions in the readers. A writer should want her readers to become engaged with her characters on an emotional level. A reader should love or hate a character, should want to see that character succeed or die horribly. If, in characterizing that character, a writer can get the readers to project a future for that character, she's got the readers and can run them through a gamut of emotions from joy to terror, precisely because she's gotten her readers to invest brainsweat in a character.

Reading critically in the field is important for yet another reason: it points out to us that the books we grew up reading, the books that made us love science fiction and fantasy, are not the books being published today. In 1997, after seeing a movie trailer for *Starship Troopers*, I bought the book and read it for the first time. This book is a classic of science fiction but, truth be told, if it arrived in New York today it would be sent back for a rewrite. The author would be asked to be more graphic and descriptive with the battle scenes, he'd be asked to pump up the characterization and it would be suggested heavily that the polemics be trimmed back.

That sort of thing can be decried as sacrilege, but various factors in the business today make it a reality. If you look at SF novels before 1983 and after, you'll find, on average, they are 50 percent larger, and most all of that increase comes in the area of characterization. There are even novels being published today that don't have a plot, but get published based on the strength of some very appealing and interesting characters. Readers now demand more than a snappy plot and a technological marvel that saves the day, and writers who deliver more than that are the ones who will sell.

Reading the current works will definitely show the trends that are hot and heating up, which leads many to believe they should jump in and write that type of book. The cold fact is, though, that by the time a trend is hitting print, the editors are already sick of it. Doing a book like that *now* is probably too little, too late. Instead of looking at the trend's window dressing, taking a glance at what lurks beneath it is vital.

Writers can be broken down into two large categories. The vast majority belong in the "lazy" category. These are writers who are still writing the sort of books they read as a child. If they decide to write an epic fantasy novel, they read *Lord of the Rings*, file off a few serial numbers, rely on the stock characters of the Western literary tradition, and write a perfectly good quest novel. There are a lot of careers out there that have been solid, even spectacular, by authors who have done just this. It certainly is one path.

The other group of writers are "dynamic." What they do is look at what has gone before, take those universal elements, then—dare I suggest it?—apply their imagination to more than naming characters and countries. They invent new elements that get woven into their work, be it creatures, places, magical systems, new sapient races, whatever. They take a staid concept and expand on it, reshaping it, making it new and, more importantly, making it their own. They do this through additional research and a desire to push themselves to grow as writers.

We've lost some of the magic of our literary tradition. Everyone knows of Robin Hood and his enemy, Guy of Gisborne, but very few people are aware that old Guy used to have his own cycle of songs sung about him. He was every bit the hero that Robin Hood was, and then some bard, somewhere, got the brilliant idea of writing a song where these two figures met and fought and one of them lost. That bard wasn't content with just rehashing the same material others had created, but he went and did something new and clever. It's that spirit that I look for in my own work and the work of other authors.

So, the third agenda, then, really is for you to become a dynamic writer. You have to work on your craft, know how to run a business and be in touch with the changes going on in your field. By studying the works of your peers you can see what works, what doesn't, and figure out ways to improve what you do. By challenging yourself to do more than others, to further our literary heritage, not just wallow in it, you will be creating works that live and breathe. Works that do that will build a solid career and keep you able to do the one job it seems everyone in the world would love to have.

FALLER

Written by
Tim Jansen

Illustrated by
Rob Hassan

About the Author

Tim Jansen is a life-long resident of Washington and has the usual odd résumé of a writer. He has been a carpenter, construction worker, janitor, and has worked as a hydroseeder driver in Alaska.

He is fascinated with quantum physics, science fiction in general, and with old movies.

Tim is currently working on his first novel, Decatur.

Lenlah wasn't bad. She was as good as people come. But the devil got inside of her and carried her away.

We lived on a dairy farm deep in the Five Valleys, nearly three hundred miles west-northwest of Omaha, Nebraska, the nearest Outside city. It was beautiful country. We had fourteen Ayrshire and twelve Jerseys. We also raised chickens. Lenlah and I tended to them and we helped with the milking, too.

Lenlah was my sister. She didn't care about the wars except, like everyone, as something to watch at night, sitting out under the stars watching ships explode. Bright little flashes, white and gold and silent. Way out in space.

Sometimes they fall and streak across the sky, all different colors. And sometimes they even crash to the ground. Years ago, before I was born, a big lunar shuttle fell near here, just over the southern hills. But it was still almost a day's ride and all on board were dead.

This ship was small. A strike ship. It had only one pilot and though injured, he survived. And he fell right onto our farm.

I was eleven that spring; old enough to try and act like a lady, Father kept reminding me, with little success. Lenlah was seventeen. She didn't need reminding. In just three weeks she was to marry Mikal Mathose, the only son of the richest man in Five Valleys.

Father liked to take credit for that catch, as he was great friends with Mathose, Sr., but it wasn't all his doing. Lenlah was very beautiful.

• • •

It was April 7. A warm Saturday night. I was out in the back field lying on a stack of green alfalfa under the stars, looking for ships but having little luck. I was just about to turn in, wishing I could be at the dance, when I heard Lenlah call from across the north pasture.

"Milly, are you out there? Wake Father—there's an injured man and he needs help!"

Naturally, I was surprised. The big dance at the Mathose ranch was practically Lenlah's engagement party, but Mikal had gotten pretty drunk, so she came home early—a good hour's walk alone in the dark with only a sliver of a new moon to see by.

She had practically tripped over the spaceman. It was that much dumb luck. That or the devil.

"I'm here, Lenlah," I shouted back into the dark, then leapt off the haystack and raced for the house. My older brothers, Josh and Todd, were still at the dance, so father hitched up the mares and tore some slats from an old crate, as Lenlah had said the pilot's leg was broken. Lenlah got blankets, a sheet and scissors. I got the lens lantern, threw some cushy straw in the back of the buckboard, and we raced off to rescue the man from space.

I'd just finished cutting the sheet into a pile of two-inch strips, as evenly as I could, given the bumpy ride, when Father pulled the wagon to a stop. We'd arrived. Lenlah handed me the lantern, leapt off the buckboard and hurried to the spaceman. Father and I followed.

He was lying on his back on the bank of the creek just behind the alfalfa field, his spacesuit gleaming white in the lantern beam. I was careful to keep it from his eyes, since he had no helmet.

His parachute, which Lenlah had managed to unhitch before she left him, fluttered mostly submerged in the gurgling creek downhill. Barely conscious, he mumbled something about prowlers as Father and Lenlah found the clasps and removed his boots, careful of his left leg, which bent at a queasy angle below the knee.

Gallons of water, it seemed, ran out of his spacesuit and back into the creek. Lenlah must have had quite a struggle pulling him out. She'd managed it by harnessing herself into his shroud lines and pulling him an inch at a go.

His suit was baggy, so once they had the waist unzipped, the bottom half slid off pretty easy. I handed Dad the scissors and he cut open the left leg of the soaking wet jumpsuit. The spaceman had no wound or bleeding. Lenlah ran to the buckboard to grab the splints. Father, very gently, slid the leg back into line. The spaceman didn't flinch.

Father held the two wooden slats in place, one on each side, while Lenlah padded and secured them with the strips of sheet, Father instructing her as they went.

When the leg was set to Father's satisfaction, Lenlah pulled off the top half of the spacesuit. Then I set down the lantern. The three of us got a blanket under the spaceman and we carefully lifted him into the back of the buckboard. I'd guess the whole operation took about half an hour.

Father drove back slow and easy, somehow missing every bump. Lenlah tucked the other blankets snugly

Illustrated by Rob Hassan

around our passenger, who shivered pretty badly now. That creek stays stubbornly cold well into summer.

Back at the house, we pulled up to the front porch and carried the spaceman on the blanket into my room. He began mumbling about the heat, even though he still shivered as we laid him on the bed.

Father rode out for Doctor Jander. I lit the lamp on the bedstand, and Lenlah cut our guest out of the rest of his wet clothing. He had a few bruises and his right knee was purple and badly swollen, but I paid more attention to the shredded jumpsuit on the floor, wondering what strange devices lay hidden within the bulging pockets. Father had sternly instructed us not to open any of them.

After we tucked the spaceman in with extra blankets, Lenlah gathered up the still-dripping jumpsuit. I looked down at the wet floor and caught my breath. Something had fallen from a pocket. When Lenlah left the room I picked it up.

I'd seen a compass before, but never anything like this. The needle showed as an image on a tiny screen that also flashed numbers in different colors. It had buttons I felt afraid to push.

It was magical, the first electronic device of any kind I'd ever seen outside of pictures in magazines that the older boys would sneak into school. It was as thin as a wafer and light as a feather. I slipped it in my pants pocket.

"Hello," the spaceman said groggily. "I guess I made it."

I spun around. He smiled at me.

"Lenlah," I screeched. "He's awake!"

•••

By the time Father returned with the doctor almost two hours later, Lieutenant Fillip Fraser was sitting up in bed, most of the blankets off, finishing the fourth cup of beef broth Lenlah had fixed him.

We waited in the living room while the doctor worked. No one went to bed. And I told no one about the compass. About a half-hour later the doctor invited us back in to see his handiwork.

Lieutenant Fraser, still sitting up, beamed us a bright smile. He'd dressed in Father's red flannel pajamas, the legs scissored off at the knee. His lower left leg was now wrapped in a proper medical splint, while he elevated the right on a stack of folded blankets with several wet cloths draped over the swollen knee.

"The lieutenant will be fine," Doctor Jander told us. No internal injuries that he could see. His left tibia had broken, but it was a clean break and should heal nicely.

The right knee had either a badly torn ligament or a closed fracture. Either way, the swelling made immobilizing it impractical, so the lieutenant had to stay off his feet until his people could come for him. A rider would be sent to Logan in the morning, so, if they were quick and rode all night, the rescue team would arrive in three and a half days.

When Lieutenant Fillip heard that, his jaw dropped. Then he glanced at the paraffin lamp by the bed.

He knew where he was now. Five Valleys.

"I thought rebels had taken out another substation," he said. "Stupid me."

"Not so much as a flashlight within two hundred miles," the doctor said. "But some of us manage without them." He glanced at Lenlah. "If it hadn't been for this young lady, you'd be dead from exposure by now."

The lieutenant looked at my big sister and smiled again.

"My guardian angel," he said, as if he were actually staring at one.

Lenlah glanced nervously at Father before she returned the lieutenant a quick, polite smile. She went red as a beet.

The doctor broke the awkward silence with brief instructions for the lieutenant's care, hardly more than keeping cool rags on the knee and dosage for the morphine tablets, then said goodnight to us all and hurried off. Lenlah, hardly looking up from the floor, stammered goodnight to the lieutenant and hurried out even faster. Father and I followed.

I slept with Lenlah, as I would for the next three nights. She didn't mind. But that first night I was too excited to sleep. I jabbered on and on about Lieutenant Fillip Fraser and exploding ships for I don't know how long before I realized that Lenlah had fallen fast asleep.

By the time I woke next morning, Josh and Todd, who had slept over at the Mathose's, were already out doing the morning milking, Father was out haying and Lenlah was setting breakfast. When I saw the table my eyes about popped out of my head.

Ham, scrambled eggs, hash browns, corn bread with maple syrup and butter, applesauce, milk—rich Jersey, no doubt—coffee and a big bowl of blueberries—our last jar—with whipped cream and sugar on the side. It wasn't hard to guess who inspired all this. It took both Lenlah and I, each with a large tray, to carry it all to him.

"Holy meteors!" he gasped, wide-eyed, sitting up and ready to eat. But after that initial surprise, he paid scant attention to his king's breakfast. Lenlah managed not to blush this time under his stare, but she hardly

looked at him as she carefully set out the meal on his bed
tray.

We left without a word, ate our more modest portions,
then returned to see how Lieutenant Fraser was doing.
He'd finished everything but the last of his blueberries
and invited us to sit down on the bed while he finished.

Lenlah politely declined and placed her hand on my
shoulder, letting me know that I should also refuse to sit.
But I had a million questions piling up in my head,
screaming to get out, and I thought, *if* she wants to drag
me out by my hair, she is welcome to try. So I screwed
up my courage and sat down on the foot of my bed.

"Tell us everything."

He smiled. And with his spoon in one hand and a
plump blueberry in the other, he showed us the whole
exciting story.

• • •

He was flying a routine low-orbit patrol. He
approached the terminator into night, enjoying the view,
when he caught a brief flash on his infrared, 300 kilometers dead ahead. Nothing registered on the other passive
systems and he had no confirmation from the monitor
satellites—probably just a sun flash reflecting off a bit of
tumbling debris.

But just in case, he ejected chaff, activated electronic
jamming and, to be extra safe, launched a couple of antimissiles. Three minutes and thirteen seconds later they
detonated.

No doubt now, it had to be a Prowler missile. Hopefully an ex–Prowler missile. But you could never be sure
with those tenacious devils. Lieutenant Fraser fired his
remaining antimissiles and both Sidewinder 12's.

The entire salvo veered wildly off course, counter-jammed. The blueberry, lighting up all scopes now, began to close on the spoon. He had eighty-eight seconds.

He took a perilous steep-angle reentry down to earth, and hoped that the Prowler would burn up before it reached him. For the first time in his career he felt grateful that they'd designed the low orbiters with emergency reentry capability.

The lieutenant jettisoned his ordnance pod, spun his strike ship one-eighty, and ignited both engines. The full-power retro burn slammed him back into his couch and roared in his ears. He was on his way.

He'd bought himself a few minutes but he knew that the Prowler was still on him and still accelerating. And the ship's ceramic outer skin wasn't even glowing yet. He reached maximum reentry angle, but pushed a full degree past that before shutting the engines down.

If he was amazingly lucky, the Prowler could burn to a cinder before he did. Four hundred eighteen seconds later a hundred alarms went off.

Shrapnel tore through his ship. He could hear it like the scream of death. The Prowler detonated. So Lieutenant Fraser popped the blueberry right into my open mouth.

I was so caught up in the story, I hardly noticed. But Lenlah giggled in spite of herself. I swallowed the blueberry without tasting it as his ship began spinning from venting gases.

Faster and faster the spoon spun, twirling between his fingers while his other hand reached for the manual stabilizer. But the centrifugal force was building so quickly that before his hand was halfway to the stabilizer it was yanked away and slammed against the cockpit wall. He figured he had less than a minute before his ship disintegrated.

But his hand wouldn't budge.

Thirty seconds passed. Very quickly. He began to black out. But just before he did, he saw a finger twitch. Then another. He tried lifting his hand off the cockpit wall. No go, but more fingers twitched.

He could feel it now—the G-force was slowly lessening. He'd fallen deep enough for the still-tenuous atmosphere to retard his spin rate.

With all his remaining strength, he pushed his hand forward. Keyboards, switches, even read-out screens, became obstacles as formidable as mountains.

It took a good half-minute. But he reached the altitude control stick at his knee and closed his fingers around it. With a few delicate twitches he stopped the multiaxial spin and realigned his ship, nose forward.

He was still on track. The temperature in the small cockpit had climbed to 10 degrees but his suit could handle that. He felt more worried about a burn-through. The self-patching resin layer just under the skin could only handle so much shrapnel damage, even at safe temperatures, which, at this near suicidal speed, he now well exceeded.

After disengaging the alarm systems to stop the damned blaring horns and flashing warning signals lighting up the cockpit like a berserk Christmas display, he released the first drogue chute—far too early, but it held. But after the third chute the entire package malfunctioned and detached prematurely. No matter. Good enough. All he had to do now was maintain stability until atmospheric drag slowed him below the sound barrier enough so that he could eject.

He extended the stabilizer fins. Not working. He had to rely on his maneuvering jets. First he extended a periscope, as his viewscreens were down. He roared over the Arctic, hurtling toward the middle of the Pacific Ocean.

Using the tiny jets, he awkwardly aimed himself at Florida, then spent the next four minutes trying to regain some semblance of stability before his nonaerodynamic ship shattered into tiny splinters. But the vibration was already so great that his teeth rattled.

At 140,000 feet, somewhere over America and practically cartwheeling, he punched out. Speed: mach 1.5. He set the spoon down on his tray.

"I must have come to long enough to unlatch my helmet and practically drown myself, but that's the last I remember until I woke up on your wonderful bed."

He smiled at me, turned to Lenlah. She quickly reached for his tray, then paused as he snatched the last blueberry out of the bowl.

"Are you in much pain?" I asked.

"I've only needed one morphine this morning. Isn't that right?"

Lenlah curtly nodded as she gathered the coffee cup, drinking glasses and syrup pitcher from the bedstand.

"Does it itch?" I asked.

"Now that you mentioned it, like blazes."

"Sorry," I said, watching his toes wiggle. "I guess your chute tangled, huh?"

"That, or I got banged up ejecting."

"Your chute was torn," Lenlah said, as she turned with the full tray for the door. "Come, Milly, there's a pile of dishes to wash. And we should hang some new lime cloth in the milking shed if we have time before church."

Reluctantly I turned to follow.

"Another blueberry?"

I spun around and opened wide. It was right on target again, but this time I crunched it before I swallowed. It was sweet and delicious. I smiled and scurried after Lenlah, who waited at the door.

•••

When we returned from Sunday service, which I hardly noticed with all the lieutenant's adventures still swirling in my head, Father sat all four of us kids down on the porch steps and gave us the lecture.

He was cheerful enough about it—I don't think he knew how far his daughters had already strayed that morning—but he paused after every sentence until both of us had nodded that we heard and understood.

We were to be civil and polite to our guest and take good care of him. He was our responsibility until his people came for him Wednesday morning. But we could not socialize with the outsider. No casual conversation. No unnecessary visits. And no lingering in his room after serving breakfast.

"I trust both you girls had enough time this morning to get all that out of your system?"

"Oh, yes!" I said, nodding to him vigorously, though his eyes, now steely, were on Lenlah.

I turned. She stared at the floor in shame. But Father just smiled.

"Good," he said and nodded his approval. "Off to work with you then. Boys, you can start the baling when you have time. Girls, clean out the stalls and milking shed, and you had better hang some fresh lime cloth."

He stooped, kissed us both on the nose, then slung his bow and quiver over his shoulder. Off he rode. Lenlah wished him luck. I shrugged.

Dad was ten times the archer Mr. Mathose was, but Mr. Mathose somehow always managed to bag the prize buck each autumn. Mr. Mathose even won the archery tournament last year, but only after his son started courting Lenlah.

The boys headed to the field and Lenlah went to the barn to mix up some chloride of lime. I went inside to dust the mantel, crowded with Father's archery and Lenlah's running trophies. I wondered how many war medals Lieutenant Fraser had.

It was hard to believe he was in league with the devil. But as Mother used to say before she ran off three years ago: "With a bit of cunning, you can fool anyone, even yourself; but eventually your deeds will betray you."

She was speaking, of course, of Outside. She had never been there, but Father had. He was born there. "It is a savage, disease-ridden world," he'd told us one quiet night years ago. "People are surrounded by countless machines, yet no one is safe."

After losing Mother, Father worked desperately hard to erase the stigma her desertion to Outside put on our family; and, especially, to secure the best possible future for Lenlah, his first eligible daughter. In both regards, he succeeded beyond what anyone could have hoped. But, even so, I think he still wished Mother had simply died instead.

I shrugged, finished dusting the base and returned a shiny sprinting maiden to the mantel.

•••

"How many ships have you blown up?" I asked, dragging a dustcloth over my woefully unadorned chiffonier.

"A few. Just a few," he said, nibbling at a square of corn bread from a tray Lenlah must have brought in for him. He stared out the window. "Lenlah. What a lovely name."

He turned to me suddenly, as if remembering I was there. "Oh—*Milly*'s nice too!"

"I hate it. More butter? We have lots of butter."

"No thanks, Milly," he said, spreading his last gob across his last square of corn bread. "Those strike ship cockpits are a tight fit."

I smiled, but stopped my laugh short when I saw how troubled he looked, staring through the corn bread he held suspended halfway to his mouth.

"Milly, does she like me at all?"

"I'm sure she does," I said, not really knowing myself. "It's just hard to tell with Lenlah. She's not the emotional type."

And that was true. Though I'm proud to say I can still rile her, I haven't otherwise seen her get excited over anything since Mother left us, except maybe her running.

I wiped the windowsill, then looked for something else to clean. He smiled and motioned for me to sit on the bed. I smiled back and plopped myself next to his broken tibia.

"I bet it's pretty exciting—shooting down ships in space, Lieutenant Fraser."

"Call me Fillip," he said, banishing all formality with a wave of his hand. "I guess you could call it that, but it can be pretty tricky."

"How's that?"

"Well, say you're pursuing an enemy intruder. But his orbit is several miles under yours. . . ." He paused to swallow, scrunching up his face. I stretched to the bed-stand and handed him his milk to wash it down.

"Thanks, Milly. . . . And you're falling farther and farther behind him. How do you catch up?"

"Fire my main engines?"

"That seems the logical thing to do, doesn't it?" he said. "But space can be a peculiar place. All firing your main rocket would accomplish is to boost you into a higher orbit—and you'd drop still farther behind because you're following a longer path around the earth."

He took another bite of corn bread and wiped his buttery fingers on one of our special-occasion cloth napkins. "So, what else might you try?"

"Fire retro-rockets," I said, waiting on pins and needles as he swallowed the last of his corn bread and gulped down the last of his milk. He set the empty glass back on the bedstand, leisurely wiped his mouth with his fancy napkin, then leaned back on his pile of pillows, folded his hands behind his head and smiled at me.

"Milly—that is exactly correct. You've just dropped yourself into a lower orbit and onto a shorter track. You're at his orbit now, but you're still too far behind."

"More retro," I said, nearly shouting.

"Right, so you drop lower. You're closing on him now. Eighty kilometers—as close as you want to risk. You apply just enough forward thrust to acquire his orbit and . . ."

He paused, like maybe he thought I was too young and impressionable for the grisly stuff.

"You blast him to bloody smithereens!" I shouted before he could change the subject.

"If you're so inclined," he said, smiling.

"With lasers and rockets!"

"And some cold water," Lenlah added, stepping into the room with a small bucket and eyeing me suspiciously. I hopped off the bed and dashed back to the windowsill with my dust rag.

"Why, thank you, Lenlah," he said, beaming at her as she set the bucket on the bed and carefully removed the stack of rags from his knee. The swelling had gone down but the color was almost black.

"Your corn bread was absolutely wonderful," he said.

"Thank you," she said, redunking the rags in the bucket.

"Plenty of butter, too. I love butter. How about you?"

"Yes. I suppose so." She lifted the dripping rags and wrung them out.

"Where are you stationed?" I asked, feeling suddenly all alone.

"Most of the time I'm on space stations," he said, watching my sister daintily drape the first wet rag on his knee. "But I'm officially out of New Canaveral, two thousand miles from here, I'd say. About one hundred and ten degrees east-southeast on your compass."

Then, as Lenlah turned to grab another rag hanging from the bucket rim, he winked at me. I almost fainted. He must have seen me snatch his electronic compass off the floor that first night. I felt like a thief but managed a smile.

He smiled back. It was all right. I made a mental note to smuggle it back in to him at the first safe opportunity—I'd hidden it in the left pocket of my sheepskin winter coat that hung in the storage closet—but I never did.

"Thanks, Lenlah," he said as she laid the last rag. "They feel cool and wonderful."

She smiled curtly, then stooped down to get the chamber pot from under the bed.

"Quite a head for orbital mechanics, your kid sister has. She's been wonderful company."

"Come, Milly," she said as she stood up and grabbed the serving tray with her free hand. "It's time to do the henhouse."

"Just shout out the window if you want anything," I told the lieutenant as I stuffed the dust rag in my pocket and scurried after Lenlah, who waited at the door.

But he didn't answer. He stared at Lenlah. She blushed again as she shut the door behind us.

"Milly, you're incorrigible."

"I know," I said, smiling. "But my room did get dusted."

• • •

With spring harvest in full swing, three Jerseys calving, and Father around to keep an eye on us at mealtimes, I had no more opportunity for unauthorized visits with Lieutenant Fraser. I would deliver a meal, say "Howdy," and go back to work. The hours between dragged like months.

And the days flew by.

• • •

The last morning I got up in time to help with breakfast. Lenlah was making pancakes.

"He's taken a real shine to you, you know," I said as I cracked an egg and dropped it into the pan. "Not that you should care. He's from Outside, you're formally engaged, and for good measure he's probably married."

Of course I knew he wasn't—at least he wore no wedding ring—but I wanted to see if Lenlah had noticed that.

"His wife got killed in a rebel missile attack five days after they were married," Lenlah said as she added more milk to the batter. "She had just finished packing to join him at New Canaveral."

"Ouch," I said as I plopped an egg from too high and splashed my little finger with sizzling bacon grease. "Sounds to me like you've been doing a bit of dusting yourself, big sister."

I always called her that when I wanted to rile her. It usually worked. I hoped she might even pitch an egg at me. She'd done it before. But she just shrugged and broke it into her batter bowl.

"That's three eggs," I said.

"I know that's three eggs. Do you have a problem with three eggs?"

"As long as they've been dusted."

"I couldn't sleep last night. He heard me up and asked me to come in. He couldn't sleep either and wanted something to pass the night, so I showed him how to cut and sew a simple appliqué handkerchief. It took me five minutes."

"That's a minute an egg," I said, tipping the pan to whiten the tops of the yolks.

"That makes no sense."

"Neither does five eggs in the batter."

She shrugged and put the fifth egg back in the egg bowl.

• • •

"Flapjacks!" Fillip exclaimed, staring wide-eyed at the breakfast tray I carried into his room. He grabbed the knife and scooped up a gob of butter before I had the tray settled over his lap.

"Where's Lenlah?" he asked, pouring syrup over everything.

"Feeding the guys. They just came in from the barn."

"I guess this is my last good meal for a while," he sighed, sawing away at his towering stack of cakes.

I watched him fork a dripping load into his mouth, then I turned and scurried for the door.

"Oh—," he said, or something like that through his food. I stopped, pulled myself together, then turned to face him. He paused to swallow, then continued. "Almost forgot . . ."

He reached behind him, under his stack of pillows, and pulled something out. "It's pretty poor work, I'm afraid, but I'm even worse at words."

I stepped forward and took it from his outstretched hand. It was a handkerchief, cut not quite square from a piece of old linen out of the attic. It was embroidered. A shaky line of uneven blue stitching served as a border. In the middle was an appliqué, just as crudely and hastily stitched.

It showed a red heart with a jagged diagonal line through the middle, breaking it in two.

My lips began to quiver. Hot tears ran down my cheeks. I felt too embarrassed to look at him. I couldn't speak to save my life.

"It's that bad, huh?" he said.

I threw myself on him, hugging his chest and pressing my wet face against his shoulder. I'd never felt so embarrassed in all my life—I'd only known him three and a half days.

"You're a great kid," he said, a slight quiver in his voice.

"Sure you don't want your compass?" I managed to blubber out as he patted me gently on the back.

"Milly, where I'm from they're a dime a dozen. But you can do me one favor."

I nodded vigorously against his wet shoulder.

"Tell your sister I'd sure like to see her before they come and drag me away," he said.

"I sure will, Lieutenant Fillip," I sniffled. "Sorry, gotta go."

I stood up, smiled bravely, stuffed my new handkerchief deep into my pants pocket so Father wouldn't see it, turned and scurried for the door.

• • •

I did tell Lenlah, as if she didn't know how he felt. But she never got the chance to pay him that last visit. Straight after breakfast, before we'd even done the dishes, Father had us clean the henhouse again just to get us out of the house.

It was pointless for anyone to try and sneak back in, as Father was only as far as his archery range in the east pasture. It's a wonder that he hit the target at all, the way he kept glancing toward us.

We didn't get much cleaning done, though. Our hearts weren't in it. I still hadn't shown Lenlah my new handkerchief.

"They're here," she said, so quietly I barely heard her. But I didn't need to be told, since I was looking out a window, too.

A team of four black horses pulled a covered wagon up the road. It was about eight-thirty. Right on schedule. The morning sky was bright and blue.

Lenlah dropped the shovel and ran out to watch. I dropped my armload of clean nest straw and followed. Our brothers, who had been busy in the hayloft, came out also, pulling straw from their clothes as they walked toward the house. Father, almost reluctantly it seemed, came last, leaning his bow against the porch.

Mr. Anderson drove, his horse tethered behind the wagon. A soldier in a blue uniform sat beside him. The wagon pulled up to the front porch and two more soldiers, one with a medical bag, hopped out the back with a stretcher. Like Lieutenant Fillip, the men were all smiles.

After Father led them in, I went to the back of the wagon and took a good peek inside, but there wasn't a machine to be seen. I shrugged and looked at Lenlah, expecting her to scold me. But she was gazing at the front door. I did the same.

A couple of minutes later the captain came out carrying the spacesuit bundled in an old blanket. Behind him the other two bore Lieutenant Fillip, strapped to the stretcher. He watched Lenlah. He looked very sad.

When they passed her, very slowly he reached out his hand. Lenlah just stood there. I was about to nudge her with my elbow when she finally responded and took his hand. He beamed with delight, then clasped her fingers firmly between both of his hands.

But as the stretcher kept moving, the tender moment was very brief. I don't think even Father, watching from the porch, paid it much mind.

I'd already said my goodbye, so I ran to the front to hold the team. Sweaty, exhausted horses can get ornery, and they pay no mind if you shed a tear or two.

As Lieutenant Fillip was slowly lifted into the wagon, Lenlah turned away and looked down at her hands. Then she looked over at the cows grazing in the field, the chickens scratching in the hen yard, a black crow wheeling lazily overhead. Anywhere, it seemed, but toward Fillip.

When the men got Fillip secured, the captain thanked Father for the good care we'd given the lieutenant and offered to pay for the trouble. Father politely declined, of course. So the captain tipped his hat, climbed back up on the wagon, and gave me a smile. I let go the bridle and stepped back.

"Giddyap, ya pack of loafers," said Mr. Anderson with a snap of the reins.

As the wagon pulled out into the road, I ran back to stand with Lenlah. She didn't even glance at me. She gazed only at the wagon now, going away.

Lieutenant Fillip was sitting, looking back at us. I waved goodbye. The two soldiers with him waved back, but the lieutenant didn't see me. He saw only Lenlah.

I clutched her hand. She was gripping something. I looked down and saw the corner of a linen handkerchief revealing itself between her tight fingers. I squeezed harder, wishing, for some reason, that it would disappear.

When I looked up again Fillip seemed to be trying to scoot himself closer to the open back of the wagon. But one of the soldiers put his hand on Fillip's shoulder and he stopped.

They moved awfully slow. It took a lifetime for them just to reach the broken rail hardly a quarter of the way down the pasture fence. What was wrong with them? The road was fine. Did they think they were leading a funeral procession?

It was like we'd all become stuck in a painting. The kind that gives you the shivers but you don't quite know why. I wanted to run back into the house, dragging Lenlah with me.

But I didn't.

Instead, Lenlah slipped her clutched hand from mine and started after him.

She wasn't running. Not at first. She wasn't even walking fast. But I couldn't have been more stunned if she'd taken off and flown.

As soon as you realize what you're doing, I thought, that your legs just started moving on their own, you'll stop. I'm not going to embarrass you further by calling out your name.

"Lenlah—," I blurted before she got four steps away.

She stopped. I sighed with relief. She half turned and looked back at me. She said nothing. Her expression was enough.

It said goodbye.

I had lost her.

She turned her hope-filled eyes back to Fillip, stuffed the handkerchief deep into her pocket, and ran.

For real this time. With all her heart. As fast as her feet could fly.

And when Lenlah put her mind to it, her feet could fly like a thoroughbred filly's. She was the fastest sprinter in the Five Valleys. She was beautiful to watch.

I looked past her to the wagon, hoping Lieutenant Fillip, somehow, would send her back to me. He tried. He practically hung out the back of the wagon, waving with both arms for her to go back. I wondered why he was so frantic.

A second later I found out.

Lenlah had reached the broken fence rail in nothing flat and was less than three posts from the back of the wagon when Father's first arrow whizzed out and clipped her right leg, just above the knee.

It didn't embed but she went down hard.

She didn't stay down though. Not on your life.

She jumped back up, blood soaking her jeans, and was off again, running even faster. Faster than I'd ever seen her run.

She flew. She was a rocket. She was streaking through the sky.

I looked back at Father.

He was nocking another arrow. My brothers were screaming at him. Todd rushed at him but Father knocked him off the porch with a sweep of his arm. Father drew the arrow back, then raised it to aim. His eyes had never left their target.

They were cold eyes. Cold enough to freeze the fires of hell.

"Run, Lenlah!" I screamed.

Fillip quit waving her away. He leaned out the back of the wagon, arms outstretched, trying to reach her and drag her in. Calling her name.

The soldiers took hold of him. But even with his broken leg and bad knee, it was all the three of them could do to keep him from jumping out after her.

Lenlah was only a moment from him now. She reached out, her fingertips only a few swiftly vanishing feet from touching his. He was ready. With all his might, he would yank her in to safety.

It couldn't be a second before it would happen.

Lenlah was a streak. No arrow could even catch her.

But, like the devil, time plays tricks. Perhaps it happened when their fingers touched. I can't say they actually did, but it looked awful close.

Heartbreakingly close.

Then time stopped.

The second arrow struck her square in the back. Almost dead center but a little left. Right at her heart. She dropped like a rag doll.

I must have started after her because someone grabbed hold of me and dragged me back, kicking and screaming. Josh ran to her instead.

She died there, my sister Lenlah. Her swift legs sprawled out ungracefully behind her. An arrow in her back. Her arms were still reaching out for him, far away now, her Fillip.

Gone.

•••

I never did find the handkerchief. But I found the cloth he had cut the appliqués from. He'd made her a red heart pierced by a blue Cupid's arrow. I'll bet it was beautiful.

•••

They hung Father that summer. Only because he could have easily rode after the wagon, or simply jogged the distance, and dragged Lenlah back. Josh and Todd took opposite sides in the court battle and became bitter enemies. They soon sold the farm and took work as hired hands on opposite ends of the Valleys. When the Mathoses heard of this, and that I wouldn't choose between my brothers, they offered to take me in. But I was leaving anyway.

● ● ●

It's very lonely now. I stay in the hills and back country, well away from the cities and paved roads. Rebel units are easy to track in the snow. I tell them I can lead them to a downed strike ship; then I eat all I can, stuff my pocket with more, and run. No one's caught me yet. Outside of the rebel camps, the only machines I've seen are abandoned vehicles. I've slept in more than a few.

I miss her especially at night, shivering in my bedroll; no one there to warm my icy feet against. And I dread the clear sky, fearing every pretty bright flash is Fillip exploding.

I prefer the gently falling snow. And when I wake in the morning to see the world so white and pure and clean that it hurts my eyes, I know there is reason for hope in this world. I know no one dies in vain.

Lenlah wasn't bad. She was as good as people come. But the devil got inside of her and carried her away. And when he was through with her, he left her to the angels.

The devil is inside me now. And I will run with him as far as he will take me.

I have a compass.

It's in the left pocket of my sheepskin coat.

I have a heading.

110 degrees ESE.

Straight on I go.

CONSERVATOR

Written by
Steven Mohan, Jr.

Illustrated by
Christopher Jouan

About the Author

Steven Mohan, Jr., spent two years of his childhood living in the Philippines, an experience that left him with a lifelong fascination for other cultures. After graduating from Northwestern University with a degree in Mechanical Engineering and a commission from the United States Navy, he completed a shipboard tour of duty in which he visited several exotic locales in the Middle East, Southeast Asia and the South Pacific.

Steven currently lives in Pueblo, Colorado, where he works for a major commercial air-conditioning company as a manufacturing engineer. While he works on his MBA, Steven writes science fiction, and recently sold a story to Aboriginal. His favorite authors include Dan Simmons, David Brin and Kim Stanley Robinson.

Susan Brock was titrating a poison she had isolated from the blood serum of a rhesus macaque when her comms suite beeped. She looked up in annoyance, pipette still in hand, and considered ignoring the call. Coded numbers crawled across the holo projector's readout. The call was from a Conservatorship subdirector. The country code revealed that the call originated on Luna. (Who did she know on the Moon? *Her* case officer was stationed in Shanghai.)

Brock sighed and put the pipette down. She stood and winced at the stiffness in her legs. (She used her neural implant to check the time; she had been working without a break for over four hours.)

She scrutinized her small studio apartment for any evidence that she wasn't Asha Patkar, a respectable Indian widow who did enough trade in arcane potions and folk cures to make a home just off the crowded streets of Old Delhi, but not enough to live anywhere else. Of course if the caller were really a subdirector, he would probably know her true identity, but Brock had learned to be wary.

Her apartment was simple and neat. The furniture was cheap, but functional; a print of blue-skinned Vishnu hung on the wall by the door. The table covered with samples and biomedical equipment had been deliberately placed outside the holo camera's pickup. She adjusted her plain orange sari, drew a veil across her face in the custom of *Purdah*, and, confident that her cover was safe, stepped toward the comms suite.

As she moved, her glance caught the holo of her and John on a white Mexican beach. Her stomach clenched. Brock stopped and turned to study the holo. She had been younger then, happier, more idealistic. Her long, dark hair was pulled back, her skin still white. Brock had looked every bit the product of the quiet suburbs of Toronto that she was. John had been younger, too. An irreverent half-smile flashed white against his California tan; his hair sandy-blond, eyes a startling blue.

It had only been a month. She still had trouble believing that he was gone. Maybe it would have been easier if she'd had some idea what had happened in Islamabad. He'd been a smart operative. How had he allowed himself to get caught in the riot?

Brock walked over to the small desk on which the holo stood and touched the button on the device's black base. The image flickered off. She stood staring at the place where it had been.

Her comms suite beeped again.

"All right, damn it," she muttered under her breath, "I'm coming."

She moved to the suite and punched a square blue button. The projector snapped to life.

A man suddenly stood before her. He was tall and thin, with drawn features, pale skin, and clear gray eyes. He looked very sure of himself.

"Ms. Brock?" His voice immediately betrayed him as an American.

"I am Asha Patkar," she said in heavily accented English.

The man nodded.

"Very good. Ms. Brock, my name is Subdirector Wilson Smith. The ID code on this transmission should verify my identity. You may drop your cover."

Her eyes darted to the code and then back to the man. She nodded and removed her veil. "What can I do for you Subdirector Smith?"

"I have a mission for you. It supersedes all your present activities."

She glanced at the pipette on the table where it waited to help her understand the toxin that was killing India's primates. "I'm doing important work here—"

"Yes, I know," said Smith. He folded his arms and frowned. "This is more important."

"What do you want me to do?"

"I'll explain when I arrive."

Unlike Brock, who had been modified to look Indian when she had been assigned to the subcontinent, Smith was an obvious foreigner. He'll fit in so well, she thought darkly.

"When will that be?"

"I'll take the next shuttle down from Diana. I'll be in Delhi in," he paused, obviously consulting his implant, "about six hours."

"You're coming directly from the Moon?" Brock couldn't think of anything more conspicuous. "You'll have to clear customs. That means—"

"Yes, yes, I'm aware of that." His impatience was thinly veiled. "It's not optimal, but as I said before, this is important."

Brock suddenly understood. This was political. Only the Political Directorate could have conceived such a stupid, melodramatic plan. She shuddered. She had no desire to become entangled in politics.

"Look, I'm Ecological Directorate. Perhaps a political operative would work out better."

"There are none available. The incident in Islamabad managed to endanger most of our political agents in South Asia. We need a fresh face for this mission."

She sucked in her breath. Islamabad. Her stomach roiled; her legs felt weak. What did Smith know about Islamabad? She glanced involuntarily at where the holo of her and John had been.

"Can't you at least tell me what's going on?"

Smith shook his head.

His cloak-and-dagger attitude suddenly made Brock angry. "This *is* an encrypted link," she snapped.

"That's not the issue," he answered smoothly. "The less you know, the less you can be made to reveal."

"But—"

"I'll rendezvous with you at the Dunston safe house at 21:30 local time. Until then minimum profile. Do you understand?"

Brock nodded. Smith studied her for a few seconds and then abruptly vanished.

She sighed. This was obviously going to be trouble. Brock felt restless. Her implant told her that it was not quite half past one, which meant she had a good nine hours of waiting before she would meet Smith. He had made it clear that she was not to go out.

A knock pulled her out of her reverie. She veiled herself again and opened the door.

Mohammed stood looking furtively from side to side. When he saw her, an eager smile grew on his young face. Brock knelt so that she was eye-level with the boy, and let the veil slip. She didn't know how old he was (she guessed six or eight) or even his family name. More to the point, neither did he.

Brock tried to push away her own anxieties. She smiled. "Would you like to come in and have a cup of tea?" she asked in unaccented Hindi.

"Mistress Asha, I have found a tiger," he said. "We must go."

Brock frowned. Her orders were explicit. Minimum profile. That meant no covert ecological transactions.

"Mistress, *please*." Urgency mingled with studied courtesy in the boy's voice.

Orders were orders. How could she explain? She put her hand softly on the boy's head. "I'm sorry. I have so much work."

"It has been a week since last we saw an animal."

She felt guilty denying him. She knew how much the boy loved the elephants, cobras, and tigers of India's magical past. She couldn't bear to disappoint him just to satisfy the paranoia of a self-important political sub-director.

Brock sighed. "Perhaps we could take a *quick* look."

Mohammed's face lit up with a smile. She refastened her veil, and stepped out into the oppressive heat.

Sol was a blinding spot of white in the cloudless sky. Only her arms and part of her face were exposed to the sun, but that didn't seem to do her any good. Brock's artificial pigmentation didn't protect her well. She had seen enough Indians with melanoma to know that natural pigmentation didn't work much better.

The boy pulled her into a street. He led her east, toward the river. "This way."

She glanced down at his small hand. A series of faint blue lines lay atop the mahogany-colored skin on the back of his hand. The tattoo looked like a bar code.

"What's this?"

The boy shrugged, as if to say "It's not important."

Brock frowned. The tattoo hadn't been there six days earlier, but then she knew very little of Mohammed's life on the street. He would have told her if it meant something significant.

She smelled the sweet odor of sandalwood. Mourners were cremating bodies on the *ghats* of the Yamuna River. She glanced up. Black smoke curled into the cloudless, blue sky. Her eyes followed the column of smoke down until it was lost beyond the striking rust-colored sandstone walls of the Red Fort. From the wall, an Indian flag fluttered in the wind: a blue Ashoka wheel centered on a field of saffron. Brock remembered when the orange of Hinduism had been joined by a stripe of Islamic green and a white stripe symbolizing unity. It hadn't taken the Priyadhavshina government long to change that.

Mohammed pulled her into the congested, narrow street that was Chandni Chowk. Loud vendors filled the bazaar, hawking everything from rice and pungent curry to religious software. Colorful silks flashed before her eyes; cloying perfumes and soaps assaulted her nose. A large holo of the great actor Dinesh morphed into a four-armed demon, exhorted them to come see the latest Bombay release.

"How much farther?"

"Almost there," answered the boy.

Soldiers carrying shouldered laser rifles pushed past homeless children and businessmen in Western suits. Bare-chested priests with shaved heads begged for coins. A rowdy crowd ringed a pit where a mongoose stalked a cobra. Ten-rupee bills flashed from one hand to the next, and back again, with each lunge of mammal and snake.

The crush of people made Brock claustrophobic. It was as if all India crowded in this narrow street. She felt drowned in sensory input. Yet, Mohammed threaded his way through the crowd as if it were the most natural thing in the world.

Finally the boy tugged her hand and pulled her through a dark doorway. Brock just had time to see a painted crimson symbol, then she was blinded by the absence of light. She felt a sudden chill.

"Mohammed," she hissed. "This is a plague house."

"No," said the boy. "The mark is just a trick to keep soldiers away."

Brock frowned in the dark, unsure. India had suffered dozens of deadly epidemics. Maybe the plague symbol was a ploy, but then maybe it wasn't. She drew her veil tighter.

She kicked a piece of debris in the dark. A rat squeaked and scurried away. Slowly her eyes adjusted. The room had obviously been abandoned.

"The trafficker said to meet him here," said the boy.

She normally conducted deals in the open, in the shops, bazaars, and markets of Delhi. She avoided places like this, hidden from witnesses. Her stomach knotted. This was the perfect place to cut a Western woman's throat and take her money.

Had it been like this for John: caught in a situation he didn't fully understand, fearing for his life? Had he looked up from supposed safety only to find himself in the center of the Islamabad riots? She pushed the thought away. Thinking about John's death would paralyze her.

"Perhaps this is not safe."

"But you have seen so few tigers."

Mohammed was right. There weren't many of them left. Each genetic sample she could acquire meant an added probability that the creature could be resurrected after it was finally driven to extinction.

Illustrated by Christopher Jouan

"What's the name of our contact?"

"Sankar."

She unconsciously rubbed her thumb against the white edge of her right ring fingernail. All she had to do was press that thumb hard on her nail and a poison-tipped needle a few millimeters long would spring through the nail. A pinprick would kill her instantly. Somehow the knowledge of the needle's existence comforted her even more than the weight of the small taser she carried in a fold of her sari. The needle made her feel like she was in control.

"Conservator?" The voice was a gravelly whisper.

Brock jumped, startled. She turned and saw the dim form of a man. "Sankar?"

"Come this way."

Brock passed through a door she could barely see. She felt Mohammed brush by in the dark. A door slammed behind them, and she heard a bass rumble. There was the sound of a struck match, and suddenly she blinked away golden after-images.

When her eyes adjusted to the light of the lamp, she studied her surroundings. The inner room was as dilapidated as the outer room. Old magazines, broken boards, and debris covered the floor. A huge black box squatted in the corner.

Sankar, a bent man, had a black patch over his right eye. He was short, but muscular, and had an unhealthy blue-black sheen to his skin. Brock realized that he was in the middle of transition to Sirian-human. Nanites in his body would modify him to live with the heavy gravity and exotic radiation of the planet Indra.

"When do you emigrate?" she asked softly.

Sankar leered at her, but said nothing. Most of his front teeth were missing.

Brock glanced down at Mohammed. He carefully surveyed the room. She looked back to the animal trafficker. "Where's the tiger?"

"Do you have money?"

"A thousand. The standard price."

"Old Delhi is a dangerous place for a pretty young thing," hissed Sankar. "Why should I not just kill you and take your money?"

Brock looked back at Sankar. She saw avarice in his eyes. Her left hand drifted toward the taser. Her heart started to hammer, but she kept her voice carefully level.

"I am not quite so helpless as you think. In any event, the Conservatorship offers you a fair price for blood, skin, and fur samples. If you killed a Conservator, you would lose all that. And for what? We offer one thousand rupees for a bit of blood that's useless to you anyway." She smiled mirthlessly. "You're practically stealing already. Now, where's the tiger?"

Sankar held out his hand. Brock sighed, pulled a few folded bills from her sari, and handed them to the man. He greedily counted them, then looked up at her. He stepped to the box and pulled away a blanket .

Lying in a cage was a great cat, perhaps three meters long, and over 250 kilos in mass. The tiger's eyes didn't track the motion of the blanket in Sankar's hands; the beast was drugged. It lay quietly on the floor, tongue lolling from its great mouth. Its magnificent orange and black coat looked washed out in the dim light. Its fur was matted and dirty.

Mohammed looked up at her expectantly.

"Go ahead," she said softly. "Be careful."

He approached the animal the way she had taught him, moving slowly outside the beast's field of vision.

The little boy put a small hand on the tiger's rib cage, touching a part of the past that usually could only be found in storybooks.

Brock, satisfied that the boy was sufficiently cautious, began pulling medical supplies from a sample kit.

She tried not to think about what would happen to this great cat, but her mind was relentless. The coat would be cleaned and sold to a Western collector who would find it all the more valuable because the species was on the brink of extinction. The bones would be ground up and sold in South Asia as a virility potion. The beast's eyes would be used as aphrodisiacs.

She knelt by the beast and carefully laid a large syringe on the floor. She leaned forward and began cleaning the spot where she would take the blood sample with alcohol and iodine. Considering the animal's future, it was a useless gesture.

Brock had once worked for the Center for Research in Endangered Species in San Diego. CRES self-righteously refused to deal with the Sankars of the world. They believed that buying genetic samples from poachers only created markets for their crimes and speeded the extinction of trophy species.

The Conservatorship had a much different philosophy. It remained carefully neutral in all things. Mankind was already lost in a wicked world. The Conservatorship aimed to preserve some of humanity's history, art, and ecology against a time when the race would treasure what it had lost. In the interim, it collected what it could and let the rest be destroyed.

Brock found the admission of defeat liberating. She put her hand on the tiger's coat. She felt its slow, measured breathing and the warmth of its huge body. She didn't have to concern herself with the depressingly impossible task of saving *this* tiger. She only had to preserve its DNA so that one day the species *Panthera tigris* might be resurrected.

She picked up the syringe. From the corner of her eye she saw Mohammed glance up. His mouth twisted in surprise. Brock suddenly felt a crystal of ice lance through the small of her back. She gasped desperately for air and probed the pain with her left hand. Something stuck out of her back. Her hand came away covered with blood. She turned enough to see Sankar behind her; his eyes focused on hers, close enough that she could smell his sour breath.

"What . . . ?" she gasped, barely able to get the word out.

"You see, Conservator, the government is going to deport me in less than a month." He smiled. "So my future relationship with your precious Conservatorship is not important. On the other hand, I could certainly use whatever money or equipment you have."

Brock fumbled for the taser with her left hand, but Sankar was ready. He stepped forward and knocked it from her hand. Brock heard it slide across the floor. He was very close. She suddenly realized that she held the syringe in her right hand. She jabbed out and up, connecting with his left eye. She gasped with pain, almost unable to breathe. The simple motion of her arm had twisted the knife in her back.

Brock looked up at the man. His right eye went wide with shock. Blood streamed from the needle protruding from his left eye socket. Sankar's hands went to his face and she noticed a strange pattern of blue lines on one of them, like a bar code. Before she passed out, Brock wondered where she had seen that symbol before.

•••

Brock woke inexplicably terrified. She was so frightened she could barely move, barely think. Why?

She was lying down. She smelled the faint odor of cleaning ammonia. She turned her head; an IV stuck out of her right arm and an electrode linked her wrist to a biomedical monitor. She was in a hospital.

Sankar had tried to kill her. Was that the source of her terror? No. She could examine that memory without fear.

Yet fear froze her mind. Even simple deductions took glacial slowness to complete. She closed her eyes and forced herself to think.

The facility was not bright and new like the government hospital that served New Delhi's elite; nor was it crowded and dirty like a public free hospital. She started to tremble. This was a parter clinic.

Brock jumped out of bed and jerked the IV from her arm, releasing a thin trickle of blood. She pulled the electrode off her wrist, causing the monitor to emit a shrill, piercing whistle. Panicked, she knocked it off its stand, sending it crashing to the floor.

She found her bloodstained sari folded neatly in the top drawer of a small, particle-board dresser. There wasn't much time. She threw off her hospital gown and quickly wrapped herself in the garment.

Her taser was gone.

She heard the door open behind her. She wheeled and braced herself, hands out, ready to fight.

The man who entered was small. He wore a white lab coat and slacks, and carried a clipboard. Brock had been prepared to see a hulking commando dressed in black, needle gun in hand.

"You don't look like a parter," she snapped.

The man's lips twitched into a slight smile. "What do you imagine a parter to look like?"

"What do you want?"

The man inclined his head toward the monitor on the floor. "I am usually concerned when a patient's heart rate suddenly speeds up and then stops."

"Patient!" Brock spit the word out. "Is that what you call it?"

The man sighed. "Whatever you may think of parters, Mrs."—he glanced down at this clipboard— "Patkar, at least at this clinic, our patients come to us voluntarily."

"So you can sell their organs."

He shrugged. "India is a desperate place. We do not make it so. We merely fulfill a need."

"I never volunteered."

"No." He glanced to his left; Mohammed stood there just outside the door. "This young one gave us a thousand rupees to repair your wound and watch over you for twelve hours. He signed a contract."

"And what if I hadn't wakened during that twelve hours? Would you have cut me up and sold me for parts?"

The man didn't answer. He only offered her his half-smile and turned to leave.

The door swung shut. She turned to Mohammed. "What were you thinking? This is a *parter* clinic!"

The boy flushed. "I didn't know where else to—"

Brock leaned forward and grabbed his shoulders. She felt a sharp twinge in her back, but was angry enough to ignore it.

"They could have killed me. Good Lord! Where did you get the money?"

"It was the money you gave to Sankar. I took it from him." Tears began to roll down the boy's face. "You were bleeding, and you were *heavy*. No one would help me." Mohammed started to sob. "I didn't know what else to do."

Brock drew a deep breath and put her arms around the boy.

"Okay," she said. "I'm sorry. Let's get out of here."

The boy sniffled and looked up at her. "Let's go to your apartment. I'll take care of you."

Dunston House.

The name popped into her head. She had an assignment. Brock frantically tried to do the math. She hadn't slept the full half-day, but how long had she slept? Was it after nine-thirty?

"Mohammed, listen. I have an appointment."

"But you are not well."

"I must go."

The boy started to shudder. He looked down. "Please do not go," he said quietly.

"I don't have a choice."

He looked up. His eyes were shiny. "Then let me go with you."

He only had a vague idea that she worked for something called the Conservatorship. She couldn't expose a subdirector to an Indian national, but she didn't know how to explain. "I just can't."

"I'm sorry." The words tumbled from the boy in a torrent. "I'm sorry I brought you to the parters. I'm sorry I took you to Sankar. I didn't know. I *didn't* know."

"I understand, but I'm already late."

"Please don't be mad at me," he whispered.

"I'll see you soon."

In one fluid motion she squeezed his shoulder, stood up, and walked out the door. Mohammed cried softly. She didn't turn around; Brock didn't want to see his face.

•••

Dunston House was a medium-sized Victorian mansion built during British rule in the early twentieth century. The Conservatorship had purchased it for use as a safe house. Brock approached what looked to be a simple wrought-iron fence. She knew that an invisible, low-power laser was tracing the outlines of her face. She placed her right hand in a slot in a meter-high post and felt a slight prick in her index finger as the device sampled her blood. In a second the fence's internal logic decided she was Susan Brock, and the gate opened.

She walked through the gate, up to double doors, pushed them open, and stepped into a well-appointed house. A Persian rug covered the foyer, light streamed from a crystal chandelier overhead, and a broad staircase curved up and to her right. She glanced left and saw light emanating from a half-open door. Brock limped toward the room she knew to be a study. She could still feel the sharp pain in her back.

"Where the hell have you been? You're almost two hours late," Smith called from the other room.

"I was involved in a little altercation," Brock called back.

"Your orders were to maintain a minimum profile. Couldn't you even do that for—" He stopped when she walked into the room with blood spattered all over her orange sari.

She glanced about. He sat on an ornate sofa before a beautiful teak coffee table inlaid with glass. He was alone.

"What happened to you?"

She couldn't think of a convincing lie. "A buy went bad," she finally answered.

"A buy." He pressed his lips together and set his jaw.

"Look, I told you before. I am a member of Ecological Directorate. I was just doing my job."

Smith seemed to be gathering himself. He spoke with a level voice. "Your actions have jeopardized the most important political mission in India in the last twenty years. But we'll discuss that after you return. For now, you are an hour late for a community reception held by Old Delhi's member of parliament at Sansad Bhavan."

"What?"

Smith drew a deep breath.

"We have to have a reason for you to be at Parliament House, and Asha Patkar is the kind of respectable member of the community with whom M.P.'s love to have their image taken."

"What am I supposed to do at Parliament House?"

"Do you know this man?"

A holo of a seated C. J. Priyadhavshina appeared in the middle of the room. A handsome man in his early forties, dressed in a conservative gray suit, he sat with legs crossed, obviously at ease with himself.

A disembodied voice that Brock recognized as belonging to a reporter said, "Mister Priyadhavshina, it has been widely reported that your government has a record of oppressing Moslems and other religious minorities."

Priyadhavshina frowned. "These charges disturb me. They are wholly untrue."

"But you have turned India into a Hindu theocracy," prompted the reporter.

"America considers itself a Christian nation, Israel calls itself the Jewish state, and of course the world is full of Islamic Republics. Yet when the people of India declare their interest in spirituality, we are subject to ugly accusations. I suggest that an unfair double standard is at work."

He's smooth, Brock thought. She turned to Smith. "You're asking me if I recognize the prime minister of India?"

Smith sighed and the holo disappeared. "All right. We don't really have time for the detailed briefing anyway. We have a source who is willing to let us verify that the Priyadhavshina government is involved in a deliberate effort to cleanse India of Moslems. We need that proof."

"Who is the source?"

"You don't need to know."

Brock bit back a sarcastic response. "So he's going to bring us the information."

"No, he wants to limit his involvement. But he's willing to look the other way while we get it."

"You want me to go get the information."

Another holo appeared. This time it was a schematic of the prime minister's residence.

"Your invitation to the reception will get you onto the grounds. Security is lax because Priyadhavshina himself is on a religious pilgrimage to Varanasi. You'll walk toward the main entrance, but take this path here." A crimson line traced its way across the schematic perpendicular to the main entrance. "It will lead you to a series of glass doors, each opening out from an office. One will be marked with a piece of red cloth. The door will be unlocked and the security system will be disarmed." He handed her a small CD. "There will be a computer on a desk. Copy the file Purification.DOC. Once you have the file, leave the room, join the party, make your excuses, and walk back out through the front gate. Return here."

"It sounds bloody dangerous," she said.

Smith shrugged. "It should be routine. As always, the neutrality of the Conservatorship should protect you."

Brock felt the pain in her back and decided she wasn't as certain as Smith. "I still don't understand what authority you have to make me do this."

"I am political subdirector for South Asia."

A light went on in Brock's head. "Then you are responsible for Pakistan."

"Of course."

"Tell me what happened in Islamabad."

Smith frowned. "Why?"

Brock hesitated. "I knew someone involved."

"Who?"

"John Evans. He was . . . a friend."

Smith studied her for a long moment. She couldn't read his expression. "Pakistan is very unstable right now," he said. "Rich against poor; fundamentalists against secularists; Sunni against Shiite. John got caught in the middle."

"What precisely was his assignment?"

"We'll discuss it after your return." Smith's voice was cold.

"But—"

"I have no more time to play games, Brock. Do you, or do you not, wish to remain a member of the Conservatorship?"

She nodded.

"Then you must hurry. You need to change. I think you'll find a new sari upstairs."

His eyes told her that she had kept him waiting long enough. He had no patience left. If she wanted any answers about John, she would have to do exactly as he said. She turned to walk back toward the stairs.

● ● ●

Sansad Bhavan, the Indian Parliament House, was an unimpressive circular structure braced by colonnades, located at the end of Parliament Street. The moon was new, and though footlights shone on the building itself, the grounds remained shrouded in darkness. Brock had never been there before; she had very little interest in politics.

A pair of guards stood before the gate that blocked off the building's grounds. The guard on the left stepped toward her as she approached. Like his companion, he wore the khaki uniform of the Indian Army, his head covered by a white turban, and he carried a matte-black laser rifle slung over his shoulder.

Brock wore a dark blue sari with a white floral imprint. It was pretty, but simple, something befitting a respectable widow. She felt the heavy paper of the invitation tucked within a fold of her sari.

She pulled it out and handed it to the guard on the left. "Asha Patkar," she said. "I am sorry I'm late, but this has been a most eventful day." You're babbling, she thought. "I spent so much time getting ready for the reception, that I almost forgot to actually come." She laughed, and hoped the guards didn't hear her nervousness.

"Scan her," said the guard on the left, who appeared to be the senior.

The guard on the right pulled out a wand and waved it over her. Brock felt a brief panic when he waved the device over her right hand, not knowing if the polysteel in the implanted suicide needle would cause the wand to alarm. After a moment, the guard on the right said, "She's clean."

The guard on the left smiled and handed her back the invitation. "Everything appears to be in order Mrs. Patkar." He turned and pointed. "Follow this path for about twenty meters, and you'll find a greeter who will direct you to the reception."

Brock nodded and stepped through the gate, trying not to limp. She walked down the path, which was lined by bushes and banyan trees, a testament to India's natural beauty.

The flora provided excellent cover for an intruder. But why should anyone be concerned about that? This was the seat of Indian government. There had to be motion detectors, laser eyes, thermal imaging devices, and God knew what else scanning the grounds.

When Brock came to the prescribed point, she stopped and leaned over, as if to smell a flower, and glanced back at the guards; they weren't watching. She darted behind the nearest tree.

Brock winced as she stepped onto the grass, expecting alarms to sound. She waited a full second. Nothing happened. Smith's source had obviously held up his end of the bargain. Even in the dark, she quickly found the path.

Smith's directions had been specific. The second path ran along the perimeter of an office annex. The office would be marked with a red flag on the handle. She found it easily. Brock grasped the cold brass handle. She turned it and heard a small click. Open.

She used the rag to wipe down the handle and then she put on rubber gloves. The lights in the office were off, but the computer workstation was on. She bent over the computer, found the file Purification.DOC, slid the CD into its slot, and hit the copy command. The powerful workstation took only a few seconds. She was almost clear. She entered a few keystrokes, pulling up the file that she had just copied, to ensure it was not a decoy. She scanned the document quickly.

Purification was a diabolical plan to rid India of its excess population by convicting "undesirables" of false crimes and sentencing them to transformation and deportation to Sirius System. There were many targets: untouchables, communists, Sikhs, Moslems, others.

Face after face, each surrounded by graphics and false records of a criminal past, flashed across the screen. The file was clearly genuine. She knew that she should leave, but something seemed wrong with the records. Her mouth felt dry. Bar codes were displayed next to the faces.

She hit the sort command and typed in the name "Mohammed." Her back was sore from bending over so long. More faces. She heard a noise, and caught her breath. She glanced at the still-closed door and waited a beat. Nothing. It was long past time for her to go. She scrolled through the faces and stopped. There he was. *Her* Mohammed. The office lights snapped on. She stood with a jerk, sending pain coursing through her body.

A man stood in the doorway. He was nearly two meters tall, and he smiled faintly, as if amused. He held a gun in his right hand.

In one smooth motion she popped the CD out of the computer, placed it in the folds of her sari, and stood.

"Excuse me," she said in her most entreating widow's voice. "I was separated from the party. I have never seen a computer and was curious. I didn't mean to—"

"That's not necessary, Ms. Brock." He spoke in English.

Brock could feel blood pounding in her temples. "Who are you?" she asked, also in English.

"I am Ramesh Garekhan, Minister of Security. I am also your source."

The gun was pointed at her.

"What are you doing?"

"I'm reconsidering my position." He nodded at the computer workstation. "I don't wish to find that information splashed all over omnidat and the world's leading editorial pages. Priyadhavshina would have my head for that."

"Why did you agree to sell the information in the first place?"

"I am not concerned with the government's place in history, and it was a chance to supplement my income. But *I am* concerned about my neck."

"Surely you know we won't release this information."

"Do I have your word on that?" Garekhan asked sarcastically.

"Look, in perhaps five or six decades, the Indian people will take a hard look at themselves, and they will want to know their true history. *Only then* will the information be released. We preserve history. Natural history. Cultural history. Political history. Those who live in the present have no need to fear us."

Garekhan laughed. "Really, Ms. Brock, I am an *intelligence* agent. Information is my currency. I know what your people did in Islamabad."

Brock felt as if she were trapped in a nightmare, where everything twisted just out of phase. "What are you talking about?"

"Your agent, John Evans, used the same appeal to a member of an Islamic fundamentalist group called God's Fist. I can almost hear the words 'I am only interested in history.' The terrorist told him about an assassination attempt against a leading moderate politician. Evans tipped off the government, the assassination was averted, and mass arrests and rioting followed."

No, Brock thought. I don't believe John violated his neutrality.

"Now, as a good Hindu, I have no love for God's Fist," said Garekhan. "But, the lesson was not lost on me."

We're not like that, Brock wanted to say. It was all a terrible mistake. John's death, Mohammed's extradition, her being here. She looked in Garekhan's eyes and knew he would hear none of it. "What are you going to do with me?"

Visions of torture filled her mind. She pressed her thumb hard on the nail of her right ring finger. Her breath caught as she felt the needle tear through the nail. She glanced down to ensure it had punched through her glove. You are in control.

"I'm sorry," he said as he walked toward her. "I promise it will be quick. Please hand me the CD." He reached out.

She dropped it just beyond his fingertips.

Garekhan sighed.

"Ms. Brock, I outweigh you by at least forty kilos and you were searched when you entered. You can't have a knife or a gun. Please don't try anything stupid. It will only make things harder."

He knelt, eyes and gun on her the entire time. He glanced down to see the CD, and she lunged forward and thrust her fingernail into his neck. His body jerked in surprise and he fell. Garekhan rolled and came up on his knees. He pointed the gun at her, but the needle's neurotoxin was quick. He had only a few seconds. Brock kicked the gun from his hand, picked up the CD, and ran out the glass door.

Brock hoped that she had a few minutes before Garekhan's disappearance would be noticed. She walked down the path; the night air cooled her flushed face.

The guards looked up and Brock's heart stopped. Brock braced herself for a fight. She had no defenses left.

A guard's hand closed on her elbow, steadying her.

"Are you all right, mother?" he asked gently.

They thought she was drunk.

Brock nodded. "Thank you, I just needed some air."

The guard nodded and helped her to the gate. Brock offered a silent prayer of thanks for the guard's discretion.

Outside the gates she walked away from Parliament House and melted into one of the crowds that were everywhere in India. Two minutes later she heard the sound of men shouting and sirens wailing in the distance.

● ● ●

In the end she decided to risk returning home. She had left no fingerprints, and they didn't have her DNA file, so any hair or skin samples left in Garekhan's office wouldn't lead back to her immediately.

Of course they would uncover her identity. She had killed a member of Priyadhavshina's staff. (Before speaking with Smith, she had never killed anyone; now she had killed twice.) They would find her if they had to interview every single person on the Parliament House access list.

But she felt pretty certain that she had some time.

Brock hid herself behind the corner of the alley that led to her front door and watched the crowd pass. No sign of the army. She turned and peered into the dark alley. She saw movement near her door. Brock felt her heart leap into her throat. She jerked her head back beyond the edge of the wall. How had they managed to locate her so quickly? She turned to leave, then thought better of it. She carefully looked one more time.

It was Mohammed, sleeping in her door jamb. Brock felt relief wash over her. Her legs suddenly felt weak. She walked down the alley and bent over the prone form pressed against her door. The muscles of his face were slack. Carefully keeping her right hand with its poison needle away from the boy, she shook him gently.

"Wake up, little one," she said softly in Hindi.

He scrunched his face into a grimace and tried to press himself further into the door. She shook him again. His eyes fluttered open, and a broad smile illuminated his face.

"Asha!" It was an exclamation of joy. Then anguish showed in that little face. "Please don't make me go away. I'm sorry. Please."

"Shh," Brock whispered. "It's all right. Let's go inside."

She touched the sensor pad on the door with her left hand and heard a click. She pushed the door open with her shoulder and led Mohammed in. He looked haggard. He might very well have not eaten in the last day. She nodded at the refrigerator. "Get something to eat."

She walked over to her computer station, slid a blank CD in one of the drives, slid the CD that Smith had given her in the other, and hit the copy command. She turned and found Mohammed looking at her.

"Mistress Asha, I am sorry about Sankar."

She looked into the boy's solemn eyes. Again she smelled Sankar's rancid breath and remembered his body pressing against hers in a struggle to see who would live and who would die. She had violated orders. She had allowed herself to be led into a dangerous place. She had killed. It was wrong to blame the boy.

She knelt. "It was a mistake." She reached out and caressed his face. "But we must both learn from our mistakes and move on. Do you understand?"

He nodded. "Thank you," he whispered.

"Now," she said more loudly. "Get something to eat."

He turned and dashed for the refrigerator.

She pushed past him and drew a pair of pliers from a cabinet. Unfortunately, the suicide needle had not been made for easy removal. She got a grip on the needle's tip, took a deep breath and pulled. The needle came free, along with most of her nail. She gasped in pain. Blood flowed everywhere. Brock grabbed a clean white cloth napkin, and wrapped her finger to staunch the bleeding. She then carefully placed the needle and the pair of pliers in plastic and threw them in the garbage.

She heard a knock at the door. Brock felt her blood freeze. She glanced at Mohammed. The boy sat at her small dining room table, happily eating. If it was the authorities, he would be caught with her. The knock came again, sharper, more insistent.

She could hide Mohammed, but she felt sure the security forces would search her small apartment. She could not think what to do.

"No matter what happens, say nothing," she said softly.

Mohammed glanced at the door. He nodded solemnly.

There was a louder knock, and this time a muffled man's voice said, "Open," in Hindi.

She walked over to her computer and pulled the original CD out of the drive and set it on the desk. She opened the door; Wilson Smith stood there. He pushed his way past her, and she shut the door.

"What is the matter with you? You were supposed to return to the safe house. Do you know that half of India's security forces are looking for—"

He stopped abruptly when he saw Mohammed, studied the boy for a second, and then turned to Brock. He said quietly, "Get rid of him."

"I will not," snapped Brock.

"Look, we don't have time—"

"No, we don't."

Smith sighed. "Does he speak English?" Brock shook her head. "Very well. What happened?"

"Garekhan tried to kill me."

"Why?"

"Because he knew what had really happened in Islamabad," Brock hissed. She glanced at Mohammed. He was watching the exchange closely, but he hadn't said anything. He was a good boy.

"Where's the disk?"

"Why did you lie to me about John?"

"Listen to yourself. You are emotionally involved. I had to protect you from that."

"Your protection almost got me killed."

"If I had known that Garekhan was going to sabotage the buy, I never would have sent you," Smith said angrily. He drew a deep breath. "Now, give me the disk."

"Why, so we can put it in a vault for fifty years?"

Brock turned to Mohammed.

"Come here," she said softly in Hindi.

The boy got up from the table and moved between her and Smith. He's protecting me, she thought.

She grabbed his arm and held it up so that Smith could see the bar code. "This boy is marked for deportation. It may not mean anything to you, but he's my friend. We could help him and tens of thousands of people like him by releasing that file *now*."

"You sound just like Evans," he sneered. "Even if you made a difference in this one case, how could anyone ever trust a Conservator again? What would be the chances of saving the tiger then?"

"So we just give up and let the world be as it will be, until some mythical time when mankind knows better?"

"If you released the information and it kept this boy from being deported, would it really do any good? You must know that you have to leave the country. What are his chances of survival alone in India?"

She looked down at the boy. Pollution, poverty, crime, and disease all conspired to kill Mohammed. She couldn't protect him.

"Give me the CD," Smith said softly.

"It's on the desk," Brock said.

Smith walked over and picked up the CD. He placed some papers on the desk. "There's a passport, papers, a plane ticket to Nairobi, and some money. When you—"

"Get out," said Brock.

"You must leave Delhi immediately."

"I'll figure it out on my own. Now get out of my apartment."

Smith nodded curtly, turned, and left.

"Who was that man?" Mohammed asked.

"It is not important."

Brock walked over to the computer and popped out the second CD. She didn't need Smith. She could release the information herself.

But to what end? Losing John had hurt so much.

She touched the little boy's head.

John's actions had only brought anarchy to Pakistan. Killing Sankar hadn't saved the tiger. It would give her a lot of satisfaction to release the list, but she had a sick realization that it might make things worse for Mohammed. He could easily be killed in the unrest that followed. This wasn't a world of heroes anymore.

"I have to go, Mohammed," she said.

Brock snapped the CD in two, and tossed it in the garbage. She put the papers Smith had left her in a fold in her sari, and pulled Mohammed into a tight hug.

A FEW NOTES
ON THIS VOLUME

Written by
Dave Wolverton

About the Author

Dave Wolverton started his publishing career in Volume III of Writers of the Future *with his story "On My Way to Paradise." In the past ten years, he has published ten adult novels, eight middle-grade books, and dozens of short stories. His science fiction novel,* Lords of the Seventh Swarm, *recently came out in paperback.*

Dave also recently wrote a comic time-travel novel based on a screenplay written by L. Ron Hubbard. The novel will be published by Bridge Publications, Inc., in 1999.

As I mentioned in my opening article, not much has changed with the *Writers of the Future* Contest over the years, but this year we do have a couple of new twists.

First, we have a few changes to the rules. Most of the items are minor, but I feel that I should take some time and point out these changes, along with our reasons for making them.

Most of the changes that we make are taking place because the contest is still growing, and we need to streamline the process for dealing with manuscripts.

In the past, we have told authors that they have to make their manuscripts anonymous. This means that you have to leave the title and page number at the top of each page, but not your name. This helps keep the judging fair and impartial. However, perhaps twenty percent of the authors who enter the contest do not follow that rule. Our gracious contest administrator then has to go through the manuscripts and either blacken out the names or cut them out. This of course takes a lot of time, and we regret that we can no longer provide this service. In the future, manuscripts that are not made anonymous by the author will be returned unread.

Another problem we've had is with authors who send in a story, rewrite it, and then send in the new corrected version with a note (or more often a frantic phone call), asking the contest administrator to please throw out the old version and put in the new. Alas, we cannot do that any longer. I would suggest to these authors that it is best to write the story, polish it as much as possible, and then send it in on the last day of the contest.

A third thing that we've done to facilitate judging is that we are now staggering our quarters in the UK and Australia, so that we can get stories mailed from those areas here in the US for more timely judging.

Beyond these rather mechanical changes in the contest rules, though, is something that is more significant. Beginning this year, we are asking authors to please look at the content of their stories and to avoid sending material that is too sexually explicit, excessively violent, or which might be normally considered offensive by the average adult reader.

Now, what exactly does that mean? Does it mean that you can't talk about sex or can't show sex? Of course not. Does it mean that no one gets hurt or maimed in the story? Of course not. You can read the stories I've selected for the past eight years and see what I've published. You'll find sexual content and violence galore, and both items may be necessary to a story.

But I have, over the years, begun to lose patience with authors whose sole purpose in writing a story seems to be to try to sicken his or her audience into putting the piece down. To such authors I say, "I surrender." I will gladly put the piece down. In spite of my desire to keep this contest as open as possible, I will, for example, disqualify stories that graphically depict sexual torture, or stories that exist primarily to serve as a sort of "hate mail" directed toward certain ethnic groups.

So, take care.

•••

I would like to thank those who have helped make this contest a success in the past year. This includes all of those who submitted stories and illustrations, along with our contest judges, administrators, and of course our prize winners.

Our *Writers of the Future* judges this year included Kevin J. Anderson, Gregory Benford, Doug Beason, Algis Budrys, Anne McCaffrey, Larry Niven, Andre Norton, Jerry Pournelle, Frederik Pohl, Tim Powers, Jack Williamson, Robert Silverberg and Dave Wolverton.

Our *Illustrators of the Future* judges this year included Edd Cartier, Leo and Diane Dillon, Vincent Di Fate, Bob Eggleton, Will Eisner, Frank Frazetta, Shun Kijima, Paul Lehr, Frank Kelly-Freas, Laura Brodian Kelly-Freas, Ron and Val Lakey Lindahn and H. R. van Dongen.

•••

Our published authors this year are

First Quarter

First Place: Stefano Donati, "Literacy"
Second Place: Carla Montgomery, "The Dragon and the Lorelei"
Third Place: Scott M. Azmus, "Red Moon"
Published Finalist: Amy Sterling Casil, "Jenny with the Stars in Her Hair"
Published Finalist: Jayme Lynn Blaschke, "Cyclops in B Minor"

Second Quarter

First Place: Richard Flood, "The Dhaka Flu"
Second Place: Steven Mohan, Jr., "Conservator"
Third Place: Ladonna King, "Agony"

Third Quarter

First Place: Brian Wightman, "Nocturne's Bride"
Second Place: David Masters, "Broken Mirror"
Third Place: Chris Flamm, "Waiting for Hildy"
Published Finalist: Maureen Jensen, "Silent Justice"

Fourth Quarter

First Place: J. C. Schmidt, "Spray Paint Revolutions"
Second Place: T. M. Spell, "Red Tide, White Tide"
Third Place: Tim Jansen, "Faller"
Published Finalist: Scott Nicholson, "Metabolism"
Published Finalist: Ron Collins, "The Disappearance
  of Josie Andrew"

Our prize-winning illustrators this year are

Dionisios Fragias
Rob Hassan
Christopher Jouan
István Kuklis
John Lock
Paul Marquis
Sherman McClain
John Philo
Eric L. Winter

NEW WRITERS!

L. Ron Hubbard's

Writers of the Future Contest

AN INTERNATIONAL SEARCH FOR
NEW AND AMATEUR WRITERS OF
NEW SHORT STORIES OR NOVELETTES OF
SCIENCE FICTION OR FANTASY

No entry fee is required.
Entrants retain all publication rights.

ALL AWARDS ARE ADJUDICATED BY
PROFESSIONAL WRITERS ONLY

PRIZES EVERY THREE MONTHS: $1,000, $750, $500.
ANNUAL GRAND PRIZE: $4,000 ADDITIONAL!

Don't Delay! Send Your Entry to
L. Ron Hubbard's
Writers of the Future Contest
P.O. Box 1630
Los Angeles, CA 90078

CONTEST RULES

1. No entry fee is required, and all rights in the story remain the property of the author. All types of science fiction, fantasy and horror with fantastic elements are welcome; every entry is judged on its own merits only.

2. All entries must be original works in English. Plagiarism, which includes poetry, song lyrics, characters or another person's world will result in disqualification. Submitted works may not have been previously published in professional media.

3. Eligible entries must be works of prose under 17,000 words in length. We regret we cannot consider poetry or works intended for children. Excessive violence or sex will result in disqualification.

4. The Contest is open only to those who have not had published (more than 5,000 copies) a novel or short novel, or more than three short stories, or more than one novelette, in any medium.

5. Entries must be typewritten and double-spaced with numbered pages (computer-printer output okay). Each entry must have a cover page with the title of the work, the author's name, address and telephone number and an approximate word count. The manuscript itself should be titled and numbered on every page, but the AUTHOR'S NAME SHOULD BE DELETED to facilitate fair judging.

6. Manuscripts will be returned after judging. Entries MUST include a self-addressed return envelope. U.S. return envelopes MUST be stamped; others may enclose international postal reply coupons.

7. There shall be three cash prizes in each quarter: 1st Prize of $1,000, 2nd Prize of $750, and 3rd Prize of $500, in U.S. dollars or the recipient's local equivalent amount. In addition, there shall be a further cash prize of $4,000 to the grand prize winner, who will be selected from among the 1st Prize winners for the period of October 1, 1998, through September 30, 1999. All winners will also receive trophies or certificates.

8. The Contest will continue through September 30, 1999, on the following quarterly basis:

October 1–December 31, 1998   January 1–March 31, 1999

April 1–June 30, 1999   July 1–September 30, 1999

Information regarding subsequent contests may be obtained by sending a self-addressed, stamped business-size envelope to the above address.

To be eligible for the quarterly judging, an entry must be postmarked no later than midnight on the last day of the quarter.

9. Each entrant may submit only one manuscript per quarter. Contest winners are ineligible to make further entries.

10. All entries for each quarter are final. No revisions are accepted.

11. Entries will be judged by professional authors. The decisions of the judges are entirely their own, and are final.

12. Winners in each quarter will be individually notified of the results by mail.

This Contest is void where prohibited by law.

L. Ron Hubbard's

ILLUSTRATORS
OF THE
FUTURE
CONTEST

 TM

OPEN TO NEW SCIENCE FICTION
AND FANTASY ARTISTS
WORLDWIDE

All Judging by Professional Artists Only

$1,500 in Prizes Each Quarter
No entry fee.   Entrants retain all rights.

**Quarterly winners compete for
$4,000 additional ANNUAL PRIZE**

L. Ron Hubbard's
Illustrators of the Future Contest
P.O. Box 3190
Los Angeles, CA 90078

1. The Contest is open to entrants from all nations. (However, entrants should provide themselves with some means for written communication in English.) All themes of science fiction and fantasy illustration are welcome: every entry is judged on its own merits only. No entry fee is required, and all rights in the entries remain the property of the artists.

2. By submitting work to the Contest, the entrant agrees to abide by all Contest rules.

3. This Contest is open to those who have not previously published more than three black-and-white story illustrations, or more than one process-color painting, in media distributed nationally to the general public, such as magazines or books sold at newsstands, or books sold in stores merchandising to the general public. The submitted entry shall not have been previously published in professional media as exampled above.

If you are not sure of your eligibility, write to the Contest address with details, enclosing a business-size self-addressed envelope with return postage. The Contest Administration will reply with a determination.

Winners in previous quarters are not eligible to make further entries.

4. Only one entry per quarter is permitted. The entry must be original to the entrant. Plagiarism, infringement of the rights of others, or other violations of the Contest rules will result in disqualification.

5. An entry shall consist of three illustrations done by the entrant in a black-and-white medium. Each must represent a theme different from the other two.

6. ENTRIES SHOULD NOT BE THE ORIGINAL DRAWINGS, but should be large black-and-white photocopies of a quality satisfactory to the entrant. Entries must be submitted unfolded and flat, in an envelope no larger than 9 inches by 12 inches.

All entries must be accompanied by a self-addressed return envelope of the appropriate size, with correct U.S. postage affixed. (Non-U.S. entrants should enclose international postal reply coupons.)

If the entrant does not want the photocopies returned, the entry should be clearly marked DISPOSABLE COPIES: DO NOT RETURN. A business-size self-addressed envelope with correct postage should be included so that judging results can be returned to the entrant.

7. To facilitate anonymous judging, each of the three photocopies must be accompanied by a removable cover sheet bearing the artist's name, address and telephone number, and an identifying title for that work. The photocopy of the work should carry the same identifying title, and the artist's signature should be deleted from the photocopy.

The Contest Administration will remove and file the cover sheets, and forward only the anonymous entry to the judges.

8. To be eligible for a quarterly judging, an entry must be postmarked no later than the last day of the quarter.

Late entries will be included in the following quarter, and the Contest Administration will so notify the entrant.

9. There will be three co-winners in each quarter. Each winner will receive an outright cash grant of U.S. $500, and a certificate of merit. Such winners also receive eligibility to compete for the annual grand prize of an additional outright cash grant of $4,000 together with the annual grand prize trophy.

10. Competition for the grand prize is designed to acquaint the entrant with customary practices in the field of professional illustrating. It will be conducted in the following manner:

Each winner in each quarter will be furnished a Specification Sheet giving details on the size and kind of black-and-white illustration work required by grand prize competition. Requirements will be of the sort customarily stated by professional publishing companies.

These specifications will be furnished to the entrant by the Contest Administration, using Return Receipt Requested mail or its equivalent.

Also furnished will be a copy of a science fiction or fantasy story, to be illustrated by the entrant. This story will have been selected for that purpose by the Coordinating Judge of the Contest. Thereafter, the entrant will work toward completing the assigned illustration.

In order to retain eligibility for the grand prize, each entrant shall, within thirty (30) days of receipt of the said story assignment, send to the Contest address the entrant's black-and-white page illustration of the assigned story in accordance with the Specification Sheet.

The entrant's finished illustration shall be in the form of camera-ready art prepared in accordance with the Specification Sheet and securely packed, shipped at the entrant's own risk. The Contest will exercise due care in handling all submissions as received.

The said illustration will then be judged in competition for the grand prize on the following basis only:

Each grand prize judge's personal opinion on the extent to which it makes the judge want to read the story it illustrates.

The entrant shall retain copyright in the said illustration.

11. The Contest year will continue through September 30, 1998, with the following quarterly period (see Rule 8):

July 1–September 30, 1998

The next Contest will continue through September 30, 1999, on the following quarterly basis:

October 1–December 31, 1998   January 1–March 31, 1999

April 1–June 30, 1999   July 1–September 30, 1999

Entrants in each quarter will be individually notified of the quarter's judging results by mail. Winning entrants' participation in the Contest shall continue until the results of the grand prize judging have been announced.

Information regarding subsequent contests may be obtained by sending a self-addressed business-size envelope, with postage, to the Contest address.

12. The grand prize winner will be announced at the L. Ron Hubbard Awards events to be held in the calendar year of 1999.

13. Entries will be judged by professional artists only. Each quarterly judging and the grand prize judging may have a different panel of judges. The decisions of the judges are entirely their own, and are final.

14. This Contest is void where prohibited by law.

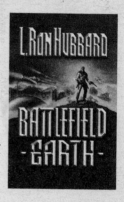